Missing Genes

Geoff Tomlinson

ISBN:- 13: 978-1517473587
ISBN-10: 1517473586

DEDICATION

For the ladies in my life, for their love and support - the residents of Basel and all those who love this amazing city.

Prologue

The study of genetics and genetic engineering is a fascinating and controversial one, involving not just science but ethics. In recent times, huge strides have been made in understanding how everything works and how diseases and handicaps could be eliminated, as well as increasing the food supply for the ever-growing population. But concerns about change and whether or not it is ethical to bring about this change hold us back.

Gregor Mendel first suggested the existence of inheritable units back in 1857. Charles Darwin too had his own theories.

The word gene comes from the Ancient Greek *pangene* meaning race or offspring. The Danish botanist Wilhelm Johanssen is believed to have first coined the term in 1909. But it was not until the 1950's that a hypothesis of genetic replication was published. Since then ideas have flowed thick and fast.

One theory is that each gene specifies a different trait. DNA replication is said to be extremely accurate, however errors do occur. These mutations, as they're called, can be caused by many things.

What if some of these genes go missing? What happens to an individual if his DNA is minimally damaged, what about the person with chromosomal abnormalities? In this tale you will meet characters who have not received the usual hand of genes. Characters for whom genes have clearly gone missing. Characters whose beliefs and behaviours are beyond the norm. Characters we may generously describe as eccentric, others of whom we are utterly terrified.

It is not the strongest of the species that survive, nor the most intelligent, but the one most responsive to change.

Charles Darwin

CHAPTER 1

The man at the front of the room drew himself up to his full height, rotated his muscular shoulders forward several times; rubbed his hands, as if washing away the sins of the world and, drawing a deep breath, gazed at the expectant faces of the people seated before him.

His audience could not fail to be impressed by what they saw, for the man had an imposing presence. Above average height, a broad, deep chest - and well-developed biceps bursting below his short-sleeved shirt. They would have taken in the lightly tanned face, the square jaw and a head topped with a wild mass of uncontrollable blonde hair. They weren't to know the colour was only possible, these days, through magic bottles vainly secreted away at the back of his bathroom cabinet. But it was the eyes that would have captured their imagination. Aryan, steely, piercing blue eyes, which, if caught, caused the beholder to turn away or look down, afraid the intense, penetrating gaze would see straight into their soul or, at a minimum, access their most intimate thoughts.

Dieter von Murren rested a hand on the olivewood lectern and looked at each person in turn. When he had completed peering at each of the fifteen people seated before him, he smiled and rubbed his nose with an exceptionally long, elegant forefinger and cleared his throat.

'Wilkomme,' he said in a deep, reverberating baritone and unnecessarily repeated the greeting in half a dozen other languages before reverting again to Swiss-German.

'I think you all know who I am. Some of you I have met before. I'm really looking forward to renewing friendships - and getting to know each of our new guests.' His eyes scanned the room before continuing. 'It is my very great pleasure to be your host for the period of your stay. According to the documentation that you completed, Schweitzerdeutsch is the majority common language and the one I will use at group meetings,' he paused and attempted to make eye-contact with the people seated before him. 'For those of you who do not speak Swiss-German, I'm sorry - but most of our time together will be as individuals or pairs when we will use your native tongue.' He then, as a demonstration of his superiority, repeated, what he had said in flawless English, French and Italian.

Positioned deferentially behind him were his eight staff members. The man half-turned and, as if well rehearsed, they stepped forward as one, to stand alongside him. The employees, neatly but casually dressed, stood with their hands clasped before them on each side of the man. They were symmetrically ordered, four to the left and four to the right. He reached for the woman at his right hand and held up her arm: a short, well-built, woman of about forty, with cropped brown hair and a no-nonsense upright posture. This was Helga, he announced, to whom all questions regarding physical wellbeing should be addressed; Helga, he continued, would also run the early-morning yoga classes. Helga forced a smile and aimed it over the heads of those seated, barely concealing how she abhorred people with mental fragility. She was made of sterner stuff.

Nearest to him, on his left side, was Martina, the administrator, who would deal with queries over finance, form-filling and travel arrangements. Martina was in her late thirties, a long, dark beribboned pigtail hanging neatly behind her, almost to her waist. She was a thin, almost anorexic looking woman, whom the man had earlier rescued from herself - and from the adoring look she gave him, eternally grateful.

Anna was introduced as the nurse, a shy nineteen-year-old slip of a girl who had never seen the inside of a hospital, never mind being professionally trained. She was another of the man's 'success' stories, whom, when her crisis was resolved, he had bought a book on first-aid and as a reward had presented her with a job - and the key of the medicine cupboard.

A fat, sallow-faced woman in an apron was introduced as the chef, together with her young assistant. The man then named the two local girls, who helped in the canteen and cleaned the rooms. The final introduction was the elderly gardener, the only other man on the premises. Each was introduced with equal enthusiasm. All were vital members of the team, he assured the seated group, whose only purpose in life was to ensure the guests wellbeing and that they were made to feel comfortable.

Formalities completed, the man nodded, smilingly to Helga, who bobbed slightly in acknowledgement of her dismissal, bowed Germanically, towards the seated minions, stepped backwards and strode purposefully towards the door. The others taking their cue, followed without a word.

'In a few moments,' the man began, once the gnarled old gardener had closed the door. 'In a few moments I will lead you around the premises. You will find that we're quite compact, little over three hectares, most of which is taken up with gardens and an orange grove. Group meetings will take place in this room; while individual or couple meetings will take place either in my office or your room or, depending on the time of day, strolling through the orange grove. Breakfast will be served at seven o'clock in the dining room, after which I will address the group and inform you of any changes to the day's plans.' As he spoke, the man looked intensely at each individual, who in turn averted their eyes, protecting their obvious fragilities.

'However,' he continued. 'Over the first two days I will meet with you individually and for these two days only, we will stick to a strict timetable to give me the opportunity to meet you and get to know the challenges you are facing.' The man paused and strode first to the left and then to the right, allowing time for what he had said to sink in. 'Remember, you are here to relax,' he continued, once his perambulations had ceased. "We are ten kilometres from the nearest habitation of any size and so it would be difficult to find a more peaceful spot. It is five hundred metres or so to a small beach and although the ground shelves steeply, it is a safe spot to swim. I recommend that once I have shown you the layout, you find time to explore - and enjoy the sunshine, the birds, the flowers - and feel free to help yourself to oranges directly from the trees. So, on your feet, if you please and let me show you our modest facilities.'

Modest or not, the facilities were comfortable and formed a rectangle around a raked, sandy-floored courtyard, dominated by an ancient olive tree, whose massive proportions threw welcome shade throughout the day, around the enclosed space. Wooden chairs and benches were spaced invitingly at intervals around the perimeter and under the tree.

Two sides of the rectangle provided accommodation for the guests, each room minimally equipped but with a small en-suite shower-room. The other two sides included the room where the group had just met, in the corner of which was a baby grand Steinway piano that the man would play at every opportunity. There was the man's office and private suite, an administrative bureau, canteen, kitchen, a library, plus smaller utility rooms.

Like the Pied Piper, the man, led his flock around the facilities, his effusiveness and hypnotic tone precluding any questions. Like sheep, rather than children, they followed closely, though one man stood out, as he dragged along at the end of the group. This man was filled with scepticism, as he battled not to be taken in with all this nonsense, like the rest of the idiots around him.

When the tour around the buildings ended, the man led his flock into the orange grove where blossom and fruit at various stages of development hung incongruously on the same tree. Underneath one particularly large tree he halted in its heavy shade, and while still holding forth waved for his audience to sit. Wordlessly they obeyed, their eyes never leaving his face. For a further half an hour his voice floated calmly, yet forcefully over his guests, leaving each feeling as if they had been smoothed with a velvet glove and bequeathing each with a residue of calmness and reassurance. Even the sceptic was calm despite the previous turmoil in his head.

Without a break in his soliloquy the leader glanced towards the setting sun and announced it was time for dinner. He invited those at his feet to return to their rooms and meet in the dining-room at the appointed time. So saying, he stretched both arms towards his flock, as if offering a blessing, gave a brief nod, turned on his heel and left.

CHAPTER 2

The next morning the blonde-headed man awoke with a pleasurable start to find his naked loins straddled by the young nurse who shared his bed. She quickly brought them both to a silent climax and rolled away. After a few moments he kissed her forehead in gratitude, climbed out of bed and into a pair of bathing trunks. Without a backward glance he left the bedroom to begin his daily routine. He jogged through the cool, fragrant orange grove to a low rocky cliff, where he carried out a few rudimentary stretching exercises and while deep breathing, cast his eyes around the stunning bay, noting the solitary small boat, from which a man was fishing, before hurling himself into the calm, turquoise sea.

For fifteen minutes the man swam up and down the small bay before wading ashore and walking back to the Centre. Back in his quarters the girl was in the shower but when she heard him return, she quickly clambered out and into a voluminous towel; she knew better than to upset his routine. They took breakfast silently together, standing in the kitchen - breakfast for him comprising of nothing more than a huge peeled orange that he'd picked on his return and two cups of black coffee.

Patients, as he called his clients, came for two weeks of 'therapy;' they were usually tortured souls with fragile personalities, many with life, marital or relational problems and the first couple of days were spent talking to them individually. He had pinned a rota to a noticeboard and, after the coffee, settled himself in his office to await the first 'patient.'

Although von Murren had been running his Centro Paraiso for several years, he always voyeuristically enjoyed the first few days, listening to all the woes of his patients, handing out tissues and encouraging each to bare their soul. He had an uncanny knack of drawing out the most private and intimate details and a way with words that provided succour for the poor demented patients. He had no training in psychology but was familiar with Jung's theories and had read enough of Sigmund Freud's work to understand that sexual issues lay behind most of his client's problems - guilt, anorgasmia, infertility, infidelity but mostly guilt!

No doubt many people who knew Dieter von Murren might describe him as a fallen angel. Not as in the myth, cast out of heaven but from society. Except that he chose to escape impending chains and gloomy darkness by running away to his secret bolthole, leaving behind everything he had ever worked for: wealth, property, prestige and a family. All lost because of his greed. But at Paraiso he had adopted a simple life, content to dispense wisdom and to bask in the admiring glow of his many followers.

At the end of the second day, the man had met each of the fifteen people: there were six couples, two middle-aged females and a solitary man. The following day he studied his notes and drew up sketchy plans of how he would deal with each, before typing up a list of names and times to meet. There were the usual problems he found with each fresh group. Couples who were basically incompatible and should never have married in the first place. For these tortured souls he had developed a standard patter for dealing with such issues. The two single women were menopausal but the single man left him puzzled. The young German had, at first, been reluctant to say anything about his past or any specific problems and then when pressed as to why he was here, had told a protracted tale so devious, the man knew it was fabricated - a little more digging was required, he decided.

On the third day, after his morning swim, the leader joined Helga's yoga class, where he successfully shut out everything around him, as he strived to seek 'union with the divine.' He was naturally supple and, at his father's expense, had once attended advanced yoga classes in India.

At dinnertime, in the evenings, he would wander around the tables, glass of red wine in hand, chatting informally. To the casual observer, it was astounding how quickly he had obtained a close rapport with each of his clients. They would stop eating, lay down their cutlery and peer into his eyes like rabbits mesmerised by a stoat, hanging onto the words of wisdom he dispensed, as fluently and, probably as nutritious, as the fresh juice spilling out of the orange-squeezing machine! Later he would sit at the piano and entertain anyone who cared to listen, his talent and repertoire drawing warm applause, when he finally closed the lid.

The next few days passed quickly, as the man pontificated and played mind games with his guests' psyche. Following several hours of emotional upheaval, except for a morning pep talk, it was his practice to leave the patients in peace for the rest of their stay, in order to put into practice what he had suggested. As his guests lounged about the property: in the sitting room, under the orange trees or on the beach, he would maintain a high profile, questioning each pair how they were progressing, suggesting new methods of behaviour, observing and manipulating.

The man met with the young German on two more occasions but at each he failed to get through the solid suit of armour with which he had surrounded himself. 'He had heard good things about Paraiso,' was all he said but it was plain to see that all was not well, he was crying out for help but wouldn't allow himself the luxury of confessing.

At the end of each week, a mini bus transported some of the guests to Palma, the nearest airport. Most stayed for two weeks but there were usually a few who only stayed for one week. As usual, they were emotional and unhappy to leave, the psychological prop the man had provided about to be removed. There were hugs and kisses and promises to return. The man, of course, encouraged this; he hardly ever advertised his services nowadays, he relied on his clientele spreading the word and returning for more of his spiritual nectar.

The last person to mount the bus was the single man. At the last moment he turned and stared over his shoulder, his face creased like a scrunched up ball of paper, the bitter expression epitomising his utter anguish and frustration.

CHAPTER 3

Dieter von Murren was the only child born to a German lawyer and his partner in the small Swiss village of Hofstetten, close to the city of Basel, during the sultry summer of 1950. His parents had never married and so he was given his mother's surname. At age five he was sent to the local kindergarten and a year later the local primary school. At age eleven, his father enrolled him at a private school in Basel, where he excelled in everything he did. His diligence and good humour ensured that he was immensely popular with teachers and fellow students alike.

With seemingly little effort, as he grew older, Dieter topped the exam tables, broke records for sprinting and jumping, led the debating team, played the piano superbly; as well as the clarinet in the school orchestra and took the lead in all the school plays. There were those who said, behind closed doors, that the whole of the school, the Freies gymnasium, revolved around Dieter von Murren. He was consulted by teachers and students alike and later, as head boy, had more influence than was wise, his eloquent powers of persuasion were doubtless inherited from the genes of his lawyer father. In truth he was manipulative and ultra egotistical but remarkably those around him either did not notice or forgave him.

Dieter's father had a successful business in Freiburg in southern Germany, and owned a vast apartment in the city centre; it was only much later he opened an office in Basel. Eventually, he decided Switzerland would be a good place to settle his partner, Isobel and bought a modest, though spacious, villa on the northern slopes of Hofstetten. The house was blessed with open views across the valley to the farmland and a mountain known as the Blauenberg.

Dieter's mother, Isobel von Murren, was an only child born into a wealthy, catholic family in Freiburg and was only eighteen when she first met Ferdinand and instantly fell under the spell of his immense charm. But Ferdinand had been briefly married previously and his wife, a devout catholic, had refused to divorce. There had been floods of tears when he explained all this to Isobel and later, rows with her father when she became pregnant and unable to save her reputation by marrying.

During his teenage years, Dieter saw little of his father, whose law practice, endless meetings and secret mistress ensured he was rarely at home. His mother, seemingly oblivious to her husband's absence, was grateful for the comfortable standard of living and place in local society that she enjoyed. She seemed content to bask in his considerable shadow. Dieter, of course, twisted his mother around his elegant pianist's fingers in such a sly and crafty manner, she didn't appear to notice that her precocious son ruled the roost and did as he pleased.

Hofstetten village was compact, surrounded by farmland to the south and west and forest to the north and east; there was nothing Dieter liked better than hiking, cycling and climbing on the Blauen with his friends or exploring the hundreds of trails through the forest. It was an idyllic childhood of privilege and plenty.

Towards the end of his school career Dieter's father had been on the scene enough times to convince his son to follow in his footsteps and study law. Dieter was such a brilliant pianist, initially he considered studying music to become a concert pianist but the promise of an early partnership in his father's successful law firm was a juicy, lucrative carrot dangled enticingly before his nose.

But first, Dieter was faced with the prospect of compulsory military service. This would involve up to seven weeks of basic training followed by a further fourteen weeks. He wasn't fazed by the idea, every Swiss male knew that this was something required – a veritable rite of passage. When the day arrived Dieter packed his bags, kissed his mother farewell and took the train to Sumiswald in a scenic area called Emmental. At Boot Camp he learned to follow instructions, learned new skills, such as the rudiments of crawling through mud while lugging a rifle and a spine-crushing backpack. At the end of this period he was offered officer training, which involved a commitment of more time. He of course accepted, despite the knowledge that this would involve him spending approximately two-thousand days in the army over the next thirty years. The further up the ranks one was promoted, the more time the officer was required to commit. A process known as 'paying your grade.'

Dieter revelled in leadership, giving orders and demanding loyalty. There is little doubt if he had decided to stay in the military, as one of the four thousand professionals leading one-hundred and thirty thousand conscripts; he would have risen like cream to the top. He was a natural leader filling his minions with confidence and a willingness to follow.

Dieter didn't find it at all bizarre that a country that had not fought a war for over five hundred years, kept such a powerful fighting force. Like many of his fellow Swiss, he believed neutrality had to be fiercely guarded.

By the time he arrived at the Law School, in Basel, Dieter was totally used to getting his own way. In the army and in other spheres of life it was either through articulate argument, force of personality, guile or a combination of all three. His father had rented him a comfortable apartment alongside the Rhine, and the fact that he had left home, albeit only fifteen kilometres away, meant he was, in theory, free to do what he pleased but the fact was not really noticeable - as for years Dieter had done exactly what he wished and lived the life he wanted to lead.

At the university it wasn't long before Dieter's intellect and talents were recognized by his law professors; he became a favoured student and basked in the glow of academic sunshine. In his favour, he worked hard, really hard, read profusely, his essays were always handed in on time - and he continued to practice the piano on a daily basis. As a result he found himself invited into the homes of distinguished professors, as a dinner guest, who would later plead that he entertain those present with a recital. Dieter loved being the centre of attention and as his fingers flew over the keys, his blonde curls hid his penetrating blue eyes, as they roamed around the guests, mentally taking notes of the most desirable women present and the men who might prove useful in his future life.

Notwithstanding his youth, Dieter had an opinion on everything and could hold his own among the prestigious and eminent guests, often politicians or prominent business leaders. In his final years at school he had been introduced to the works of the one-time Basel University professor, Frederick Nietzsche and annoyed teachers and students alike by continually quoting from his books. On his bedroom wall hung a poster of the heavily moustached philosopher; and underneath it read 'There are no facts, only interpretations.' A philosophy to which he subscribed.

Dieter's striking good lucks, courtesy and talent fascinated almost all the beautiful, intelligent, or vivacious females he met - they fell under his spell and often, unwittingly, found themselves in his bed and then gently discarded in such a tender manner they usually remained friends, anxious to be invited back to his attic room again. And it wasn't just the ladies he charmed, men of influence left their business-cards, with requests that he contact them once his studies were over, emphasizing that they would be delighted to discuss career opportunities.

Despite being the brightest star in the universe, as at school, Dieter was popular among his fellow students and he was equally at home bashing out drinking songs in sleazy underground bars, as playing Mozart or Rachmaninov in professorial parlours. But unlike his drunken acolytes, he could down as much beer as they but remain sober, find the energy to bed the pretty barmaid – and having returned to his attic abode, continue to complete his essays on time to the highest standard. Not surprising, that it was to Dieter his fellow students turned when they were struggling and seemingly without effort he would point each in the right direction. His generosity in sharing his intellect and talents with even the most modestly endowed student endeared him to all; while his wealthy cohorts often invited him for glamorous weekends in luxurious alpine chalets to meet their parents.

Dieter's closest friend and fellow law student was Marco Kaufmann; they had been students together at the Freies Gymnasium. Marco came from one of Basel's old, monied families, though you would never know it. The wealthy, Calvinistic folk of Basel kept their fortunes well hidden; preferring to dress modestly, no fur-coats or diamonds; take the tram and travel economy class – none of the trappings of wealth on view that you might find in other European cities.

One autumn evening Dieter and Marco were out drinking in their favourite haunt: a restaurant in Basel called the Fischerstube. Each was savouring a huge glass of Ueli beer, a beverage actually brewed on the premises. Marco was explaining to Dieter what went on at his local Clique and trying to persuade Dieter to join. Dieter of course knew all about the local tradition of Fasnacht, the three days of celebration that took place each year in the week after Ash Wednesday. He had attended Morgenstreich as a child, more times than he could remember. The excitement of taking the crowded tram into the city when all good people should have been abed. Leaving from the nearest tram station of Flüh at three in the morning, so that he and his mother would be in the city-centre ready for the four o'clock, morning start.

He remembered how the hairs on his neck would stand to attention when the clocks of three nearby churches, as well as that on the City Hall, rang out. On the fourth stroke, all the street lights were extinguished, and like the crowd around him, in the freezing, pitch blackness, he held his breath, listening. Eventually, faintly, in the far distance, the haunting sound of piccolos and drums would be heard. The evocative sound gradually growing louder, as the group of players slowly drew near. The high-pitched notes and steady beat of the Basler drum reverberating around the ancient mediaeval buildings and down the narrow alleyways. To a small boy, it was utterly magical.

Marco was explaining how his Clique of piccolo and drum players met regularly to practice for Fasnacht at their cellar headquarters, and how the clique was split three ways: the old men, the main group and the youngsters. Marco had joined when he was sixteen and was taught how to play the Basler-drum properly and a couple of years' later graduated into the main group.

'You can already play the clarinet,' he argued, 'so you'd be in the same group as me right from the start. Think about it, it's great fun, we have lots of laughs,' persuaded Marco.

It is true, thought Dieter; every resident of Basel loves Fasnacht. Although it only lasts for three days, some people spend the other three-hundred and sixty-two days preparing for it. In Swiss German, a rough translation is: the night before fasting; referring to the beginning of Lent. In medieval times people dressed up in costumes, put on masks and noisily roamed the streets eating and drinking, before the religious festival of Lent began.

He'd learned at school that when the Protestants gained control of Basel in the sixteenth century they tried to stop the event. The locals objected and controversially started parading through the streets on the first Monday in Lent - and have done so ever since.

Later it became more formalised and the different trade guilds formed pipe and drum cliques. Each clique dress differently and as they process, carry a painted lantern poking fun at politicians or social issues.

'You really should come,' Marco was nagging. 'We need more fife players.'

By the time they left the 'stube' that evening and laughingly rolled across the Mittlere Rheinbrücke, the bridge across the Rhine, Dieter had been persuaded he would go with Marco to the next meeting of his Clique.

When Dieter did indeed accompany Marco to a meeting, soon after the discussion, he was introduced to the Dambuurmaioor, the group's leader, who was also the drum major and conductor. He was grilled as to why he wanted to join this particular Clique. Marco had primed him with the right answers; this was after all, the most prestigious of all the groups! He was then requested to demonstrate his ability with the pipe. As he played, the old man looked towards his older colleagues and nodded - there was no discussion, Dieter was accepted into the Clique, and as Fasnacht approached, the intensity of the practices grew, as well as the anticipation of the much-loved annual event.

This marked the beginning of Dieter's participation in the Fasnacht celebrations, which continued every year, without fail and, as with every other aspect of his life, he was welcomed and appreciated.

CHAPTER 4

In the summer following his second university year, Dieter persuaded his father that a couple of months in London would help improve his already competent English - to iron out his accent, as he put it. His father agreed to write the cheque and so Dieter arranged a course and suitable accommodation. By the end of June he was happily ensconced in an expensive, though tiny apartment in the city centre and at the language school placed in the top group with a dozen or so similarly able students.

For eight weeks Dieter planned to attend lessons in the mornings and explore London's galleries and museums in the afternoons - and hopefully attend as many concerts as possible in the evenings. He soon grew to love the cosmopolitan flavour of the metropolis and the scores of cultural events on offer.

In his language class there was only one student of a similar age, the majority were several years older. Initially he hadn't given her a second glance - unisex scruffy clothes and lank blonde hair tumbling onto the desk, hiding her features but one day in the canteen he took the only vacant chair and found himself sitting opposite the most intensely blue eyes he had ever seen, other than his own. He introduced himself and shyly she, the girl, mumbled her name was Katarzyna. Her transparent skin was so pale, her hair so blonde, that it was almost white. Dieter knew she must be Polish. He told her he was from Switzerland and asked where she was from.

'Gdynia, the port on the southern Baltic coast,' she had replied, confirming his intuition. He found that she spoke passable German and they switched between English and his native tongue, as they sipped their cappuccinos. Soon she was laughing at his outrageous stories and jokes and coyly drawn onto the same wavelength. He discovered that she was a kindergarten teacher, who in her spare time played the cello in the town orchestra. The conversation moved on to the latest concert Dieter had seen and their mutual love of classical music soon became apparent. Dieter told her that he had a ticket for a concert at the famed Albert Hall in two days' time. Katarzyna groaned with envy - such events were out of her budget she complained. Later, as they wandered back to class, he asked her what she was doing later that afternoon.

'Walking,' she had replied. 'Every day I walk, either by the river Thames or in one of the many parks.' He asked if today he might join her, and as they re-entered the classroom she nodded, pleased at the thought of spending more time with such a courteous and charismatic companion.

The following day after a class comparing the complexities of Shakespeare's language with the modern-day idiom, they set off for Trafalgar Square and the National Gallery. As they wandered round the many rooms Dieter enjoyed demonstrating his depth of knowledge, particularly of the Impressionist painters, his erudition leaving Katarzyna suitably impressed. After some three hours they collapsed with coffees in the spacious tearoom, where Katarzyna kicked off her shoes, gigglingly complaining that there was too much to see.

Later that evening they went to the cinema in Leicester Square and afterwards fell into a bar, where they stayed, until she reminded him there was reading to be done before tomorrow's lesson. As they strolled back towards the hostel where Katarzyna was staying, she kept glancing slyly from under her impossibly long lashes, at her companion, knowing that she had fallen under his spell. His never-ending chatter and fund of humorous stories drawing her in, as if snared on the hook of a fisherman's line. It suddenly struck her that despite his maturity, he must be at least five years younger than she. Was this an issue? She eventually persuaded herself that it was not.

As for Dieter, at that particular moment, he wasn't seriously considering how he felt about his companion, as he studied the ground, avoiding stepping on the breaks between the flagstones. For sure, he liked her softly-rounded features and blue eyes. It was flattering the way she hung on his every word, made complimentary comments and laughed out loud at his jokes. He loved an adoring audience and, for the moment, Katarzyna conveniently provided the attention his personality demanded.

At lunch on Friday he told her to shut her eyes before removing her empty plate and laying a ticket on the grubby green tablecloth. He commanded her to open, which she did with a giggle, immediately picking up the ticket and examining it with great care - and then gasping with pleasure.

'It's for the concert at the Albert Hall, I was telling you about; I managed to get a second ticket,' explained Dieter. 'I was lucky, they first told me they had sold out but then someone couldn't go.' Katarzyna reached across the table, her eyes moist, and squeezed his hand:

'The Berlin Philharmonic… how wonderful…thank you so much,' she breathed. 'But, really, as I explained, I'm on a very tight budget.'

'That's okay,' said Dieter, 'my treat, it's no fun attending such a concert on your own.'

The concert in the Albert Hall's famed, cavernous auditorium left them both breathless and overwhelmed. Outside, mingling with the chattering masses, Katarzyna buried her hand into Dieter's, before reaching up to peck his cheek, proclaiming it was the best concert she had ever attended in her whole life!

Neither was surprised that they found themselves back in Dieter's narrow bed that night, nor that the following day Katarzyna moved out of the hostel and into his tiny apartment. She was like putty in Dieter's hands and like his mother before her, scurried around ironing his shirts, cooking delicious meals on the single hotplate or utilising the miniscule oven, pandering to his every whim. Their lovemaking was wild and noisy, provoking a neighbour to rap loudly on the wall, shouting for them to behave - at this they fell about laughing, only to begin again, resulting in more banging and bellowing.

When the English course ended they celebrated together with a meal in an expensive restaurant; Katarzyna knew her lover was only just setting out on his university career and it would be years before he was in a position to settle down. Dieter realised this too but promised he would visit her in Gdynia during the Christmas break. That night they fell asleep in each other's arms, Katarzyna weeping silently to herself, convinced that life would never be the same again.

When Dieter awoke the next morning Katarzyna was

standing by the door, her packed suitcase by her feet, she was gazing down at him, a solitary tear sliding down her cheek. He leapt out of bed, gave her a quick hug before struggling into his clothes, declaring that he would go with her to the airport.

'I'm not going to the airport,' she said. 'The son of a friend is giving me a lift.' She picked up her case but Dieter took it from her and dropped it on the bed before wrapping her in his arms. 'I must go,' she said, tears rolling unchecked down her cheeks. 'He's outside on the street, I'd rather he didn't see you; he might tell my father!' She looked at him appealingly before opening the door and slipping out.

Dieter put on his shoes and slowly descended the circular stairs. When he peered around the doorjamb he was bewildered to see a huge truck, with Slavic writing on the tilt, parked on the busy street causing chaos, and Katarzyna climbing up into the cab helped by a tall young man wearing a green T-shirt and a baseball cap. As the huge vehicle pulled slowly away into the early morning traffic, he saw the Polish number plate and Katarzyna's pale, pouting face reflected in the driving mirror.

Back in his room, he was struck how empty it felt, the absence of littered lingerie and Katarzyna's warm persona was tangible. He saw that she had left her address written on a scrap of paper, prominently displayed on an old chest of drawers where he couldn't miss it. Dieter picked it up and gazed at it for several moments, walked to the window and peered down on the continuous line of vehicles below - and then deliberately tore the paper in half and then quarters and finally into eight small pieces, which he icily scattered like snowflakes into the waste-basket.

CHAPTER 5

The weeks and months slipped quickly by, in which Dieter continued to study and play his beloved piano. His father, in an attempt at matchmaking, introduced his son to the daughter of one of his wealthy clients. She was a trainee fashion designer, hoping to make a name for herself in Paris and for a while they saw each other regularly and even holidayed together one scorching summer at a small hotel in St Tropez. While Dieter could find no faults with his attractive, well-heeled companion, he refused to become totally committed, purely because she was his father's choice. Eventually the distraught girl realised that the relationship was going nowhere and the weekend trips from Paris ceased and Dieter's Saturday nights were spent back in the smoky bars beneath the city, hammering out drinking songs with his fellow students.

After three and a half years of study Dieter completed his thesis and sat the final examinations. He passed with the highest marks, graduated from university and immediately signed up to complete a Master's degree. As it would be several months before these courses started, his father had insisted he gain experience working at the Basel office. Dieter was dismayed, he wanted to travel, lie on an isolated beach somewhere and forget everything to do with law. But in the end blackmail won out, his father's promise of a bigger apartment and the latest Porsche helped decide the issue!

One bright summer morning Dieter left his new apartment and walked across the bustling Market Square, where the early morning sun illuminated the red façade of the wonderful City Hall. He then strolled on through the medieval back streets and alleyways to his father's office, to begin, what he thought would be, several months of misery under his father's thumb.

Fortunately for Dieter, his father still spent most of his time in Freiburg; as this was the busier of the offices. Dieter had many times visited his father's modern offices in Basel's old town, where the medieval façade concealed a skilful renovation. The office was run by an elderly, bald-headed man, named Walter Klein. Walter had been a regular dinner guest during Dieter's teenage years and obviously a trusted retainer. He greeted Dieter with enthusiasm, saying what a great day this was for the company to have Ferdinand's son beginning his apprenticeship. He showed Dieter into a small, brightly lit room and introduced him to a lively middle-aged lady, who was to act as his mentor.

During those first weeks, Dieter quickly moved from completing mundane legal tasks to more sophisticated cases; he really enjoyed the intellectual challenge. A delighted Walter Klein glowingly reported his rapid progress to Dieter's father.

Dieter worked tirelessly throughout the week, concentrating on the job in hand, while reading and studying legal tomes each evening. But on Friday and Saturday nights, he continued the routine of meeting with his old cronies from university to carouse in the noisy, smoke-filled basement bars. Sundays, when the weather allowed, he would hike with friends through the neighbouring forests, usually ending the day by dutifully sharing dinner with his mother at home in Hofstetten.

Following the split with the Parisian designer, a succession of eligible women flowed in and out of Dieter's life, attracted by his wild good looks, courtesy and glowing future prospects. But while he took advantage of their charms, Dieter skated on the surface of the thin-iced relationships before eventually sliding on to pastures new.

During one particularly long break between girl friends, perhaps only as little as fourteen days, he found himself thinking of Katarzyna. He was lying on his bed and it was the first time since their parting, he thought of her but had no idea what had triggered the little grey cells. The memory of her quick smile and warm personality suddenly and nostalgically overwhelmed him; she was so different from all the other women he had dated since - most of them had been much better looking and yet... He found himself contemplating a trip to Gdynia - before remembering he had destroyed the note she had left with her address. He thought of playing detective and tracking her down but realised that he knew nothing about her, except for the fact she was a kindergarten teacher who played the cello. As he lay remembering those few weeks he shared with Katarzyna, over two years before, he wondered how many people lived in Gdynia, what was the population; how many schools were there, how easy would it be? The more he thought about her, the more determined he became that he would try and find her. But during the following week the further he went with his enquiries, the more complicated he realised it would be.

To start with he would need a visa from the Polish embassy and was told this could take weeks. He was required to provide a valid reason for the journey, addresses of the people and places he was visiting. He knew it was no use providing false information, because for certain, every detail would be checked.

He learned that, while in theory, it was now easier to get through Berlin's border crossing points from west to east and all he would need was a passport, he should expect to be grilled and have his papers checked at regular intervals all the way. Although cracks were showing in Honecker's East Germany, it was still a Soviet-style police state and certainly no place to be driving an expensive Porsche with Swiss number plates.

CHAPTER 6

It was typical of Dieter's von Murren's personality that the more difficult or unattainable the goal, the more enthusiastically he refused to take no for an answer. He had made several trips to the Polish embassy in Berne and in the end his perseverance was rewarded and three weeks later he had a visa stamped in his passport to visit Poland, his covering letter stating he had urgent business to discuss with Gdynia's largest law firm.

He arranged with Walter Klein to take a week off work, and having packed an overnight bag, he left Basel early one morning and drove his Porsche the eight hundred and seventy kilometres to Berlin, where he left his car with an old university friend and took a train to Warsaw.

Peering through grubby windows, as the train crawled through East Berlin's sprawling suburbs, Dieter's morale sank, as he entered a drab, poorly lit, disturbing nightmare, peopled by grey, zombie-like figures, slouching, full of threatening resentment. He congratulated himself on his decision to take the train; at least in the stuffy, battered compartment he felt somewhat safer. Seven hours later the train pulled into Warsaw's brand new, not quite completed, main station but it was late and he missed the connection to Gdynia. He sat in the station's sparkling new coffee bar fretting and the two beggars that wandered in and approached him got short shrift, and sensing his mood each quickly moved on.

It was dark by the time Dieter arrived in Gdynia, he found a taxi outside the station and instructed the driver to take him to his pre-booked, centrally located hotel, where he collapsed and slept.

The following day, he asked a taxi driver to take him to the education department where he charmed his way into the inner sanctum, showed his business card and spun a yarn about needing to contact a young teacher about a personal legal matter.

He was surprised how readily the information was supplied by the stocky battle-axe who guarded the data; no doubt his charm had worked its usual magic. An hour later a taxi dropped him in a leafy suburb close to a concrete monstrosity that was the school. On the pavement, outside, Dieter strolled up and down the street. He glanced at his watch, it was almost lunchtime. Perhaps this would be a good time.

High-pitched shouts indicated caged animals desperate for freedom, and Dieter grinned, as he watched tiny figures erupt through a door, as if escaping from a monster, screaming with joy as they raced to the perimeter fence without stopping. A couple of grim-faced female adults emerged, followed by even more noisy children. There was a gate in the fence but it was locked. Dieter shouted and one of the ladies walked towards him. He explained he needed to speak to one of their colleagues. The older of the women looked him up and down and asked who he needed to see, he seemed respectable enough, even if he was German.

'Katarzyna,' he replied, 'Katarzyna Kaminski.'

The girl nodded, drew a large key from her apron pocket and unlocked the gate. Dieter thanked her and followed, as she led him into the building. They were only just through the door when Dieter saw Katarzyna walking down a corridor towards him, her arms full of books, carefully watching where she put her feet, avoiding satchels and outdoor shoes. He had grown a full beard since she had last seen him. Will she recognise me, he wondered? She glanced up and saw him.

'Moj Bozel,' she cried in Polish, frozen to the spot, seemingly unaware of the books slipping from her grasp and scattering among the muddy boots. 'My God, Dieter, what are you doing here?'

'Looking for you,' he replied quietly, stretching out his hands invitingly. Ignoring the books, Katarzyna flew into his arms where they clung to each other, oblivious of the tittering children spilling down the corridor.

'You didn't write,' she said accusingly. 'And I couldn't write to you, you didn't give me your address!'

'I'm sorry,' he replied. 'I lost the piece of paper.' She let him go and stood back, she had forgotten how good-looking he was. She hardly noticed the beard.

'How long are you here for?' she asked breathlessly?

'A couple of days maybe three,' he answered.

'Gowno! I have to work,' she cried despairingly. 'You should have warned me!'

'I'm sorry - I told you. I lost your address!' Dieter was bending down, gathering up the books strewn at their feet. Katarzyna ran her fingers through his blonde curls.

'I missed you,' she murmured.

'I missed you too,' he lied, standing up, holding a neat pile of exercise books. 'Where do you want these?' She led him into a classroom, where a tubby assistant was busy washing paintbrushes in the sink.

'Anka,' said Katarzyna, 'I'm going out for an hour.' The girl at the sink looked over her shoulder grinned and said something that Dieter could not understand. Katarzyna collected her coat and they made their way out onto the street, once out of sight of the school she snuggled her hand into his, reached up and kissed his cheek.

'I thought you had forgotten all about me,' she whispered. 'Two years is a long time!'

'I thought you might already be married - or at least have a boyfriend.'

'Not married but a boyfriend ... well sort of.'

Katarzyna led them towards to a small café she knew and for the next hour she quizzed him about the real reason for his visit, not believing he had come specially to see her. Suddenly she glanced at her watch, 'I must get back' she said, 'the children.' Dieter paid for their coffee and they dashed back towards the school, laughing and out of breath. At the school gate she kissed him hard on the lips, not caring if anyone was watching.

'Be back here at three-thirty,' she commanded and ran inside, turning to wave when she reached the main door.

The next few days flew by; during the day Dieter explored the comparatively new city, while during the early evenings Katarzyna walked him along the foot of the cliffs, or down the impressive promenade, explaining that the huge docks had only been built in the nineteen-twenties, at a time when Gdynia was an insignificant fishing village.

'And now she said proudly, 'it's one of the largest shipyards on the Baltic.' Dieter gazed at the huge cranes, his arm loosely around Katarzyna's waist:

'Was Gdynia affected at all by the war?' he asked, gazing at the Lego-like stacked containers.

'Oh yes,' replied Katarzyna, 'in nineteen forty-five it was totally destroyed, flattened. The Germans executed more than twelve thousand people, when they first came, including many of my family.' Walking further on Katarzyna pointed out a statue. 'Not just the Germans who killed our people,' she sighed. 'Polish troops…the police… killed and injured hundreds of striking shipyard workers in the 1970's, it was the beginning of the end of the government … and the old ways.' She turned towards Dieter. 'Enough of all this morbidity, she laughed and pulled his arm. 'Come on, let's go back to your hotel, I need you to make love to me!'

At the end of the three days, Dieter took the train to Warsaw, leaving a weeping Katarzyna on the platform. He leaned out of the window waving, until the isolated figure; arm aloft clutching a fluttering handkerchief became an unrecognisable, insignificant dot. As Dieter settled down to read, he found his eyes skimming the page but not registering what he was reading. He was weighing up whether or not he really wanted Katarzyna in his life. Gazing at the pages of Gore Vidal's best-selling *Burr*, he found himself mentally listing pros and cons of continuing the relationship.

On the plus side, she was attractive, an exciting lover, shared his passion for music, loved children, was even-tempered. The contrary side was more difficult: she was from a different culture, he couldn't decide whether or not that might be an issue in the future; her father was a communist official in the dockworkers union and wouldn't approve. Katarzyna had said as much. The main problem he decided was the distance between them and the impossibility of spending time together in order to be sure.

And then there was America! He had plans to apply to Harvard to study for a doctorate - and that would take another two years and he still hadn't started his Master's course! By the time he had changed trains in Warsaw and was en-route for Berlin he was beginning to think his impulse to try and rekindle the relationship was a mistake. If Katarzyna lived in Basel, it would be different, there would be time for the relationship to slowly build and time for him to study but being so far apart … it made no sense.

CHAPTER 7

At about the time Dieter von Murren was beginning his Master's course, in the small, attractive town of Todtnau, scenically squeezed between the mountains of the Belchen and Feldberg in Germany's famed Black Forest, a small boy clung to the wire fence surrounding the school playground. As usual, he was isolated, ignored by the other children, left to his own devices. It was the same every day both in the playground and in the classroom. If you don't understand something or someone, his schoolmates thought; stay away, don't look, don't speak and perhaps the problem will evaporate and go away, just like a bad dream.

The boy gazed through the diamond shaped wire at the river rushing by, hypnotised by the way the water turned to foam, as it splashed over rocks and formed mesmerising whirlpools. Whirlpools that gathered leaves; dragged them inevitably towards the centre and sucked them under.

Another young boy, even smaller, strolled up to the wire trying to see what the attraction was. He was new to the school and didn't know about staying away, not looking and not speaking.

'What can you see?' he asked. No reaction. He repeated the question, this time louder. Still no response. He dug the older boy in the ribs. 'Can you see fish?' The larger boy clinging to the wire suddenly let go and swung an arm, his elbow caught the younger boy in the throat with a sickening crack and the innocent child fell, poleaxed. Mindlessly the older boy let go the wire and began kicking the prostrate child in the body and head, until the crying stopped. The screams of the children who had gathered around brought the duty-teacher running. She dragged the sweating, bulbous-eyed boy away but by now he was screaming and struggling. He was strong and he slipped from her grasp, climbed over the fence and ran.

This incident, the like of which, had never previously been witnessed at the small village school, horrified teachers and parents, and traumatised those children who witnessed the cruel violence. All demanded: something must be done. Bruno Schmidt was expelled, psychoanalysed and spent the rest of his school life in a Special School for special boys. He was eventually diagnosed as a schizophrenic, fed pills and made manageable.

CHAPTER 8

Following the trip to Gdynia, Dieter wrote a lengthy letter to Katarzyna detailing the plans for his Master's degree and his ambition to gain admission to Harvard to complete a doctorate. He didn't spell it out but he was letting her down gently, letting her know that she didn't really figure in his future plans. There was no mention of further visits or hints that she should visit him. There were no outpourings of love or any words that he might be missing her - purely the facts of how the next few years of his life were already clearly mapped out.

Anyone reading Katarzyna's reply would have felt the emotion and the disappointment, despite the fact that she wrote in English, not trusting her German but her carefully chosen words sailed over Dieter's head, unappreciated that here was a woman desperate to be an integral part of his life.

Dieter deigned to send Katarzyna a couple of postcards in response to her lengthy missives, which over the following weeks landed in his post-box at regular intervals. But on the whole, the memory of his hasty visit grew fainter and more distant.

Dieter's time working in his father's office came to a welcome end and on his final day, after the office door was locked, Walter Klein produced a bottle of champagne and as the employees stood awkwardly around the cluttered office, he congratulated Dieter on his achievements, told those assembled what a wonderful day it would be when Dieter had finished his Master's course and joined them fulltime. As he raised his glass and toasted Dieter's future; Dieter knew one thing for certain, he would never work in his father's office, he was determined to do something totally different - he felt convinced he was destined for something far greater than this mundane, parochial business could offer.

* * *

In the summer after Dieter had completed his Master's degree, he rented out his apartment, moved some of his belongings to his parent's home and flew to Boston. He was excited on two counts, one, he had never visited America. And two, Harvard, in his eyes at least, was the world's most prestigious university. He had never doubted that he would gain a place and didn't know that the acceptance rate for the Business School was under twelve per cent. He was enrolled for the Ph.D. programme to study business economics at the HBS facility, located in Allston, approximately a mile and a half across the Charles River from Harvard Yard, the centre of the main campus.

After living in his own apartment for several years he was somewhat surprised to find that all students were required to live on campus, even doctoral students. But it wasn't long before he understood the reasoning and enjoyed being on the spot, close to the lecture rooms, the library, his fellow students and the professors.

The days passed quickly. Dieter thoroughly enjoyed the intellectual challenge of his course, the American way of life and all the wonderful cultural possibilities that Boston had to offer. His piano playing ability was soon recognised and became a passport into the homes of the great and the good, exactly as it had in Basel.

At one of the many functions he attended, Dieter met an assistant professor of business administration; she taught first-year MBA classes and in a distinctly southern drawl, introduced herself as Charlene. She was not the type of woman he usually dated, despite being a leggy, slim blonde - for she was noisily strong-willed, articulate and far too clever for her own good. It seemed, when she wasn't teaching, she was always out determinedly running or cycling - definitely not his type.

Dieter really upset the woman when, at their second meeting over cocktails at a professor's home, he asked if it was correct to describe her as a WASP? Charlene choked and almost spilled her drink and went to great lengths to explain that it was usually used as a derogatory term.

'But you're white,' he protested 'and the last time we met, you told me you're a Christian and that your ancestors came from Germany.' He could see, as he tried to explain, that he had made a faux pas and so tried to make amends by inviting her out to dinner.

Dieter's invitation and the resulting dinner in a dimly lit, carefully chosen restaurant led to regular assignations. Despite the spinsterish, prim and proper persona that she projected; in Dieter's company she soon melted, became less argumentative and allowed herself to be manipulated. She admired his endless stream of anecdotes and courteous, though determined, manner. She liked the way he always had clear ideas of what he wanted and it came as a surprise that she quite enjoyed the new experience being told what to do and ordered about, for it was always Dieter who planned their weekend activities of concerts and visits. As for Dieter, it was a game, as he prodded and gently teased. He knew that he only had to snap his fingers and she would fall into his arms without a second thought but he cruelly kept her just far enough away, waiting to see if she would eventually beg.

At the beginning of December Charlene invited Dieter to spend the Christmas period with her, at her parents' home in Alabama. It was not an easy decision, for he knew his mother would expect him to spend the holiday period in Hofstetten. In the end he wrote to his mother explaining that he was going to take the opportunity to travel and see more of America.

Charlene's parents lived near Birmingham and her father was at the airport to meet them and transport them to the family home in the countryside. Charlene's father was a rugged, retired quarry manager of few words, though obviously very proud of his clever daughter.

Dieter was surprised when they rolled off the highway, through large wrought-iron gates and down a long drive surrounded by fields where grazing horses raised their heads in greeting; Charlene pointing and excitedly reciting many of their names.

Her mother was on the steps of the sprawling, ranch-style home - a jodhpur-clad, cloned, older version of her daughter, though obviously much younger than her husband. She greeted Dieter enthusiastically, such that Dieter had the feeling this was the first time her only daughter had ever brought a male friend home! Over supper Dieter was grilled and spent much of the time describing his home country and answering awkward questions concerning his future ambitions.

After breakfast the next morning Charlene suggested a ride

and led Dieter out to the elegant stables, where two young girls were busy, one mucking out, the other grooming a gleaming gelding. Dieter had to admit that he had never been astride a horse, which caused Charlene to laugh uncontrollably, as if something unbelievably vital had been omitted from his education. She assured him that he wouldn't have a problem and chose an elderly, experienced mare that would, as she said, 'look after him.'

Having saddled up, she held the horse steady and told Dieter to put a foot in the stirrup. He was soon in the saddle and tried to ignore how far away the ground was below him. One of the girls had saddled a beautiful, gold-coated palomino, which Charlene hugged lovingly before nimbly leaping onto an upturned bucket and into the saddle, ignoring the stirrup. Side by side they left the stable yard and rode towards the open countryside; Charlene issuing instructions for controlling the horse, suggesting that Dieter practice turning right and then left. The horse obediently did as requested and Dieter's confidence grew. He liked this he decided and it wasn't long before he had urged the horse into a trot, which brought cheers from his tutor.

At the top of a hill, Charlene suggested they stop and slid elegantly from her mount, tying the reins around the saddle horn. Dieter climbed down more carefully, asking if they needed to fasten the horses to an overhanging branch. Charlene assured him this would not be necessary and that the well trained horses wouldn't wander far and would come when she called. She was dressed in a stylish windcheater, a silk scarf around her neck, the Stetson pushed to the back of her head, jodhpurs emphasising her ample, though shapely hips. Dieter took this in before gazing down into the valley where the ranch they had just left was comfortably nestled. He loved the wide-open expanse of countryside, the surrounding forests and the glimpse of a lake in the distance - it almost reminded him of home.

'Were you brought up here?' he asked.

'No,' replied Charlene. 'My parents bought the place when Dad retired. We lived in the suburbs of Birmingham but it was always Dad's ambition to move to the country when he finished in the quarry business.'

'But you learned to ride as a child,' said Dieter. 'You must have done.'

'Oh yes, I went to riding school almost as soon as I could walk. My mother used to take me every weekend - she'd been brought up on a farm and ridden all her life.' Strange, thought Dieter, that never once had he himself ever contemplated learning to ride, it never entered his head and now after only an hour or so in the saddle, he was hooked.

Dieter spent five days as a guest at the luxurious ranch house in Alabama. Each day he and Charlene, and occasionally her mother, rode for miles. His proficiency improved and he relished the magnificent scenery and wide-open spaces. But on the fifth day he made his excuses, explaining that he wanted to see more of America while he had the chance. Charlene's mother was very disappointed to see him go, she already had this charismatic young man earmarked as a prospective son-in-law. As for Charlene herself, she offered to accompany Dieter but he eloquently explained that he intended to 'slum it' by touring the southwest by Greyhound bus and staying in motels. She wasn't put off but he rebutted all her overtures and in the end she consoled herself that she would see more of him when the new term started, just a few weeks away.

Driving her mother's pick-up, Charlene delivered Dieter to the bus station in downtown Birmingham and waited patiently while he bought a ticket. It wasn't long before an early morning Greyhound pulled into the bay, heading for New Orleans; he thanked Charlene profusely for the hospitality he had received, hugged her and pecked her cheek - promising he would take her out for dinner in a couple of weeks' time, when term started again. Once he had found his allocated window seat, he turned to wave but Charlene was already back in the pick-up, miffed that he wouldn't take her with him and deep down already convinced that she was wasting her time.

CHAPTER 9

Throughout the Spring, Dieter and Charlene spent time together, attending concerts, visiting museums with the occasional daytrip to Cape Cod. But Dieter used the excuse of his studies to limit the contact. In the summer, halfway through his course, Dieter returned to Switzerland and stayed with his mother at Hofstetten. His father was home at weekends and quizzed his son about his research and described the role he could play in his company when he had finished. Dieter bit the bullet and sowed the seed that he might want to gain experience in some other line of business before joining his father. It had led to an argument that saw his mother slide quietly away to bed and left his father grumpy for the rest of his visit.

By the beginning of September, he was pleased to be back in his small but well equipped apartment and telephoned Charlene to let her know he was back but she wasn't home. He left a message on the answering machine but a week later she still hadn't called.

A few days before the course was due to start again, Dieter ran into Charlene on the campus, she seemed flustered, explained that she had spent the summer in Hawaii, asked after his trip but unusually for her, kept the conversation short, made excuses and left.

It was almost four weeks before their paths crossed again, and this was one evening at a cocktail party. Charlene briefly introduced him to the older man she was with, before making an excuse and dragging him away. Obviously, thought Dieter, Charlene had found herself a new escort. Later that evening, as he contemplated events, he felt a pang of something he didn't recognise, could it be jealousy? More likely selfishness for he had lost an amiable companion - he would have no one to accompany him to concerts and galleries - and he had totally underestimated her, for she had never begged!

A month later, at yet another monotonous social event, he spotted Charlene. He decided that she looked very subdued but as elegant as ever, as she stared thoughtfully into her large glass of white wine. She was on the fringe of a group of people Dieter didn't know. He was pleased to see a familiar face - in fact, he decided, he was very pleased to see Charlene. As he watched, he realised that she was on her own. Dieter approached her from behind and spoke her name. From her expression, it was apparent that she was very pleased to see him and offered her cheek. After asking how she was, he enquired about her escort, he couldn't remember the man's name.

'I was a fool,' she said, taking a sip of wine. 'Turned out he had a wife to go home to!'

'Oh dear!' said Dieter, hiding a grin. 'I'm sorry.'

'It get's worse,' she continued, 'the woman works in the administration, in my building, I actually know her but didn't know she has a husband!' Dieter put an arm around Charlene's shoulder and squeezed:

'Do we really have to be here?' he whispered. 'Would anyone notice if we just slipped away and had dinner somewhere?'

They found a quiet table in a small restaurant that they had visited before and in no time Charlene's mood changed, as Dieter told stories of his trip back home and she about her vacation in Hawaii with two girl friends and her couple of weeks in Alabama.

'My mother kept asking why I hadn't invited you again!' she said, catching his eye. 'You obviously made quite a hit.'

After the meal they strolled arm in arm back to Charlene's apartment, where at the door, she invited him for a coffee. Dieter hesitated but only for a moment. They never did get the coffee, for the moment they were through the door and into the hallway of her apartment she dragged him into her arms and kissed him passionately. Coats, gloves and scarves dropped to the floor. Gradually the remainder of their clothes were scattered, leaving a sensuous trail from the hallway to Charlene's bedroom.

CHAPTER 10

By the early summer Dieter had completed his thesis. Later he defended his research and graduated - Doctor Dieter von Murren Ph.D. had a elegant ring about it he thought smugly - a certain je ne sais quoi!

Dieter, although filled with satisfaction at his achievement, was consumed with a feeling of sadness that the heady, academic life at Harvard had ended. He had blossomed in the intellectual stratosphere and had taken every opportunity to glean all that was offered by the brilliant minds that had surrounded him. After a hectic round of farewell parties, he reluctantly packed his belongings and bid farewell to his many friends.

Charlene offered to drive him to Logan Airport, where she hugged him briefly, hiding her tears with a noisy show of bravado, convinced that she would never see or hear from this man again. He was about to fly out of her life forever; a nagging thought, that for some weeks, she repeatedly tried unsuccessfully to put to the back of her head. Inside the terminal there were the usual proclamations of meeting again but both knew they weren't really meant. And as Dieter's flight to Zurich climbed into the sky, Charlene was parked in a layby allowing herself the catharsis of a wet, noisy weeping and swearing session; just to get the bloody, self-centred, arrogant but lovely man out of her system, she justified to herself.

After a few moments Charlene calmed and watched the relentless traffic hurrying by with moist, unseeing eyes.

'I've had a lucky escape,' she eventually thought. He would have broken my heart. Dieter von Murren doesn't have a heart, or if he does it is made of stone. It's amazing, she decided, that someone could be so charismatic, good-looking, academically brilliant and yet be worth nothing because at the core he was rotten, egotistical, calculating, and untrustworthy. In a relationship, she murmured to herself, I wouldn't trust him an inch. Charlene kicked the car into life. Checked her makeup in the mirror, stared into her own eyes and shouted unconvincingly:

'Thank God he's out of my life!' As for Dieter, settling back into his business-class seat, he did think about Charlene on the long flight - for about five minutes flat. She had been great company he agreed, and since that fateful, boring cocktail party, a regular and exuberant, if inexperienced lover but the idea of a long term relationship with this young lady was certainly not on his agenda.

Dieter took the train from Zurich airport to Basel; peering out of his first-class window and comparing the neat fields and picturesque houses, all so calm and orderly after the frenetic city life he had just left. Both, he decided, had their place, he needed to plan his future to include time in both. He loved the excitement, noise and sense of danger that he felt in the cities. He liked America; he liked Americans, even if at heart, they were all frustrated wild-west cowboys. He loved their spontaneous generosity, openness and friendliness and failed to reconcile these attributes with their politicians and alien foreign policies that caused him and the rest of the world to despair.

His mother met him at the airport, she had missed him and was overjoyed and full of questions. His father would be home in a few days time, she told him and pleaded that he be patient with his father and not upset him. He tried to explain, as she drove carefully through the Binningen and Bottmingen suburbs of Basel, how he needed to gain experience with a large multi-national company before joining his father's firm. His mother said nothing, she followed the logic but knew Ferdinand would be livid; he was relying on his son taking over the business.

After exactly twenty-four hours of devoting every waking moment to his mother, Dieter made excuses and drove his Porsche down the hill through Ettingen and into Basel. He made his way to the Headquarters of one of city's largest pharmaceutical companies, Ciba Geigy, where he had arranged an appointment with the Director of Human Resources, an ebullient Swiss, named Weber. The interview went well and ended with the pair heading off to the canteen for lunch. By the time the meal had ended, Weber knew that Dieter was exactly the kind of person to whom he would like to offer a job. A top job. However, he would need to fire someone first and as they sipped their coffee, he was mulling over in his mind who that might be. Later, in the spacious reception area Weber handed Dieter his business-card and as they shook hands, he told him to telephone in a week's time, when he would have some news.

At precisely two o'clock, the same day, in another part of Basel, Dieter was shown into the luxurious offices of Hofmann La Roche, another of the city's major pharmaceutical firms. The hunched up figure of the Human Resources Director did not stand but pointed to an empty chair. He was perched like a hungry sparrow behind a massive glass-topped desk, upon which an elaborated carved nameplate announced - Axel Koch. Herr Koch, thought Dieter, seemed in danger of disappearing into the enveloping arms of his massive armchair - although he couldn't see, Dieter was convinced that this powerful little man's feet probably didn't touch the floor. In a pronounced Bavarian accent, the man plied Dieter with searching questions, as he worked his way through the eight page curriculum vitae, that Dieter had supplied a week earlier.

At last satisfied with the answers, he invited Dieter to accompany him and walked him through the spacious open-plan offices where La Roche's elves scurried about, files of paper in hand, brows furrowed in mock concentration. Dieter was introduced to a number of department heads, though Axel Koch was careful not to say why his guest was visiting. At the reception area Koch handed Dieter his business card with the same request as Weber from Ciba, call in a week's time. Only Koch was not considering whom he could fire but whom he could persuade needed an assistant.

The following day saw Dieter back out at Basel's airport, incongruously situated across the Swiss border in France. He caught an early morning flight to Berlin and by ten o'clock was seated, waiting for his appointment with the Human Resource Director of Pfizer, another huge pharmaceutical company. At the end of the two-hour interview Dieter was offered a position with the vague title of Assistant Business Planning and Strategy Director. It sounded good and the attractive salary and perks very tempting, nevertheless he politely explained he was testing the waters and was given two weeks to decide whether or not he wanted the position. Dieter left the palatial offices and spent a couple of hours exploring the Kurfürstendamm shopping area, though the only thing he bought was a small gift for his mother.

He caught the late afternoon flight back to Basel and arrived in Hofstetten at the same time as his father. His mother fussed around them both before disappearing into the kitchen leaving the two men in the living room. The pair of them stood in the bay window looking out across the fields towards the Blauen, sipping single malts, which Dieter's father had poured.

'I hear you've been to Berlin today,' said Ferdinand. Dieter nodded and grunted. 'Are you going to tell me why?' enquired his father.

'I went to Pfizer's headquarters to see what kind of job they might have for me.' Ferdinand was silent. Eventually, he half-turned towards Dieter and said:

'You must realise that I make a very good living … and if you will join the business, I promise that, provided you do well, I am willing to hand over the task of running the company to you. Within twelve months I'll be ready to retire.'

'Yesterday I also went to the big two in Basel. Seems they are interested in offering me a job too,' said Dieter, ignoring his father's proposal.

'Did you hear what I said?' said Ferdinand draining his glass.

'I did Father,' replied Dieter. 'But I need to spread my wings, gain some experience of life in the corporate world before joining your company.'

'They'll chew you up and spit you out!' snarled Ferdinand. The discussion grew into an argument until Dieter's mother entered the room, drawn by the loud voices. She shouted and hushed the pair, threatening there would be no dinner if they didn't behave themselves. A threat she had used since Dieter's childhood, which caused him to smile and give her a hug, though the disagreement continued all evening, right up to the moment Ferdinand climbed into his Mercedes and headed back to Freiberg.

The following day Dieter received a telephone call from Luther Weber, the Human Resource Director that he had met a few days earlier, inviting him for another meeting. This time Weber was accompanied by two other smart-suited men. The three of them probed and prodded and in the end offered him a position with a title even grander and more obscure than that offered in Berlin a few days earlier. The two men shook Dieter's hand warmly and left, leaving

Weber to work out the details of the contract.

'I've already been offered a similar position with Pfizer, in Berlin,' said Dieter.

'How much are they offering to pay you?' asked Weber? Dieter told him.

'Chickenfeed,' laughed Weber, 'I can double that.' Momentarily, Dieter was shocked by the generosity but his face didn't flicker - he was after all Dieter von Murren Ph.D. and worth every last penny.

CHAPTER 11

Dieter celebrated his twenty-sixth birthday with a group of his university friends at the luxurious hotel: *Les Trois Rois*, perched impressively alongside the River Rhine in Basel. There had been a hotel on this spot since the 1600's and even Napoleon was supposed to have been one of many famous visitors. All of his friends had successfully graduated from the local university and most swallowed up by the local pharmaceutical companies. These giant companies had a never-satisfied hunger for talent and were already having to seek fodder from abroad. It was a topic of discussion among the young men, worried that one day these monoliths that poured money into the local economy, as well as its museums, galleries and theatres, might eventually fall into foreign hands. Decades of company generosity had made Basel wealthy and a delightful place to live. Living standards were high; no one wanted to see that change.

A week later Dieter joined the queue of cars pouring through the gates of Ciba Geigy, excited about starting his first day. He had an allocated parking space, into which he gingerly steered his Porsche but as he strolled across the tarmac to the main entrance he decided he would in future use the tram. From his Rhine-side apartment it would be an easy commute, much simpler than sitting in his car crawling through the busy early-morning streets.

At reception his identification badges were waiting and after a word with security he made his way up to Weber's office. There were more papers to sign but when that was all completed, Weber took his arm and guided him towards an elevator and the top floor, where he was directed towards a spacious, corner office. Inside the clinically stark room, decorated with the obligatory metre-high aspidistra-style plant, Weber smirked and introduced Dieter to Gloria, an extremely attractive, raven-haired woman, whom Weber said would be Dieter's personal assistant. She smiled shyly, balanced the papers she was carrying with one arm and her chin and wrung his hand. Weber soon made his excuses and left. Gloria followed but not before pointing out a button on Dieter's desk, which she told him to press if he needed her; at which point Dieter settled himself into the comfortable, enveloping arms of the enormous office chair and gazed at the pile of papers the glamorous Gloria, had meticulously placed before him. His eyes strayed towards the panoramic windows and Basel spread far below him and with a push of his foot he sent the chair into a spin. After several chuckling rotations, he grabbed the desk, took a deep breath and picked up the top sheet of paper - his working career had begun.

CHAPTER 12

During the first week Gloria was constantly in his office, as he learned the routine. The close contact stimulated the usual lustful thoughts to leap, uninvited, into his cerebral cortex, as he devoured her from the top of her head to the tip of her moderately-heeled stilettos. But when she left his office for the last time on the second day, he gave himself a good talking to.

In retrospect, perhaps it was Weber's smirking introduction that set warning bells ringing. Spending one's working day in the company of such a luscious companion could easily lead to innocent after-work, drinks and progressively, to less-innocent activities and then the gossip would start and his planned career targets might be compromised.

And so it was, that after only two days in the job, Dieter determined that he would never mix business with pleasure and after all, there was a whole world of women waiting for him outside the factory gates, he could almost hear them clamouring - he just needed to make time to meet them.

For the next twelve months Dieter's life was consumed by his new job. Meetings and travel, usually backwards and forwards to the east coast of the USA, consumed every waking moment. Many a person would have complained or resisted the demands but Dieter relished the challenge. His talent, confidence, enthusiasm and knack for solving the most intricate problems instantly drew him close to senior management, such that his immediate superior began to fear for his job. The fool, in order to protect his position, fed Dieter even more work and more complex issues to deal with but the ploy totally failed to work, as Dieter was like an ever-hungry caterpillar devouring everything his superior put in his way. The man was right to fear, for

Dieter was only in the job for twelve months, when indeed, his superior was fired and Dieter moved up a notch and into a larger, more luxurious office.

Despite his promotion he took his personal assistant, the glamorous Gloria with him. They now had a thoroughly professional relationship; she was efficient, usually at least half a step ahead, didn't complain if asked to work late and was, after all, not known as glamorous Gloria for nothing. He liked her haughty, piercing gaze, clipped manner of speaking and the fact she didn't flaunt her obvious attractive female charms but kept her body carefully wrapped in stylish but thoroughly appropriate business clothing.

In the November of that year, Dieter's friend Marco telephoned to inform him that clique rehearsals were starting in earnest in preparation for the Fasnacht celebrations the following March. He managed the first practice without difficulty and thoroughly enjoyed the camaraderie, as the rusty band ploughed through the long list of old favourites. The next day, however, Dieter spent a great deal of time with Gloria trying to reorganise his agenda to allow him to attend as many practices as possible. It was fortunate that it was usually he who called for meetings these days and so much easier than if he had been lower down the pecking order.

One grey afternoon, in the middle of December, as he slouched wearily in the corner of the taxi taking him home from the airport, he barely noticed the twinkling Christmas lights, reminding shoppers how few days were left to spend their hard-earned francs. He had flown from New York's JFK airport to Heathrow, hung about for two hours before the Crossair flight to Basel. He was very fond of the small airline that flew out of Basel. Crossair's charismatic founder and CEO, Moritz Suter, demanded that his staff really go out of their way to ensure a top-class service, which he found so refreshing after the adequate but impersonal service offered by the larger airlines.

It had been a long day and he still found it bizarre that he could fly from Basel to New York and back in the same day. The Concorde flight from Heathrow was expensive but still he believed it was good value when one considered how precious the company saw his time. Although tired, he was feeling very satisfied, in the knowledge that the meeting had gone really smoothly and he had probably saved the company several hundred thousand francs - definitely justifying the Concorde fare.

He paid the taxi-driver outside his apartment block and shivered as he picked up his overnight bag from the pavement and turned towards the steps leading up to the front door. The temperature was well below zero and a keen northerly wind added to the chill. He was somewhat startled to see a tiny figure slumped on the steps, alongside a rucksack of equal size, together with an unwieldy ski-bag. The figure suddenly stood as he drew near and as he peered at the small amount of face showing beneath a woolly cap, realisation suddenly dawned.

'My God … Katarzyna! What are you doing here?' Later, in the comfort of his apartment, sipping coffee, Katarzyna explained that she had arrived at Basel's railway station during the morning, with the intention of heading for the Bernese Oberland and two weeks of skiing. On the spur of the moment, she decided to explore and see if Dieter was at home.

'Do you realise,' she said accusingly, 'that it's over three years since you last wrote to me!'

Katarzyna never did get to the mountains that holiday. Except for Christmas day, spent at Hofstetten with his parents, they never left the city. In retrospect, Dieter thought that his parents had been amazingly welcoming towards Katarzyna and, in fact, as they left at the end of Christmas day, his mother had congratulated him on finding such a wonderful young lady and that she hoped to see more of her.

Dieter delighted in showing off Basel's many charms to Katarzyna. They spent hours visiting the various art galleries and Dieter was surprised to learn that among her many talents, Katarzyna was a keen painter. When the bitter weather eased, he took her walking alongside the Rhine and through the narrow medieval streets.

'How is it possible to have so many old houses,' she had cried. 'I saw one with a date that said 1382. Why weren't they flattened in the war?'

'There's a lot to be said for neutrality,' replied Dieter. 'Mind you the whole city was razed to the ground by an earthquake in 1356 … so most of the old buildings date from soon after then.'

'Wow,' she exclaimed, 'imagine how wealthy countries would be if they didn't go to war. Why do ordinary people allow their leaders to …' She stopped abruptly, 'but what would I know, I'm just a simple kindergarten teacher?'

'And a talented painter and cellist,' cried Dieter, pulling her close and planting a kiss on her forehead.

Dieter took her to the ballet one evening, a special Christmas production of the Nutcracker. Before entering the theatre Dieter walked Katarzyna towards a large, shallow pool filled with water, where ten bizarre sculptured machines creaked and groaned as they sprayed water in all directions. Katarzyna laughed at the ingenious fusion of cogs, paddles and weird shapes, made all the more incongruous being coated with thin layers of ice.

'This is so clever,' she cried.

'They were made by Basel artist, Jean Tinguely,' Dieter explained.

'I love it,' laughed Katarzyna.

'Rumour has it that this is where the stage was located in the old theatre and when they pulled it down and built the new one, Tinguely designed this to represent all the actors, dancers and other artists who had performed on the stage … so they're all in conversation with each other.'

'Um,' sighed Katarzyna. 'What talent … and to think I've never heard of him.'

'He's most famous for blowing things up,' said Dieter.

'You'll have to explain that,' replied Katarzyna.

'Better than that,' replied Dieter. 'They are planning a museum to display his work, When it's finished I'll take you.' The ballet performance had been intoxicating and Katarzyna was in seventh heaven.

'How can such a small city, have such a wonderful theatre and fabulous ballet company?' she questioned later, as they wandered back to Dieter's apartment.

'Mainly thanks to the pharmaceuticals, like the one I work for,' explained Dieter. 'The arts here are heavily subsidised.'

'Well, I think that's a brilliant way to spend their profits,' Katarzyna responded. Dieter agreed.

On her last day as Dieter drove Katarzyna to the airport. Tongue in cheek, she asked if it would be another three years before she saw him again? Dieter didn't answer. He was busy calculating.

At the departure gate, they were holding hands but not saying much. Katarzyna apologised for the hundredth time for turning up unannounced. And for the hundredth time Dieter had replied that he was glad that she had. Katarzyna was amazingly in control, no tears - no expectations. It had been a wonderful two weeks of lovemaking and laughter, just like London, she thought and she tried to convince herself that she was happy to settle for that.

Later that night, Dieter lay in his bed analysing his thoughts about Katarzyna. He had thoroughly enjoyed her company and additionally he felt that that she would enhance his standing within the company; for he had noticed that men with stable, family backgrounds seemed to progress faster and further up the corporate ladder than the fly-by-night bachelors. From that point of view she could prove a useful asset. The fact that she had an easy-going, compliant nature was important. He didn't want an independently minded woman complicating his life. Katarzyna, he felt sure, would be an admirable companion but happy to remain in the background, competently organising the household and not keeping too close an eye on his life-style.

The next morning, before leaving for work, Dieter wrote Katarzyna a long letter inviting her to quit her job at the earliest opportunity and come and live with him in Basel.

'So that we can spend more time together and see if we are compatible for a long-term relationship,' he had awkwardly penned.

Katarzyna was quite overwhelmed when she received the invitation but didn't hesitate to see her supervisor at the earliest moment and hand in her resignation. Soon after she travelled to Warsaw to obtain a visa to visit Switzerland. By Easter she was settled in Dieter's flat, at every moment exuberantly exclaiming that she had never felt so happy in her whole life. Dieter paid for her to attend intensive German classes, so that in no time her already competent level of the language improved dramatically; though the spoken dialect, the Schweitzerdeutsch, proved somewhat slower.

Dieter arranged a meeting with the leader of one of the many amateur orchestras in the city and so for one night each week, Katarzyna played her beloved Cello. His final gesture was to rent a small room in the apartment building that had a single window looking out over the Rhine and Kleinbasel that she could use as a studio for her painting. Dieter now felt that Katarzyna was well set up to deal with his many absences, for work was as ever demanding and the amount of foreign travel increasing.

By the time her three-month visa was due to expire, Dieter was already convinced that Katarzyna was living up to his expectations. She provided everything he needed and coped uncomplainingly with his long absences. Rather than renewing the visa and the trip outside of Switzerland that would be required, he suggested that they visit the local council offices and get married. Although she had always thought that one day she would have a traditional church wedding, with a long white dress and a dozen bridesmaids, she cried in gratitude. And so on a sunny May day, much to his parent's delight, Dieter and Katarzyna were duly married in a simple ceremony in the fabulous red-facaded City Hall, the Rathaus, the five-hundred year old building that dominates Basel's market square. Afterwards, fifty or so guests toasted the couple's health in *The Three Kings* and another phase in Dieter's life began.

* * *

It wasn't planned but eighteen months later Katarzyna found herself pregnant. Dieter feigned delight, though secretly he wasn't sure how he felt about fatherhood. But in reality, because of his work commitments, having a baby at home did not impact dramatically on his life and he quite enjoyed showing off photographs of the beautiful Stephanie.

Twenty months later Claudia was born and reluctantly it was decided the apartment was too small. Katarzyna needed help, preferably someone who would live in and be on call day and night. Dieter made time to visit an old friend who owned an estate agency.

A week later Dieter was shown a wonderful property close to a small village called Burg im Leimental, on the edge of the Jura Mountains, some thirty-minute drive from Basel. The ancient houses of the tiny village scrambled up a steep incline, overlooked by a solid, rectangular castle dominantly perched above limestone cliffs. Right at the end of the village, was situated a six-bedroomed house, tucked away down a long drive. The property, known as Les Peupliers, presumably after a line of tall poplar trees running along the southern perimeter, boasted a stable-block for a dozen horses, a couple of sizeable paddocks, an indoor riding area - and an unbelievable view across the Belfort Gap, to the mountains of the Vosges.

'It's the last house in Switzerland,' said the agent, pointing to the faint outline of the Grand Ballon, the highest peak in the Alsace. 'You are surrounded by France,' he continued, waving his arms expansively. Dieter was delighted; this was exactly what he had in mind. He smiled when he heard traditional Swiss cow bells echoing across the hillside – it was just perfect.

The price was negotiated and Dieter returned to his apartment and informed Katarzyna that he had bought a house and that they would be moving. He gave her the brochure, which she studied carefully. Her eyebrows rose, as she read about the impressive property but her only question was whether it was wise to be so far away from the city and its many amenities. Dieter had grunted and said thirty minutes was nothing.

A couple of months later Dieter arranged for Katarzyna and the children to stay with his mother, while the apartment was cleared. He then hired an interior designer to furnish the new property. It took her a month! When the woman had finished the work, she walked Dieter around the house and he smiled with satisfaction and told her that she had done a good job. Needless to say the large living room boasted a Steinway baby grand piano.

Dieter then drove to nearby Hofstetten to collect Katarzyna and the family moved in. Katarzyna was understandably disappointed that she had not been asked for any input about furniture or decoration, but she fought off a desire to complain, by pragmatically convincing herself that it was Dieter's money that had bought the home and she and the children were fortunate to be invited to live there.

A week after they had settled in together, Dieter made a special trip to London where he interviewed half a dozen fully trained nannies at an agency that specialised in such things. One of the English girls caught his eye; she was small, vivacious, spoke fluent French and had a smattering of German.

'From an earlier position in Bavaria,' she had told him, where she had worked for a German prince and his family. Dieter checked her impressive references and hired her. The girl, Maria Beckett, accepted, though thought it odd that Mrs von Murren was not being consulted or asked for an opinion.

Fortunately, Katarzyna took an immediate liking to Maria - and Maria in turn to her new employer and the children. She was delighted with her own room, with its en-suite bathroom situated alongside the nursery. In no time Maria had made herself invaluable and quietly helped organise the household, as well as caring for the children.

Dieter was very happy with his new home and the efficiency with which it functioned but there was one more item on his wish-list. He had noticed that at the top of the village was an old house with a stable that always had horses and girls in and around. One day he stopped and introduced himself to the old man who was busy grooming a stocky mare. The man explained that he lived in the house and made a living by looking after other people's horses and he walked Dieter around to the rear of the house where there were further stables and a field that ran down the steep hillside, divided into sections with railed fencing. It was clear to Dieter that the man, who had introduced himself as Jacques, was very knowledgeable about horses and so Dieter explained that he wanted to buy a horse for himself, one for his wife and later a pony for his daughters.

Jacques led Dieter into a small room that he used as an office in one of the stable blocks. There were two chairs and Jacques pulled out a pad, asked Dieter numerous questions about his exact requirements and made notes. He knew the property where Dieter lived and explained that he had looked after the previous owner's horses, organised their grooming, exercise and feeding. Dieter was delighted and in no time a deal was struck that Jacques would find three suitable horses and take over the responsibility for their wellbeing.

Katarzyna had ridden horses when on holiday in the Masurian Lake District in eastern Poland and although not an expert, she was a competent rider and delighted when Jacques delivered two middle-aged horses and a tiny white pony.

Maria joyfully told Katarzyna that she had ridden since she was a small child and even spent some time teaching riding to beginners. Throughout the following summer Dieter and Katarzyna explored the forests and mountain tracks on horseback and when Dieter was away, the cleaning lady would be left in charge of the girls while Katarzyna and Maria trekked around the neighbourhood. Life for all the von Murren family was going well.

CHAPTER 13

At the special school for special boys, Bruno Schmidt played the game; he was a clever boy, he quickly realised that if he followed the rules, life was made easier. He always said what his minders wanted to hear and before long he was described as a 'good' boy. He was given little perks that over time grew into larger ones; he was let off routine chores, given the easier jobs. As a young teenager he behaved so well he was occasionally allowed into town on his own, which was totally against the rules.

The year Katarzyna gave birth to Stephanie, Bruno turned sixteen. After all the years spent on the psychiatrist's couch discussing his problems, he understood the issues and, provided he remembered the pills, for most of the time he was developing into a normal, useful member of society. When he left school the authorities found him a place in a hostel in Stuttgart and a job in a huge supermarket warehouse, where he was taught to drive a forklift truck and spent his days mindlessly stacking the warehouse shelves. Once a week, as a condition of his release, he had to attend night-school. To begin with it was a tedious chore but lately he had been enjoying the sessions, there was a new teacher, about his mother's age and she usually brought cakes, told jokes and singled him out for extra work.

At the hostel he was befriended by a petty criminal nicknamed Kolt, some three or four years older. Occasionally Bruno accompanied him breaking into parked cars, his companion seeking anything he could sell to feed his drug habit. Except for sharing a few drags of marihuana out in the grounds of the hostel, away from the prying eyes of the warden, Bruno had no interest in drugs; he had been brain-washed sufficiently to know that mixing unknown chemicals with the magic ones that kept him on an even keel, would put him back into care - or worse.

A few days after his seventeenth birthday, during the weekly lesson, his teacher pulled him aside and asked him to stay behind when the others had left. He did and she explained that she felt Bruno was capable of taking some exams that might help him get a better job but it would need commitment and lots of homework. Begrudgingly he said he'd think about it; not that he thought for a minute that more reading and writing was likely to improve his prospects, nevertheless he took the books she offered and promised to look at them.

Back at the hostel, he was lying on his bed leafing through the books his teacher had insisted he take, when Kolt entered without knocking and flopped on the bed beside him. He demanded to know what Bruno was looking at and grabbed one of the books. He took one look at the pages of unintelligible words and flung it down.

'What's that about?' he snarled.

'War and Peace,' replied Bruno.

'Bloody crap,' spat Kolt. He picked up another, this was more interesting it had pictures, after a few moments he started laughing. 'Who gave you this?' he demanded.

'The night-school teacher,' replied Bruno, engrossed in the first page of Goethe's Sorrows of Young Werther.

'She must fancy you then,' he grinned.

'What are you gabbing about?' asked Bruno.

'Well it's a dirty book, full of women with nothing on.' Bruno tore his eyes away from the Goethe to see what Kolt was going on about.

'They're paintings you stupid wally, famous paintings, hanging on gallery walls.' Kolt's eyes were glued to a picture of Goya's *La Maja Desnuda.*

'God, I can't remember the last time I saw anything like this - real I mean.' He fumbled in his pocket, pulled out a few notes and started counting. 'Let's go and get us some tail,' he urged.

'Don't be stupid,' responded Bruno, who knew nothing about the opposite sex.

'If you've got a tenner, I know someone who'd oblige,' continued Kolt.

'I'd rather spend a tenner on several glasses of beer,' laughed Bruno nervously, beginning to feel threatened that his inexperience would be exposed.

After another intense barrage of badgering, Bruno piled the books up on his bedside table, sat on the side of the bed and pulled on his shoes. In the hallway they signed the book, left the hostel and made their way into the city. Kolt obviously knew where he was going and he led Bruno into an area he had not visited before. It was poorly lit and the buildings were tall, dark and threatening.

'Where the hell are you taking me?' asked Bruno.

'Shut up and keep walking,' ordered his companion. As they rounded a corner a blinking neon sign drew attention to a sleazy looking bar, seemingly squashed under a towering block of flats. Kolt pushed open the door letting it crash back into Bruno's outstretched hands.

It took several moments for his eyes to adjust to the dim, dingy interior. There was a long bar with a prize-fighter imitating a barman, busy filling glasses. Kolt ordered two glasses of beer and they sat in a corner; the room was almost empty, just three men leaning on the bar talking football to the singlet-clad, tattooed wrestler. After a few moments a young woman in a flimsy dress pushed her way through a curtain at the rear of the room and leaned wearily against the bar. The barman slid a glass of clear liquid towards her, which she downed in one gulp and slid it back towards him. He ignored it. Realising nothing else was forthcoming she flopped onto a chair and rested her elbows on a table, an expression of utter exhaustion sullying her once pretty features. Kolt drained his glass.

'Let's go,' he ordered getting to his feet. Bruno quickly followed; they nodded to the barman and went out into the cold, damp night. Round the corner was the entrance to the same apartment block that housed the bar. Kolt tried the door, he seemed surprised, it was unlocked. The hallway was a desolate, graffiti covered hellhole, eerily lit by a single flickering, cold florescent tube, with nothing more artistic than swear words creatively displayed in rainbow colours. At the foot of the stairs, Kolt pointed to another door.

'That's the way into the bar - punters use it to visit the girls upstairs but we aren't going to pay that bloody, greedy pimp.' He set off up the stairs, two at a time.

Reluctantly Bruno followed; he was so worried about what was happening, he lost count of the floors they climbed. All he knew was that he was out of breath and sat on the top step while Kolt examined the nametags by the doors.

'Bugger!' he swore, 'It's the floor below, we've come too far.' He turned and made his way back down the stairs where he began hammering on an apartment door. Bruno remained seated, waiting and wondering, his head in his hands. Everything was spinning, he felt out of control. It was a long time since he had felt like this. Suddenly, with a start, he remembered he had forgotten to take the little pink pills that morning. How could that be? he wondered. I never forget. Never!

Even through the whistling in his head, Bruno heard the door open. He watched through the bannisters, as a tall, thin man hurried out, struggling into an oversized coat, pulling up his hood to hide his face. Bruno heard Kolt call a girl's name and he reluctantly got to his feet. The man had gone and Kolt was holding the door open. Bruno was surprised when he shuffled inside, for the room was quite tidy with pink walls, a large bed and a chest of drawers. There was even a print on the wall, depicting young lovers strolling alongside a river, probably the Seine, he thought.

Kolt was introducing the anorexic girl, with dyed red hair and carmine painted lips, who was perched on the edge of the bed wrapped in a blue dressing gown and incongruously, purple, high-heeled shoes but all this didn't really register. Bruno was like a rabbit caught in the headlights.

'Livia here owes me a favour, don't you Livia,' said Kolt. She didn't respond.

'You go first,' offered Kolt generously, glancing towards Bruno.

'I have to go to the bathroom first,' said the girl. From her accent, she wasn't German but from somewhere further east. She stumbled across the room and closed the door.

'Get your pants off then,' ordered Kolt. Bruno didn't move, he was still standing by the door.

'It's okay, I'm not in the mood,' he replied. Kolt raised his voice.

'We haven't come all this way, just for you to get cold feet. Get your pants off?'

'I don't have a condom,' argued Bruno. Kolt strode up to Bruno, pulled an evil looking knife from his jacket and waved it threateningly under Bruno's nose.

'Just do it!' he snarled.

'You go first,' stammered Bruno. ' Perhaps watching you will put me in the mood.' Kolt laughed and punched Bruno's shoulder:

'Bloody pervert!' he said, unfastened his belt, pulled the trousers off his sticklike legs and lay on the bed.

'Come on girl,' he shouted. 'We haven't got all night. That bloody pimp of yours will be sending up your next customer before we've finished.' The girl came back into the room and poutingly peeled off the dressing gown.

Poor Bruno's head pounded, as the girl bounced up and down on Kolt's painfully thin body. He became dizzy as they rolled first one way and then the other. There was no sound except for Kolt gasping for breath and the bed squeaking, as if in pain. He thought they would never end, where did his scraggy companion find all that energy? Bruno shut his eyes, his body was not responding, he needed some fresh air. He needed to be out of this room with its sickly pink paint and fluffy teddy bears seated on the chest of drawers; their beady eyes witness to the daily depravity.

He hadn't realised, Kolt was done, and already on his feet, the girl flat on her back, legs impossibly wide - waiting.

'Get on with it!' nagged Kolt. Bruno backed up towards the door. Kolt picked up the knife that he had left on the bedside table and once again waved it under Bruno's nose. He snarled and swore. Bruno undid his belt and allowed his trousers to fall to the floor. The girl hadn't moved. He knelt between those thin, wide, outspread legs, Kolt settled back in the armchair to watch. Flat on her back the girl had no breasts, he glanced at her face, the carmine lips smudged but widening, as if to swallow him up. Bruno's head was in turmoil, his body limp and unresponsive. Realising nothing was happening the girl wrapped her legs around him, still nothing.

'This is a waste of time,' she said gasping for breath.

'Don't rush him, be nice' said Kolt.

'Roll over,' murmured the girl into Bruno's ear. He did as he was told and the girl toiled and bounced until she collapsed exhausted and then burst out laughing.

'Funny friend you've got here, it's a record - the first time I've failed.' She lay on her back and laughed unmercifully, cackling like a demented chicken. Kolt joined in.

'He's still a kid,' laughed Kolt.

'Perhaps he prefers men or little boys,' the girl giggled. Bruno was sitting on the edge of the bed; the girl wrapped an arm around him. 'Would you like me to go and find you a little boy to play with?' Something snapped. The taunting, the whistling pain in his head, the shame, it was all too much. Without a thought or any warning, he swung an arm, as he did when he was just nine years old and the elbow had the same dramatic effect. The girl was poleaxed. Kolt leapt to his feet.

'Good God, you've killed her! I heard her neck snap!' he cried in a panic. He started punching Bruno's body but Bruno ignored the blows, reached across to the bedside table, picked up Kolt's knife and with one blow plunged the blade straight into Kolt's heart. With an agonised, wide-eyed expression of disbelief, Kolt crashed heavily to the floor, blood pumping violently through the hole in his shirt.

Bruno clambered slowly to his feet and pulled on his trousers. He went into the bathroom washed the blood away from his hands before pouring water over his face. Miraculously, the pain in his head had suddenly stopped; exactly as if someone had pressed a switch. Returning to the bedroom he looked round taking in the chaotic scene, he checked the girl; there was no pulse, her head twisted at an unnatural angle, she was definitely dead. The knife was still in Kolt's chest; Bruno took a tissue from his pocket and carefully wiped the handle until he was satisfied it was clean.

He then went into the bathroom where he carefully cleansed the taps, and door handle and, as he left, polished the inside door knob and the outside handle. Nonchalantly, he descended the stairs and made his way back to the hostel, where he calmly signed himself in. Back in his room he shook three pink pills into his hand and swallowed them, reminding himself that he really must never forget to take them again.

CHAPTER 14

Three days passed by before the police visited the hostel. They interviewed everyone and then turned their attention to Bruno.

'You signed out at the same time as the victim,' said the burly detective.

'That's true,' agreed Bruno, 'and we walked to the end of the street and then he went one way and I went the other.'

'Did he say where he was going?'

'No. He just said: see you later and walked off.'

'Where did you go?' Bruno said that he wandered around the city centre for a while and then went into a bar and had a drink. He had carefully chosen the name of the busiest bar he knew, where it was always so hectic, everyone was anonymous.

The police did not bother him again. He went to Kolt's funeral with the warden; except for the undertaker and a priest no one else was there. Later he read in the newspaper that the girl's pimp had been arrested and charged with double murder, the article said it was believed he had attacked the girl for entertaining Kolt without going through the normal channels. Bruno felt nothing, if he was schizophrenic then his other half had carried out the atrocity and that was nothing to do with him.

* * *

Bruno's studies went well, such that his teacher entered him for the examinations early. He sailed through them and to celebrate she took him home to have dinner with her husband. It transpired that the husband worked on a local newspaper and he offered to ask if there was a suitable job for Bruno.

A week or so later he dressed in his best clothes, cleaned his nails and went to meet the woman in charge of human resources.

She gave him some tests to complete and asked many questions. A day later she telephoned the warden and left a message that he call her back. He did and another interview was arranged. This time she had a colleague with her, after more questions he was walked around the facility and at the end offered a trial as a junior reporter. The offer left him cold but he accepted, mechanically thanked the ladies, returned to the warehouse and handed in his notice. That evening he telephoned his mother and told her about the new job, she was delighted; Bruno promised that he would travel to Todtnau before too long to see her.

Over the next few months Bruno grew into the new job, he had no real feelings about whether or not he liked it better than driving the forklift truck. He carried out his duties almost with the same attitude, as when he was stacking shelves at the warehouse. There he had concentrated, worked hard and eventually he could make the forklift truck do anything he wanted. In this job he concentrated, worked hard and eventually got the information he wanted and then wrote it down and polished it until his supervisor was satisfied.

Bruno was good at writing, fluent, with an observant eye and an appealing turn of phrase. But for someone of his demeanour, to be a journalist was a disastrous decision - he had difficulty grasping the 'bigger picture' and there were too many awkward characters and too much injustice to write about. There were days when he just needed to kick the life out of some corrupt local politician or wring the neck of some wayward employer. Today, today especially, he had an overwhelming urge to beat his father to death.

CHAPTER 15

Dieter was really delighted with his new home and took to inviting his friends and work colleagues to lunch or dinner. He preferred lunch, for then his guests could wander around the manicured grounds, pet the horses and admire the wondrous view. Later as guests lounged with their glasses of champagne, he would entertain by playing his beloved piano. Katarzyna proved a brilliant hostess thought Dieter, at one such gathering, as he watched her deep in animated conversation with the CEO of one of Basel's largest companies. Yes, he decided, he had made a good choice.

One sunny autumnal day Dieter drove out of Basel to a small village in the surrounding countryside. Hidden among trees on the side of a mountain was a large modern factory, with a spacious car park and access to several loading bays. Dieter had a meeting planned with the owner, Beat Graf. He knew him well, as he was a member of the same Clique and a talented piccolo player. A few weeks earlier Graf had invited Dieter to the factory and taken great delight in showing him around the modern premises.

In Graf's modest office, Dieter commented on five new paintings that had been added since his last visit.

'Keith Haring, I see,' he said, drawing closer to inspect the detail. 'That will have put your insurance premium up a few francs,' he grinned.

'I've had them a long time,' smiled Beat Graf. 'They've been out of sight in a bank vault for years, seemed such a shame.'

'You may consider it sacrilege,' smiled von Murren. 'But in my opinion they're an improvement on the Picasso you had on the wall, the last time I was here.'

'Well,' responded Graf, 'As I'm sure you know, we Baslers have a special relationship with our friend Pablo.'

'Remind me,' said Von Murren, puzzled.

'Some years ago there were a couple of Picasso's hanging in the Kunstmuseum but they belonged to a private collector and then he announced that he needed to sell them. The good citizens of Basel were so upset that they voted to pay an increase in their taxes to buy them.'

'Oh yes, I remember,' interjected von Murren. 'And Picasso was so touched he gave the City four more.' Graf nodded. Anyway, enough of Picasso, sit down, I've a lot to say.'

Driving home two hours later, Dieter had a great deal to think about. Beat Graf had explained that he had set up the company, Begrafica, twenty years ago and now, at the age of seventy, he was looking for someone to take over the running of the company - he had no children and had offered the opportunity to Dieter. Graf had assured Dieter that he would have full control and a fifty per cent share in the profits, with the option to buy the company at a later date. It was very tempting. So tempting that he telephoned Walter Klein, the man who ran his father's Basel law office.

The next day, Walter Klein set one of his legal team the confidential task of due diligence, with instructions to employ a finance man from an office in the same building to go through the latest balance sheets.

'I want a proper and detailed report one week from today,' Dieter had instructed Walter Klein. 'No short cuts!'

Five days later Walter Klein telephoned Dieter to say the report was ready. Dieter sent Glamorous Gloria in a taxi to collect it. As he pored over the figures, Dieter realised that Beat Graf had built up a very successful company. It was highly profitable and had full order books. He telephoned Graf and made an appointment to visit again.

Three months later, to the chagrin of his superiors, Dieter resigned from Ciba and began to work alongside Beat Graf, as a partner. The business plan was simple, the company made vitamins and mineral supplements, as well as a limited number of generic drugs, usually best sellers, as soon as their twenty year patent had expired.

After four weeks of working together, Beat Graf shook Dieter's hand and told him that he was going on a world cruise, and didn't expect to hear from him, unless there was a dire emergency.

Dieter couldn't have been more pleased, he was now his own boss and in the knowledge he was entitled to a fifty per cent of the profits, determined from that day he would double them.

CHAPTER 16

The first thing Dieter did, once he was on his own and in charge, was to lure the Glamorous Gloria away from her position, to join him as his personal assistant. Over the next four years Dieter threw himself wholeheartedly into his new project. New buildings were constructed, the latest robotic machines installed, talented staff recruited, many others ruthlessly 'let go!' Sales soared, as did the profits but Dieter knew they could grow even more.

Despite the long working hours, Dieter still insisted on entertaining most Sundays. Katarzyna now had help in the kitchen, provided by a lady from the village called Beccy Blom but if it was to be a very special occasion, Dieter would insist that she ask the chef at the local hotel-restaurant Bad Berg to provide something exceptional.

One fateful Sunday in December Dieter had invited the chief operating officer of each of Basel's major pharmaceutical and chemical companies to dinner and was delighted when each accepted. They arrived with their glamorously gowned wives in their chauffer-driven limousines at the appointed time and admired the tasteful twinkling lights that decorated the exterior of the house and the magnificent Christmas tree standing in the spacious hallway. There had been a sprinkling of snow, which added to the magic but not deep enough to make negotiating the hill up to the house life threatening. All of them had visited previously, some several times. Each knew they would be in for a relaxing evening; Dieter was a great raconteur who would no doubt keep them well entertained.

It was a lively dinner where a great deal of the chatter was about the demolition of the Berlin Wall, a few weeks' earlier and what affect this might have on their respective companies. Afterwards, replete, the guests sprawled in the comfortable armchairs nursing their brandy goblets, while Dieter played the piano. Eventually he stopped to a round of spontaneous applause and cries of approval. The end of the recital was the pre-arranged signal for Katarzyna to gaily announce that she had gifts for the ladies and that they should follow her. As they trooped obediently from the lounge, Dieter moved around the room offering cigars.

'So,' he asked, 'How's business for you all, will you be celebrating a happy Christmas or drowning your sorrows?' There was a chorus of varying replies, followed by some intense discussion. Eventually one of the men said:

'The trouble is that it is companies like yours that eat into our profits, make the shareholders restless and threaten our jobs.'

'I agree,' replied Dieter, so we need to be pragmatic.' He turned to one of the men and wagged a finger. 'You can't compete with our vitamin C, on price, so why do you bother?' He turned to another of the guests. 'And now that your cardiac arrest drug is out of patent, you need a change of strategy.' There was a pause in the conversation. 'I don't have to tell you that the huge amount of money you invest in research eats into your profits and yet research is your lifeblood. My company spends nothing on research, sells drugs around the world at half the price you charge, which national health schemes love. We need a gentlemen's agreement.'

'What do you mean?' asked one man. Dieter turned towards the speaker:

'Well for a start, let's take Brazil. You stop trying to sell vitamins there and I'll stop selling cardiac arrest drugs. As I said, let's be pragmatic, divide up the world markets.' Dieter's suggestion was greeted by ironic laughs.

'Brazil's a poor example,' said the man. 'We have a factory there, I couldn't just close it down, it would cause an uproar. Anyway you'll get us all sent to jail, the Federal Drug Administration would be on to us in a shot.'

Beccy Blom, the woman who helped Katarzyna in the kitchen, walked in with a tray and began collecting the empty glasses. Dieter ignored her.

'This isn't something that could happen quickly,' said one man. The others agreed.

'You're right,' said Dieter. 'This is a long-term arrangement, country by country, drug by drug.' There were several dissenting voices, the others were quiet, contemplating Dieter's preposterous proposal. 'Think about it,' continued Dieter, 'and then call me to make arrangements to meet - nothing on paper. No phone calls. Only face to face! Believe me - between us, we can take over the world.'

CHAPTER 17

Bruno Schmidt had not seen his father since he was about eight years old and had forgotten all about the overweight stranger who sometimes came to stay. But, one day when Bruno was older, under intense questioning, his mother had reluctantly told him the name of his father and that he was a successful businessman. She did not mention that he left her when Bruno's troubles at school began. During their relationship his father had paid the rent on his mother's spacious, well-located apartment. But after the trouble at the school his father's visits became less frequent, until they ended altogether and a year later he stopped paying the rent, causing his mother to move into a small two-roomed apartment in a shabby block, inconveniently too far out of town. She had been overwhelmed by her son's wicked actions and his absence, compounded by the loss of her lover, drove her in a downward spiral. It wasn't long before she began drinking heavily and her health deteriorated.

Now that Bruno worked in Stuttgart, he only travelled to Todtnau occasionally to see his mother, the two-hour drive, in his mind, a real disincentive and the town had such dark, disturbing memories. His last visit had left him particularly angry and he knew that anger spelled disaster.

He had become incensed when he saw how poor his mother was, the dirty state of her kitchen and the empty bottles partly hidden under the sink. He couldn't bear to see how her health was suffering but despite his badgering she refused his demands that she contact his father to ask for financial support. He had shouted at her, telling her how ridiculous it was that she should have to struggle to pay the bills. 'The man, his father, must be asked to help,' he had yelled. After all, she had said her ex-lover was supposedly loaded. In the end, cowed by his bullying, his mother agreed that she would write to his father and ask to see him. But a couple of weeks later, when he telephoned, she lied and said that she had written to his father but that he had not replied. This was the reason he had this overpowering urge to beat the life out of the man who had deserted his mother. But first he needed to do some research, to find out more about him and where he lived.

CHAPTER 18

Bruno produced his business card, which was inspected by the matronly receptionist and he was asked to wait. He'd had no trouble locating the man his mother had said was his father but now his heart was beating too fast and the damn tic affecting his left eye was playing up.

The woman returned, said with a smile that he was expected and showed him into a large, luxurious office. He glanced around the room noting the expensive-looking, original paintings on the walls. The man behind the desk, rose momentarily to his feet, indicated a chair and asked how he could help. The question went unanswered. Bruno was intently studying the man, seeking similarities that might indicate that this was indeed his biological father. The man was fat, he noted, so it was hard to tell if the jaw line was similar, he was also as bald as coot; Bruno had a thick brown thatch. There was, however, something about the eyes and the timbre of the voice but Bruno was not convinced. He wondered if his mother had told him the truth. Had there been other men in her life at that time? Bruno's musings were interrupted by a second:

'How can I help?'

'Forgive me,' muttered Bruno, clearing his throat. I'm new to the area and my editor informed me that you are the town's most prominent philanthropist and he wishes me to write an article about you.' The old man chuckled, self-consciously:

'I wouldn't say that,' he protested.

'I have a list here,' said Bruno fumbling in his pocket. 'My editor says you are extremely generous and give to a wide variety of charities, as well as supporting less prominent but needy causes and individuals.' The old man smiled:

'I'd be interested to know from whence your editor drew his

information!' he said pompously.

'Is it true that you support local environmental and educational schemes?'

'Well… yes,' admitted the man. 'I do support the work of a couple of schemes; one trying to reintroduce a wider range of wildlife into the area. And…'

'Oh yes sir,' interrupted Bruno, appearing to check his papers, 'I see that I have that information.' Bruno went on to read out a list of national charities and the man reluctantly agreed that from time to time, he did support their appeals.

'I think our readers would be more interested in the personal aspects of your charity work,' said Bruno. 'Could you perhaps give me some names of private individuals that you have helped. Perhaps I could speak to them and hear their side of the story - and just how grateful they are ... and what a difference you made to their lives?'

'No, I don't think that would be a good idea,' blustered the man, not knowing what the untidily dressed man wasting his time, was on about.

'Oh, that's a pity,' sighed Bruno. 'One of my sources tells me that you have been especially generous to a woman in Todtnau.' Bruno glanced at his paper and pretended to read his mother's name… 'A Martha Schmidt!'

Bruno watched intently as the man took a violent deep breath, while his pudgy face and fat neck slowly turned an angry shade of puce, as blood suffused through his veins. He was holding his breath and for a second Bruno thought that the old man might expire.

Showing enormous self-control, the man allowed his tortured lungs to relax and the air escaped through his clenched teeth with a barely audible whistle.

'That's not a name I recognise,' he said flatly.

'Oh my informant must be mistaken,' said Bruno quickly. Bloody liar, he thought to himself, you know exactly who she is. He continued: 'May I ask if you donate to any of the political parties?'

'You may ask,' replied the man, regaining his composure. 'You may ask but I will not be telling you.' He smiled broadly, like a benevolent father dealing with an impertinent child! Bruno asked a few more questions, made copious notes before pulling a small camera from his pocket.

'May I?' he asked, indicating the camera: 'Just for reference.' If my editor decides to go ahead with the story he will send down a professional photographer to take a proper picture. Bruno snapped a couple of photographs before pushing the camera into his pocket, thrusting out an unwilling hand and thanking the man for his time, by now convinced that the man was indeed his father.

Back in the office, in Stuttgart, Bruno quickly completed a draft describing the major traffic accident that he was meant to be reporting that afternoon and showed it to his sub-editor.

'Not enough detail,' he had snapped. 'You were meant to interview the police-chief, what happened?' Bruno made excuses that the man wasn't available.

'Well keep trying. Telephone and make an appointment. You don't give up.' There were times when the sub-editor wondered about Bruno Schmidt and whether he really had the drive that was needed to be a reporter. As for Bruno he couldn't have cared less about the traffic accident, he'd spent all day out of the city and now, single-mindedly, was trying to decide how best to deal with the man he had just met - his biological father.

That evening Bruno telephoned his mother and his stomach churned, as he listened to her slurred voice. She had been at the bottle again. He glanced at his watch, it wasn't even eight o'clock. He half-listened, as she described how she had reluctantly been to the doctor who had informed her that she probably needed surgery to replace a hip and had made an appointment for her to see a consultant. Bruno listened with dismay, her breathing was so laboured, as she struggled with the pain in her leg and the asthma, which had plagued her for years; he couldn't imagine her surviving a general anaesthetic unless her chest improved and she stopped drinking. She really needed to get treatment for her alcohol problem, he thought and get out of that miserable apartment block - and move away from the damp valley that for half the year lay in heavy shadow, never seeing the sun. Later Bruno lay on his bed brooding: a month in a sanatorium was what she needed he thought; and he needed to persuade his father to pay for it.

CHAPTER 19

Beccy Blom helped Jacques Wolf with the horses when she wasn't required at Katarzyna's home. Sometimes she would exercise them around the country lanes and forest paths or cheerfully scrub the mud away from their flanks, after they had been rolling around in the fields. Once groomed, she would plait their manes and comb their tails. She had loved horses all her life but had never had sufficient income to actually own one.

Beccy, born in the village of Burg, had never married and still lived in the same tiny attic flat, where she was born, wedged under the roof of an ancient timber-beamed house, directly on the street, a hundred metres or so below Jacques' home and stables. But tonight she was in Jacques' bed. They made an unlikely pair, he in his mid-sixties, with almost as much hair on his naked chest as his full-bearded face. She, twenty years younger, thin, wiry, angular but with an appetite that persuaded Jacques to limit sharing his bed, to about every second week. It was an arrangement that suited them both admirably, for each valued their independence.

'You been helping out at the big house again,' said Jacques in Beccy's ear, as she attempted, one-handedly, to plait the hair on his chest.

'More bigwigs than ever,' she replied, deciding it was easier to plait the mane of a horse.

'I wonder who pays for these shindigs - Mr Know-all or his company?'

'Dunno,' replied Beccy, ' but they don't go short of nothin,'

'Don't know what his wife sees in him,' murmured Jacques.

'She's lovely,' agreed Beccy. 'A real lady, so kind and thoughtful. But him,' she paused unable to find the words. 'You know what him and his posh friends were talking about tonight?' she continued.

'No... what?' sighed Jacques, not really interested. He'd been wondering where he could find some more grazing space for his growing number of horses.

'They were talking of how he and his pals could take over the world ... a bit for you ... in exchange for that bit, for me!'

'I don't know what you mean,' grunted Jacques.

'Well they seemed to be sharing out the world, as if it was a pack of cards. You know ... clubs for you, diamonds for me,' she sang.

'You ain't making any sense woman,' complained Jacques, suddenly aware that her hand had left his chest and was nestled between his thighs, gradually driving all thoughts of people plotting world domination from his mind.

Later that day, Jacques was up at the von Murren house checking the horses. Maria returned from a hack, while he was bent over checking one of the horse's hooves. They exchanged pleasantries as Maria removed the saddle and began to brush down the sweating animal. Jacques always spoke to Maria in French, her German, while improving, was still limited.

'I hear you had a big party here last night,' Jacques said, making conversation.

'Yes,' she replied, breathless from the exertions of her brushing. 'Not that I get invited.'

'I suppose you have to keep the kids out of the way,' he continued. She agreed. 'He's a funny fellah, that boss of yours,' said Jacques, leading the horse back into the stable.

'He's okay,' replied Maria, 'not that I see much of him, he's always working.'

'Plotting and scheming no doubt,' went on Jacques. He was thinking of what Beccy had said.

'What do you mean?' asked Maria.

'Well rumour has it he's planning on taking over the world,' said Jacques. Maria laughed,

'You'll have to explain that,' she said, 'I don't understand.' Jacques decided that he had said too much.

'I don't understand neither,' he said. 'Just village talk.' He held the door open and Maria led her horse into the stable, bid Jacques goodbye and went into the house for a shower.

Standing under the scalding water, washing her hair. Maria began to think about what Jacques had said. She'd always thought him a sensible man, not one to bother with idle gossip. What did he mean about Dieter von Murren was going to take over the world? She was puzzled.

CHAPTER 20

Some months later Maria was at her German lesson in Basel. Katarzyna, as generous as ever, allowed Maria to take her Range Rover down the mountain to a small village called Flüh, where she could catch the tram into the city.

Once the lesson was over, it was usual for most of the group to walk to the nearest bar but tonight only two men and another woman, a French-speaking Belgian, said they could stay. Seated around a small table, it was a rule to speak as much as possible in German, with the penalty for the first person to break the rule, having to pay for the drinks. Eventually the strain became too much for one of the men, an American called Joe, and he burst out laughing, complaining that the conversation was too stilted and nothing interesting was being said or asked. The Belgian woman, who was fluent in English nodded,

'I don't have enough vocabulary yet to ask the interesting questions,' she giggled. The other man, a Scot, with a broad Glaswegian accent and such an unpronounceable name, they all called him Jock, agreed and so the conversation continued in English.

'What are you doing here in Basel?' asked the Scot, looking at each person in turn.

'I work for a Belgian bank,' volunteered the woman. Joe said he was a reporter for the International Herald Tribune. Maria explained that she was an au-pair, while the Scot admitted that he worked for one of Basel's pharmaceutical companies.

'A motley crew,' cried the American rising to his feet, accepting his penalty and heading for refills at the bar.

Settled back down with their drinks, Joe turned to Maria and asked if she worked for anyone rich or famous.

'I'm always looking for an angle,' he added.

'Not famous, answered Maria but rich … yes, I suppose so.'

'Tell me more,' demanded Joe. Maria explained about the von Murren's, Joe looked thoughtful,

'I read something about Dieter von Murren in the BAZ, a long time ago,' he said. 'I think the article said that he was a high-flyer heading for the top at Ciba but threw it away to run a factory somewhere in Baselland.'

'That's the man,' agreed Maria. 'But remind me, what is the BAZ?'

'The Basel Newspaper … Basler Zeitung … B..a..Z,' they all spelled out together, accusingly. 'Have you already forgotten your first German lesson, when the woman went on at length and telling us we should read the BAZ every day?' questioned Joe.

'I thought she was Bats, expecting us to do that after just one lesson,' laughed the Scot.

'Back to Dieter von Murren,' said Joe. 'What's he like? Do you think it would be worth me interviewing him for an article in the Tribune?'

'Why not?' replied Maria. 'He seems to be well-known in the area. He's good looking, successful, some say charismatic ... and certainly ambitious from what I hear, with plans to take over the world!'

'What do you mean … take over the world?'

'I don't really know, just village gossip about some big plans that he has.'

'Aaw, thanks Maria,' said Joe. 'I think I'll follow up on that, do a bit of research, see what I can find out about your charismatic employer. Does he have a place for you in his world plan do you think?'

'You're joking,' laughed Maria. 'He doesn't even know I exist.'

CHAPTER 21

A week later Joe Leman drove his ancient Toyota out to Burg im Leimental, parked at the restaurant Bad Berg and ordered a coffee. He sat outside on the empty terrace and enjoyed the weak sun, while chatting up the waitress in his limited German, conscious of the air filled with birdsong. At some stage, an attractive, pale blonde woman, of indeterminate age, appeared at the door, as if checking up on the young waitress. Joe called out and asked if she was the owner. The woman dismissed the waitress with an authoritative nod, introduced herself as Barbara and sat opposite Joe. After tolerating Joe's limited German in silence for a few moments, the woman then spoke to him in fluent English. Joe had noticed this many times, when local Baslers would let him ramble on in German until they made up their mind that their knowledge of English was better than Joe's German - and then they would switch, without any warning or introduction. Some of his friends took exception to this habit but Joe was just grateful, he often thought that he would never get to grips with the complex language.

He introduced himself and said he was going to write an article about the village, perched, as it was, on a hill complete with castle - almost an outpost of Switzerland, watching out for any marauding French, coming across the plain. He asked about the castle and any well-known residents. The woman was a mine of information and it wasn't long before Joe had pulled the notebook from his pocket and was filling the pages with shorthand notes.

'Where does Dieter von Murren live?' he asked.

'Right at the top,' she replied, 'as far as you can go.'

'Do you know him?' asked Joe.

'Not really,' replied the woman. 'We cater for some of his parties and he occasionally drops in for a glass of wine when he comes to settle his bills. No more than that.'

'I hear that Albert Hofmann lives here, the LSD man,' continued Joe.

'Yes,' replied the woman. ' He lives up the top as well.'

'Do you know him?' asked Joe.

'Better than von Murren, he comes in here some times with his wife, or friends, for a meal. Nice couple!'

'So … von Murren. Who in the village would know him best do you suppose?' asked Joe.

'Well a woman from the village, Beccy Blom, helps out up there, in the kitchen and that. And Jacques Wolf looks after their horses. But I don't suppose they really know him. He just flies up and down the hill in his fancy car, I wouldn't think anyone here really knows him.' Joe thanked Barbara profusely, paid for his coffee and began walking up the steep main road. After five minutes, with his calves aching, he decided it had been a mistake and went back to collect his car and drove to the top of the village, and parked by an old, covered water trough. On the way up, he had passed a man grooming a horse. Joe wandered back down the road, as he drew near, he called out:

'Herr Wolf? Jacques Wolf?'

'That's me,' replied Jacques in German dialect, putting the brush down and rubbing his hands down the side of his pants before pumping Joe's hand. Joe introduced himself and again explained that he wanted to write a piece for his newspaper. Jacques walked him round the building, to his small office, offered a chair and pulled a half-full bottle of white wine and a couple of dubiously clean glasses from a shelf behind his seat. He carefully placed them on the roughly hewn plank of wood that served as a desk. By now the pair were conversing in English and Joe asked how Jacques came to be so fluent.

'As a young man I went to Australia,' explained Jacques. 'I travelled, surfed, worked … stayed there for about four years.' His watery blue eyes misted for a moment, as the thoughts of a beautiful, auburn-haired girl, drifted into his mind. 'I came very close to spending my entire life there,' he murmured. With an effort he dragged himself back to the present, took a swig from his glass, before waxing lyrical about the village where he had been born and brought up, he needed very little prodding from Joe. Once again Joe was able to fill several pages in his notebook. And, as with the woman at the restaurant, he asked after any well-known local residents and of course received the same two names. Joe explained that he knew quite a lot about the world-renowned scientist but what about Dieter von Murren? What did Jacques know about him?

Jacques liked to pontificate but spending his days alone with the horses in his care, he rarely had an audience. In Joe he had a willing listener and he spoke at length about anything and everything he knew about von Murren and his theories of why he was so rich.

'He's a very ruthless and ambitious man, so I hear,' said Jacques. 'Sacked a lot of people when he took over the factory and replaced workers with machines. Now there's a story going round that he has plans to become even richer.'

'Doing what?' asked Joe.

'Well, he's always entertaining bigwigs from them big companies in Basel and folk believe he is plotting with them to take over the world.'

'I don't understand,' said Joe but he had that faint tingling feeling around his chest that he always got when he thought there was a good story in the offing.

CHAPTER 22

Bruno Schmidt was desperately trying not to lose his temper with the woman who was patiently trying to explain that her employer had left specific instructions that he did not want to see the reporter again. She kept repeating that she was sorry but her boss was adamant. Bruno kept glancing across to the door leading into his office and contemplating whether or not he should just barge in. Suddenly he changed tack.

'This is nothing to do with the article my editor wants me to write,' he gushed. 'This is a personal problem, I need his advice … it's urgent.' The woman wilted, she was not used to dealing with such aggressive demands. She told Bruno to take a seat while she went to see her if her employer would agree to see him. As the woman walked to the office door, knocked and let herself in, Bruno was contemplating what he would say. But his head was spinning, thoughts bouncing from one side of his skull to the other, giving him a headache. He closed his eyes tight in an attempt to stop the tic and held his head in his hands, perhaps he thought, it would be safer just to run. The woman reappeared:

'He says he can spare you five minutes,' she said. Bruno stood, looked at the door and drew in a deep breath, before striding purposefully across the room. The man was engrossed in some papers and only looked up when Bruno noisily closed the door.

'Ah … Mr Schmidt, my receptionist says you need some advice,' he said coldly. 'Please sit down and explain how I can be of assistance.' Bruno cleared his throat.

'I'll come straight to the point,' he blurted. 'My mother has told me that you are my father …' The silence was tangible, as the man assimilated the roughly spoken words that reverberated around the room.

'That's not possible,' he eventually stuttered, staring at Bruno, calculating if this could possibly be the child who had been sent away for the heinous crime he had committed at school. 'What is your name?' he eventually asked.

'Bruno Schmidt … and my mother is Martha Schmidt.' The man slumped in his chair, the young man before him was about the right age, had Martha's colouring and even some features he recognised from gazing in the mirror at his own reflection.

'What do you want?' he wheezed.

'Her health is suffering, she needs an operation but before they can operate she needs treatment for her asthma.' He didn't mention the drink. 'She lives in a dark, dank apartment, she needs somewhere better to live.'

'I'm sorry to hear that she's not well,' said the man, sounding as if he meant it.

'Sorry is not good enough, you need to do something about it,' said Bruno tersely. The man thought carefully before he spoke:

'When we parted,' he stopped and cleared his throat. 'When we separated, I put several thousand marks in her bank account to help take care of you and to tide her over… we discussed it … she was quite satisfied with the arrangement.'

'Well things have changed, she needs a couple of months in a sanatorium and somewhere better to live.'

'I'm sorry, when we went our separate ways, we agreed that was the end of a chapter, as I said, I paid her generously, she was quite happy with that.'

'You paid her?' sneered Bruno, ' ... like you were finished with a whore!'

'It wasn't like that …' the man struggled for words, he could hardly tell this miserable little man in front of him that he was the cause of the breakup … and he had his career to think of.

'I wonder what your wife would say if I turned up on the doorstep and explained who I was?' said Bruno in a threatening whisper.

'You'd be wasting your time. I don't have a wife,' replied the man, thrusting out his jaw.

'Oh I think you do,' hissed Bruno, suddenly so calm, that the tic had stopped dancing.

'I'll tell you what,' said the man, after some moments, rising to his feet, I'll go and see her. Write your mother's address on here.' He thrust a pad towards Bruno and handed him a pen. 'You say she still lives in Todtnau?' The offer rather took the wind out of Bruno's sails, but he scribbled the address and stood for a moment staring at his father. He had no words. His head ached. He felt helpless, as he did on the rare days he forgot to take his pills.

Suddenly without a word, he turned on his heel and left. As the door closed the man peered at what Bruno had written and then slowly walked across the room towards a large ornamental cabinet. He pulled open a door, reached inside for a brandy decanter and poured himself a large measure, which he downed at one go. He was thinking of Martha Schmidt. He'd been very generous at the time. But her son … his son … There was a history. He had wild eyes and the air of a madman, it might be safer to at least go through the motions.

CHAPTER 23

Soon after Joe Leman had the discussion with Maria Beckett, about Dieter von Murren, he had been recalled to the head office in Neuilly-sur-Seine, a suburb of Paris. He didn't complain, he loved Paris; it was where he had started with the Herald.

When he was only nine years old Joe's father had been posted to Paris as a junior diplomat, so by the time he returned to Washington, six years later, Joe spoke French like a native. He was an avid reader in both English and French and had an addiction for Hemingway's novels. After college, with a bright, shiny degree in Journalism, Joe took himself off to Paris, where he styled himself on Jake Barnes: Hemingway's protagonist in his favourite book: *The Sun Also Rises.* He bought the Herald each day from a kiosk, and like Jake would sit in the sun, reading the paper, while sipping a glass of Chardonnay and watching the world go by. For some weeks he haunted the areas that Hemingway so vividly described but society had moved on, the sleazy cafés with their decadent customers had faded away; Paris, he rued, had changed dramatically since the nineteen-twenties.

When after a few months Joe ran out of funds, he took himself round to the International Herald Tribune's offices and asked for a job. His cheekiness paid off, he was offered a two-week probation and started straight away. His competence and knowledge of all things French ensured that at the end of the two weeks he had impressed the editor sufficiently to be offered a fulltime position and sent out to gather news - the paper's life-blood.

The only problem with this current assignment, as far as Joe was concerned, was that he was standing in for a colleague who mostly covered all the boring parliamentary stuff at the Palais du Luxembourg and the Palais Bourbon. The poor guy had developed stomach cancer, which didn't surprise Joe, because he thought all the garbage that was spouted in these two elegant buildings would make anyone ill. The only advantage was, that the sessions were widely reported and from these he could extract the juicy bits and elaborate. His editor seemed satisfied, which gave him more time to explore and seek out more interesting snippets, even if they never made it into print.

Some three weeks later Joe was called into the Human Resources' manager's office and asked if he would like to stay for a couple of months, until they found someone else. The guy he was replacing would not be returning to work. Joe immediately agreed, though he asked if there was any way he could share the job of reporting the boring stuff and do some real investigative journalism? He was assured that this might eventually be possible but it never happened.

Over the next few days Joe moved out of the modest hotel, where he had been staying and into a tiny company flat on a side street off the Avenue du Route. His heart sank when he opened the door of the second-floor, high-ceilinged flat. It comprised of one small bedroom, with no space to swing the proverbial cat, a bathroom straight out of the 1920's and a pokey, claustrophobic living room that was poorly lit and patterned with dismal brown wallpaper. In the corner of the living room were a stove, a sink and a cupboard with just enough crockery for one person. The only agreeable feature about the place was the large bay window, with an exterior low wrought-iron balustrade, looking out on the busy street. Joe couldn't help but think of his bright, comfortable apartment back in Basel. Having taken stock, he heaved the solid walnut table alongside the window, set up his typewriter, poured himself a glass of wine and sat watching the masses making their way home from work.

Two weeks flew by before he found himself thinking about what Maria, the girl at the language school in Basel, had said about Dieter von Murren. He remembered the tingling sensation that he had felt, convinced that here was a real story. So far there had been nothing like that here. He had meant to do some research on von Murren but except for typing his name on a file, he had not added anything, the move to Paris had put a stop to that.

Four weeks later a young American was appointed as the local correspondent and Joe spent two weeks showing him the ropes before he bid his Paris colleagues farewell and headed back to Basel.

On the evening of his second day back, Joe headed into Basel, planning to have a meal at one of his old haunts. As he stepped off the tram in busy Barfüsserplatz, he remembered it was the day he used to have his German lesson and wondered if the girl still went. He checked his watch and realised the lesson should be ending. He quickly made his way through the quiet streets and into the building where the classes were held. He waited in the foyer, watching people coming and going and then he heard a shout, it was Jock who had spotted him, Maria was behind him. There was much hugging and many questions: where had he been, why was he missing the lessons. In the end they headed for the usual bar and Joe was able to explain his absence, it was obvious that he had been missed.

At the end of the evening Maria and Joe bid farewell to Jock and caught the same number-ten tram. As the modern, yellow streetcar worked its way passed the Zoo, Joe asked if Maria had heard any more about her boss taking over the world. She laughed and said not that she knew, though the bigwigs of Basel's industries were still regular visitors. They exchanged telephone numbers and he said nothing more but kissed her cheek before leaving the train at Binningen, leaving Maria to continue to Flüh, where she had left Katarzyna's car. As the tram rumbled through the darkened suburbs she decided she was really pleased that Joe was back, he was good company and perhaps she would take up his offer to have a meal out one evening.

The next day Joe went to the main library and began searching the newspaper achieves for any news about Dieter von Murren - there was lots and it wasn't long before he had pages of notes and a sheaf of photocopied articles, albeit mostly in German, causing him to regret his scant knowledge of the language but making him even more determined to keep up his lessons. He felt sure Dieter von Murren would provide him with a story; he was definitely someone he really needed to know more about. His mind flicked over to Maria - and he concluded that she also was someone he would like to know better. On his return to his apartment Joe filed away the information that he had gathered and placed the file on a shelf among his books, where it gathered dust, as Joe persevered with the task of trying to interpret the niceties of Swiss politics and culture for the Herald's readers.

CHAPTER 24

A week after the confrontation with his son, Bruno, Ferdinand Brandt drove out to Todtnau. At the edge of the small town he stopped and consulted the scrap of paper where Bruno had scribbled the address. He had no idea where to go. He wound down the window and stopped a woman passing by, pushing a pram and asked if she knew the street. She pointed back the way he had come and so he reversed his Mercedes and drove until he found the side street the woman had described. He soon found the small block of flats with its sad, crumbling façade and overgrown gardens. He drove past, parked a short distance away and sat contemplating whether or not he really wanted to meet the woman he had not seen for almost twenty years. He wondered if he would even recognise her?

Martha Schmidt had been an entertainer at a hotel in the city, where he regularly took clients. She always seemed to be there, seated in a corner, playing a piano while softly crooning popular pop songs. After a while he took to asking the waiter to deliver her a glass of wine or chatting with her, while waiting for his clients to arrive. And the rest, he thought to himself, as they say, is history. He had been really fond of Martha; she was so different from his Isobel. And although shocked when she announced that she was pregnant, he had stood by her and if it hadn't been for that wretched son of hers … theirs, he might still be seeing her.

Eventually he picked up courage and made his way to the front door where he let himself into the foyer and studied the row of named bell-buttons. There were six apartments; he found Martha's handwritten label, all the others were neatly typewritten. He took a deep breath and rang the bell. It was some moments before the intercom crackled into life.

'Mrs Schmidt?' he asked. He thought she said yes. 'Your son asked me to see you,' he said.

'Bruno?' she replied.

'Yes, Bruno, can I come up?"

'I'm on the second floor, number three,' she replied. The man looked for the lift, only to find it was out of order. He found the stairs and slowly plodded his way upwards, stopping every few steps to catch his breath. The landing was bare and like the exterior, the paint was peeling. He was surprised to see a freshly painted door with a large number three, a token of Bruno's handiwork. He knocked, rather than using the bell and after a few moments the door was flung back to reveal a dishevelled woman in a dressing gown. Her grey hair was uncombed, a slash of scarlet lipstick leaping out of a pallid, wrinkled face. She lifted a hand holding a wine glass:

'What do you want? Where's Bruno?' she wheezed, clinging to the door with the other hand, so that she wouldn't fall. Brandt's mouth fell open and he gasped like a fish, no words articulated. The woman leaned forward.

'Come in ... come in and have a drink,' she grinned, her whole body shaking. Brandt stepped back:

'I'm sorry,' he muttered. 'I've rung the wrong bell,' he turned visibly shaken. It was along time since he had seen anyone so drunk.

'No matter,' the woman called, 'Come in anyway … where's Bruno?' Brandt turned away mouthing apologies and staggered down the landing. He was too horrified to look back. The woman's raucous voice was echoing down the corridor - inviting him to 'come in.'

Back in the car he sat eyes closed, breathing heavily while cursing for putting himself in such an embarrassing situation. He pictured the woman in his head. She was not the woman he had known and loved. She had been a lady - and yet he knew. He knew in his heart that the broken shadow of a woman he had just seen, was indeed Martha Schmidt.

Driving back to Freiburg the man was agonising about what he should do. He now understood why the man Bruno, he couldn't bring himself to call him his son, wanted his mother in a sanatorium, she needed to dry out, to be cured of her obvious alcoholism but should he help or turn his back and walk away. If he helped out would that mean he would have Bruno on his back for ever more - but if he didn't help, would that in fact be worse. He wearily decided that he would sleep on the dilemma.

CHAPTER 25

Brandt had a very restless night, as he dreamed of pursuing his former lover, only to find that each time he caught her and drew close to kiss her, the face that he remembered transformed to reveal the hag-like features he had seen the day before. Soundless screams echoed in his head, as he scrambled to free himself from her clutches.

Brandt's working week was also fraught with frustration and as he left his office Friday evening he bristled, tense and disgruntled. He walked towards the car park, his head down, concentrating on where he placed his feet. A man blocked his way, as he turned into the car park. He looked up angrily - it was Bruno.

Earlier that day, amid angry scenes, Bruno had been fired from his job, he had then attacked his boss and the police were called. He had been admonished and told to go home. Instead he had jumped on a train. Since then he had been roaming the streets seething with anger, seeking an outlet and eventually found himself outside his father's office.

Brandt tried to sidestep the man but Bruno mirrored his movement blocking his way.

'Well?' Bruno challenged. 'Have you seen her yet?' Brandt swore.

'I've been too busy,' he lied.

'You have no intention of going … do you?' snarled Bruno, roughly pushing his father in the ribs. Brandt stumbled and fell against his son, grabbing his arm.

'If you keep threatening me, I certainly won't go to see her,' he gasped.

'If you don't go to Todtnau this weekend … you'll be sorry … really sorry,' Bruno said pushing his father away.

'I will not be intimidated by your thuggish behaviour,' said Brandt firmly, pulling himself upright.

'I'm warning you!' said Bruno, thrusting his face right up against his father's.

'You'll do what?' queried Brandt sarcastically. 'What exactly will you do?' Bruno kept his face pressed up against his father's, almost touching.

'Go and see your wife, for a start,' he snarled, pushing his father again. 'How will you like that?' He kept repeating the phrase, each time pushing his father harder and harder, 'What do you say to that?' Overcome with rage, he punched his father in the stomach, causing Brandt to stumble to his knees, gasping for breath. Bruno stared down angrily before pushing him vigorously with his foot, causing his father to roll on to his back.

Unfortunately for Bruno, his actions had been witnessed by a slowly cruising police-car, which immediately stopped. For a second, the policemen watched but the moment Bruno swung his leg for a second time, they leapt from the car and raced across the road. Bruno made a run for it but was outstripped by the more athletic policeman, his colleague helping Brandt to sit up and rescue his broken spectacles.

Brandt was back on his feet, though still slightly bent because of the pain in his stomach, watching, as his handcuffed son was frogmarched to the car and forced into the backseat.

'Was he trying to rob you sir?' asked the policeman kindly, holding a tissue to a cut on Brandt's cheek. He had already recognised Brandt from his court appearances.

'No,' Brandt replied breathlessly, 'he just attacked me for no reason.' The policeman commiserated.

'Any chance you could keep him locked up for the night and I'll come and see you at the station tomorrow, when he's had time to calm down?'

'No problem,' replied the constable, 'I'll tell the Chief to expect you.'

The next day Brandt talked his way into the cell where Bruno had spent the night. Unshaven, hair uncombed, owl-like brown circles around his eyes - he looked a mess. Brandt gingerly eased himself down onto the empty cot opposite his son, his stomach muscles still hurt. Bruno was lying stretched out, staring at the ceiling, seemingly oblivious to his father's arrival. After some moments of silence Brandt spoke:

'I thought that they might have taught you how to behave at the school you went to.' Bruno didn't show any sign that he had heard. He'd not been able to take his tablets … and he had forgotten the day before. The contents of his head were swimming. 'The Inspector tells me you've lost your job … I'm sorry to hear that.' No response. 'Taking out your anger on innocent people won't help you know.' The one-sided conversation went on for some time, until Brandt grew tired of the charade and left. Back in the police-inspector's office, Brandt was asked if he wanted to press charges against Bruno. Brandt shook his head. The inspector then asked if he knew who Bruno was. Brandt replied that he was a reporter who had come to see him some months earlier about a story. The inspector nodded and enquired if he knew why the man had attacked him.

'Probably just because I accidentally bumped into him in the car park', replied Brandt. The inspector nodded.

'There had been trouble with him earlier, yesterday morning, when he attacked his employer. He was formally cautioned and let go … but now it seems his boss realises that he has two broken ribs and a broken cheekbone, so he's going to press charges. Looking at his records, I see that he's been violent before, though a long time ago. If you pressed charges, I think we could take him off the streets for a spell.' Brandt thought for a while and then shook his head.

'No, I won't make matters worse. Seems he'll get locked up anyway.'

And so, Bruno Schmidt was sentenced to six weeks imprisonment but after only two weeks inside, he slashed a fellow prisoner's face with a razor, wounded a warder and had his sentence increased to four years. Four years in which to maliciously brood and plan.

CHAPTER 26

Joe Leman was seated at his desk, in what he called his office, pondering over some papers. It was, in fact, the second bedroom of his two-bed apartment. One wall had a floor to ceiling bookcase, bulging with books and files. The other wall was covered with a huge poster advertising the Basel Art Fair, together with a pin board, covered with flapping papers. Joe's desk was under a window, through which there was a glimpse of a turret on the local Schloss.

He had filed his weekly report early and had time to spend on his special project. He was busy translating some of the information that he had gleaned on Dieter von Murren. The file that he had opened on von Murren was full and he had already started a second one. Pausing to sip from a cold cup of coffee, he leaned back in his chair contemplating his next move. It was obvious from everything that he had read; Dieter von Murren was the golden boy and not a smidgeon of dirt anywhere. But Joe still had this tingling sensation whenever von Murren's name arose. Peering into the distance, his eyes unfocussed, it wasn't long before he decided that before he could move further, he needed to meet the man and he reached for the telephone directory.

The woman at the other end of the line spoke fluent English and in no time he had an appointment, arranged for the following week. Now he would be able to find out for himself, what this man von Murren was really like and if he was capable of taking over the world, whatever that meant?

* * *

Dieter was his usual expansive self as he showed Joe Leman

around his highly mechanised factory, explaining what each machine did and how many potions, pills, tablets and capsules each was capable of producing. Back in his office, Dieter introduced his personal assistant, Gloria, still as glamorous as ever, when she arrived with a tray of coffee. A few moments later, he apologised, as Gloria placed urgent papers on his desk to be signed.

Joe couldn't take his eyes off the woman and while sipping coffee, he watched carefully for any body language, which might indicate a less than business connection between the pair. He noted how close Gloria stood to Dieter but not quite touching. The almost adoring glances she threw his way but Dieter only had eyes for the papers she had placed before him. She glided out of the office, smiling and fluttering her eyelashes in his direction. Unrequited love perhaps, Joe wondered?

Dieter expounded his theories of cheap drugs for developing countries, while acknowledging that pharmaceutical companies needed fat profits to fund research.

'It's a catch twenty-two situation,' he kept reiterating. 'Everyone wants drugs, as cheaply as possible but everyone also wants new drugs to combat the many diseases that plague the planet. If the pharma's don't make profits they can't carry out the research.'

'So your factory produces drugs that are no longer protected by patent?' asked Joe. Dieter nodded. 'Am I right in thinking that the major pharmaceutical companies continue to manufacture the same drug, under their brand name - and charge twice as much?'

'Correct,' replied Dieter, 'more or less.'

'I would have thought that your business must upset the big companies in Basel that rely on these sales to fund their research,' continued Joe. 'Especially, as you're right on their doorstep. I could imagine them sending out their hitmen to finish you off.' Dieter laughed. 'You really must be so unpopular with Basel's pharma leaders and their shareholders,' said Joe. 'How do you sleep at night?'

'Oh I sleep soundly,' laughed Dieter. He gently rebuffed all the questions that followed, his charming disarming manner clearly registering with Joe. Maria was right, this man did have charisma and he could talk. Joe had long since given up making notes, drawn in by Dieter's lucid arguments about the inevitability for business and medicine to be interlinked.

'You make it all sound like a game,' said Joe. 'Do you ever

meet with the leaders of the major pharmaceutical industries in Basel to discuss these issues?'

'Rarely,' replied Dieter. 'Obviously we bump into each other from time to time at conferences and seminars and such.'

'So you don't meet socially?' queried Joe. It was painfully obvious to Joe that Dieter ducked that question, as he skilfully changed the subject, bringing the discussion round to Joe's opinion of life in Basel.

An hour later, as Joe drove back to Basel, mentally sieving all the information he had gleaned that afternoon, he decided that he almost liked Dieter von Murren. He was highly intelligent, had an enormous ego and yet tried to appear modest. It was plain that he was extremely successful but … but thought Joe, I wouldn't trust him an inch.

The following day Joe telephoned Dieter von Murren's factory, made up a story for the receptionist and asked for Gloria's surname. He then searched the telephone book and found her home number in the suburb of Muttenz. That night he called the number but failed to get an answer. He was more fortunate the next evening. He explained whom he was and that he was writing a piece about her boss's business. He had questions that he had forgotten to ask, was there any chance that they could meet for a drink one evening, to save worrying her boss again. After an initial reluctance, Gloria eventually agreed and a date was fixed for a meeting at the International Hotel in downtown Basel.

CHAPTER 27

'Gloria,' Joe kept singing the name in his head, as he sipped a beer in a corner of the International Hotel foyer, one eye monitoring the swing doors. He was humming the hit-song, while trying to remember the name of the girl who had belted out the number in the film Flashdance. 'Gloria, you're always on the run now. Running after somebody, you gotta get him somehow.' Hmm, he wondered, was Gloria after Dieter von Murren? He'd be quite a catch, wife or no wife!

With impeccable Swiss timing, Gloria Gabric swung in through the doors, her long fashionable black coat almost sweeping the floor. The concierge stepped towards her but she had already spotted Joe's waving hand. Ten minutes later, greetings complete, Gloria was settled in an armchair with a glass of white wine.

'Gutedel,' she murmured, 'My favourite.' Joe asked if she had visited the vineyards of Markgräflerland, just north of the Swiss/German border. She had - and proceeded to inform Joe that fifty per cent of the grapes grown on the hills above that part of the Rhine were Gutedel, and listed all the best vintners. Joe inwardly groaned, realising that she was far more knowledgeable than he, and quickly changed the subject.

The topic of the International Herald arose and Gloria quizzed Joe about his role and some of the more salacious stories currently being aired. He brought the conversation around to herself, her schooling and career. As she began, Joe found himself drawn again towards this attractive woman and her husky clipped manner of speaking. He slyly studied the shoulder-length, raven coloured hair, the full lips and bottomless eyes. It was obvious, he thought, that Gloria knew that she was being scrutinised but she didn't bat an eyelid - she was used to it.

Her parents were from Croatia she told him but she had been schooled in Basel and trained as a secretary.

'Did you consider university?' asked Joe, for it was apparent to him that she was highly intelligent.

'Yes but my father was unemployed at the time,' she replied. 'We needed the money.'

'Does he have a job now?' asked Joe.

'No, he has old injuries from the 1970 troubles. He was a student at the time, thrown into prison for five years and badly beaten. He has trouble walking, never mind working.'

'I don't know about that period of Croatian history,' admitted Joe.

'It's complicated,' sighed Gloria. 'Students protesting about the way Croats were being treated by Yugoslavia - and the usual police brutality. When he came out of prison he and my mother came to Switzerland and applied for asylum.'

'And your mother, does she work?'

'She has a cleaning job ... despite a degree in Serbian & Croatian Literature - not a qualification that has been any help here!'

'So you still live at home with your parents?' enquired Joe.

'No,' she replied. 'I share a flat with a girl-friend.'

'Anyone special in your life?' asked Joe. 'A boyfriend?'

'There are lots of special people in my life,' she said sharply. 'But no boyfriend.'

'That surprises me,' said Joe. 'You're a very beautiful woman.' Gloria tossed her head ignoring the compliment.

'You said on the phone that you had questions about my boss, not about me?' She drained the glass and Joe walked over to the ornate circular bar and ordered another.

'Okay, Dieter von Murren … your boss!' began Joe. 'I have all the facts about his career. I need some input about the man himself, what's he really like. What makes him tick?'

Gloria sipped her wine and studied her glass. Joe noticed the purple fingernails that matched her necklace and bracelets.

'He's a good man to work for,' she said in a non-committal tone.

'How long have you worked with him?' asked Joe.

'About twelve years, I suppose' replied Gloria. 'That's a scary thought!' she mused. Where does the time go.'

'Then you would know him better than anyone,' pressed Joe.

'So you say he's a good guy to work for … but he strikes me as being unbelievable egocentric. Some people say he's ruthless. Capable of anything!'

'He treats me well, I have no complaints,' Gloria interjected. 'In fact he treats me very well.'

'Buys you presents does he?' suggested Joe.

'What are you insinuating?' Gloria said sharply.

'Well, as I said, you're a very beautiful woman … he must have tried it on!' Gloria tensed; Joe noticed that she was holding her breath.

'He has always been a complete gentleman, as regards our relationship,' she hissed. 'Our relationship has been nothing but professional.' Her voice was rising. 'Why is it you journalists are so obsessed with sex?' She was draining her glass, preparing to leave.

'It's what makes the world go round,' thought Joe but profusely apologised, begging her to stay. He asked if she had eaten and suggested that he buy her dinner. Initially she refused but Joe persisted and in the end she agreed.

They ate dinner in the adjoining restaurant, where one wall was all plate-glass looking out on the busy street. Joe turned on the charm and kept Gloria amused with anecdotes of his former life in Paris. Following dinner and another glass of wine Gloria noticeably relaxed. Joe began again probing for information about her boss. She let slip that she thought he had extra-marital affairs but not with anyone in particular. There had been times when she had been asked to book air-tickets for female 'business consultants' to accompany him to seminars or meetings. She admitted she was only putting two and two together.

'I've heard rumours that he intends to take over the world,' said Joe starkly. Gloria smiled.

'Where did you hear that?'

'From people in the village where he lives.'

'Gossip, idle village gossip,' said Gloria.

'Gossip or not - what do you think they mean? I haven't been able to pin anyone down,' said Joe. 'All I'm told is that he and all the other big bosses in Basel are going to carve up the world and I'm presuming they mean the world markets. Do you think that's feasible?'

'No. They'd all risk going to jail,' she replied with a laugh.

'Big fat profits and bonus's might persuade the more greedy that it was worth the risk,' continued Joe. 'Your boss strikes me as being a risk-taker. He has the ego to convince himself that he could get away with anything.' Gloria was staring into her glass:

'True - for Dieter von Murren, anything is possible,' she murmured. Joe leaned towards her:

'Would you be willing to help me find out what he is up to? I'm absolutely sure he's up to no good, I feel it in my bones, they're never wrong.'

'What could I do?' whispered Gloria sceptically.

'Be my ears and eyes,' replied Joe. 'If we get a good story there could be a lot of money in it for you.'

'How much?' asked Gloria. 'My father needs an operation, extra cash would be useful ... but I can't risk losing my job.'

'Perhaps five figures, if we get a good story,' said Joe. 'But be careful. No calls from the office, where you might be overheard.'

'I don't really know what I'm supposed to look for,' complained Gloria.

'Signs that he is doing deals with other drug producers. Anything out of the ordinary.' Joe said earnestly. Gloria looked at her watch.

'Will you do that? Will you look out for anything unusual and let me know?' Reluctantly Gloria eventually agreed.

'I really must go,' she said rescuing her handbag from under the table and standing upright. As they headed for the door, Gloria thanked Joe for the meal and the pair walked out into the foyer. Joe kissed her cheek and escorted her towards the door.

'I'm going to use the facilities before I catch the tram,' he said, bidding her farewell and returning towards the rear of the lobby. Before turning down a side corridor, he looked towards the door, in time to see Gloria fall into the arms of a short, athletic looking woman and watch them hold hands, as they made their way through the swing-doors.

'Ah,' thought Joe, surprised. 'Perhaps that's why she doesn't have a boyfriend.'

CHAPTER 28

Over the next few months Joe Leman spent many hours researching how the pharmaceutical industry worked. He interviewed the chief marketing person at each of the companies and read copiously about the strategies involved, as well as about the generic companies, like Dieter von Murren's that produced drugs once their patent had expired. On his office wall he affixed a huge world map and methodically started sticking in coloured pins, indicating which local companies operated where and what type of products they sold. It was a tediously slow process, a real labour of love. But when it was completed he hoped that it might indicate if there were any noticeable changes, should von Murren and his cronies start to change their marketing strategies.

Joe continued with his German lessons and looked forward to seeing Maria each week. He never saw her on her own; Jock was always with them, except for the short ride home on the tram, when they sat together for about ten minutes before Joe reached his stop.

On one occasion Joe asked Maria if she ever had a day off. 'Rarely,' she had replied but her boss was flexible and she felt sure she could ask for a Sunday off. And so a date was fixed and Katarzyna told Maria that she must never be afraid to ask for time off. Maria was an invaluable member of the household and Katarzyna would do anything to make sure that she stayed.

On the appointed Sunday, Joe was waiting at the tram stop and joined Maria on the tram when she arrived at ten in the morning, dressed in jeans, sweater, walking boots and carrying a small rucksack. The pair of them continued to the railway station, where they changed trams and travelled out to the pleasant suburb of Riehen. From there they set off among the mediaeval buildings and climbed towards a local landmark: the ancient Chrischona clinic and the adjacent two-hundred and fifty metre high communications tower. At the top they nibbled sandwiches that Maria had brought and admired the view across the Rhine valley. After spending some time wandering around the old buildings they strolled back down the hill towards the Rhine, following a bubbling man-made stream. Maria told Joe that she had been born in York and studied childcare in London. She'd always been good at French in school and at age eighteen had taken a job in Strasbourg, in so doing becoming fluent in the language. She told how she stayed with the family of a British diplomat for two years but when they were moved to Asia, she landed a job with a family in Bavaria. It turned out the man was a German Prince with business interests all over the world, which meant lots of international travelling, which she had thoroughly enjoyed. The wife was Spanish and the family communicated entirely in English and because of all the travelling Maria had only acquired a smattering of German.

Basel was unusually quiet by the time they had walked back into the city but they found a back-street café and ordered a meal. Joe asked Maria how she got on with the von Murren's? She replied that the wife, Katarzyna and the girls were delightful but the husband more aloof.

'I think that I told you that I'm trying to write an article about Dieter von Murren,' said Joe. 'He showed me around his factory and we had a good chat. But somehow he wears a mask - the persona he presents is hiding something. A handsome façade covering the real Herr Doctor von Murren.' Joe swigged his beer. 'I'm not entirely sure he's honest. What do you think?'

'I couldn't say,' replied Maria, surprised. 'I live under the same roof but the only contact I have with him is through the girls. He seems nice enough. But it's funny you say that, the man who looks after the horses insinuated Dieter was up to something?' Joe's ears pricked up.

'I understand that he entertains a lot,' said Joe, not admitting that he had met Jacques Wolf, the man she was referring to. 'Is it always the same people?'

'I guess,' answered Maria. 'He has a close circle of about three or four friends, I suppose. Sometimes there are many more.'

'Listen,' said Joe in a secretive whisper. 'There's a story going round that he and some of his mates are up to no good. I'd really like to find out if it's true. Would you be prepared to help?'

'How could I possibly help? As I said, I have hardly have any contact with him.'

'Well, for a start, would you make a list of all the people that he socialises with and the dates that they meet?' Maria thought:

'I suppose I could do that but I wouldn't want to do anything to hurt the family.'

'No of course not,' said Joe hastily.

'I don't really see how that would help you, I mean they have dinner and he plays the piano and that's the evening gone.'

'Would you ever be able to listen in on what they are talking about?' asked Joe.

'No.' replied Maria quickly. 'I'm never invited. My job is to look after the girls and stay out of the way.' Joe looked pensive,

'Well maybe there's nothing in it but it would help if you would be my ears and eyes, make a list of his guests and keep me informed if anything unusual happens.' Maria, though feeling uncomfortable, nodded in agreement.

Later Joe had taken Maria back to his apartment where, after coffee, he had ridden with her on the tram, out to Flüh and then walked with her to Katarzyna's Range Rover. In the unlit car park Maria fell into his arms, until they parted promising to meet up again soon. Joe watched the tail lights fade away before making his way to the empty platform, his head awash with possibilities.

There had been several girlfriends over the years but he had never been in what might be described a proper relationship. The demands of his work and a driving ambition to succeed had always got in the way of anything more permanent. Perhaps he had never met Miss Right he thought. His musings were shattered by the rattling arrival of the tram, returning from its furthest destination, Rodersdorf.

Lying in his bed that night, Joe was feeling slightly smug. He had two spies at work. He really liked Maria, a really practical and loving personality - so different from the very attractive, sexy Gloria. Both, he hoped would prove useful but it was Maria he knew he could trust. All he could do now was to sit back and spiderlike, patiently wait for the victim to land in his web.

CHAPTER 29

Over the next year Joe met with Gloria about once a month, usually over coffee in a quiet Basel side street. She rarely had anything useful to report about her boss but the thought of a possible substantial payment kept her coming. At one meeting she told Joe that a senior executive from one of the Basel companies had visited von Murren and she had heard them rowing but other than that, nothing out of the ordinary.

Maria, on the other hand, Joe saw every week, as she stayed the night after their weekly German lesson, a routine they both enjoyed. But according to Maria, nothing eventful was happening in the von Murren household. Joe was irritated; nothing was happening with his coloured pins either - the pins that he had so carefully stuck in his wall map, to chart any changes to company marketing strategies.

One evening, in a moment of frustration, he ripped out the pins, rolled up his wall map and stared at the bare wall. Gathering the information from the companies was too time consuming and the published information always months out of date. He needed a different approach.

At Joe's next meeting with Gloria, he asked if her boss was likely to be travelling soon. She responded that he would be in Mexico the following week.

'Who's in charge, when he's travelling?' asked Joe.

'A man called Hahn,' replied Gloria. 'Doctor Hahn, the production manager.'

'Any chance I could have a poke around among your boss's files, while the cat's away?' Gloria paled:

'I don't think that's a good idea,' she said quickly. 'Anyway, he wouldn't be so stupid as to put anything in writing.'

'I'd like to get a feel for where his major markets are, said Joe. 'Unlike the major pharma companies, he doesn't publish much - a couple of hours among his files might give me some idea.'

'Well I can answer that,' gushed Gloria. 'Almost every developing country you can name, plus most of Europe.'

'Please Gloria, I'd really like to look,' persisted Joe. After a great deal of persuasion Gloria finally gave in and a date fixed.

'The office staff tend to work late,' said Gloria. 'And the machines don't close down until nine pm. Doctor Hahn is a workaholic, he's sure be around tinkering with his toys - and then there's security.' Gloria was obviously concerned.

'Don't worry,' said Joe reassuringly. 'It'll be okay. I'll come when the office staff has left. What time do you suggest, when will they be gone?'

'The office-manager usually leaves about six-thirty but because Dieter's away, she might go earlier,' said Gloria.

'Okay,' said Joe. 'Six-forty five.'

''What about security?' said Gloria suddenly. 'You'll have to sign in?' 'I won't use my real name. Stop worrying. I'll think of something,' replied Joe squeezing her arm in an attempt to calm her obvious anxiety.

'I don't like this,' she whispered, shaking her head. Joe continued to reassure Gloria, as they stood ready to part. He pecked her cheek, once to the right, once to the left and back to the right, in typical Swiss manner and was treated to a triple waft of Jasmin perfume for his troubles.

On the appointed day, Joe rolled up at von Murren's plant and wound down his window to speak to the burly security guard, seated inside his warm cabin. He was asked his business and he replied that he an appointment with Miss Gloria Gabric. The guard picked up the phone and gabbled in Swiss German, after which he gave Joe a pass fastened to a ribbon to hang around his neck and pressed a button to raise the barrier. Joe was relieved that he hadn't been asked for his name?

Inside her office, Gloria greeted Joe calmly but he could tell she was tense. He asked if everyone had gone and she told him the office manager had left with her staff and, as far as she knew, only Doctor, Hahn was still around. She locked her office door and took

Joe through into Dieter's office. In front of a substantial glass-fronted cabinet, she chose a key from a ring attached to her belt and unlocked the door. Inside she extracted a heavy file and placed it in the desk.

'That's the latest personal correspondence concerning orders,' she said. Joe thanked her and settled down in Dieter's chair.

'Don't sit there,' she cried. You'll be seen, take it through to my office. She looked round wildly. The office had glass on two sides, affording a view over the whole factory but now it was dark, it resembled a goldfish bowl.

Over the next two hours, the pair of them flicked through many files, Joe filling pages of his notebook and Gloria making photocopies of the occasional document.

'I won't forget this,' he said, closing the last file and putting his notebook into his pocket. He rose and stretched, Gloria replaced the files and locked Dieter's office door. They left together and made their way across the car park.

'Do you think you found anything?' asked Gloria.

'I think I may have,' replied Joe. I need to check my other sources.' He thanked Gloria profusely and leaned across to kiss her farewell but she pulled away, formally thrusting out her hand.

'The security guard,' she hissed. Joe nodded and wrung her hand.

The following week Joe was tied up researching and writing a series of articles his editor wanted in a hurry. He knew he would have some free time once that was completed and so managed to contain his impatience.

CHAPTER 30

At the crack of dawn on Friday morning, after her overnight stay, Joe walked Maria to the Binningen tram-stop. He wrapped his arms around her shoulders, as they waited on the empty platform. Their Friday morning timing had been perfected over several weeks and dead on time the gleaming yellow tram pulled alongside the platform. A quick kiss and Maria was gone, en-route to Flüh and Katarzyna's parked Range-Rover.

Back in the apartment Joe made himself a coffee and settled at his desk, surrounded by the mountain of literature he had collected about Dieter von Murren. In front of him he had the notes and photocopies from his trip to the factory, together with a list of names Maria had provided him with; the names of people who had visited Dieter's home for dinner. He also had Dieter's appointment diaries from the past two years - and they made very interesting reading. For the rest of the day, Joe meticulously pieced together the puzzle. At one stage he tacked paper to the wall and covered it with flowcharts showing who was connected to whom; as well as another large sheet showing a date line.

Joe was so absorbed the hours evaporated, until sudden stomach pangs reminded him that he had not eaten. Reluctantly he stopped and headed for his tiny kitchen where he loaded a plate with cheese, grabbed a packet of biscuits and opened a can of beer. Back in his office he stood nibbling and studying his handiwork. Joe was convinced that the document Gloria had copied showing Begrafica had stopped trading in Sierra Leone and rented their vast warehouse to one of the companies run by one of Dieter's dinner guests, was significant. Another document showed that the same company had stopped trading in South Africa and that three months later Begrafica had taken over the rental of their warehouse. In his mind it was truly significant but it didn't prove anything, he needed more. He glowered at price lists for different products. It was impossible for him to tell if price-fixing was going on - pills, tablets and capsules were all different weights and the packaging contained varying amounts. It would need an expert to decipher all this stuff. Joe flopped back onto his chair and took a gulp from the can. Even with all this material before him and all his theories, he knew he didn't have a story. His heart sank, as he glanced at his watch and was shocked to discover it was almost three in the morning. He dragged himself to his bed convinced he was wasting his time and fell asleep fully clothed.

* * *

Joe woke up the next day in time for lunch and as he spooned bircher muesli into his mouth he flicked through the yellow pages. He'd awoken with an idea. He found what he was looking for in the directory and wrote an address on a slip of paper. Half an hour later he was on the tram and heading for Kleinbasel, an area of the city across the river. He left the tram near the huge exhibition area, known as the Mustermesse and consulted the street map that he had pushed into his pocket. It took him another twenty minutes before he found himself in front of a tired looking block of flats. At the entrance he scrutinised the list of occupants alongside the bell pushes.

Raziel Stavi, on the fifth floor, that was the name he had written on the paper. Joe pushed the bell. Almost instantly the speaker crackled into life.

'My name's Joe, I called earlier.' A heavy accented, whiskey worn voice told him to take the elevator to the fifth floor. A black-bearded broad shouldered man was standing in the corridor, as Joe exited the elevator. He waved.

After introductions Joe sat in an upright chair in front of a desk where Raziel Stavi had turned the living room into an office. Instantly the phone rang, Stavi mumbled an apology and gabbled into the phone, Joe presumed in Hebrew. Joe glanced round the room; it was scantily furnished, there was a couch where a crumpled duvet indicated it was regularly used as a bed. There was small mat on the marble floor and a coffee table, with a dirty mug, half-filled with cold coffee, together with a copy of Blick, the sensational, local tabloid newspaper. The walls were bare and the curtains only half drawn across the windows. Joe's musings were interrupted, as Stavi noisily replaced the phone, cleared his phlegm-ridden throat and asked how he could help.

'The Phone Directory says that you're a private detective,' stated Joe. The man nodded. 'I'm a journalist ... working on a,' Joe searched for the right words. 'Working on a rather delicate investigation.'

'My specialism is divorce cases, getting information on adultery. They don't get any more delicate than that,' Stavi stated seriously, sticking out his jaw and looking Joe in the eye for the first time.

'Well for the moment, I don't actually want your expertise,' said Joe. 'I wondered if you had any special recording kit, voice recording that is. Something I could borrow or rent.'

'You want to spy on a private conversation?' said Stavi. Joe nodded. 'I got cameras, video-recorders, microphones, stuff like you never seen. What exactly do you want to do?'

'Well, I need to set up some equipment in a room where four or five people will be relaxing, having a drink, chatting. I need to know what they are talking about.'

'You got any proof you're a journalist?' asked Stavi abruptly. 'You sure you ain't an industrial spy?' Joe fumbled in his pocket and found a business card and handed it to Stavi. The man peered at it: 'So you work for the Herald?' Joe nodded. 'Do I get a cut, if you get a good story?' he asked, with almost a grin. Joe ignored the comment with a laugh.

'Well, can you help me?'

'How big's the room?' asked Stavi. Joe had never been in Dieter von Murren's living room; he had no idea of its size. He considered what Maria had said about how many people had been entertained - and the fact there was a grand piano.

'Huge,' he replied. 'At least three times the size of this one.'

'You have to be more precise,' said Stavi. 'Spying is an art.'

'How did you learn?' asked Joe with a chuckle. He'd never thought of espionage as an art-form.

'Mossad,' came the monosyllabic reply. Joe did not pursue the answer; it might be a story for another day.

'Look,' he said, 'for the moment, all I need is a microphone and a tape recorder.'

'You don't get it,' said Stavi getting to his feet. 'I got directional microphones so sensitive; they'd pick up the faintest fart at a hundred metres. If you got five or six folk sitting about, facing in different directions you'll need more than one microphone. You need a diagram of the room and where folks will be. You need to plan.' Stavi headed across the room and down a corridor leaving Joe slightly confused.

A toilet flushed in the distance and a kettle whistled. A few moments later Stavi reappeared with two mugs of steaming coffee.

'Being American and a journalist, I presume you'd like this.' He placed a mug in front of Joe and sat down again. 'Well?' he continued. 'Have you thought about it?'

An hour later Joe left Stavi's apartment with three mini microphones a tiny recorder, and a host of verbal instructions reverberating around his head. If this didn't work, he thought to himself, at least he now had an excellent contact that he could call upon to help.

CHAPTER 31

The only thing that brightened the dull, October day in Katarzyna's mind, was the fact that it was her older daughter's tenth birthday. Stephanie had inherited her mother's genes with regard to looks and personality: she was calm, thoughtful and kind. She spoke Polish with her mother, German with her father and English with Maria. She was also an accomplished pianist and school reports placed her at the top of her class. Next year she would have to change schools and there had been discussion between her parents, whether this would be the time for her to join her father's old school or whether they should send her to the English-language international school. In the end Dieter and Katarzyna had agreed that they would visit both schools nearer the time and let Stephanie choose.

Stephanie's birthday fell on a school day but on the following Saturday Katarzyna and Dieter took both girls into Basel to enjoy the Herbstmesse, a tradition dating back more than five hundred years. The Autumn Fair was not just an amusement fair, though the dozens of exciting rides were by far the greatest attraction for the girls.

The various public squares, including Petersplatz, Barfüsserplatz and Munsterplatz were ringed with stalls selling not only food but also anything and everything imaginable. The fair attracted thousands of people but because it was spread out around the city, the atmosphere was friendly and familial.

The girls screamed with excitement as they hurtled through the air on some of the more scary rides that left their parents happy to be spectators. But in the Munsterplatz they all rode the big wheel that gently spun them close to the sandstone tower of the cathedral, affording views over the nearby Rhine and the mediaeval roofs. Later they ate sausages from one of the stalls before heading back to the car park and home, with Stephanie proclaiming what a wonderful birthday it had been.

Family outings had become a thing of the past, as Dieter seemed to be travelling more than ever, as his empire grew. Katarzyna became used to his long absences and gradually her life revolved more and more around her daughters and her horses, rather than her husband.

Christmas came and went and before he knew it, Dieter was carefully scheduling his diary to allow regular practices with his Fasnacht Clique. The musical and drinking sessions with Marco and his cohorts, contrasting vividly with his business life, a real opportunity to relax and let off steam. Over the following years and no matter how busy his schedule, Dieter always, without fail, managed to find time to join his clique for the annual Fasnacht celebration.

Each year Katarzyna and the children religiously attended the ridiculously early morning Moorgestraich, which signified the start of Fasnacht and once Dieter's clique had been identified, the three of them usually pushed their way through the crowds to follow the clique around the city. Shortly after seven o'clock the family usually fell into a restaurant for an early morning breakfast, revolving around a bowl of traditional Basler mehlsuppe - flour soup. Not exactly the girls' favourite! Afterwards the females would make their way home but Dieter returned to clique headquarters and a lively drinking and singing session.

CHAPTER 32

The unmistakable squeak of a key in the lock woke Bruno Schmidt. The warder had unlocked the cell door. He slid his legs over the side of the bed and stretched, he had slept well. He slipped his feet into an old pair of brogues, opened the cell door and made his way to the toilets, as he did each and every boring morning, day in and day out. A warder standing at the bathroom door, nodded in greeting. Bruno ignored him. A dozen men in various states of undress were busy washing or shaving. Bruno found an empty sink and turned on the tap. Despite years of living in institutions, he hated the lack of privacy and after a quick shave and wash, he made his way back to the cell and dressed. In the canteen he collected his food and sat between two men he knew he could trust not to bother him. The stilted conversation was about the soccer match many of the inmates had watched the previous night, when Bayer Munich had once again triumphed. Bruno had not watched the game and only half listened to the expert pundits.

The prison was located in Freiburg and known locally as Café Fünfeck, due to its pentagonal design. Bruno had not told his mother he was locked up and consequently had no visitors. Martha Schmidt spent most of her days in an alcoholic stupor and only occasionally remembered she had a son. In a lucid moment she might telephone him. But he was never at home, she would complain to herself, before making excuses for his absence.

At the prison Bruno was being trained as a carpenter and spent most of each day in a workshop learning basic techniques. This apprenticeship was meant to provide him with skills to find useful employment after his release. He was being pragmatic, he knew he could never again find employment as a newspaper reporter, his previous editor would see to that. Not that he cared, he had hated most of the people he had to interview or write about. They were either: pompous, self-righteous, corrupt or downright uninteresting. He'd be just as happy mindlessly driving his forklift truck.

The psychiatrists who had tracked his progress through his teenage years had concluded that, although intelligent, Bruno lacked the gene that controlled empathy, sensitivity, wonderment and the tap that controlled the flow of milk, the milk of human kindness - he had no concept of conscience and an inability to socialise. The case-notes had included the word 'alexithymia,' a disorder that seemed to cause a short-circuit in the brain, leading to emotional blindness. What he did have, however, was the ability to loathe and despise. Each night as he lay on his cot he honed his ability to hate, he had no need to stick pins into symbolic dolls. Staring unseeingly at the ceiling, he could do it more effectively in his head. The target of his revulsion was his father. The man who had sowed the seeds of his being in the garden of his mother's womb and then deliberately shirked his responsibilities. He had walked away - neglecting the nurture both so obviously needed. Well he would suffer. In a few short months, he would suffer.

Bruno was playing the game that he had played at the Special School. He was becoming a model prisoner, this way he knew his sentence would be reduced, he might even get an early parole. And then! He spent hours considering how he would kill his father, not that he thought of Brandt as his father - he was just someone who had fucked his mother. Killing him would be the easy bit - first, he had to suffer. Maybe there would have to be other deaths, deaths of those Brandt loved and cared about. He needed to plan, in less than nine months, with any luck; he would be out of this god-forsaken place.

CHAPTER 33

Dieter von Murren was feeling pleased with himself. He was relaxing in the rear of a company limousine, as it weaved its way along Morgartenring, heading for the westerly suburbs of Basel and home. He had just flown in after a long, boring flight from Buenos Aires to Zurich and the final hop to Basel. He was feeling satisfied, having signed a contract to take over a factory in the suburbs of that megacity. He had persuaded one of his pharma cronies to pull his business out of Argentina, in return for Dieter quitting Sierra Leone! You didn't need a degree in economics to know who had got the better part of that deal? The other company's operation in Argentina had fallen foul of the unions and one dispute had followed another, disrupting production. In the end they were pleased to pull out. Dieter knew he had the skills to deal with union leaders, he'd already met with most of them and would soon have them eating out of his hand. His profit margins were wider; he didn't have shareholders to worry about. He could afford to be generous - to start with.

Dieter had been away for two weeks and so he received a hero's welcome back in Burg. Katarzyna and the girls took turns to hug him, the latter demanding to know all about Argentina and had he seen any gauchos? Later in bed, Katarzyna slid into his arms but Dieter immediately fell asleep. How many women has he bedded this trip she wondered, as a silent tear slid down her nose and across her chin.

Over breakfast Dieter told Katarzyna he was planning a dinner party for Saturday evening and please would she organise dinner for eight guests, plus themselves. When she asked who would be coming, he replied that he wasn't sure but that he planned to invite the 'usual crowd.' Rather than being upset at his manner and curt instructions, Katarzyna was pleased; she enjoyed having a houseful and had got to know one or two of the female guests quite well. Occasionally she met them for coffee in Basel, either alongside the Rhine at Les Grand Hotel Trois Rois, or Café Huguenin in Barfüsserplatz.

When Maria walked into the kitchen later that morning, having taken the girls to school, Katarzyna asked her if she would mind taking a note down to the Bad Berg restaurant at the bottom of the hill.

'We're entertaining again,' she said gaily.

'Oh, who's coming?' asked Maria.

'The usual crowd,' repeated Katarzyna. 'But I think something special from the chef would be nice.'

'Do you mind if I ride down? It will save me having to exercise Beauty later.'

'Of course not' replied Katarzyna. 'Good idea.'

Outside the Bad Berg restaurant, later that morning, Maria tied her mount Beauty to a rail, climbed the steps onto the terrace and into the restaurant. The owner was in deep discussion with the chef but she looked up and greeted Maria with a smile. The chef waved and turned to leave, Maria called for him to wait, explaining that her boss had a request. The owner opened the envelope that Maria handed over and read the contents to the chef. He nodded and took the note.

'How many this time?' asked Maria with a laugh.

'Dinner for ten,' replied the owner.

'Cheese on toast for me then on Saturday night,' Maria joked.

'No,' said Barbara. 'Mrs von Murren, says to send enough for you and the children, as well.'

'Oh, that's nice' replied Maria. ' She's such a thoughtful person.'

On the way back Maria was thinking of Joe and his requests for information on Dieter's activities. She hadn't had much to tell him over the recent months but she supposed the dinner party was something he would be interested in.

Thursday, after the German class and a beer with her fellow students in the nearest bar, Maria and Joe rode the tram back to his Binningen apartment. As she busied herself making coffee in Joe's kitchen, she called out that the von Murren's were entertaining on

Saturday night. Joe immediately shot into the kitchen full of questions. She told him that there would be eight for dinner and it sounded as if it would be the usual guests. Maria had already supplied Joe with a list of previous dinner guests, there were usually four men from the major pharmaceutical companies together with their wives, totalling eight. Joe dived into a drawer and pulled out a small box holding the listening equipment that Stavi, the private detective, had given him. He spread the items out on the table and he explained what he wanted to do:

'I need to hear what they are talking about,' he said. 'Any chance I could get in to the house on Saturday and set it up?' Maria stared at the tiny microphones, deeply troubled:

'So this is how you get your information by snooping on people,' she hissed. 'I suppose you've got cameras as well. Wouldn't surprise me if you've recorded us in bed.' She was really very angry and close to tears.

'Maria,' said Joe pleading. He reached for her. 'Maria I have no cameras and this is the first time I have ever used such equipment - it's not mine, I've hired it from a private detective.' Joe held Maria's face between his two hands. 'Maria, just this once … help me.'

'No way,' Maria almost shouted. 'I don't want to be a party to this. If he's a criminal you should tell the police.'

'There's no proof. The police wouldn't be interested,' replied Joe his excitement rising. 'Look Maria,' he wrapped an arm possessively around her waist and pulled her round to face him. 'This could be a real scoop … but I need your help.' Maria tried to pull away but Joe held her tight.

'If you get your, your scoop,' she said loudly. 'If you get your bloody scoop … and he's found guilty … and sent to jail … then I've helped destroy the family. Those two lovely girls without a father. Katarzyna ... the nicest person you could ever meet...' she was struggling for words, close to tears.

'Look,' said Joe quietly, trying to peer into her eyes but she was avoiding his gaze. 'Look, if there is nothing suspicious in the conversation then I'll stop looking for a story. But I need to know.' Maria had gone limp in his arms. 'Help me set up these microphones just this once. I'll never ask you again.'

* * *

The following Monday, Maria rode Beauty across the fields to a small village called Metzerlen, where she used a public telephone to call Joe. She explained where she was and that she had his eavesdropping equipment with her. They quickly agreed that she would make her way slowly back towards Burg and Joe would meet her at a quiet spot near the edge of the village. She arrived at the appointed place and had to wait; each minute driving a nail of guilt into her conscience. She tied Beauty's rein to a gate and walked up and down, her mind in turmoil.

By the time Joe arrived and parked off the road, under the trees, Maria was extremely agitated. Joe quickly grabbed her, swung her around and planted a kiss on her unresponsive lips. She struggled free without a word and took the tiny box containing the listening equipment out of the small rucksack she carried and thrust it into his hands. Joe could see that there were tears in her eyes. He pushed the box into his pocket and again wrapped his arms around her:

'I'll never ask you to do that again,' he whispered. By now she was limp in his arms and he could feel her sobbing.

They sat in his car for a while, where Joe held Maria's hand and questioned her about the Saturday night dinner party. Afterwards, he tried again to explain what he thought Dieter von Murren was up to and why it was illegal. It made no sense to Maria who just felt that her secure life with the von Murren's was slipping away; that the ship was sinking and that she, Katarzyna and the two girls were hopelessly fighting the waves. It appeared they would all drown - and it was her fault.

CHAPTER 34

Joe spent all Monday night listening to the tapes; he was amazed at the quality of the recordings and was grateful for the advice Raziel Stavi had provided. He had removed his shoes and socks, convinced that unfettered metatarsals increased his ability to think clearly. From time to time he marched around the room wiggling his toes, concentrating hard.

Much of the stuff was useless, just idle chitchat in the local dialect, Baslerdeutsch. But about one o'clock in the morning, Joe suddenly sat upright and replayed a portion of the tape. Von Murren was playing Gershwin on the piano, the tuneful medley drowning out much of what was being said. He could picture one or two of the guests leaning over the piano watching, as von Murren's slender fingers flew over the keys.

Over and over again Joe replayed the tape, scribbling down the odd words that he caught. They were speaking English; something about someone was 'playing the game.' Joe was having to concentrate hard; perspiration was running down his neck. It really was a case of one word at a time. Thirty minutes later Joe switched off the recording-device and stared at the paper in front of him: 'Baumann has pulled all his business out of Argentina in return for Begrafica pulling out of Sierra Leone,' he read. 'I'm prepared to pull out of Kenya, if you stop selling in South Africa.' Joe leaned back in his chair and grinned:

'Gotcha,' he snarled and waved a fist in the air. At about two in the morning, Joe eventually fell into bed and lay thinking of how best to move forward. This was a scoop; he needed to plan carefully, before approaching his editor.

The following morning Joe rose early and took the tram to

Kleinbasel, where he made his way to Raziel Stavi's apartment to drop off the recording equipment. Stavi made coffee, despite Joe's protestations, he wanted to get back and start on his article but Stavi wanted to talk. He wanted to know if Joe had managed to gain the information he needed and whether or not the equipment had proved effective. Joe sipped the coffee and assured Stavi the equipment had done exactly what Stavi had said it would do and thanks to his advice about microphone placement, he had the information he needed.

'I've kept the tape,' said Joe. 'And I've made transcripts, so I don't think I'll need to listen again but if I do, can I use the replay equipment.'

'Of course,' replied Stavi. 'No problem.' Stavi started to probe. Was the victim anyone he knew? Had he bugged an office or a private home? What was he going to do with the information? From his side of the net, Joe batted away the questions, like the pro he was. Saying a lot but not giving anything away. Growing impatient, Joe emptied his mug and clambered to his feet. He thanked Stavi for the coffee and equipment and handed over a bundle of notes. Stavi counted them carefully before stuffing them into his pocket. Walking to the door, he shook Joe's hand and told him not to hesitate to call, if he could help in any way.

Before Joe was even outside the building, Stavi had the equipment, that Joe had returned, connected to a piece of special kit and through a pair of earphones was busy listening to the conversations that Joe thought only he possessed. 'Amateurs!' Stavi sarcastically hissed aloud. Poor Joe, little did he know that since his first visit, Stavi had been bugging his telephone and knew all about his interest in Dieter von Murren. And now, as Stavi listened, he was considering how he himself could best use this latest information.

CHAPTER 35

Joe spent the following two weeks building a case against Dieter von Murren. Point by point, chapter by chapter, he outlined the events leading towards a condemning conclusion that Dieter von Murren and his cronies were manipulating the market. At the end of the two weeks he had what he considered a watertight case. Obviously he couldn't use the fact that he had illegally taped conversations but that was just the proof he needed, in is own mind, to confirm the paperwork, which he attached as appendices.

During these two weeks he had missed the German lessons and Maria had not called. After some heartache he decided that he couldn't call her until the case was out in the open, it might be safer for Maria if they didn't see each other. He didn't want the link between himself and Maria to be exposed.

Satisfied that his report was as complete as it could be, Joe took the tram to the railway station and caught a train to Zurich for an appointment with his editor, Murray Majors, who was visiting from his Paris headquarters.

Later sitting with Major in an office, Joe spelled out what he had uncovered, going through samples of the papers - and suggesting that the story might be gradually rolled out over several editions. For several moments they sat in silence, as the editor read Joe's introduction through half-glasses perched precariously on the end of his nose. While he read, Joe gazed at his boss, a legend in the newspaper industry. He was looking old, Joe decided. What little hair he had was scraped thinly over his bulging forehead. The hair he lacked on top was more than made up for by a thick, grey, droopy moustache and uncontrollable eyebrows, giving him the appearance of a shaggy sheepdog. But for all this, he was highly respected, especially by Joe, who almost regarded him as a father figure.

'You realise this is dynamite Joe?' stated the editor. Joe nodded. 'Can't afford to get it wrong.'

'I've been working on this for months,' replied Joe. 'I'm confident the story will stand up.'

'What about your sources? Are they reliable?' Joe nodded again:

'Sure … they're good.'

'Okay, leave it with me. I'll read it thoroughly and then get the legal team to give it the once over. We must be sure.' Majors stood, the meeting was at an end. As they edged towards the door, Majors shook Joe's hand. 'Great work Joe, you done good!'

The following Thursday, after much thought, Joe decided he would attend the German class and hopefully try to explain the situation to Maria. During the class she avoided his eye but afterwards, together with Jock and the Belgian woman they headed for their regular bar. Jock was pulling Joe's leg for playing truant, Joe explained that he had deadlines to meet and had been busy. At ten o'clock they parted company and Maria and Joe climbed onto the number ten tram together.

'I've missed you,' said Joe, as they sat side by side. But you know I couldn't call. I hoped that you might telephone me.'

'You're not the only one who's been busy,' said Maria somewhat huffily. As the tram rumbled past the Zoo, Joe asked:

'Will you stay?'

'I can't tonight,' replied Maria. 'I'm needed early in the morning. Mrs von Murren is going away for a few days.'

'I wanted to explain,' said Joe.

'You've got less than five minutes,' replied Maria. 'And then it's your stop.'

'I've nailed him,' whispered Joe excitedly. 'He's as guilty as hell.' I've written the article and given it to my editor.' Joe, glanced out of the window, realising he had less than two minutes to explain. 'It may take some weeks before they decide whether or not to publish.' He looked at Maria and tried to hold her hand but she eased out of his grip. 'It might be better … better for you, I mean, if we didn't see each other until this has blown over.' The tram was slowing, as it pulled into the Binningen stop. 'Please call me, when you can.' Joe was pleading. 'Please call. I want to see you again once it's over.' Maria did not reply. The tram stopped, a couple of people were waiting for the door to open. Joe snatched a kiss on Maria's cool cheek and sped towards the already closing door.

The tram pulled smoothly away from the platform, where Joe stood in the gloom waving to Maria but she wasn't looking, her eyes were closed fighting back the tears. She was not worried for herself but for Katarzyna and the girls. She felt sure that their comfortable life in Burg was about to disintegrate.

CHAPTER 36

Raziel Stavi had always been good at his job. He had flair for languages and had worked for Mossad in many different places but mostly in Africa. He had hoped to eventually settle in the USA but while on assignment in Washington there was an unfortunate fatality. The man he was supposed to be investigating was found battered to death and Stavi had been quickly and quietly removed from the country. Back in Israel his boss did not accept his explanation or protestations of innocence and he'd been allocated mundane jobs in insalubrious, far-flung places.

It was while he was in Kinshasa he had met a shady, Swiss entrepreneur in a dingy bar, who said he needed a bodyguard and made an offer Stavi could not ignore. Stavi resigned from Mossad and moved to Geneva. It did not take him long to realise that his employer's business methods bordered on the criminal and Stavi was not entirely surprised when after only six months his employer met an untimely end, knifed in a dark alley off the Postgasse in Bern, leaving Stavi with the keys of his boss's Geneva flat and the combination of his safe. Looking back on his career, it would be true to say that the grim-reaper was always a close companion of Raziel Stavi.

With the cash that Stavi removed from the safe, he moved to Basel where he set up his private detective agency. The job kept him in beer money but little else. The income from cuckolded husbands, suspicious wives, plus a little industrial espionage didn't exactly support a lavish lifestyle; consequently he was always on the lookout for a new angle. Joe's visit had perked his curiosity and now that he had listened to Joe's recorded conversation with a man named Baumann, plus the bugged conversations with some bird called

Gloria, he had developed a plan. And today he had an appointment with Kurt Baumann, Chief Executive Officer of Global Vigour Products, a large pharmaceutical company, known locally by its initials GVP, with its head office in Basel.

Before leaving his apartment Stavi glanced at himself in the mirror, nodded with approval and ran a hand through his unruly hair. The image in his head did not match the image in the glass. Despite the clean shirt and tie - and his only suit, he looked more like a 1920's gangster, than the suave entrepreneur he hoped to project.

The burly doorman at GVP politely stopped Stavi and asked his business. Stavi replied that he had an appointment and was directed to a reception desk at the end of the foyer, the vast, muted, open space decorated with polished marble floor tiles and expensive-looking ground to ceiling murals. The woman behind the desk asked how she could help and Stavi produced a business card, entirely in Hebrew, carefully designed to confuse, rather than enlighten.

'I have an appointment with Doctor Baumann,' he said. The woman checked the name, spoke it aloud and looked at a diary.

'Ah yes,' she said and called to a smartly suited youth standing nearby. 'Christian, take Mr Stavi to Mr Williams' office.' The lad almost clicked his heels and politely requested Stavi to follow.

'But my appointment is with Doctor Baumann!' he objected.

'You'll see Mr Williams first Mr Stavi, please follow Christian.'

Stavi was taken to an elevator, which whisked them to the sixth floor. Halfway down a wide corridor, Christian knocked on a door with a sign proclaiming: Andrew Williams. He waited a moment until he heard a shout and then flung open the door.

'Mr Stavi for you Mr Williams,' he announced and stood aside to allow Stavi to enter.

A tall young man with a pronounced Welsh accent came forward thanked Christian, shook Stavi's hand and pointed to a chair.

'You wanted to see Doctor Baumann, I believe,' he began.

'Yes, I specifically told the woman I needed to speak to Doctor Baumann when I telephoned,' said Stavi, easing the unaccustomed collar away from his neck with his index finger.

'You will appreciate that Doctor Baumann is a busy man. A very busy man. I am one of his personal assistants, I'm sure I can help you.'

'I have some important information that Doctor Baumann

would want to hear,' continued Stavi.

'What kind of information?' asked Williams.

'It's for his ears only,' replied Stavi quickly.

'If you tell me, I can assess whether or not we need to bother Doctor Baumann. It's usually the case that I am able to help,' continued Williams, with a smile.

'Sorry, it's confidential, I need to speak to Doctor Baumann.' Stavi was irritated.

'I see,' said Williams. 'May I ask what kind of work you're in Mr Stavi? Who do you work for?'

'Am I going to see him or not?' replied Stavi, ignoring the question. There was a pause.

'I'm afraid not Mr Stavi, unless you give me some idea of the nature of your business with Doctor Baumann.' Stavi breathed deeply in an attempt to control his emotions.

'It's more of a personal matter,' he said. 'Tell you what,' he said suddenly. 'You give me his home address and I'll write to him.

Yes, that might be the best way - I'll write.'

'I'm sorry, I'm not permitted to give you information about his private life - and certainly not his home address.'

'This is crazy,' exploded Stavi. 'I only want to speak to the man. Anyone would think he was a bloody emperor or something!'

'You will appreciate Mr Stavi that the world is full of cranks.' Williams eyed Stavi's ancient, crumpled suit and ill-fitting shirt. 'Doctor Baumann must be protected. He is, as I said, a very, very busy man.' Stavi started to speak but Williams cut him off. 'It is my job Mr Stavi to ensure Doctor Baumann's time is usefully employed and he is not distracted from his very important job of guiding this very important company in a way its shareholders would approve of.' Williams drew breath; he was not used to this kind of confrontations and was shaking. 'Unless you can spell out for me why you want to speak to Doctor Baumann, then it is useless for this meeting to continue.' Stavi was quiet for a moment.

'All right, if you insist.' He paused dramatically and leaned forward: 'It concerns his boyfriend.' Williams visibly paled:

'What do you mean … his boyfriend? Doctor Baumann is happily married.'

'Now you can understand why I need to speak to Doctor Baumann personally,' said Stavi, his face creased with apparent concern. 'Now you understand why I didn't want to tell you the reason I need to speak to him.'

'I can't comprehend what you mean,' Williams stuttered, open-mouthed.

'There's a problem with his boyfriend,' explained Stavi. The sort of problem that could lead to a scandal.' Stavi was enjoying the look of total bewilderment on Williams' face. 'Look,' said Stavi conspiratorially. 'If he nips it in the bud, he might, he just might be able to save the situation - and his reputation - and that of the company.' Williams looked like a deflated balloon. 'You now understand why I need to see Doctor Baumann.'

Stavi left the palatial GVP building with a grin on his face and a piece of paper in his pocket, upon which Williams had reluctantly written his boss's address and private, unlisted telephone number. It transpired that Doctor Baumann was away in Sierra Leone and not expected back until the end of the week.

Stavi did not own a vehicle, so the following day he hired a small car and drove out into the hills outside of the city looking for Baumann's home. He climbed the twisting road up to a hamlet called Gempen, where he parked and studied the map. The address gave the house a name, rather than a number on a road called Hochwaldstrasse. He decided that must be the name of the road leading to the next village, Hochwald.

He hadn't driven far out of the village, when he spotted a pair of wrought-iron gates at the end of a winding drive, in the distance he could just glimpse the roof of a large house. Stavi continued past until he found a space at the side of the road where he could park. Once he was satisfied he was far enough off the road he pulled on a pair of walking boots, an anorak and baseball cap, easing the brim right down over his eyes, before striding back towards the gates.

On a pillar were a bell push and a speaker, as well as a nameplate, giving just the name of the house. This was Baumann's home. Stavi noticed the security cameras, one on each pillar and moved away. Stavi's knew from his research that Baumann was married and had two sons, both grown up and working in the USA. He also knew there was a resident housekeeper.

He walked on down the road until the high hedge stopped and there was a field. A little further on was a gate; Stavi vaulted over and looked towards the house. He could still glimpse the roof hidden behind a line of trees. Making his way towards these trees he began circumnavigating the property. At one point he came across an empty stable-block and a track, overhung with trees, leading towards the house. It seemed likely the field and stables belonged to Baumann, he decided. He looked inside the stable, it was unlocked and unused. Stavi walked some twenty metres slowly down the track, until he had a view of the house. He pulled a pair of field binoculars from his pocket and surveyed the elegant building noting that here were lights and cameras on each corner. Satisfied that he had seen enough, Stavi made his way back to the car, considering his next move.

***

Doctor Kurt Baumann was seated in his study the evening after his return from the African trip, scanning a heap of papers. The visit had gone well and the initial apprehension, that had plagued him since agreeing to work with Dieter von Murren, had eased a little. Von Murren's premises on the outskirts of Freeport were clean, bright, functional and empty. Von Murren had kept his word. For his part, he must now finalise the process of closing down the operation in Argentina. It would be a relief; he thought, to be rid of the pestilent unions and their constant, unrealistic demands.

He was slightly startled when the phone on his desk began its muffled ring. He glanced at his watch, it was ten pm. There must be an emergency he thought picking up the phone.

'Baumann,' he said quietly.

'Good Evening,' said the voice the other end of the line. 'We haven't met but it's imperative we do so, as soon as possible.'

'Whose this?' said Baumann annoyed. The number was only known to his closest staff.

'You don't need to know,' said Stavi firmly. 'I have vital information about your dealings with Dieter von Murren. We need to meet so that I can explain before the authorities find out.' Baumann's face paled under his expensive-looking tan and somewhere, deep in his intestines, a muscle involuntarily contracted, the spasm causing him to snatch a breath.

'What do you mean, I don't understand?' he gasped.

'There's a problem over your deal with Begrafica,' continued Stavi.

'I don't know what you are talking about. What kind of

problem,' wheezed Baumann.

'This isn't something we should talk about over the phone. When can I see you?'

'What kind of problem?' repeated Baumann, an edge of fear in his voice.

'Unless you act quickly, the deal may become public knowledge - that kind of problem.' Baumann swore.

'Come to my office tomorrow … about eight o'clock.'

'No - we shouldn't be seen together. I'll come to your home,' replied Stavi.

'No - I don't want you to come to the house. My wife …' argued Baumann, his mind was whirling.

'Do you own a stable in the field next to your home?' asked Stavi.

'Yes,' replied Baumann, surprised. 'Not that we have horses any more.'

'Right I will meet you there at ten o'clock tomorrow night.' Stavi ordered. After some argument, Baumann agreed and Stavi hung up, leaving Kurt Baumann staring at the phone in his hand, cursing himself for listening to Dieter von Murren and his stupid ideas. He paced the room for a few moments before stopping in front of a large ornate mirror. His bald, polished, dome-shaped head gleamed in the low light, his piggy blue eyes, pinched tight.

'Damn you to hell von Murren,' he hissed. 'Damn you, damn damn, damn!'

The following evening Stavi again drove to Gempen and parked in the same spot. It was trying to rain and so Stavi zipped up his anorak and wedged the cap tightly on his head before setting off down the road towards the gate. He made his way across the field towards the stable block, occasionally switching on the powerful torch that he had brought with him.

The moment he had the stable block in sight, a dog began barking, soon followed by another. Stavi stopped and listened; he heard a hushed voice commanding the dogs to be quiet. Carefully Stavi edged nearer and reached out a hand towards the corner of the stable. Immediately the dogs burst into a bout of ferocious barking. Stavi called out :

'Doctor Baumann?' From inside the building a muffled voice replied:

'Yes, I'm inside. It's quite safe, the dogs are leashed.' Stavi made his way towards the entrance and looked over the half stable-door; the tidy interior was illuminated by a single, dim fluorescent tube. In the gloom he could just make out the figure of a slight man, wearing a baseball cap, muffled in a bulky overcoat with two Rottweilers at his feet, coiled ready to spring if their master gave the order.

'Come in,' said Baumann, stiffly. One of the dogs stood and threateningly sniffed at Stavi's legs. Baumann immediately pulled on the leash and snapped at the animal to sit. It did.

'What's this problem you spoke about last night?' queried Baumann calmly; he was after all, used to dealing with crises, though not of such a personal nature.

'Do you mind if I sit?' said Stavi easing himself down onto a straw bale, noticing that as he did, the dogs dropped onto their bellies but their eyes never left him. Baumann ignored the request.

'This problem?' he questioned. Stavi cleared his throat:

'In the course of my work I came across the fact that you and Dieter von Murren have an illegal arrangement,' he paused for dramatic effect. 'And this arrangement,' Stavi emphasised the word. 'This arrangement is the subject of an investigation by an American journalist.' Baumann's blood turned cold, he didn't respond immediately.

'How do you know this? What exactly is your line of work?'

'It's better you don't know,' replied Stavi. 'Let's just say that I fix things when things need fixing.'

'How far along the track is this reporter? Who else knows, do you have any idea?' asked Baumann, his mind was spinning around all the possibilities.

'My guess is that he hasn't told anyone, he's still at the information gathering stage,' replied Stavi.

'Which paper does he work for?' asked Baumann, his head down, peering at the dogs at his feet.

'It says the International Herald Tribune on his business card,' answered Stavi, also eying the dogs, who in turn were still watching him with an unbroken gaze, ready for any untoward movement.

'So,' said Baumann after a few moments. 'So, you fix things do you Mr …? I'm sorry I didn't even ask your name.'

'It's better you don't know,' replied Stavi.

'Have you come across this type of problem before?' asked Baumann cautiously. 'Do you have any suggestions for the best way to deal with the situation?'

'In my experience newspaper reporters do not listen to sense. They tend to be righteous about such things and the usual methods of persuasion, like large sums of money, don't usually work,' pronounced Stavi.

'But worth a try?' questioned Baumann.

'Waste of time,' replied Stavi.

'Perhaps I should speak to him,' suggested Baumann.

'Appeal to his better nature?' he almost smiled.

'I think it's better you keep right away from the man and leave me to try and persuade him to drop the story,' said Stavi. Baumann nodded.

'I have a feeling that this is going to cost me a great deal of money,' said Baumann pragmatically.

'Certainly if the story becomes public, you will go to gaol,' said Stavi. 'You will lose your job. Be heavily fined. Be disgraced. Never again find work. Probably lose your family.' Stavi was almost enjoying spelling out the disaster in store for Kurt Baumann. 'And as for the company; well who knows? The level of fine the authorities might impose may well put it out of business. Seems like the Anti-Trust folk are always on the lookout to clobber someone, as a warning to the others.' Baumann knew Stavi was right and his eyes never left the dogs.

'For two million Swiss francs, I can save your bacon,' Stavi said slowly. 'Chickenfeed in comparison to what will happen if the article gets published!' Stavi let his words sink in. Baumann didn't flinch. The silence between them was palpable, only broken by the gentle sound of the dogs' breathing. 'Do we have a deal?'

'You haven't actually provided me with any proof,' said Baumann quietly. 'How do I know that you haven't concocted the story to swindle me out of a large sum of money?'

'Because,' replied Stavi, 'I have heard the reporter's recording of you agreeing to give up doing business in South America, in exchange for von Murren pulling out of Africa - and read the transcript.' Baumann started to object. 'And I know that you have just come back from Sierra Leone.'

'That doesn't prove this so called reporter is going to print a story,' objected Baumann. 'And how could he have possibly taped such a conversation, if there was one.'

'He bugged von Murren's home when you were there for dinner,' replied Stavi. Baumann gasped.

'I don't understand how you know all these things. Are you working together?'

'No,' responded Stavi quickly. 'But he came to me for help. I didn't like what he was up to, so I bugged his flat and when he was out, took a look at his files.' Stavi fumbled in an inner pocket and drew out a sheaf of papers. He handed them to Baumann: 'Take a look.' They were copies of part of the transcript Joe Leman had made from the recording. Baumann frowned, as he read, von Murren had been careless, he thought. Very careless.

'So,' he sighed, as he handed back the papers. When you learned all this, you decided I was an easy target - a source of some easy money?'

'As I said,' began Stavi pragmatically. 'I'm a problem solver. A fixer of things. But this particular problem might demand a rather extreme solution and as such, costs money.'

Baumann was deep in thought, staring at the dogs at his feet, as if hoping that they might provide him with an inspirational solution.

'How do you propose to solve this situation?' he asked.

'You don't need to know,' replied Stavi quickly. 'I want a million francs, in thousand-franc notes, by next week - and another million in cash the day after the problem is solved.' Baumann's eyes wandered all around the dimly lit stable.

'How do I know the trail won't still lead back to me … after you have,' he paused. 'After you have solved this problem?'

'Because I'm a professional,' stated Stavi bluntly. 'There will be nothing to connect you to this reporter.'

'Except for the fact I will have drawn out a huge sum of cash from the bank,' replied Baumann. 'That can't be disguised.' There was silence as both men contemplated a solution.

'I'll tell you what,' began Baumann after a few moments. 'I have an account in the Cayman Islands. There's not enough in it, for this transaction but the manager there knows that I have been considering buying property.' Stavi looked doubtful. 'I could transfer the cash to that account and if you opened an account, in your name, in Grand Cayman, the money could be transferred. Believe me, your money is safer there, than here in Switzerland,' Baumann explained. 'You could fly down there, open an account and fly back the next day. You said this reporter is still gathering facts for his story … surely we have time?'

'I only operate in cash,' said Stavi dourly.

'You'll have to make an exception,' said Baumann authoritatively. 'I can't be seen to be withdrawing such large amounts of cash from accounts here; there'd be questions. It won't be a problem in Grand Cayman.' Stavi was about to argue that Baumann was in no position to set the rules, when he interrupted: 'I'll give you an extra two-hundred thousand, in cash, which you can collect here … once the problem is solved,' he said quietly.

In the end this is what the pair agreed. They stood and uneasily shook hands. Only the dogs witness to their conspiracy.

'I need to have some way of contacting you,' said Baumann, 'in case of emergencies.'

'As I said,' began Stavi. 'It's safer for you if there is nothing to link us.'

'You can't just walk out of here and disappear like so much dust. Anything could happen.'

'Okay,' replied Stavi reluctantly. 'I'll call you when the issue is solved and when I collect the money I'll give you a telephone number.' Under the suspicious gaze of the two dogs, now on their feet and straining at their leash, Stavi left, promising to call within a week.

CHAPTER 37

Maria and the two girls had the house in Burg to themselves for a week. Katarzyna had flown back to Poland, where her father was unwell. Dieter von Murren was away in Helsinki. Maria drove the girls to and from school each day and in the evenings, after homework was completed and dinner cleared away, they played games. Hide and Seek was a favourite and the three of them scampered around the empty rooms giggling and laughing. But each evening, as she lay abed, Maria was shrouded with a sense of foreboding. What would happen when Joe's article was published? She didn't fully understand what Katarzyna's husband was supposed to have done but Joe had made it sound very wicked. He had said there would likely be court cases and prison. She wept at the thought of her girls' lives being turned upside down; for it was obvious they thought the world of their father.

Wednesday evening, after the girls were in bed. Maria telephoned Joe. He wasn't there, so she left a message on the answerphone, explaining that she would be missing Thursday evening's German lesson. Despite what Joe was doing to the von Murren's, she missed him and dialled the number again, just to hear his voice.

The following Thursday Joe did not show up for the German lesson and afterwards, as she rode the tram back towards Flüh, there was a holdup in the suburb of Binningen, to allow howling police cars and rushing fire-engines to cross the track. Gazing through the window she could see flames biting dramatically into the night sky, an apartment building was ablaze. As the tram pulled away, she looked back horrified and then anxiously realised that the fire must be very close to where Joe lived.

The following day Maria rode one of the horses through the village. On the spur of the moment, she stopped at the public telephone box and called Joe's number. It was over three weeks since she had last seen or spoken to him. Instead of a ringing tone, all she heard was a voice in German telling her the phone number was 'ungültig' - out of order. Maria remounted the horse and as they plodded their way back up the steep path Maria worried and wondered what had happened to Joe and why his phone was out of order?

Once back at the house she made her way to the kitchen, where Beccy Blom was busy mixing the ingredients for a cake, while Katarzyna was gaily chatting, as she arranged flowers in a vase.

Katarzyna greeted Maria and asked about the hack before suggesting Maria made them all a cup of coffee. When Beccy left the kitchen to place the vase of flowers in the living room, Maria explained to Katarzyna that she was worried about Joe. Although she hadn't met him, Katarzyna knew about Maria's friendship.

'I'd really like to go and see what's happened to him. I haven't heard anything for three weeks,' explained Maria, 'and his phone's out of order.'

'Of course you must go,' said Katarzyna generously. 'Take the Range Rover … but remember to pick up the girls from school.' Maria thanked Katarzyna and rushed to her room to shower and change.

An hour later, Maria was slaloming around the parked cars in the narrow streets of Binningen, as she picked her way towards Joe's apartment. Maria was shocked to see that the end of the street had a tape across and a no-entry sign. She had to reverse and drive around nearby streets before she found somewhere to park. It took her several minutes to make her way back to the blocked-off street where she ducked under the tape and made her way towards Joe's apartment building. With each step that she took, the more horrified she became. The building was scarred with black marks around and above many of the windows. She stopped to stare, filled with apprehension. The air was filled with a pungent, sickening smell of devastation. She picked out one of Joe's windows on the third floor and her heart stopped when she saw the smashed glass and blackened walls. There were a number of skips outside the building and workmen were carrying out scorched furniture. An armed policeman was standing near the entrance. Maria walked quickly towards him and climbed the half-dozen steps. He held out a hand and in the Basel dialect told her that she couldn't go in.

'I'm looking for my friend,' said Maria. 'He lives here.' The policeman spoke again in German before he took a couple of steps into the building and called out.

A few moments later a tall, angular man in a suit and open-necked shirt appeared. He greeted Maria in English and ushered her away from the doorway and the busy workmen.

'I understand that you are looking for someone?' he said. 'All the residents are either staying with relatives or in a nearby hotel.'

'Was anybody harmed?' asked Maria, her face creased with worry. 'Fortunately, except for one broken ankle caused by a lady falling down the stairs, everyone seems to be all right,' replied the man, who explained that he was a policeman and part of team working with experts to determine the cause of the fire.

'So everyone is accounted for?' asked Maria, her voice shaking. 'Because I haven't heard from my friend.'

'Which apartment was your friend living in?' asked the policeman.

'He was on the third floor - an American.'

'Ah,' began the policeman. 'Mr Leman, Joe Leman ... we haven't been able to contact him, which we need to do because the fire seems to have started in his apartment.' Maria blanched. The policeman reached out a hand and laid it reassuringly on Maria's shoulder.

'I'm sure he's okay; he's certainly not in the building. I'd like to know more about your friend - do you mind if we continue this discussion in my office, so that I can make some notes.'

* * *

'So tell me about Joe Leman,' began the plainclothes policeman, who had introduced himself as Silvio Belloni. 'How well do you know him?' They were sitting in a harshly-lit, grim office surrounded by grey filing cabinets at a police-station close to Basel's railway station, Maria nursing a cup of espresso. She explained that they had met at German lessons and that they occasionally went out to the cinema or a restaurant. Belloni nodded and asked where Maria lived. She explained about her position working for the von Murren's. Belloni looked up from the pad, where he was scribbling notes, at the mention of the name.

'You said that you think the fire started in Joe ... Mr Leman's apartment,' she said.

'Yes, we're sure of it,' replied Belloni.

'Why are you so sure?' asked Maria. Belloni looked at her, considering how much he should say. He cleared his throat.

'Because someone spread petrol all around a room that we think he used for an office and deliberately destroyed everything - and I mean everything!' Maria gasped:

'Then … where's Joe? What's happened to him?' Belloni looked at Maria:

'I was hoping that you might be able to tell me that.'

Over the next half an hour Maria told Belloni all that she knew about Joe. Not that she knew that much about him, though the most significant information was the fact that he worked for the International Herald Tribune. Belloni nodded and said that he already knew this and was waiting for Joe's boss in Paris to get back from a business meeting.

'He will be at the Zurich office the day after tomorrow, I'll go up to Zurich to see if he can shed any light on Joe's movements.' Maria glanced at her watch and started:

'If there's nothing else, I must go,' she said nervously. 'I have to pick up the von Murren children from school.' She rose to her feet. Belloni asked for her telephone number, which he scribbled on the pad.

'Please call me if Mr Leman contacts you,' he said. 'Here's my card.' Maria nodded and left.

Driving to the girls' school, Maria's head was in a whirl. Who would have set Joe's flat on fire? Certainly not Joe himself. In which case, where was he?' Oh how she wished that she had not been so offhand and angry the last time she saw him!

CHAPTER 38

The following Thursday Maria attended her usual German lesson but found it hard to concentrate, glancing across the room at the empty desk, where Joe usually sat. Afterwards she joined Jock and the Belgian woman at the usual bar. She explained about the fire and how Joe was nowhere to be found. Both were visibly shocked but tried to reassure Maria that Joe knew how to look after himself and would eventually turn up.

Almost a week later, while she was in the stable-yard brushing down one of the horses, Katarzyna came out of the house and said a policeman named Belloni wanted her to call him back. Maria dropped the brush, mumbled her thanks, and raced into the house.

Belloni sounded serious and asked if Maria could meet him at the police station where they had chatted before.

'Do you have any news?' she pleaded.

'Nothing definite yet,' he replied. 'But I have a few more questions for you.' They agreed to meet Friday after lunch. 'By the way,' continued Belloni. 'Do you know if Joe Leman ever went to a dentist in Basel?' Maria was confused, what sort of question was that?

'Well actually yes, he goes to the same dentist as me in Bottmingen. The surgery is over the dairy on the main street.' Belloni thanked Maria and hung up, leaving her wondering what other questions he might have. In reality, she knew so little about Joe. Back in the stable yard Katarzyna was fondling the head of the horse that Maria had been brushing.

'Did your policeman have any news?' she asked.

'No. No news but he wants to see me again on Friday. He says he has more questions. I'm really sorry.'

'No, it's not a problem,' responded Katarzyna. 'You must go.' Maria picked up the brush to resume her task.

Tell me about your missing friend,' said Katarzyna. 'All you have told me is that he is an American and called Joe!'

'Well he's in my German class,' began Maria. 'He once lived in Paris … he speaks fluent French.'

'Well, what does he do for a living? Why is he in Basel?'

'I think he's a writer of some sort,' replied Maria.

'What sort of writer" persisted Katarzyna.

'I don't really know,' she lied. 'I'll ask him next time I see him.' Maria was hoping against hope that there would indeed be a next time.

* * *

Friday after lunch, Maria drove to the police station and made her way to Belloni's office. She accepted his offer of coffee and while he was away, she gazed around the dismal room, wondering if all Swiss police stations were the same - filled with grey filing cabinets, cluttered desks, overflowing wastepaper baskets, tatty pin-boards covered in flapping papers and grimy cups on almost every flat surface.

Her musings were interrupted by Belloni's return, elbowing his way through the doorway, an espresso cup in each hand. Settling behind his desk, he asked after Maria's health, took a sip of the coffee and carefully replaced the cup on the desk.

'I went to Zurich but that was a waste of time,' he said. 'Mr Leman's boss, the editor, couldn't or wouldn't tell me anything useful.' Belloni peered into Maria's eyes and reached out a hand and laid it on top of Maria's. She began to draw it away but Belloni grasped it tightly. 'Miss Beckett,' he said quietly. 'I have some bad news!' Maria tensed, her eyes filled with tears. 'I'm sorry. There's no easy way to say this … but Joe Leman is dead.' Maria gasped and the tears streamed unbidden down her cheeks.

'I had this feeling that's why you asked me to come today,' she sobbed. Belloni reached behind him and picked up a box of tissues and handed her one. Maria blew her nose noisily and wiped her eyes. 'How did it happen?' she asked.

'How it happened, I don't know,' replied Belloni. 'He was

found in the river near Kembs.'

'The river, she gasped. 'I don't know where Kembs is,' whispered Maria.

'It's about twenty kilometres downstream from here, close to a lock.' Belloni twisted a pen around in his hand. 'We think he'd been in the river for a week, possibly longer.' Maria was struggling to comprehend what Belloni was telling her - Joe dead, drowned?

'The dental records helped prove his identity,' explained Belloni.

'Joe drowned,' she murmured. 'But he was a good swimmer. He took part in the Rhine swim each year ... you know when half of Basel jump in the river and swim through the city.' Belloni was nodding.

'I'm afraid that we don't think he just drowned.' Maria asked what he meant. 'Well Joe Leman had a fractured skull. Looks like someone hit him with a hammer or something similar and then dumped him in the river.' Maria burst out sobbing again, at the thought of something so wicked being perpetrated against someone so gentle and kind.

'But who?' she began and stopped.

'Exactly,' said Belloni. 'Who? Who has Joe Leman upset enough that they would want to take his life?'

Maria jolted upright, as if a blade had slid straight into her heart and she gasped. Dieter von Murren, she thought. He must have found out about Joe's newspaper article. He must have killed him. She sobbed uncontrollably for a few moments. Belloni stood up and lit a cigarette. He proffered it to Maria but she shook her head. Belloni took one long drag and snuffed it out, smoking indoors was meant to be taboo.

'Well … do you have any ideas?' he asked. 'Did he ever say anything to you about his work" Belloni was wandering around the room, shoulder's hunched, hands thrust deep into his pockets. 'His boss said he was an investigative journalist. Did he ever tell you about anyone he was planning to write about.' Maria was gazing at the floor, her mind in turmoil, unsure of what to do or say. 'Please think Maria, did he ever mention any names.' Maria stopped sobbing; she was considering whether or not to implicate Dieter von Murren. If he murdered Joe then he should face justice but if she gave his name and he was innocent? Maria suddenly climbed to her feet:

'Thank you for telling me what happened to Joe,' she began quietly, suddenly in control. 'I have to pick the girls up from school. I'll think about what you've said and try to remember if he talked about anyone.' Belloni took her arm and walked her towards the door.

'Please do think really hard about this,' he said. 'You're our only hope.'

For the next week Maria's every waking moment was spent thinking about poor Joe. Was it possible Dieter von Murren was implicated? Obviously he hadn't been personally responsible, he wasn't even in the country but could he have paid someone to get rid of Joe, to prevent the article being published? Obviously, she thought, the fire had been set to destroy all his research into the article. Her mind was in turmoil and she went about her daily tasks as if on autopilot. Katarzyna had asked about the visit to the policeman and had been wonderfully sympathetic, which hadn't helped Maria think straight about Katarzyna's husband. Nevertheless, she said nothing about Joe's demise.

'Take a few days off,' said Katarzyna. 'Do you have any friends you could stay with? Do you want to go and visit your mother?' Maria shook her head,

'Thank you but I'm all right,' she replied.

'Please,' repeated Katarzyna. ' I'll pay for you to stay in a hotel for a few days. Get away. I understand, it's such a terrible worry for you.'

That evening Maria decided that she needed to speak to Joe's boss. He had once mentioned that he was based in Paris but that Joe met him occasionally at the Zurich office. The following morning Maria telephoned the Editor's secretary and her heart skipped a beat when she explained that her boss was away in Zurich for a few days.

Later, when Maria and Katarzyna were riding side by side on a forest path they came to a clearing affording the wonderful view across the Belfort Gap to the Grand Ballon Mountain. During the ride Maria had been thinking about Katarzyna's offer:

'Perhaps you're right,' she suddenly said. 'A few days away might help clear my head.'

'Excellent,' responded Katarzyna enthusiastically. 'Take yourself off somewhere nice; up in the mountains maybe?'

At the end of the day, Katarzyna had given Maria an envelope bulging with notes.

'Here,' she said. 'This should be enough to pay for a hotel for a few days. Come back at the weekend.' Maria fell into her arms weeping and muttering her thanks.

The following day Katarzyna dropped Maria at the station in Flüh, where she caught the tram to the main railway station. She bought a return ticket to Zurich and spent much of the journey reading the International Herald Tribune that she had bought at the kiosk. On the inside page was the office address and that was where she was going. She was determined to speak to Joe's editor and find out if what Joe planned to publish, was so devastating, it would drive someone to kill him. Peering, unseeing, out of the window at the rural landscape rushing by, Maria contemplated what she would say and wondered what kind of reaction she might get.

She found the offices in a suburb called Oerlikon. There was a lot of construction work going on in the area, towering cranes hovered over each site and she smiled at the thought of Joe's regular comment that the crane should be Switzerland's national bird.

Inside the building, she explained to the receptionist that she needed to see: 'whoever was in charge.' The petite girl, with a heavy Swiss accent, asked what exactly was her business.

'I need to discus Joe Leman's death,' she said.' The girl froze, then leapt to her feet and disappeared down a long corridor.

Maria didn't have to wait long and was shown into an office, where an old, tired, walrus of a man half rose and indicated a chair.

'You knew Joe Leman?' he asked intently, leaning forward. Before she could answer, he apologised for being rude, introduced himself as Murray Majors, thrust out a hand and asked Maria her name. 'Would you like tea, coffee, a glass of water?' Maria declined. 'So … you knew Joe Leman,' he began again. Maria nodded.

'Yes, we were good friends.'

'I'm sorry,' said Majors with a frog in his throat. 'A good man,' he blew his nose in a large linen handkerchief. 'And a bloody good reporter too?'

'Do you have any idea why anyone would want to kill him?' asked Maria. 'And burn all his belongings?' Majors shook his head:

'It's a mystery to me,' he said, still dabbing his nose with the handkerchief. 'A total mystery!'

'So you don't believe that he was working on something for

the paper that upset someone enough to bash him on the head with a hammer and throw him in the river?' said Maria breathlessly, fighting back the tears. Majors removed his half-glasses and looked at her, his head tilted slightly to one side.

'You seem to know a lot about the case?' he said quizzically.

'I've spent a lot of time with the policeman investigating Joe's death,' replied Maria.

'Ah,' said Majors reaching into the drawer of his desk, where he extracted a business card. He pulled the glasses back on his nose and read: 'Silvio Belloni.' Maria nodded:

'Yes, Belloni - He told me that he had been to see you but you couldn't tell him anything.'

'Did he?' replied Majors. 'Well no, I couldn't help him.' Maria took a deep breath and blurted out:

'We both know that's not true!' Majors looked at her but said nothing. 'We both know that he was working on something he thought was very important … and that whatever it was that he wrote … you have a copy!' Majors cleared his throat.

'Miss Beckett,' he said quietly. Î think you need a cup of coffee.' He rose to his feet and wandered over to an old filter coffee machine perched on top of a filing cabinet, where he proceeded to fill two plastic cups. 'Cream?' he asked.

'Yes please,' replied Maria. Still with his back towards her, Majors said:

'I think, Miss Beckett, that you'd better tell me all that you know about our friend Joe Leman.' He turned and placed the coffee on the desk in front of her.

'I know he investigated the business dealings of a man named Dieter von Murren in Basel and gave you the article to publish,' Maria stated. 'And then the next thing we know is that poor Joe is dead.'

'What else do you know?' asked Majors, sipping his coffee and indicating to Maria that she too should drink.

'He thought the case was serious and that von Murren would probably go to jail,' Maria explained. 'He told me that you would make the decision whether or not to publish.'

'Joe does indeed make serious accusations in his article,' began Majors, peering at Maria over his glasses. 'The article is with our lawyers. They're checking it out, before advising me whether or not we would be within the law if we published. One has to be very careful in this day and age.' Maria sipped the bitter, unsweetened coffee with an involuntary shudder and replaced the cup on the desk. Her head was full of questions.

'But,' she began. Majors held up his hand.

'What I don't understand is why Joe told you about his investigation. In my experience Joe is extremely careful with what he says and whom he shares his information with.' He drained the cup and deftly flicked it into an overflowing wastepaper basket. 'Why did he tell you what he was up to?'

'Because I work for the von Murren's … I look after their children. But … he, Joe, persuaded me to spy on them.' Maria choked back a tear. 'I even helped him set up some sort of tape-recorder, so he could hear what was being said.' Majors grunted and settled his rheumy gaze on Maria:

'Well, he was wrong to ask you to do that … if the law found out, we'd be in trouble,' he said. 'None of what he has written in his article refers to anything that he personally heard. And certainly no mention of hidden recordings.' Majors rose slowly to his feet and wandered like a hippo to a watering hole and poured more coffee; his normally creased brow was crunched into a hideous scowl. 'The accusations Joe made are very, very serious,' he flung over his shoulder. 'It's why we are being very careful before we make any decision whether or not to publish.' He returned to his desk and wearily lowered himself into his chair, spilling the coffee, as he placed it on the desk. He pulled out the linen handkerchief from his trouser pocket and absently began mopping up the mess. 'Who else might have known about his investigation?' he asked. Maria thought for a moment.

'I've absolutely no idea,' she said. 'He only told me that he suspected von Murren of being a criminal and would I help by telling him about the people that came to dinner and things like that.'

'He never once mentioned talking to anyone else?' asked Majors.

'No never.'

'He must have talked to lots of people to find out as much as he did and to confirm his suspicions,' said Majors.

'Well, he never told me,' said Maria. Majors picked up a pencil and began twiddling.

'Tell me about the fire; Belloni didn't say much about that.'

Maria shuffled uncomfortably in her seat.

'Well Joe and I had,' she stumbled trying to find the right word. 'We had a disagreement. I was very upset about his investigation. I felt guilty about spying on the family,' she paused. 'Mrs von Murren and the children are lovely, I was upset about what might happen to them, if all this business came out. And all the pain and unhappiness that would be caused.' She rubbed a hand across her face, 'and it would all be my fault!'

'Not your fault at all,' interrupted Majors kindly. 'But go on.'

'Well Joe said it might be better for me if we did not see each other until the matter was out in the open. He was trying to save me, to protect me from appearing to be involved.' Maria took another sip of the bitter coffee. 'Consequently we hadn't seen each other for a while. I tried phoning but the phone was out of order. I thought this was odd, so one day I went round to the apartment and ran into Belloni, who told me about the fire. He said it had started in the bedroom that Joe used as an office and the whole flat was gutted.' Major's nodded; he suddenly looked ten years older.

'How much of what you have told me did you tell Belloni?' he asked, peering over his glasses.

'Nothing,' replied Maria quickly. 'I said nothing, I was afraid he would start investigating von Murren's affairs. I don't want that to happen unless I am perfectly sure in my own mind that Dieter von Murren was responsible for Joe's death.' Major's mind was ticking over:

'You said that Joe asked you to set up some kind of tape-recorder in von Murren's house.' Maria nodded. 'Tell me more about that.'

'We had a big row,' she said quietly. 'I really didn't want to do it. But … but in the end I gave in.'

'What exactly did you do?' asked Majors.

'I hid a small box and one microphone on a book shelf,' explained Maria. Another microphone close to the piano, because I knew all the men liked to stand around the piano and sing … once they'd had a drink or two. And the third I fixed on the lamp over the dinner table. Later when everyone had gone I collected the bits and the next day rode to a nearby village and phoned Joe. He drove out from Basel and collected the stuff.' Maria sniffed, 'I only saw him once after that ... and we hardly spoke.' Major grunted.

'Someone other than you must have known what he was up to ... for sure his death was no accident.' His eyes wandered around the room, as he mentally sifted through all that Maria had said. After what seemed an age his gaze settled on the distressed young woman in front of him. 'I wonder where he got the listening devices from?' he thought to himself, certainly not from the Tribune! 'Well young lady,' began Majors. 'Until I've heard from our lawyers I don't think either of us should say anything to anyone. If the legal team give us the go-head and we publish, then you and I should meet again. Maria felt frustrated but understood the reasoning,

'I feel so helpless,' she said quietly. Majors thrust a business card into Maria's hand.

'I've written my private number on the back,' he said. 'Go through in your mind everything you can remember Joe saying, he must have met other people during his investigation. See if you can remember anything that he might have said. I feel sure someone out there found out that he was about to blow a few people's careers out the window but they got to him first. Young lady ... you're our only hope of finding the truth!'

CHAPTER 39

Kurt Baumann, to say the least, was a brilliant but complicated man. A clinical psychologist could have a field day analysing the way his mind worked. An only child, his adolescence had been marred by continual arguments with his father, his schooldays tarnished by fights and punishments for bullying. But his brilliant mind and later obsession with chemistry, together with natural cunning had seen him through. He had slithered his way through higher education and to the top position of a major company with uncanny ease. He was ruthless and most people were afraid of him. He utilised this fear to maintain a tangible distance in all his relationships. It was no coincidence that his two sons were living in America and his wife sleeping in a separate room.

Baumann's grandfather, Theodor, had been a senior officer in the Nazi Schutzstaffel, the dreaded SS and served under Himmler. Through most of the Second World War he had been attached to the concentration camp at Dachau, where he revelled in causing pain and misery. At the end of the war, he escaped punishment by cleverly slipping away to Argentina, where he disappeared, never to be heard of again.

If that same psychologist analysing his grandson also studied Theodor, he would doubtless conclude that for both there was a vital gene missing. The gene that includes, among other qualities, that of compassion, empathy and a love of one's fellow man.

Kurt Baumann had hardly slept since his discussions with Stavi. He believed what the man had said. Von Murren was an idiot and he cursed himself for listening to his wild plans. He had no doubt that Stavi was capable of solving the problem with the journalist - he had recognised a certain evil gleam in his eye that he sometimes saw in his own mirror. But what about this Stavi - he was what he might call: a loose end. He didn't like loose ends.

Five days after their first meeting, Stavi had called Baumann's private number late at night and whispered:

'The problem we discussed is no longer an issue – I'll see you tomorrow night at eleven.' And had promptly hung up. Baumann's pulse was racing. The problem was solved but the hole had suddenly got deeper.

In the empty stable the following night Baumann gave Stavi a bag containing two-hundred thousand Swiss francs and explained that it would be necessary for them to meet in Grand Cayman to ensure the two-million Swiss francs was successfully transferred to Stavi's new account. Stavi began to object but Baumann silenced him by lying that the bank manager was insisting on his presence to sign away such a substantial sum. They discussed dates and once they were agreed, Baumann wrote down the name of a hotel and told Stavi that he would be in the bar at nine in the evening. If there were problems either of them would leave a message at the desk.

Back in his apartment Stavi laid out the bundles of notes in neat rows on his bed and gloated. His financial problems had been solved at a stroke. Once Baumann had paid him the remainder of his bounty, he mused, he would buy himself a nice apartment in the Florida Keys and disappear. The thought of sun-downers, as he stretched out on a terrace, listening to the surf, after a day's fishing, filled his head. He deserved an easier life, after what he had been through.

With a jerk he returned to the present, gathered up the notes and took the bag into his bedroom, where he prised up a loose floorboard under the carpet and neatly stacked the notes away. The next day he visited a travel agent and booked an economy return flight to Grand Cayman.

By contrast, Kurt Baumann had arranged for the company jet to fly him to Washington, where he had quickly arranged meetings with FDA officials at Silver Spring. Usually he sent one of his minions to do battle with the Federal Drug Administration, as his company tried to introduce one of their new products to the American market. He had easily found an excuse for the visit but had upset his Personal Assistant when he had informed him that he would not be needed and that he would be travelling alone. The pilot was informed that Baumann would be in Washington for three days. On the morning of his departure, a company limousine whisked Baumann to the outer reaches of the Basel/Mulhouse Airport, where he was greeted by the two pilots and a smartly-uniformed hostess.

The flight went smoothly and Baumann slept most of the way on the confortable full-length bed. Six hours later he was awoken by the hostess gently shaking him, announcing that they had started their descent. He showered and dressed before the hostess returned with a lightly boiled egg, warm toast and coffee.

Once the formalities at the airport were completed, Baumann bid farewell to the crew, saying that he would contact them at their hotel in three days time; after which he took the waiting taxi to Silver Spring some forty minutes away.

By lunchtime his meetings were over and he was back at Washington National Airport. He quickly found the toilets, locked himself in a cubicle and from his overnight bag extracted a short, brown wig. He eased the wig onto his head and smoothed the unruly hair. From a compartment in the bag he withdrew a false German passport, which he exchanged for his usual Swiss one. He listened carefully, and eased open the door. The room was empty. Quickly he moved to the sinks and stared at his reflection. He didn't use the disguise often but was always amazed what a transformation a head of hair brought to his appearance. He pulled off his tie and made a few adjustments before heading out onto the main concourse and towards the American Airways counter, where he bought a ticket to Miami, insisting on using cash, much to the annoyance of the saleswoman.

At Miami International Airport, little over two and a half hours later, Baumann took the escalator to the second level and made his way to the Cayman Airways' desk, where a bright young woman sold him a return ticket to Grand Cayman.

He only had an hour to wait and so he hurried through Security and settled himself into a seat in the holding area, where he closed his eyes remembering the one and only time he had visited Grand Cayman. This was when his boys were young and he and his family spent ten days at an expensive resort alongside the azure sea. It was typical of his nature that within twenty-four hours he was bored. He hated sitting on the beach or by the pool and he had never been one to read for pleasure - in his mind, time spent reading novels was time wasted.

Unknown to his family his main motive for visiting Grand Cayman was to open a bank account where he could hide some of his wealth from the Swiss tax authorities. He had paid income tax on his hard earned salary and in his mind, what he chose to do with his savings was his business and giving the Swiss government a second bite of the cherry seemed grossly unfair.

He was shaken out of his musings by the tannoy announcing his flight and he joined the queue of economy passengers heading anonymously towards the gate. An hour and a half later the plane was skimming over the turquoise sea before bouncing along the runway of the Owen Roberts International Airport. Baumann took a taxi for the short ride into the capital city Georgetown and walked into the first hotel that he came to.

The receptionist apologised that the hotel was full and so he headed back into the street and made his way through the crowd of tourists, many from the three huge cruise ships he could see moored offshore. He wandered along the waterfront, perspiring in his unsuitable clothes. Passing a shop filled with gaudy shirts, swimsuits and other holiday gear, he ducked under a row of hats and made his way inside. He soon found what he was looking for and a few moments later emerged back among the crowds, dressed in shorts, T-shirt and beach shoes; the clothes that he had been wearing, inside a bag. A little further down the street he came across a small hotel where he took their last room, the receptionist apologising that it was small. No matter he had replied and paid with cash for three days.

At eight o'clock that evening Baumann took a taxi to the Holiday Inn, the rendezvous that he had arranged with Stavi. He had particularly picked this hotel because he recalled that it was relatively isolated. The orange red sky was quickly dissolving into blackness and by the time he arrived it was already pitch dark.

He made his way to the poolside Tiki bar and ordered a beer. Only a few of the tables were occupied. The pool was invitingly lit, though a notice said it was closed from seven-thirty pm. The humid air was filled with the noise of the palm leaves rattling on the constant breeze, as well as the incessant piping call of Cuban Tree-frogs. Dozens of tall palms were scattered strategically around the area, no doubt providing welcome shade in the daytime. In the distance he could hear the steady beat of Reggae music, carried softly on the warm breeze. Baumann had arranged to meet Stavi at nine pm., time enough to finish his beer.

A few moments before the appointed time, he watched, as a man came ambling into view, picking his way through the tables. As he passed under a lamp Baumann recognised Stavi and called out. The man half raised a hand but turned towards the bar to order a beer, before making his way towards Baumann. They briefly shook hands and by the time Stavi was settled into his chair, the waiter had delivered his beer.

'I'm sorry gentlemen,' he said 'but I need your room number.'

'One hundred and six,' replied Stavi.

'I'm sorry too but the bar is now closed, you can get more drinks inside, if you wish.' The man waited while Stavi signed the chit. Once they were alone, Stavi asked Baumann where he was staying. 'In town,' he had replied.

'Thought I'd book a room here, since you suggested it as the place to meet. But it's a bit far out' he grumbled. Baumann looked around, now only one table was occupied, a young couple were hunched conspiratorially over the table. Baumann asked about his trip and how long Stavi intended to stay.

'What about the money?' asked Stavi, getting to the point.

'I have an appointment at the bank at ten tomorrow,' lied Baumann. 'Have you already opened an account?'

'Of course! The first thing I did when I arrived - and it couldn't have been easier!' Stavi emptied his glass and placed it carefully on the table.

'I shall need details of you account,' stated Baumann.

'Of course,' grinned Stavi and took a piece of paper from the breast pocket of his shirt. Baumann reached for the paper and stuffed it into his trouser pocket nodding his thanks.

'You're in the clear,' said Stavi. 'No worries.'

'I hope so,' replied Baumann quietly, noticing with some relief that the young couple were leaving, walking hand-in-hand towards the main building.

'Let's take a stroll,' said Baumann, 'I fancy dipping my toes into the sea.'

'No proper beach here, I'm afraid. It's stony. They run

regular mini buses to Seven-Mile beach, which isn't far away.'

'There must be somewhere guests swim. Can you show me?' persisted Baumann.

Stavi led the way towards the sea and before long they were standing on an area of gravelly sand where loungers were stacked against the ubiquitous palm trees. It was poorly lit but Baumann picked his way carefully down a rough path between the coral rocks down towards the water's edge. Stavi followed, somewhat reluctantly.

'Do they have snakes here,' he called out. Baumann felt among the rocks until he found a solid piece of coral the size of a baseball. He stood at the water's edge rolling it from one hand to the other.

Stavi joined him,

'Man, it's so black out there.'

'Nothing between us and Cuba,' replied Baumann, easing back from the gently lapping water. 'Have you swum since you've been here?'

'No, not even in the pool,' replied Stavi.

'Is the water warm?' asked Baumann tipping the piece of coral into his right hand. Stavi crouched down in front of Baumann, sat on his heels and ran his hands through the water:

'Yes, it's really warm,' he said - and then glancing up. 'Wow! Just look at all those stars!'

CHAPTER 40

Baumann was savouring a glass of his favourite brandy, a Courvoisier twenty-one year old cognac. He was seated in a comfortable armchair in the lounge area of the company jet, some two hours out from Washington, over the Atlantic. Marta, the hostess, had cooked him a small fillet steak and he was feeling replete, though somewhat tired, after his secret travels. Despite the weariness, his synapses were working overtime, as he racked his brain for any possible loose ends; going over everything that had happened since that first fateful telephone call from Stavi. Mentally he ticked off all the contacts he'd had with Stavi and convinced himself that there was nothing to link him to the private detective and his dirty deeds.

His musings were interrupted by Marta, appearing at his elbow, asking if he needed anything else. He politely dismissed her, insisting she get some sleep and poured himself another generous measure of brandy.

Grasping the goblet with two hands, he leaned forward, savouring the pungent aroma; as he wondered how long it would be before Stavi's body was found? He could picture the scene as some unsuspecting fisherman caught more than he bargained for. And later the whole area teeming with police and gawping guests hiding their children's eyes. The press with their intrusive lenses and reporters armed with their notebooks and sharpened pencils, while the more technically minded wielded mini-recorders and pushed microphones into the faces of anyone prepared to speak. Bedlam, he smiled, utter Caribbean chaos.

Baumann thought about the moment he had actually swung that piece of solid coral, the satisfying thud as he landed the blow, the way Stavi had collapsed, falling forward silently into the water. Baumann had then quickly stripped off his shorts and shirt and dragged Stavi away from the shore until the sea was waist deep. He held the unconscious Stavi's head under water until there was no air left in his lungs. And then, using his long-unused but well remembered life-saving technique, he towed Stavi's body well clear of the shore. Gasping for breath, he gently trod water for a moment before he vigorously pushed the corpse away into the darkness, muttering to himself:

'Thanks for your help … see you in Hell!' Back on shore, he had quickly donned his shirt and shorts and made his way cautiously to the front of the hotel where a number of taxis were lined up. He climbed into the leading cab and asked for a well-known bar in the centre of Georgetown. From there he backtracked to his hotel, where he showered and fell into bed. Not once did his recent vicious actions enter his head. Not for a second did he consider the life he had taken. Not one ounce of remorse, only satisfaction that he had successfully completed what he had set out to do. His grandfather would have been proud.

The following day, back in his ivory tower, Baumann stood at the window gazing at the panoramic view over the industrial landscape of multi-levelled buildings, all seemingly connected by pipes of every description. It looked like some preposterous musical organ capable of producing a cacophony of shrieks and whistles to match the evil, sulphurous odours that issued from the thrusting chimneys. His gaze was towards the horizon of green hills covered in Kirsch-producing cherry trees. The notes he had made at the meeting in Washington had been neatly typed by his secretary and were sitting on his desk. He was waiting for his Head of Research to appear, so that he could discuss his visit to Washington - and cement his alibi.

CHAPTER 41

Maria Beckett, lay on the hotel bed and thought long and hard about what Murray Majors had said to her. How could she possibly be the only hope for finding Joe's killer? Joe hadn't confided in her, he had been trying to protect her, by deliberately saying as little as possible. Majors had told her that Joe's article made no mention of any sources. He had no idea how he had gained all the information - except from the recordings she had helped with.

She leaned across to the bedside table and picked up a notebook she had brought with her. She peered through her scribbles until she found the names of the four men who had attended the dinner party the night she had recorded the conversations. Nessi, Hagler, Foster and Baumann. Although she had seen all four of the men two or three times, she couldn't match faces to the names. Who had the most to lose, she wondered, if The Tribune published the article? Her own boss, von Murren, was out of the country, so he couldn't have done it. The thought struck her that in fact, none of them would have killed Joe but one of them, or perhaps all of them, had hired someone to do the dirty work. She flung an arm across her eyes and swore. How could she possibly help, she didn't even know where to start? Maria thought about giving the four names to the policeman, Belloni, and let him see what he could find out. But once again the thought of the consequences for Katarzyna and the children held her back.

Maria delved into her handbag seeking her diary. She had kept a diary since she was about twelve years of age. Each day usually remembered with a single cryptic comment. She lay back and flicked through the pages until she found the entry for the first night she had spent with Joe. Her mind replayed the feelings she had that evening and a tear spilled over her eyelid. She'd had several boyfriends but for the first time she felt a long term relationship might have been possible with Joe. Maria closed her eyes and the diary dropped to her lap, she allowed herself a self-pitying sob.

Eventually, gathering herself together, she blew her nose and resumed reading. Suddenly an entry caught her attention: 'Is Joe seeing another woman?' What had stimulated that comment she wondered. She cast her mind back, until she recalled that Joe had casually mentioned that he'd had dinner with von Murren's secretary. And instantly her head was filled with a picture of the glamorous woman having dinner at the von Murren's home. Maria also remembered the stab of jealousy and envy she had felt. It wasn't fair; Gloria was not a woman she could compete with. She ought to be a world-famous model or film star or something. Following her questioning look, Joe had said he had hoped she might help his enquiries. But Maria wondered how any man could not be attracted to such a woman. The issue was soon forgotten and Gloria's name had never arisen again. But had Joe seen her, had she supplied him with information about her boss? Might she know something? The more she thought about Gloria, the less likely Maria thought she could help … but it was worth a try. Another thought struck her; Majors had said they hadn't supplied Joe with the recording equipment. She actually knew that because Joe had said that he had hired it from a private detective. When she was back in Burg she would look in the Basel telephone book to see if any such detectives were listed.

The next morning Maria caught the train back to Basel but instead of heading back to Burg, she took a bus to von Murren's factory. She knew von Murren was away, so there was no danger of running into him. At Reception she asked to see von Murren's secretary and after a few moments was escorted to her office. Gloria rose from behind her desk and thrust out a hand:

'We've met before,' she said. 'You look after Dieter's,' she quickly corrected herself: 'Doctor von Murren's children.' Maria was surprised that Gloria remembered her. 'Must be a wonderful job, the girls are so sweet.' Maria agreed about the children and decided to jump in the deep end.

'I believe that you know Joe Leman,' she burst out, watching Gloria closely for a reaction. There wasn't one.

'Joe Leman?' Gloria questioned. 'I don't think so.' Gloria took Maria's arm and guided her towards a comfortable looking sofa.

'A reporter from the Herald Tribune,' said Maria, sitting on the edge of the seat.

'No I don't think so but why do you ask?' questioned Gloria, with a smile.

'Because he was a good friend,' said Maria quietly. 'And now,' she paused and took a breath. 'And now he's dead … murdered!' This time there was a reaction. Gloria sat bolt upright:

'Murdered?' she echoed!

'You didn't know?' asked Maria.

'I … I didn't know him,' blustered Gloria.

'Sorry but I know that you did,' said Maria, in a matter of fact tone. 'He told me that he had dinner with you.' Gloria rose to her feet.

'Look, I was about to leave, let me just tidy up and I'll drive you back into town. We can talk on the way.' Maria watched as Gloria closed down her computer and threw a file into her in-tray. 'Right let's go,' she murmured, picking up her handbag. They made their way to the car park without a word, Maria trailing in Gloria's wake.

For the first few moments Gloria concentrated on the traffic and only made conversation, confirming Maria's name and asking where she came from. Suddenly as they approached a layby, she braked sharply and pulled off the road. Switching off the engine, she turned to face Maria.

'You said that Joe was dead,' a pained expression creased her perfect features.

'You said you didn't know him,' Maria said brusquely.

'I'm sorry,' replied Gloria. 'That was silly. I only met Joe twice. I don't think I even knew his surname. Once we had dinner … and once he came to the office.' Gloria cleared her throat. 'But tell me what happened.' Maria recounted the details of Joe's death and Gloria recoiled in horror. 'But why would anyone want to kill him?' she asked.

'I hoped that you might have some idea,' replied Maria. Gloria shook her head. 'Did he tell you that he was working on an article that might implicate your … our boss in wrong doing?' Gloria looked at Maria but said nothing. Maria continued: 'Joe told me that he had dinner with you, hoping that you would help him find out the truth. Did you?' she asked bluntly. Gloria took a deep breath.

'If this gets out, we'll both be fired,' she said flatly.

'So you did help him,' stated Maria.

'Nothing much,' said Gloria. 'He came to the office when Dieter was away and I let him look at some files.' Gloria suddenly looked sharply at Maria: 'Surely you don't think this had anything to do with his death. Are you insinuating that Dieter killed him?'

'Is he you lover" asked Maria.

'Who?' replied Gloria, flustered.

'Dieter.'

'Of course not ... men don't interest me.' Gloria replied uncomfortably. Maria, surprised, made a mental note.

'He had a lot to lose if the Tribune published the article,' she went on.

'He wouldn't kill,' interrupted Gloria.

'Who're you kidding,' responded Maria. 'We both know he's totally ruthless.' For a moment a silence fell between them, as each reflected on the unthinkable possibility. 'If you remember, he wasn't in the country when Joe was killed,' said Maria quietly. Gloria threw Maria a relieved glance. 'But you wouldn't expect him to dirty his own hands, would you? More likely he paid someone else to kill Joe. But who?' Gloria's shoulders slumped, as she pondered the possibility. 'The von Murren's entertain regularly,' continued Maria. 'Especially four particular businessmen from Basel.' She listed their names. 'Do you know if Dieter saw any of these men more than the others?' she asked. Gloria didn't answer the question but said:

'How much of this do the police know? How much are you going to tell them?' She looked Maria in the eye.

'I don't think the police know anything about Joe's article,' replied Maria. 'They probably think it was a robbery gone wrong. I'm not saying anything that would harm the family - unless I'm sure Dieter von Murren is implicated in Joe's death. That's why I need your help.' Gloria half turned and gripped the wheel with both hands and stared straight ahead, her mind racing.

'I really can't afford to lose my job,' she choked, half to herself. 'My family ...' her voice trailed away.

'And I don't want to see Katarzyna and the children hurt,'

said Maria. 'Though the matter might be taken out of our hands if the Herald Tribune decide to publish Joe's article. Their lawyers are trying to make up their mind if it's safe to do so.'

It was growing warm in the car and Gloria lowered the window an inch and with a deep sigh made up her mind:

'Joe looked at some files and decided von Murren was in league with Global Vigour Industries,' she said breathlessly. 'He was ecstatic and photocopied several letters and said something like: it wouldn't be long until he had von Murren nailed to the wall.' Maria recognised the phrase.

'So, this Global Vigour Industries,' questioned Maria. 'Who was von Murren's contact? Who was he conniving with?' Gloria turned and looked Maria in the eye:

'Baumann,' she said, 'Kurt Baumann.'

CHAPTER 42

On the tram, winding its way out of Basel city towards Flüh, Maria mentally sifted through all the facts she had gathered. Gloria had certainly been helpful, in fact, despite the envy she felt towards the woman and her striking good looks, she rather liked her. She was a genuine person, someone who inspired trust. So, she thought, Joe had decided the Head of Global Vigour was up to no good with her boss. Global Vigour, she mused, what sort of name was that to give a company? Gloria had said that Kurt Baumann was its CEO, but no matter how hard she tried, she couldn't put a face to the name.

Maria had telephoned Katarzyna and told her she was catching the tram to Flüh and that she would take the bus to the village. Katarzyna would not hear of it and when Maria arrived at Flüh, Katarzyna was waiting on the platform.

'I told you to take the week off,' she said, an arm around Maria's shoulders; 'You've only been gone three days.'

'I know, you're very kind - but I'd rather be with you and the girls,' said Maria.

'Did you find out any more about your friend. Has he been found?' asked Katarzyna. Maria only just stopped herself blurting out the truth. Instead she shook her head. Tears, unbidden, suddenly spilling down her cheek.

'Don't cry,' said Katarzyna sympathetically. 'I'm sure he will turn up.' She squeezed Maria's shoulder. Maria shook her head but said nothing. She was not crying just for Joe but for Katarzyna and the girls and the bottomless abyss she was slowly but surely pushing them towards.

The next few days flew by as Maria dropped, seamlessly, back into the household routine. One afternoon, before driving off to collect the girls from school, she found a telephone directory and took it to her room. She needed to see if there were any private detectives listed in the book, though she thought it highly unlikely. First she looked through a German dictionary for the German translation. Privatdetektiv - well that's a pretty literal translation, she thought and thumbed her way through the telephone book.

'Oh my God,' she exclaimed and began counting. 'There are twelve.' Twelve private detectives in a small city like Basel. What did they all find to do? She looked more closely. Five called themselves security contractors. What did that mean? The others were obviously smaller concerns. Any one of these companies could have loaned Joe the recording equipment, she thought and her heart slumped. This really was a job for the police.

Maria made her way downstairs where she could see Katarzyna was outside talking to Jacques. Taking a deep breath she stole into Dieter von Murren's study and switched on the desk-size photocopier. Why did the damn thing take so long to warm up? Maria slipped back into the hallway, where she could see Katarzyna was still outside. The first copy was lopsided; the telephone book was fat and unwieldy. She screwed up the copy and dropped it into the wastepaper basket. The second was better. She rushed back into the hall, placed the directory on a shelf near the phone and dashed upstairs with the copy, which she placed in the drawer of her bedside table.

Outside, she told Katarzyna she was off to collect the girls, leapt into the Range Rover and headed off down the tree-lined drive. Her thoughts revolved around the list of detectives she had discovered. She needed to ask each one if they had hired equipment to Joe but she worried that her German wasn't up to it. She thought of Gloria and wondered if she would be prepared to help. But that would involve telling her about her personal involvement with the eavesdropping and the traitorous feeling circulated through her brain again. The following afternoon, on her way to pick up the girls from school, Maria stopped in Flüh to use the public telephone. She had the photocopied sheet with the numbers she needed. Feeding coins into the machine she dialled the first number. A female voice answered.

'Excuse me,' began Maria. 'Do you speak English?'

'Of course,' was the brusque reply. 'How can I help you?'

'Sorry it's complicated … but a friend of mine ... who's left the country,' blustered Maria. 'He hired some recording equipment from a firm of private detectives and I wondered if it might be your company?'

'We do hire out surveillance equipment to authorised companies but not private individuals,' said the woman.

'Well I suppose he hired it for his employer,' said Maria hesitatingly. 'Is it possible you could check your records and see if it was your company he dealt with?' she continued.

'I'm sorry madam,' replied the voice at the other end of the line. 'We don't disclose that kind of information.' The coins ran out and the line went dead, leaving Maria frustrated. There was nothing for it, she decided, she would have to trail around each one of the companies and try to persuade them to check the records.

The following day Maria asked for the afternoon off and took the tram into Basel, where she headed for the most centrally located security company on her list.

The woman on the reception desk had been very helpful and after Maria's impassioned pleading had looked at her records. No surveillance equipment had been hired out in the last twelve months she said. She also assured Maria that it was very unlikely any company of repute would hire out such equipment. Except to another security company.

Savouring a coffee in the busy restaurant of a department store, Maria pondered what the woman had said. Either one or more of the companies on her list was somewhat unscrupulous or Joe had a personal contact. Joe had tried to assure her that he had never done any 'snooping' before but she had no idea if he knew a private detective well enough to hire equipment. He had used the word hire, she remembered, not borrowed - which seemed to indicate a business arrangement. There were just two names on her list that did not appear to be companies but individuals. If they were one-man outfits perhaps they might be more flexible about hiring equipment. She decided to try these. She found the office of James Syfrig easy enough and rang the bell. A middle-aged, hawkish-looking man opened the door and looked enquiringly at her.

'Herr Syfrig?' she enquired. The man nodded and threw the door wide open.

'Please come in,' he said in German. Maria stepped into a

hallway and the man guided her into a tiny office, dominated by a huge desk upon which sat an illuminated globe. The man pointed to a chair and settled himself behind the desk. Having confirmed that the man spoke English, Maria paused thinking about what she would say.

'Having trouble with your husband?' said the man sympathetically, leaning forward, his face creased into a phoney expression of concern.

Strolling away from Syfrig's office, Maria was feeling frustrated. The man had insisted he didn't own the type of equipment that Maria had described and even if he had, he certainly wouldn't lend it to anyone he didn't know. Maria didn't believe him and was certain that she would never utilise the services of such a shifty character, no matter how desperate she was.

Maria glanced at the list, 'Raziel Stavi,' she read. He was the only individual left on the list. On the back of the sheet she had written down the address and the approximate location of the street where Stavi lived. She sighed, this would require catching a tram across the Rhine to Kleinbasel, not an area she knew.

After about ten minutes, the tram rattled across the multitude of points and came to a halt outside the Mustermesse, Basel's vast exhibition centre. Maria left the tram and gazed around, totally disorientated by the enveloping buildings. A woman wearing a Hijab hurried by, wheeling a pushchair. Maria called to her and asked if she knew the name of the street. The woman shrugged her shoulders but Maria pushed the paper under her nose and pointed to the street name. The child began crying. The woman spoke sharply to the child in a language Maria didn't recognise, before she pointed and indicated with her hands that Maria must go straight and later turn left. Without a word but casting a smile in Maria's direction, the woman bent towards her child, spoke soothingly and continued on her way.

Maria took two wrong turns before she found the street she sought and the block of flats. At the door she peered at the bell pushes and the nameplates, some neatly engraved others mere grubby labels. She found Stavi and pressed the bell. There was no reply. She pressed several times more before becoming frustrated that she had come all this way just to find him out.

By the end of the following week, Maria had visited all the names on the list and drawn a blank. She had tried telephoning

Raziel Stavi twice but each time there was no reply. What would she have thought if someone had informed her, that at this moment, Raziel Stavi was thousands of miles away, lying neatly filed in the icy morgue of the capital city of a group of tropical islands that she had barely heard of?

CHAPTER 43

Unusually for Dieter von Murren, he was feeling anxious and somewhat confused. The unease had all begun one evening the previous week when, after dinner, he had settled in his study to read some documents that Gloria had prepared for him, when he noticed his photocopier was switched on. There was an unwritten rule that Katarzyna and the children kept out of his office, so why was the machine switched on? He shouted his wife's name but no one heard, they were busy watching television. Then he'd noticed the screwed up paper in the wastebasket. When he realised what had been copied, he broke out into a cold sweat. What did Katarzyna want with private detectives? Was she looking for a divorce? He thought back. Surely his only recent 'indiscretions' had been in South America and once in New York. He felt confident that Katarzyna would know nothing of these. Though there was always the possibility that one of the women had contacted her. But surely that would be highly unlikely, he tried to convince himself.

For a week he took to peeking at Katarzyna when she wasn't looking. She was her normal cheerful, chatty self, reading to the children, helping with homework. He became even more confused when he sensed that she was treating him in her usual adoring manner, always giving his hand a squeeze, a loving smile, constantly thinking one step ahead to ensure his wellbeing.

Today's lunch with Kurt Baumann hadn't helped his psyche either. Baumann had been cold and offhand, his mind obviously elsewhere and he had refused Dieter's proposal that they should start planning further 'collaboration.' He had even made excuses and left before dessert had been served.

That evening, after dinner, Dieter went out and wandered

around the stables. The horses each had their heads hanging over the door, silently watching the world go by. As one their heads turned, as he walked into view. He rubbed each of their noses and promised himself that he would get in the saddle at the weekend. It had been months since he and Katarzyna had been on a hack together.

Leaving the horses he strolled to the edge of the property and gazed at the view, the sun had set, dark clouds were gathering over the distant mountains of the Vosges. He shuddered. With the setting sun, the temperature had dropped. He needed to confront Katarzyna about the photocopying he decided, as he strolled back to the house. But how could he raise the issue without upsetting her. He knew that tact was not his strongest suit.

Later, after Maria had collected the children to get ready for bed, Katarzyna made them both a cup of coffee and they settled into the luxuriously cushioned armchairs facing each other. Katarzyna asked her husband how his day had been?

'Fine,' he replied. 'By the way, did you notice if the photocopier needs a new cartridge? Is it still printing all right?' Katarzyna looked puzzled.

'What do you mean?'

'The copier on my desk, does it need a new cartridge?' An inane conversation ensued before Dieter accepted the fact that Katarzyna had not used the copier, in fact had never used the copier and didn't know how. He believed her. Then who had? At that moment Maria knocked and walked in.

'The girls are settled, if you want to wish them goodnight,' she said to Katarzyna. Katarzyna rose and both women left, leaving Dieter von Murren to ponder the likelihood that it was Maria who had used the copier. In which case, why did she need the services of a private detective?

Thirty minutes later Katarzyna returned to the lounge and asked Dieter if he wanted another coffee. He declined and she settled back into the armchair.

'About Maria,' he began. 'Are you still pleased with her?'

'Good heavens yes,' replied Katarzyna, surprised. 'I couldn't do without her. Why do you ask?'

'I thought that she seemed … pre-occupied lately,' Dieter continued.

'Well, that's not surprising. If you remember I told you her friend has disappeared. She's been to the police station several times trying to help.' Dieter searched his memory but couldn't recall what Katarzyna had told him.

'Of course,' he lied. 'Remind me what happened.' He rose and poured himself a brandy. He didn't ask if his wife wanted one, he knew she would decline.

'Well there was this young American writer Maria met on her German course,' Katarzyna began. 'He didn't turn up for lessons so she went looking for him and found his apartment had been burnt out, totally destroyed and he had disappeared.'

'How odd,' commented Dieter.

'More than odd,' snapped Katarzyna. 'Very mysterious. Maria is very upset. It seems the police believe it was arson and have no idea what has happened to him.'

'Were they close?' asked Dieter.

'Yes,' replied Katarzyna. 'They'd been seeing each other on her days off.' Dieter grunted, perhaps it had been Maria who had used his copier. Maybe she was thinking of asking a private detective to look for this man. Dieter breathed a sigh of relief.

One evening, a couple of days later, Dieter followed Maria outside, as she went to check on the horses. He watched from a distance as she stroked the forehead of Katarzyna's horse before walking up behind her.

'She's a lovely animal, isn't she,' he said. Maria jumped, she hadn't heard him coming.

'Yes,' she replied. 'Such a gentle personality.'

'Katarzyna told me about your missing friend,' he said, coming straight to the point. Maria flinched.

'It's so horrible, I've been trying to put it out of mind,' she choked.

'American, I believe?' said Dieter.

'Yes,' replied Maria, 'though he'd lived in Europe a long time.'

'He was a writer, I understand,' said Dieter. Maria nodded. 'What kind of writer? Maria turned and looked at the horse, she desperately wanted to share her burden. To blurt out that that Joe had been murdered. But she reminded herself, just in time, that this man might be responsible.

'I don't really know,' she lied. 'He never explained.'

'Did he make a living from his writing?' persisted Dieter.

'I'm sorry Doctor von Murren, I really don't know. I was only just getting to know him.' Dieter grunted.

'Well, is there anything I can do? Would you like me to have a word with the police… try and find out if they have any clues?'

'No,' said Maria sharply. 'Thank you … they promised that they would call me if there was any news.'

'My wife told me you have been interviewed several times by the police,' Dieter went on. Maria silently cursed, why wouldn't the man drop it. 'Was it always the same policeman? Do you remember his name?'

'No,' she lied again. 'It was a different man each time.'

Dieter suddenly realised that tears were streaming down Maria's face. He stopped his inquisition and walked on to the next stable.

'Remember,' he said. 'Don't hesitate to ask, if you think I can help.' Maria blubbered her thanks and ran indoors.

The following day, once the initial morning rush had eased and he had a moment to breathe, von Murren called Gloria into his office. He invited her to sit and took secret pleasure, as he eyed the shapely, neatly crossed, black-stockinged thighs. He marvelled that his self-control had never allowed his manicured fingers to follow the enticing diamonds disappearing beneath her black pleated skirt. Gloria sat expectantly clutching her notebook, conscious but unmoved by his gaze. Dieter cleared his throat.

'There's a young woman who works at the house, looks after the children, helps my wife,' he began awkwardly. 'She's been with us for some time,' he added. Gloria nodded but said nothing. 'It seems she had a male friend called Joe. An American. And she's upset because he's gone missing.' Von Murren was twisting a pencil in his fingers. 'I believe his apartment was gutted by fire…he wasn't in it… but as I said, he's gone missing.' For a fleeting moment Dieter's gaze returned to the thighs, he tore his eyes away and looked out of the window. 'Try and see if you can find out this Joe's surname and who he worked for . . . the girl said he was a writer.' Dieter deliberately placed the pencil on his desk and turned towards his computer. Gloria rose and headed towards the door. 'Oh,' called von Murren. 'And see if you can find out the name of the policeman whose in charge of the case … and his phone number.'

Back in her office Gloria was fretting. Why did her boss want this information, she was worried? At the first opportunity she telephoned the von Murren residence and left a message for Maria to call her at home. When Maria did eventually call, they arranged to meet later in the week, when Maria next came into the city for her German lesson.

Seated in a small, cosy bar a few days later, the two women leaned conspiratorially over the table, heads almost touching. Gloria was repeating what Dieter von Murren had instructed her to do.

'But why?' whispered Maria. 'Why is he sticking his nose in?'

'Perhaps he wants to find out how much the police know?' suggested Gloria.

'Yes … but if he murdered Joe … or organised someone else to do it, surely he'd know Joe's surname!' Gloria leaned back and picked up her glass:

'You're right. Of course he'd know. He'd be bound to know Joe's surname.'

'Does that mean, he's just trying to be helpful?' suggested Maria. 'Have we misjudged him?' Gloria looked pensive, as both women leaned back and looked at each other. Maria thought for a moment and then made a decision. 'You know,' she began, looking round to check she could not be overheard. 'Joe made me hide some microphones at the house; he said it would help him prove Dieter was guilty.' Gloria looked incredulous:

'You did what?' Maria shared all that had happened, concluding with Joe's Eureka moment, when he had repeated that he had nailed their boss. He had said it substantiated some documents that he had.

'They must have been the ones you copied for him?' said Maria. Gloria nodded. 'On the strength of that he completed his article and sent it to his editor,' she said.

'Then that probably means the matter is out of our hands,' said Gloria anxiously.

'Please don't repeat what I've told you,' whispered Maria.

'Not about the microphones. I feel awful about doing that.'

'Don't worry, smiled Gloria. 'Discretion is my middle name.' She emptied her wineglass, waved at the waiter and ordered two more drinks. 'So you think it's okay if I give Dieter the information he asked for?'

'I suppose so,' sighed Maria. 'The policeman's name is Belloni, by the way.' Gloria nodded and made a mental note.

'What about the fact that Joe worked for the Herald Tribune … that he was a reporter. Should I tell him that?' Maria thought for a moment.

'It would be interesting to see his reaction, if you told him.' she said. 'Oh go on,' she continued rashly. 'Tell Dieter who Joe works for.' She stopped, the words caught in her throat. 'Tell him who Joe used to work for,' she choked.

'Were you very close?' asked Gloria sympathetically, reaching across the table and squeezing Maria's wrist.

'Well yes and no,' said Maria, 'usually I only saw him after the German classes … but … I felt that something more …' she swallowed hard and struggled to find the words. 'I felt something more permanent might grow.'

'I understand that,' said Gloria. 'He seemed nice.' Adding with a laugh 'For a man!'

CHAPTER 44

Belloni rose wearily to his feet, though his interest suddenly spiked, as the young constable stood aside and introduced the visitor. The numbness besetting his brain, caused from lack of sleep, the blind alleys, the countless people he had interviewed, the rude and the belligerent, suddenly lifted. Belloni eased his lanky frame around the desk, moved towards the man and thrust out a hand.

'Doctor von Murren, pleased to meet you. Do sit down.' Belloni indicated the chair facing his desk and resumed his own seat. 'May I offer you a coffee?' Dieter politely refused. 'I got your message that you would like to see me. How can I help?' Belloni studied the man in front of him. The very figure of understated wealth, breeding and brimming with self-confidence,' he thought. Dieter cleared his throat:

'I understand that you are in charge of the case relating to the disappearance of one Joe Leman,' he said.

'I am indeed,' replied Belloni, wondering what was coming next.

'Î learned about the fire and his disappearance from a young woman employed by my wife. I believe you've met her.'

'Ah yes,' replied Belloni. 'The young English woman.'

'That's right, Maria Beckett. She looks after the children.' Dieter shifted in his chair. 'May I ask if you are any further forward finding the man?'

'Why do you ask?' replied Belloni cautiously, suddenly aware that Maria couldn't have told her employer that Joe Leman was dead.

'Well,' began Dieter, picking his words carefully. 'I only discovered this week that I had in fact met Joe Leman. He came out to my factory saying he was planning to write an article for the Herald Tribune about Basel's pharmaceutical industry. When Maria told me about Joe's disappearance, I didn't make the connection, she didn't seem to know who he worked for.'

'Did he ever write the article, do you know?' demanded Belloni.

'No idea,' replied Dieter. 'I'm not a regular reader.'

'When was this?' continued Belloni. 'When did he visit your factory?' Dieter thought back:

'Well quite some time ago, my secretary would have a note of it in the diary, if it's important.' Belloni nodded:

'I'll call her, if it seems useful to the case. But I don't see that is likely to have any relevance. We have a good idea of his movements up until a couple of days before the fire, obviously his visit to you was well before that.'

Dieter took his wallet from an inside pocket, pulled out a business card and handed it to Belloni.

'The office number is there, just ask for my personal assistant, she'll tell you what you want to know.' Leaning back on the uncomfortable chair, Dieter looked directly at Belloni. 'So, Inspector, you're no further forward? No nearer finding this Joe Leman?'

Belloni looked at the man before him. The BAZ, the local newspaper, had carried the news of a body being found in the Rhine but he had not yet given permission for the name to be released.

'We have several strong leads,' said Belloni, stretching the truth. 'But we fear the worst.'

'Well that's very sad,' replied Dieter. 'Seemed a nice enough chap and certainly Miss Becket was very fond of him.'

'This article he planned to write, did he give any hint of what line he was exploring. Any particular angle?' asked Belloni.

'Not that I remember. He just seemed interested in what medicaments we produced in our factory, our markets. And how the major companies fund their research. I remember he seemed very interested in that.' Belloni scratched his ear.

'So you didn't know him well enough to know if he had any enemies? Someone who might benefit from his death?'

'Good heavens no,' replied Dieter. 'As I said, I only met him that once.'

'So why exactly did you come to see me today Doctor von Murren?' Belloni asked quietly.' Dieter was unflustered by the question.

'I thought there might be things you would be prepared to tell me that you wouldn't tell Miss Beckett. She's very upset, I thought you might be able to tell me something that would reassure her he will be found alive.' Belloni looked unconvinced.

'Joe Leman had no history of going anywhere without informing his boss in Paris. He says that he hasn't heard from him, which is why I fear the worst.' Belloni realizing that von Murren had nothing useful to add about Joe Leman, began shuffling on his seat.

'Well, if you'll excuse me, I have a further appointment,' he said.

'Yes, of course,' replied von Murren, looking at his watch; I need to get moving too. 'Thank you very much for seeing me.' They shook hands and Belloni escorted his visitor towards the door. A sudden thought struck him:

'Never heard of an Israeli, called Stavi have you, Raziel Stavi?' Von Murren glanced over his shoulder and shook his head.

'No, I think I'd remember such a name. Why do you ask?'

'No reason really. He lived locally, worked as a private detective but was recently found drowned in suspicious circumstances.'

'A private detective, you say?' said Von Murren puzzled, thinking of the list he had found in his study.

'Yes, he operated on his own, as far as I can see.'

'No … sorry, can't help you Inspector.'

Making his way towards the parking area where his chauffer waited, von Murren considered what Belloni had just said. Surely it was only a coincidence that someone, probably Maria Beckett, had photocopied a page of private detectives from the phone book - and one had been found dead! Surely a coincidence?

After von Murren had left, Belloni made himself a thick, black espresso, dropped heavily on the seat behind his desk and pulled out a thin file with the name STAVI written on the cover in block capitals. He read again the cryptic message he had received from the police chief in the Cayman's describing how a fisherman had pulled Stavi's body from the sea. The cause of death was drowning but like Joe Leman, he had an unexplained gash on the back of his head. He was fully clothed but his pockets were empty, he was identified because he was found close to the hotel where he was staying but hadn't been seen for two days. The message went on to give details of his arrival in Georgetown and the fact he had a flight booked to leave the day before he was found. Also that he had visited a local bank and opened an account, depositing the minimum amount needed to open such an account. Belloni looked up from the file, sipped his coffee and contemplated what had happened the previous day.

His sergeant had no trouble finding Stavi's address; he was publicly listed in the Basel phone book. Together with two policemen, Belloni and his sergeant had gone to Stavi's flat where the concierge had unlocked the apartment door. The old man had lingered inside nosily watching, as the four men began a methodical search, until the sergeant had ushered him out locking the door.

It was one of the keen, young policemen who had suddenly whistled with surprise when he had found the loose floorboard under a carpet in the bedroom and the wad of notes hidden below. The notes were now locked away in the police safe but what had intrigued Belloni was that they were brand new, so bright and crisp, he wondered if they were forged. But they had a Credit Swiss band around them and were consecutively numbered, all one-hundred and ninety-five thousand!

Earlier that morning Belloni had a frustrating meeting with the bank manager of the branch in Spalenberg. Frustrating because the manager kept insisting a client's bank transactions were private. In the end Belloni had left him the list of bank-note numbers, having explained that they had been found in the home of a man he believed had been murdered. And if Credit Suisse didn't provide him with the name of the client who had withdrawn such a huge amount, Belloni would make sure someone would be prosecuted for obstruction. The manager had countered that he would speak to someone further up the hierarchy. Fuming, Belloni left, threatening that he would return the following morning.

'Twenty-four hours you've got,' he had hissed 'or I'll get a judge to put the squeeze on you!' Belloni left, easing his frustrations by slamming the door behind him, fracturing the cathedral calm of the bank's interior and causing looks of alarm on the assembled congregation.

Belloni looked again at the slim file. One of his men had knocked on each door in the apartment block where Stavi lived but not a single soul even knew he had existed. No one could recollect seeing the man, except the concierge who said he had never been inside the apartment since Stavi had moved in and had only once had a conversation with him and that was regarding a minor plumbing matter.

The Israeli embassy wasn't much help; they had a record of Stavi's registration in the country but that was all, no next of kin listed. The local authorities said he was officially registered; he had a resident's permit and had paid his taxes.

Belloni threw down the file in disgust. In any one year, Basel rarely produced more than a couple of murders and usually they were straightforward domestic issues or drug-dealers falling out. Now there were two Basel residents dead and absolutely nothing to go on. He rested his chin in his hands and wondered if it was remotely possible the two crimes were related. Could he prove a link between Joe Leman and Raziel Stavi? He clambered to his feet and poured himself yet another thick, black, bitter espresso. Gazing at the evil mixture swirling around his mug, he resolved to go and see Joe's boss again. He wasn't convinced the man had been as forthcoming as he might be.

'Yes,' he spoke aloud,' 'it's time for another chat with Murray Majors.'

CHAPTER 45

Silvio Belloni decided to take the train to Zurich. He had set a late morning appointment and the non-stop service would, he saw from the timetable, provide him with fifty-three minutes of peace and quiet and a chance to study his case notes, uninterrupted. As the train hurtled alongside the Rhine, he asked himself why he didn't use the train more often, rather than choosing to battle with the traffic that constantly clogged up the country's highways. He opened his briefcase, pulled out a pad and started compiling questions to ask Murray Majors, the Herald Tribune's editor. He hadn't got very far when the warmth of the carriage and the soothing rhythm of metal wheels on rails lulled him to sleep. He hadn't had a proper night's sleep for weeks and unsurprisingly his chin dropped onto his chest and his pad to the floor.

He woke with a start and cursed, as the train pulled into Zurich's main station, on time to the minute. He shook his head and rubbed his eyes, cursed again, damning himself for having lost the opportunity to go through his case-notes and prepare properly for the forthcoming interview. For a moment he scrabbled on the floor retrieving his pad and pen before taking a deep breath, gathering himself together and exiting the carriage. Outside he summoned a taxi and during the trip to the Oerlikon offices mentally ticked off the questions he needed to ask.

Belloni had discovered that the premises in Baumackerstrasse were almost entirely given over to the printing of the International Herald Tribune newspaper, its distribution and subscriptions. The editorial work was done in Paris. Belloni had called Majors at his Paris number and he had heard the deep sigh the other end of the line, when he said that he needed to see him as soon as possible. A meeting meant another day away from his desk, thought Majors, and time, in the life of a newspaper editor, was as precious as life itself. He had a deputy of course, whom every one in the office thought utterly competent, except that is, for Majors himself.

Belloni proffered his card to the receptionist and she nodded, obviously having been briefed to expect him. She guided Belloni to the rear of the building, where she tapped on a door, letting herself in and closing the door behind her. After a few moments Majors himself opened the door, thrust out a hand, boisterously exclaiming:

'Come in Inspector, come in.' The receptionist left and as she did so Belloni saw the outline of a woman seated before Major's desk. She turned, it was Maria Beckett.

'Good heavens … Miss Beckett,' stammered Belloni, puzzled. Maria rose and shook Belloni's outstretched hand. She had been crying. 'What are you doing here?" Maria didn't answer but blew her nose with the tissue Majors had given her. Majors pulled up another chair and offered Belloni a coffee.

'Only got plastic cups I'm afraid,' he said with a laugh.

'Is there any other kind?' replied Belloni.

Once Majors was settled behind his desk he looked intently at Belloni.

'Inspector,' he began. 'Inspector, when you asked to see me, I called Maria and asked her to come and see me as well. There's something you should both know.' Majors sipped his coffee, before removing his half-glasses and holding them up to the light. 'You see Inspector, I didn't exactly come clean with you the last time we met … I'll explain in a moment.' Majors blew mist on his glasses and began polishing with a large white handkerchief. 'You see Inspector, Joe was working an article for the paper that would … that will … implicate at least two well-known men in Basel for illegal activities. Initially I couldn't believe that … if published, the article could have led to Joe's death. Now I'm not so sure.' Belloni started to ask a question but Majors held up a hand. 'Let me finish Inspector,' he said replacing his glasses. 'Because the article is dynamite, our legal team have been going through it with a fine toothcomb to ensure there are no expensive comebacks. A couple of days ago, I was given the all-clear and so we plan to publish the article and its allegations.' He looked at Maria. 'I just told Miss Beckett before you arrived and as you can see, she is distressed about the affect this might have on the family she works for.'

'You mean von-Murren is involved?' said the bemused Belloni. Majors nodded.

'He seems to have instigated the crime.'

'Who else is involved?' asked Belloni.

'A man called Kurt Baumann,' replied Majors. 'He's the CEO of another pharma company.' Belloni nodded.

'What exactly is this crime they have supposedly committed?' asked Belloni.

'They've been manipulating the pharmaceutical market, breaking competition rules relating to foreign distribution etcetera,' said Majors.

'It sounds as if this would need someone with expert knowledge to bring a case against them,' said Belloni, realising this was all over his head.

'I'm not even sure they have actually broken Swiss law,' interrupted Majors. But without doubt the Americans and the European Commission will be after them.'

'The Americans?' queried Belloni.

'The Department of Justice,' replied Majors. 'They'll be after blood!' Maria who had sat quietly through this exchange, suddenly said vehemently:

'But what about Joe?'

'Yes,' agreed Belloni. 'What about Joe.' But in his head he was cheering, another piece of the jigsaw puzzle had dropped into place. 'So if and when you publish and the Americans invade Switzerland, you think there will be major casualties?' he continued, looking at Majors, who nodded in agreement,

'The shit will hit the fucking fan!' he said vehemently, before looking towards Maria and apologizing.

'And the knowledge of this ... flying shit, as you delicately put it,' said Belloni, 'might have been enough for one of the culprits to have set fire to Joe's apartment and disposing of Joe himself, in order to save his own skin?'

'Its unlikely but possible,' replied Majors. 'There are some big egos at stake, not to mention personal fortunes.'

'So what's the timetable? When do you plan to switch on the fan?' asked Belloni.

'Well first, out of courtesy, I will meet with the two people who will be named and inform them about the article,' said Majors. 'And publish the first part a week later.'

'There's more than one part?' questioned Belloni. Majors nodded:

'It will be in two parts, the second section a week later.'

'How does all this help Joe?' said Maria quietly, her voice unsteady.

'Don't worry Miss Beckett,' said Belloni. 'Things are becoming clearer. We'll find out what happened to Joe.' He turned towards Majors: 'Would it be possible to have a copy of the article before you publish?' Belloni asked.

'I thought that you might say that,' smiled Majors and delved into his briefcase and brought out a large envelope. 'Hot off the press as you might say,' and handed it over to Belloni. 'So I will be coming to Basel tomorrow and plan to see the two men involved the day after. I've called their personal assistants and apparently they are both around.'

'Are you planning to see them together?' asked Belloni.

'No, separately,' replied Majors. It will be interesting to gauge their reactions.'

'Do you think it wise to see them on your own . . . knowing what they did to Joe? asked Maria. They both looked at her. Majors smiled:

'Don't worry Miss Beckett. These aren't the sort of men who do their own dirty work. I think I'm safe enough.' He glanced at Belloni. 'The Inspector here, will keep an eye on me, I'm sure.' Belloni wasn't listening, there was evidence he wasn't going to share with either Majors or Maria but with the knowledge of this article, he now knew his suspect had a motive.

Shortly afterwards the meeting broke up and as they walked towards the door, Majors explained that he would be staying at the Hilton and he arranged to have dinner with Belloni there, following his meeting with von Murren and Baumann. Later, standing outside on the pavement, Belloni asked Maria if she was in a hurry? She shook her head.

'Well,' smiled Belloni, 'Let's get a taxi back into the city centre and I'll buy you lunch.'

Seated in a corner of a busy but chic Italian restaurant, Maria sipped her glass of fizzy water and looked at her fellow diners. They were office workers who had poured out of the surrounding tower blocks and banks to make the best of their precious hour-long break. The wine-waiter, she noticed was kept pretty busy. After discussion, Belloni summoned the waiter and ordered pasta for them both, and sipped the beer he had ordered.

'It was a waste of my time coming here today,' said Maria.

'He could have told me on the phone that he was going to publish. He really didn't say anything else and there was no discussion.' She looked at the bubbles fizzing round the edge of her glass. 'It doesn't sound such a terrible crime to me ... certainly not worth killing for.' Belloni reached across the table and laid a hand upon Maria's.

'I don't pretend to understand how serious the accusations are. We have experts who will decide that.' He squeezed Maria's hand. 'But I am now convinced Joe's death was related to his research. Though how they found out, I can't begin to imagine.'

'Joe told me that he visited von Murren's factory and talked to him, so they knew each other,' said Maria.

'Yes, I know that,' replied Belloni.

'How do you know?' asked Maria.

'Because your dear boss came to see me . . . and he told me.'

'Why did he come to see you?'

'That's a good question. He made the excuse that he was enquiring on your behalf - that I might tell him things I wasn't prepared to tell you.' Belloni was still holding Maria's hand. 'And then it became clear that you hadn't told him about Joe's death.' Maria withdrew her hand, fumbled in her bag for a tissue and blew her nose.

'I didn't think I could trust him,' she said.

'Well I didn't tell him either,' replied Belloni and I'm sure that he didn't know.' The waiter came with their pasta and for a moment they ate in silence.

'Inspector,' Maria suddenly blurted out.

'Please call me Silvio,' said Belloni gently. Maria was startled but ignored the invitation.

'Like Mr Major,' she continued, there is something I haven't told you.' Belloni smiled but said nothing, waiting.

'Joe borrowed or rented some spying devices; voice-recorders and he persuaded me to set them up at von Murren's home. I didn't want to but …'

'But you did,' said Belloni kindly. Maria nodded.

'There was this dinner party . . . and . . . well Joe said the recordings proved von Murren was guilty.'

'Did you ever listen to these recordings?' asked Belloni. Maria shook her head.

'Presumably they were destroyed in the fire,' said Belloni, thinking aloud.

'I was very angry with Joe; it was why I hadn't had any contact with him for a while. Also he'd said it was better no-one knew that we were friends until things were out in the open.' Maria swallowed a mouthful of her pasta before continuing. 'I had this idea that he may have got this equipment from a private detective and so I found a list in the phone-book and started going round asking.'

Belloni's fork stopped on its journey towards his mouth and the penne dropped back into the dish.

'You did what?' he exclaimed.

'I asked if they had rented any equipment to Joe. But they said they only lent stuff like that to other security people. There were a few individuals but I only saw one . . . and he said no.'

'Was Raziel Stavi on your list,' asked Belloni, raising an eyebrow.

'Yes . . . but he was never in. I didn't see him. Is he someone you know?' asked Maria, surprised.

'No,' replied Belloni, tempted to explain. 'Just a name I came across.'

'Joe told me that he had never used such equipment before, which is why I think he must have hired it in Basel,' explained Maria. 'I thought if I could find out who he got it from, they might know something.' Her brow creased, as if in pain. 'But I don't what,' she added despairingly. Later, after coffee, Belloni looked at his watch.

'I should get moving,' he said. 'Even though I am enjoying your company.' Maria was surprised and looked more closely at her black-haired, handsome companion. 'I have another appointment,' he added quickly, almost embarrassed by her scrutiny. 'What time are you planning to return to Basel?' Maria thought for a minute and decided that as charming as he was, she didn't want to spend an hour or so seated on the train being polite and answering his questions. There were bound to be questions.

'Not until evening. I think I'll browse around the shops for a while. I rarely come to Zurich, so as I'm here, I may as well take advantage.' Belloni felt a pang of regret but nodded in agreement.

'There's some lovely shops here, trouble is that you need deep pockets.' He paid the bill and pecked Maria on the cheek before hurrying off towards Paradeplatz and the headquarters of Credit Suisse, leaving Maria to stroll along the Bahnhofstrasse. The one and a half kilometres, said by some, to be the most exclusive shopping avenue in Europe.

At Credit Suisse Belloni was shown into the plush suite occupied by one of the banks' vice presidents. He settled into a deeply cushioned armchair and relished the espresso served in a fine china cup, provided for him by a smartly suited secretary. Herr Muller would be with him in a moment she reassured him. In fact it was five minutes before Herr Muller showed up and when he did he was red-faced, puffing and full of apologies.

'Our man in Basel asked us to deal with your request about the money you found,' he began. 'We're really not happy about divulging client information.' Muller settled behind his desk, sitting bolt upright fixing Belloni with a glare. 'If the request had come from your superior …' Belloni interrupted the silly man's whining.

'We're dealing with a murder case here Herr Muller. It's a very simple question. Who withdrew the money with the numbers that I supplied?'

'We would rather inform the client first and ask his permission . . .'

'Oh for goodness sake,' said Belloni, his voice shaking with annoyance. 'If I said to you I had found the money and wanted to return it, would you still give me so much trouble?'

'He's a very important client,' Muller said quietly. 'Very influential, a personal friend of the bank's president.' Belloni rose to his feet.

'I'll be back tomorrow with a warrant from a judge and a squad of policeman to search your premises,' he threatened, making for the door.

'Inspector,' Muller called. 'Inspector, please sit down.' Belloni turned and dropped reluctantly into the chair again. 'Please bear with me,' said Muller. 'This client has millions invested with us, if he is innocent of any misdemeanour - and I'm sure he is. Well if he finds out that we have been sharing his private affairs with you, he will obviously take his business elsewhere.' The guy is sweating, observed Belloni. He decided to ease the poor man's suffering:

'If it makes it any easier for you, I think that I already know the name of your client. I just wanted to hear it from you.'

'Who Inspector, tell me who you think it is,' said Muller, peering intently over the top of his glasses.

'Von Murren,' announced Belloni. 'Dieter von Murren.' Muller shook his head, disappointed. 'Not Dieter von Murren I'm afraid, he doesn't bank with us.'

'Okay, try this one,' said Belloni. 'Kurt Baumann.' Muller almost smiled.

'You see Inspector, you knew all the time, and I didn't need to tell you.' Belloni ignored him.

'I have one-hundred and ninety-five thousand francs in my possession. How much did he withdraw?' Muller sifted the papers on the desk and handed a sheet of paper to Belloni. It was a copy of a receipt for two-hundred thousand and the date of withdrawal. 'Do you often get requests for withdrawals for so much?' asked Belloni.

'You'd be surprised Inspector,' replied Muller. 'There are still an awful lot of customers who like to deal in cash.'

'Yes,' thought Belloni. 'All the crooks and drug dealers for a start.'

On the train back to Basel, Belloni pulled the document out of the envelope that Majors had given him and began reading. He soon realized that this really was going to be a job for the experts but before he spoke to his boss, he planned to start investigating Kurt Baumann's recent activities.

The following morning he summoned two of his officers and told them what he needed: Baumann's recent movements, his phone records, details of his family.

'Paint me a picture of the man,' he demanded.

That evening Belloni made his way towards the Hilton Hotel in Aeschengraben, close to the railway station. He had decided to walk and strolled up the wide, traffic-free street called Steinenvorstadt. Besides being full of shops, there were dozens of eating places that spilled invitingly out onto the street. Multi-coloured seating, umbrellas and canopies; together with the joyful hubbub of conversation, gave the place a distinctive Gallic air.

Further on he passed the impressive cotton-reel shaped Bank for International Settlements. Locals called it the Bankers Bank and knew that it housed representatives from the central banks from over sixty countries. Though what they actually did was a mystery, probably only understood by academics with doctorates in finance. Belloni had read enough to know it was a controversial institution that some people believed had helped Hitler loot assets from conquered countries - and after the second world war, there had been many calls for its dissolution. But it had survived and over the years its reputation enhanced and now was an institution providing kudos to the city and its elegant building a much-loved landmark.

At the Hilton's reception he asked the girl behind the counter to connect him with Murray Majors' room. They met in the City Bar and had a drink together, before Majors suggested they make for the Wettstein Restaurant for a meal. Having loaded their plates from the buffet they settled at an isolated table and a waiter delivered two glasses of beer.

'So,' began Belloni, 'Did you manage to meet with von Murren and Baumann?' Majors grinned.

'I did.'

'And?' questioned Belloni.

'And I thought Baumann was going to have a heart attack. I don't understand German but he ranted and raved, so I clearly got the message - he was not happy.'

'Did he say anything that you did understand?'

'Oh yes, plenty, once he had calmed down. Told me it was all lies and that he would be able to prove it. He then threatened to sue the Tribune for every penny it's got and that I should go away and check my facts.'

'And von Murren?' asked Belloni. 'What was his reaction?'

'Calmness personified,' replied Majors. 'The exact opposite to Baumann! He listened quietly until I'd finished, then he stood up, came round his desk, took my arm and led me to the door.'

'He didn't say anything?'

'Yeah, as he closed the door he said, thank you for coming Mr Majors, you can expect to hear from my lawyers.'

'That was it?'

'That's all he said.'

'Are you really sure about these accusations?' asked Belloni.

'Yup, our lawyers tell me that Joe Leman found enough to prove they were manipulating the markets and that's a no no.'

'So when are you going to publish?' asked Belloni.

'Wednesday, first part on Wednesday.' replied Majors. 'And then . . . stand well back.'

'You said something about the Americans getting involved?' said Belloni.

'I did and I have already sent a copy of the article to the Department of Justice - and had a reply. Two guys will be here early next week.'

'I don't understand what this would have to do with the Americans,' said Belloni puzzled.

'Well, as I understand it,' replied Majors, wiping his droopy moustache with a serviette. 'Both of the companies involved are global companies, they operate all over the world, including the USA - money passes through US banks, so in theory US citizens are affected - and it's the duty of the Justice system to look after its people.'

'Sounds like an excuse to put more money in the government's coffers to me.' said Belloni.

'Of course . . . and once again the lawyers will line their pockets. God, if I had kids I'd sure as hell tell them to train as lawyers, can't go wrong.' Belloni nodded, his mouth full of pasta.

'But what about you, how's your enquiry going?'

'We're still at the information gathering stage,' replied Belloni. 'But I shall be visiting our wealthy friends in the next few days. It's going to be hard to find a link between these men and Joe's death. Obviously they wouldn't dirty their own hands.'

'Not too many hit-men in Switzerland I suppose' said Majors with a smile.

'Certainly, I've never come across one,' replied Belloni. 'Though probably, if the price was right, half the male population of Basel would take on the job.'

* * *

The following morning found Belloni seated in his office, together with the two officers he had tasked with finding out what they could about Baumann. At the end of the session Belloni decided the only thing he had learned, that he didn't already know, was that Baumann had access to a company jet and had been in the USA at the time of Stavi's death. He dispatched one of his men to talk to the crew in an attempt to discover Baumann's movements while away. Reluctantly, he then decided that he better go and see his boss and spill the beans about these two high-flying Basel stalwarts who were about to spectacularly crash to earth.

At lunchtime, Belloni grabbed a sandwich and a bottle of water and made his way to the Rhine. It was something he liked to do, if time allowed. He wandered along the bank deep in thought, oblivious of the grand historic buildings standing majestically on the far bank and beyond them the skyline-piercing chimneys of the chemical factories - the industry that over generations had provided the city with its wealth. He found a seat and unwrapped his Gruyere-laden sandwich, thinking about his boss's reaction to the news of the forthcoming Tribune article and the death of its writer. His boss had told him not to worry about the implications of the article. And to stay away from von Murren and Baumann. The specialists from Zurich would take care of that, he had said. Belloni's mission was to concentrate solely on finding Joe Leman's killer.

Belloni bit viciously into his sandwich and grunted. He had no intention of staying away from von Murren or Baumann; they were key to his investigation. He had objected and said as much to his boss but his superior had insisted Belloni stay away. He's worried about their reputations, thought Belloni. He's afraid of the almighty fuss they could cause if the accusations made in the article fell through.

He looked at the broad river rushing by; it was full, brown and ugly. He thought of Joe Leman being swallowed up by this impatient, gurgling, swirling monster. Somewhere along this bank, Joe must have been hit over the head, stripped and flung into the river. Belloni shuddered as he remembered the shrivelled corpse lying in the morgue, features distorted and partially eaten away. He'd seen enough dead bodies not to be squeamish but that didn't mean to say he found it easy. He could never ignore the link between the carcass stretched out before him and the life it had once so preciously housed. He was determined to bring the callous killer to book. There was no place on the streets for people with such a disregard for human life. Tomorrow he would go and see Baumann. The man had withdrawn cash from his account - that cash had been found in Stavi's house - and Stavi was dead. Obviously there was a link; it was up to him to prove it.

Belloni's thoughts were disturbed by a group of joggers trotting by. He followed their progress, as they moved away, admiring their willpower of choosing to run during their lunch break, rather than eat. Pangs of mild guilt assailed him because he knew that if he didn't take more exercise he would develop a paunch like his father and grandfather before him. He stood, deliberately pulled in his stomach, took a final swig from his water bottle and headed back to the office and reality.

CHAPTER 46

The following morning Belloni drove out to Dieter von Murren's factory. He'd taken the trouble to discover that von Murren was on site but he had not made an appointment, he needed the element of surprise. Gloria Gabric, von Murren's secretary, asked him to wait while she went into von Murren's office. Her heart was beating fast; she desperately wanted to know the reason for the visit.

Dieter von Murren was amazingly calm, thought Belloni after they had shaken hands and he was seated before von Murren's desk. Belloni couldn't help but think of a similar situation when he was a child, meekly standing at his Headmaster's desk, awaiting a reprimand for missing school. Today, the boot was on the other foot, he was in control.

'I believe that you know, Doctor von Murren, that you may be charged with illegal activities under the laws relating to competition?' Von Murren shuffled in his seat, rested his elbows on the desk and placed his hands together as if praying, his thumbs supporting his chin. He gazed unwaveringly at Belloni.

'Just the newspapers hungry for a story,' he replied slowly. 'You know how they are. Ravenous monsters always hungry for some scandal. There's no truth in the accusations.'

'These accusations,' continued Belloni - true or not, will prove very damaging, I imagine. Both to you and your company?' Von Murren didn't reply. 'They were made by Joe Leman,' Belloni paused for effect. And Joe Leman is dead . . . murdered.' There was no doubting von Murren's surprise and anxiety, as Belloni's words and their implication sank in.

'Inspector,' he said, rising to his feet and walking around the desk. 'Surely Inspector, you don't think I had anything to do with Leman's death? You told me he was missing; now you say he's dead.

What happened to the poor man ... does Maria Beckett know?'
He seems genuine, thought Belloni.

'Let's just say that his body has been found ... and it's obvious that he was killed by one or more persons ... at the moment, persons unknown.'

'Oh God,' breathed von Murren, 'poor man. No wonder you have come to see me.' He sat heavily in his chair and held his head in his hands. Belloni watched but said nothing. After what seemed an age, von Murren lifted his head and looked directly at Belloni. 'It was just a simple business arrangement. Baumann's company was having trouble in Argentina. He decided to move out and my company moved in. There's nothing criminal in that?'

'That will be for the others to decide,' said Belloni. I'm only interested in Joe Leman and who killed him . . . and why.'

'Well there's only Baumann and me involved in these accusations, neither of us would gain anything from Leman's death - it would just complicate everything.'

'How well do you know Kurt Baumann?' Belloni asked.

'He's been to dinner a few times and we've met at the odd business lunch. My knowledge of the man is all,' he paused seeking the right words; 'very superficial, I suppose.' Belloni prodded:

'You must know more.'

'Really Inspector, I don't. I'm totally consumed by my own business and family. I know that he is married; not that he and his wife seem to get on very well from what I've seen. I know he has two sons abroad somewhere. His company is very successful . . . and that he has a reputation for getting things done - not that he's very popular.'

'Have you ever been to his home?' asked Belloni, worrying, like a dog with a bone.

'Funny, you should ask that. No I haven't. Never been invited.' Belloni grunted and changed tack:

'If you and Baumann are charged following this article and found guilty, no doubt huge fines and jail sentences will follow.' He paused and let the thought sink in. 'From where I'm sitting Doctor von Murren, that provides a pretty good motive for trying to silence Joe Leman and destroying his evidence. Trouble is, that he had already filed the story and so his death and the destruction of his apartment was all in vain.'

Dieter von Murren was shaking his head;

'There's utterly no logic in trying to connect Joe Leman's death to the problems Baumann and I may face,' he said vehemently. 'None whatsoever.'

Driving back towards Basel and the sprawling facility of Global Vigour Products, Belloni rewound the interview with von Murren. He had cross-examined enough people during his relatively brief career, to be able to assess whether or not a suspect was lying and he was convinced von Murren was not involved with Joe Leman's death. 'No,' he thought, 'whatever von Murren is guilty of, it's not murder.'

Belloni negotiated his way into the GVP company car park and made his way into the reception area. He told the girl that he needed to see Kurt Baumann, produced his identity card and said there was an emergency. While the girl anxiously telephoned one of Baumann's minions, Belloni gazed at the expensive-looking murals and wondered if this was a wise way to invest the company's profits. A few moments later he was in a sixth floor office, explaining to the same protective personal assistant, whom Raziel Stavi had met, that it was imperative he saw Baumann immediately.

Belloni sank into a deep sofa while the young man disappeared back into the corridor armed with Belloni's card. He soon returned and led Belloni down the corridor, through a deep-carpeted outer office, where a smart-suited young woman glanced up from her computer. Williams, the personal assistant, introduced Belloni and left. Baumann strolled round the huge desk and thrust out a hand. Belloni registered that it was cold, small and the handshake limp.

'Inspector, they said there was an emergency?' said Baumann.

'Yes,' replied Belloni. 'I'm sorry about that. It was the only way I could persuade them that I needed to see you urgently, without an appointment.' He glanced around the room, noting the Picasso behind Baumann's desk and the Cezanne on another wall, doubtless originals. One side of the room was entirely glass and provided a view towards distant hills. Baumann grunted, indicated a chair and returned to sit behind the desk.

The lord in his castle, protected by the ramparts of his desk, thought Belloni; noting the two fat gold rings on Baumann's fingers and the expensive Rolex glinting under the cuff of the Italian suit.

The bald pate, a nice shade of brown, did not go unnoticed; causing Belloni to wonder where Baumann had acquired his tan?

'How can I help you?' questioned Baumann. Belloni took a deep breath and concentrated on the eyes of the man seated before him. They were bright blue but too close together.

'Two-hundred thousand Swiss francs,' he said quietly. 'I have found two-hundred thousand francs that I believe belongs to you.' Momentarily, the eyes narrowed and the lips tightened.

'You'll have to explain that Inspector, I don't understand,' replied Baumann.

'Nothing to explain Doctor Baumann, it's quite straightforward I have found a large sum of money and I have good reason to believe that it belongs to you.'

'I think I'd know if I lost that amount of money,' snorted Baumann. 'What makes you think it belongs to me?' Belloni gaze was still honed in on the eyes but they were pinched together, almost closed.

'Let's just say, for the moment, that I have proof the money is yours.'

'This is nonsense,' blustered Baumann. 'What proof? And where did you find this money?'

'If I were you Doctor Baumann,' said Belloni deliberately, 'I would think carefully before you continue to deny any knowledge of the money. As I said, I have proof. If you continue to refute the fact, you may find yourself charged with perverting the course of justice.' Baumann's mouth opened and closed like a goldfish drowning in carbon dioxide. He wasn't used to being dictated to.

After what seemed an age, Baumann rose to his feet, walked over to the window and gazed out over his empire. Making up his mind he suddenly turned.

'All right Inspector,' he said, almost in a whisper. 'I admit that I may have lost two-hundred thousand francs.' He sighed heavily and retuned to his chair.

'Where did you lose it?' asked Belloni.

'I've been such an idiot,' said Baumann, ignoring Belloni's question. 'Here I am responsible for billions of dollars of company money and I have been careless with a substantial amount of my own money. If the shareholders knew, I'd be out of a job.' Belloni was puzzled:

'You'll have to explain.'

'My wife and I once visited the Cayman Islands for a holiday and I always wanted to buy a property there,' began Baumann. 'The years passed but then there was an opportunity. I drew money out from the bank, sufficient for a deposit and gave it to a man to take to the Cayman's to complete the deal for me. The trouble is that since I gave him the money he seems to have disappeared. If you have found the money, hopefully you have found the man as well?' He looked questioningly at the inspector.

'Yes,' replied Belloni thoughtfully. 'The man has been found.'

'Good,' replied Baumann. 'He'll have questions to answer.'

'Start from the beginning,' said Belloni pulling out his notebook. 'Beginning with details of the property you wanted to purchase.'

'Well Inspector, you see there were several properties that seemed suitable for my . . . our . . . purposes. The man's brief was to look at each, decide which was best, according to a list of priorities that I gave him. He was supposed to open a bank account, in his own name, pay the money into this account and then use whatever was necessary as a payment.'

'And the man's name?' asked Belloni.

'Raziel Stavi,' replied Baumann unflinchingly.

'And Why Doctor Baumann did you ask Raziel Stavi to do such a task?'

'He had once done some security work for us. He was a private detective. Seemed a reliable sort of chap. I trusted him,' replied Baumann. 'And then the weeks passed and I heard nothing. I felt so utterly foolish, I thought that he had absconded with the money.' Belloni was fuming inside, though his expression remained unchanged. Baumann's alibi sounded plausible. He decided to try another tack.

'Doctor Baumann, I believe that you were in the United States . . .' he glanced at his notes, 'between April fourth and seventh.'

'Sounds about right,' replied Baumann. 'My secretary will confirm.'

'May I ask why you travelled to the US?' continued Belloni.

'Business,' replied Baumann in a what-the-hell-do you-think tone.

'Please explain sir,' replied Belloni, unruffled.

'I had meetings at the Federal Drug Administration, the FDA headquarters in Washington,' Baumann said, swivelling slightly side-to-side in his chair.

'That was on the morning of the fifth,' said Belloni, focusing closely on Baumann's eyes. 'What did you do in the afternoon - and the following day?' Baumann stopped swinging. His demeanour suddenly changed. His eyes flared and he snarled:

'Why are you quizzing me, like some common criminal - and what about my money? You came here to tell me you had found my money?' Belloni was unmoved.

'Please explain Doctor Baumann. What you did on April sixth and then we can discuss your money.' Baumann spluttered:

'I don't think I did much in the afternoon, I was tired and slept.'

'And the following day?' Belloni persisted.

'I want to make it clear Inspector,' bellowed Baumann, 'that I don't like you accusing attitude and I shall be reporting you to the Chief of Police. Keep on like this and you'll be back walking the streets?' Baumann was leaning across his desk, eyes wild, his face screwed up, as he thumped the desktop.

'There's no need to take that attitude sir,' replied Belloni quietly. 'We both know that I am just doing my job. What did you do on April sixth?'

'I don't get much time to myself in this job,' shouted Baumann. 'But I took this opportunity to do what ordinary people do, wandered the shops and art galleries.' Delusions of grandeur, thought Belloni but asked:

'Is there anyone who could corroborate that sir?" Baumann leapt to his feet, his face resembling a pickled beetroot and leaned once more across the desk.

'Right,' he threatened. 'You've asked for it. By tomorrow you'll be out of a job. Get out of here!' He yelled, pointing at the door. 'Get out!'

'I take that as a . . . no,' Belloni responded calmly, not moving.

'You're bloody right, it's a no . . . Get out.' For a moment Belloni did not move but decided Baumann was out of control and to prolong the interview would be counter productive. He unwound from his seat and stared at the quivering man leaning over the desk.

'Thank you for your cooperation Doctor Baumann. It was a pleasure to meet you. I will be back . . . and the next time we'll talk about your money.' Belloni's hand was on the door handle when Baumann recovered his composure sufficiently to call out.

'Wait, wait . . . what about the money?'

'Stew you bastard,' thought Belloni, let himself out and closed the door. The secretary grinned at him, as he crossed the office.

'Thanks,' she said, 'you've just ruined my afternoon!'

'Is your boss prone to losing his temper?' Belloni asked.

'I'm his confidential-secretary,' she smiled and returned her attention to the computer.

Seated in his vehicle in the car park, Belloni pulled out his notebook and began recording the interview. So Baumann said he had given the money to Stavi to buy a house in Grand Cayman. But while Stavi was in the Caymans the money was stashed under his floorboards in Basel. So what was the money really for? And what was Baumann up to after his meetings in Washington. So many questions, this is going to be a long job, he sighed and turned the ignition key.

The following morning, as Belloni strode through the outer office towards his inner sanctum, the duty officer called out and told him the Chief needed to see him. Fearing the worst, Belloni made his way upstairs and tapped on his superior's door. It was suddenly thrown open and Steiner, his boss hissed in his face:

'Get in here.' Belloni shuffled inside and waited. 'What do you mean disobeying my orders?' Belloni started to explain but was cut short. 'I told you in no uncertain terms to stay away from Baumann . . . and you deliberately disobeyed. Baumann has complained about your attitude and threatening manner . . . and I have been jumped on from upstairs. My job is under threat and my God . . . so is yours!'

'You told me to concentrate on Joe Leman's death,' began Belloni. 'And Baumann is a key witness. My visit had nothing to do with whatever blows up over the Tribune article.'

'That's beside the point . . . I told you to stay away!' The Chief made his weary way to his desk and flopped down. He sorted through the neatly stacked files, picked one up and handed to Belloni. 'You're off the Leman case . . . and back on the stolen vehicles' investigation.' Belloni began to object, he was at a key stage he cried.

For the second time in two days he was ordered out of someone's office but this time he was consumed with anger.

CHAPTER 47

Wednesday morning Belloni stopped at the kiosk on Barfüsserplatz and bought a copy of the Herald Tribune. Once in his office, he settled in his battered chair with a coffee, heaved his feet up onto the desk and spread the newspaper out on his knees. The enquiry relating to scores of stolen cars being whisked over the border and down to Lyon could wait.

The headlines were about yet another bomb going off in Jerusalem and the inevitable bloodletting revenge in the Gaza Strip by the Israeli army. Halfway down the page was a piece about Joe Leman's death and reference to his last piece of journalism, to be found on page three. All very bland and no reference to a connection.

It took Belloni an hour to wade through the article; he'd had to use a German/English dictionary to understand some of the unfamiliar vocabulary. His English was good enough to realize that this was a well-written and damning piece. As Majors had so eloquently put it, the fan would be scattering the proverbial faecal matter in all directions, even as he read.

Belloni drained the last of the already cold coffee, folded the newspaper and closed his eyes. Step by step he went over all that he knew about Joe Leman's death, right up to the moment he had left Baumann's office. He considered again whether or not Baumann's story about buying property and dispatching Stavi to do his dirty work seemed likely. More probable the money under Stavi's floorboards was to pay for Leman's disposal. He needed to know more about Stavi the man, he decided and whether or not he was a possible assassin. Opening his eyes he saw the file about stolen cars lying on his desk and swore, as he remembered Joe Leman was no longer his responsibility. He snorted with frustration, as he dragged his feet off the desk, picked up the phone and asked a constable to bring the file they had put together on Stavi.

'Sorry Sir,' replied the constable, 'Inspector Moret has all the paperwork.'

'Damn!' Belloni slammed down the phone and held his head in his hands. After a few moments he stood and made his way down the corridor to Moret's office. He tapped and walked in. Paul Moret's close cut grey hair was all he could see, as the man had his back towards him and was busy posting photos of Leman, Maria Beckett and Stavi on a board.

'Not much to go on,' commented Belloni. Moret turned and frowned. 'Judging from the notes, you hadn't got very far,' he muttered.

'I felt the picture was becoming clearer,' replied Belloni. I'm sure Baumann has something to do with the case.'

'According to Chief Steiner, Baumann's in the clear,' came the laconic reply. Belloni grunted:

'No one's in the clear, as far as I'm concerned.' He walked up to the board and focused on Joe Leman's smiling face. 'Listen Moret, can I have a look at Stavi's computer? There's something I need to check.'

'If the Chief finds you're interfering, he'll fire us both,' replied Moret.

'Can I take it to my office?' asked Belloni, ignoring Moret's comment. 'I'm not looking,' replied Moret and returned his attention to the board.

Back in his office, Belloni hooked up the computer to his screen and pressed the power switch. He gritted his teeth and waited impatiently for the tell-tale glow. He swore, cursing all computers, Stavi's machine was even older and slower than his own. After what seemed an age the screen was filled with folder-icons with unintelligible names. He opened one of the folders and files spilled onto the screen; he clicked on one of the files. It took an age to open and when it did the content was entirely in Hebrew. Belloni groaned and sank back in his chair; this was going to take a long while.

Late in the afternoon, the Chief came into Belloni's office, accompanied by a clean cut, sharp-suited American, who was introduced as being from the FBI.

'He's here concerning the accusations of malpractice made in the international newspaper,' said Steiner. 'I explained that you had handed over the case concerning the death of the reporter, the author of the accusations, to a colleague. But he'd like to talk to you anyway, as you made the initial enquiries.' With a nod towards the visitor he turned towards the door: 'I'll leave you together. Do look in before you leave.' Belloni waved towards a chair and settled behind his desk.

'I'm Silvio Belloni,' he said flatly.

'Jed Hoover,' replied the agent and thrust a hand across the desk. Belloni grunted.

'Following in the family business?' he joked.

'Sadly, no relation,' replied Hoover. 'I guess you know that I'm here, with two colleagues, to look into the business practices of two pharmaceutical companies?' He was an intense young man, as demonstrated by the way he sat perched, hawk like on the edge of the chair. 'I didn't know that the guy who wrote the article had been murdered, until I met with the editor in Paris.' Belloni nodded.

'Hit over the head and thrown in the river.'

'Your boss says there isn't a link . . . you know between the murder and the article. What do you think?'

'I know that I upset Baumann sufficiently with my questions that he went right to the top and got me thrown off the case.' Belloni said resentfully. Hoover whistled.

'Think you hit a nerve?' he asked.

'Possibly. He had alibis, stories and excuses. It's going to take a whole lot of time checking out each one.'

'And now that's not your job,' said Hoover sympathetically. Belloni shook his head. 'What about the guy whose taken over? Is he any good?'

'Yes, Moret's good. It's just that he has a reputation for taking the easiest option. And not upsetting Doctor Baumann any more than you're going to, might just be the easy way out.' Hoover extracted a business card from his wallet and wrote a number on the back.

'I'm staying at the Hilton, that's my room number. Let's stay in touch.' Belloni produced a card of his own and Hoover left to talk to Moret.

While Hoover was with Belloni his two colleagues were grilling Dieter von Murren in his office; the two Americans accompanied by two senior Swiss policemen from the special squad in Zurich. The more senior of the Swiss led the interview and went to great lengths to explain that this was a provisional visit to inform von Murren what the charges might be and that a team of investigators would follow to search the offices and go through all the files. He was told the enquiry would probably take several months. Throughout the interview von Murren was quiet, contemplative. He knew that if they decided to throw the book at him, they could - and disaster would follow. He answered the questions in monosyllables and as they trooped out through his door, he didn't move. He was stunned. His world was about to come crashing down.

Later that week Dieter von Murren did something he rarely did - he thought about the wellbeing of someone else - his wife! He visited his lawyer and made all the necessary arrangements to transfer the ownership of his home in Burg-im-Leimental, from his name to that of Katarzyna. He feared the worst and didn't want his family without a roof over their heads. He then visited the bank and transferred funds into Katarzyna's account, as well as a considerable sum of money to an account he held in Spain. There was no way he intended to spend any time in prison, life was too short and precious to be locked away for something he considered entirely inconsequential.

While all this was going on the enquiry team had visited Baumann, leaving him in an uncontrollable rage and a psychological mess. Once the door was closed his reaction mirrored Edvard Monch's Scream. His hands were tightly over his ears and he banshee-bellowed, as if being murdered. And then he began smashing things, first the photos of his family once neatly arranged on his desk. Followed by a huge, professionally arranged vase of flowers. Shards of glass scattered across the expensive carpet

The poor secretary the other side of the door, switched off her computer, grabbed her coat and ran down the corridor. As she passed personal assistant Williams's office, she poked her head around the door and shouted:

'He's gone mad, stark staring mad . . . run!' With that she continued along the corridor and down the stairs, not prepared to wait for the elevator. Williams meanwhile took a deep breath and headed for his boss's office. He tapped, opened the door and gasped at the scene of devastation. Baumann was seated quietly at his desk, as if nothing had happened.

'Ah . . . Williams,' he said clearing his throat. 'I need the company jet tomorrow night, had a call from the FDA, they need me in Washington. I'll only be gone twenty-four hours, no need for you to come.'

'Of course Sir,' mumbled the confused Williams.

'Oh . . . and could you get hold of a cleaner, I've stupidly knocked over that lovely arrangement of flowers and made a bit of a mess.' Williams nodded, dumbfounded, backed out of the door and returned to his office, asking himself why he continued to do this silly stupid job?

CHAPTER 48

Bruno Schmidt walked purposefully out of the prison doors, hunched into an anorak, the hood pulled over his head; he was carrying a small holdall. At the massive door, he ignored the warder's outstretched hand and the well-meaning call of 'Good Luck.'

Gazing straight ahead he made his way into the city, towards a hostel recommended by the administrator, who had written the address on a piece of paper, now clutched tightly in Bruno's sweaty palm. Once again, Bruno had played the game, he had been polite, helpful, become a 'trusty,' given perks - and let out early. At the hostel he was fed, shown to a small single room and told that in a few days someone would help him find a job, meanwhile, he was told, relax and get accustomed to being free again.

The next morning he ate breakfast early, before most of the other hostel dwellers were about and made his way towards his father's office. He walked purposefully through the old town and with each step his anger built. A couple of months earlier he had been informed that his mother had died. They generously let him attend the funeral. A miserable drab affair it was, with only he and the priest in attendance. It just wasn't fair!

Bruno rehearsed what he would say and once he found the office, he rang the bell and waited. The receptionist looked up and pressed a switch under her desk to unlock the door. Bruno was confident she wouldn't recognise him from his previous visit, as he had grown a moustache.

'Is Doctor Brandt here yet?' he asked with a disarming smile, a smile produced, as if at the flick of a switch, masking the inner rage. It was infectious and the elderly lady smiled back.

'He's going to Basel this morning, I'm afraid. I'm not expecting him in the office until tomorrow. Do you need an appointment?'

'No,' stammered Bruno. 'Doctor Brandt called me earlier to say he had a leak in his bathroom and could I come round and fix it. I'm a plumber,' he added. 'Trouble is, I was rushing and I didn't make a note of his address. He did say that he was going out and could I hurry.'

'Oh,' said the woman and immediately wrote her employer's address on the back of a business card. As Bruno left, he called goodbye over his shoulder and the woman waved in acknowledgment. Once out of sight, Bruno examined the card, the address was quite central. He decided it would take him about fifteen minutes to walk.

Brandt's apartment was on the top floor of an old four-storey building. Inside the porch, alongside the letterboxes were nameplates and bell pushes. He pressed the bell alongside Brandt's name. As he expected, there was no reply but the door into the foyer was locked. Bruno wandered around to the back of the building where there was an entrance to an underground car park. The folding-door was open. Inside he found an unlocked door leading to a staircase. In no time he was up two flights of stairs and found himself in the foyer. He continued upwards until, breathing heavily, he found himself at Brandt's apartment door. He knocked and waited. Confident that Brandt had left, he examined the eye-level lock. It was old and not particularly sophisticated. Bruno reached inside his coat, pulled out a large screwdriver and began levering. He couldn't shift it; frustration elicited a silent curse. A noise on the landing below, caused him to stop and hold his breath, someone was sweeping. Bruno made a quick decision and called down the stairs:

'Hello. Do you have the key to Doctor Brandt's apartment?' His cry brought a surprised response and a few minutes later a middle-aged, heavily bearded man came into view.

'Who are you?' he demanded. 'What do you want?'

'Doctor Brandt called and said he needed his lock replaced.' Bruno bluffed. The caretaker looked suspicious.

'He didn't say anything to me.'

'Well look here, someone has tried to get in.' The caretaker examined the damage that Bruno had just caused and swore.

'Why didn't he tell me?' he asked.

'The woman in his office said he was away for a few days and sent me round to fix it,' said Bruno.

'You said Doctor Brandt called you,' said the caretaker, staring accusingly at Bruno.

'He did,' lied Bruno. 'I came here first but he'd gone, so I went to the office and his secretary said you would let me in.' The caretaker grunted, he was still suspicious.

'You ain't got no tools,' he continued.

'They're in the van,' answered Bruno promptly. I need to see what kind of lock it is, whether to repair it or whether or not I need to replace it.'

'The wood here will need fixing,' said the caretaker rubbing a finger over the damage.

'No problem,' replied Bruno. 'I'll have that done in a jiffy. Are you going to let me in or not?' Reluctantly the caretaker pulled a bunch of keys from his overall pocket and unlocked the door. Bruno went inside and made great show of examining the lock. The caretaker didn't move.

'I don't think it's damaged,' said Bruno ' but while I'm here I take it off, clean it up and oil it. I'll repair the door jamb as well.' The caretaker visibly relaxed. 'Where will you be, if I give you a shout when I've finished?' asked Bruno.

'In the garage,' replied the caretaker and moved towards the steps.

Later that evening, lying on his bed, back at the hostel, Bruno studied the crumpled envelope upon which he had written two names and two addresses. Isobel and Dieter von Murren. He'd found these names and addresses in his father's apartment when he'd searched a bureau. Among other things, he had discovered a file full of bills and official letters for a property in Switzerland. Some of them referred to this Isobel, others to Dieter.

On a shelf and on top of the bureau, Bruno had studied a number of photographs of his father with a woman. Some photographs showed his father, the same woman and a boy, growing older. He had picked up a silver framed photograph of the same boy, as a man, wearing a graduate's cap and gown. There were several photographs of the same young man with a family. Was this his father's latest mistress and their love child, he wondered? It suddenly dawned that if this was the case, this Dieter must be his stepbrother.

It had come as a shock when he realised that he may indeed have a brother. This was something he hadn't even considered. His emotions ran wild; at first there was almost a warm glow at the thought of having a sibling. It didn't linger long. He was angry and jealous that he and his mother had been left to struggle, while his brother obviously lived a life of luxury.

He pulled a stolen photograph from his pocket and studied the happy smiling faces. Bruno glowered at the picture of his prosperous looking father with a woman who must be his wife and the young man standing alongside a beautiful woman and two young girls, obviously their daughters. The more he stared at the young man, a few years older than himself, the more he was convinced that he could see a resemblance to himself. It just wasn't fair, he and his mother doomed to spend their lives in poverty - poverty that had eventually killed her, while his father and those close to him were surrounded with all the trappings of wealth.

Bruno's mind began sifting the possibilities of how best to extract revenge against his so-called father. Perhaps, he considered, the route was through those dear to him. He peered at Dieter and the beautiful woman next to him, before he closed his eyes and allowed his thoughts to run wild.

The following day Bruno packed his meagre belongings into his holdall, together with a wallet containing several-hundred Swiss Francs that he'd stolen from his father's apartment. He left the hostel without seeing anyone and made his way to the railway station, where he bought a single ticket to Basel.

* * *

Once outside Basel's impressive, neo-baroque station building, Bruno stood, somewhat bewildered, watching bright yellow and green trams squealing in and out of the huge plaza. He bought a map from a kiosk and settled at a street-side bar with a beer. He quickly saw that the two addresses on his crumpled envelope were some way out to the west of the city and though not on a tram route, were connected by buses. He finished his beer and the moment the waitress went inside, he left without paying. He had plenty of cash and could easily afford his beer but hidden somewhere deep inside his psyche was the innate instinct to defraud society and cheat his way through life.

At the tram-stop he studied the timetable and a few moments later boarded a gleaming, yellow number ten, heading, according to the sign, to its furthest destination, somewhere called Rodersdorf.

While the tram rolled purposefully past the Zoo and through neat and tidy suburbia, Bruno watched passengers come and go; elderly, blue-rinsed ladies with baskets of groceries and harassed young mothers with prams and pushchairs. It was early afternoon; schoolchildren were still at their desks.

At Flüh he dismounted and boarded a waiting post-bus bound for Burg-im-Leimental, the village where his half brother lived. There were eight other passengers, Bruno counted - all elderly females.

The bus wound its way up a narrow tree-lined gorge until the landscape opened up onto a high plateau and the village of Mariastein, where all the other passengers dismounted and painfully made their stick-assisted way across the attractive square towards an ornate church which, judging by the spacious car-parks, was a place of pilgrimage.

A young man wearing grubby overalls climbed into the bus and stood passing the time of day with the driver until the church clock struck and the engine coughed into life. Punctuality was king, even in this deadest of dead places.

Once in Burg, the young man called out a cheery farewell to the driver, as he leapt nimbly from the bus and began to climb the steep street. Bruno followed and once clear of the bus, called out. The young man stopped. Bruno asked him if he thought there might be any casual work to be found in the village. The young man shook his head but then as an afterthought, suggested Bruno try at the hotel-restaurant, they might need someone in the kitchen. He pointed Bruno in the right direction and continued on his way.

At the Bad Berg restaurant, the owner told him that she didn't need anyone, explaining that when they were busy, there were ladies in the village she could call on.

'You might try Jacques Wolf, near the top of the hill,' she

called out as Bruno descended the steps. 'He looks after several horses, he might want some help mucking out stables, he's not as young as he used to be!' Bruno groaned inwardly - horses, he wouldn't know the front end from the rear.

Fifteen minutes later, Bruno stood, hands on hips gasping for breath. This was a bloody steep hill, he thought. He was outside a building with Wolf spelled out above the portal. He walked across and tapped on the door. There was no reply. He wandered around the side of the building and into a yard. A voice called out through the open door of an outbuilding. Bruno followed the voice and found Jacques Wolf slumped over a table, a mug in his grasp half filled with brandy. The empty bottle lying on its side.

'Mr Wolf,' asked Bruno.

'That's me,' replied Jacques breathlessly, his face creased with pain.

'You don't look well,' said Bruno. 'Can I do anything?"

'No . . . no, it's just my back. Been lifting bales of hay and buggered it up. The brandy will kill the pain . . . eventually. If I drink enough of it.' He snorted, as he attempted to drain the empty bottle into his mug. Bruno commiserated. 'Anyway, never mind me,' said Jacques, 'How can I help you?'

'Well,' began Bruno. 'The woman at the restaurant said you might have a job for me. I'm looking for some casual work, perhaps in return for somewhere to stay?' Jacques looked sharply at Bruno; certainly he could do with some help until he got his back sorted out.

'Well, as you can see, I'm not much use to anyone at the moment. Do you know anything about horses?'

'Only that they eat hay and produce a lot of muck,' joked Bruno.

'Well, as you can see, I could do with some help until my back's fixed,' Jacques responded with a grimace. There's a small room with a bed over the stable. There's a toilet and washbasin next to this office. Not exactly five star but I can find you a duvet and a towel.' He offered. 'I can't afford to pay you though,' he added.

'Sounds good to me,' replied Bruno . . . 'Until your back's better.'

On her way home, after working at Katarzyna's house, Beccy Blom called in to see how Jacques was feeling. He introduced her to Bruno and she was immediately smitten by his brooding good looks.

'Listen Beccy,' said Jacques. 'It's no good; I'm going to have to take to my bed with some painkillers. Can you find Bruno here a duvet and a towel - he's going to sleep over the stable.' She began to protest, that it was unhygienic and no one had used it for years. Bruno interrupted her and convinced her the room would be just fine. 'Then,' continued Jacques, ignoring Beccy's objection. 'Will you show Bruno the routine, collecting the horses from the field and feeding them.' He scrambled agonizingly to his feet. 'It's no good, I have to go.'

Beccy led Bruno down to the fields and he was amazed that the six horses all came when she called and followed the pair of them back to the stables. Beccy explained about feeding and then disappeared into the house to return a few minutes later armed with bedding and towels.

She led him up some steep steps at the side of the stable and into a tiny room housing a narrow bed and dressing table. There was a large skylight in the roof, affording an open view across the valley. All the time she was making up the bed, Beccy was tut-tutting about the unsuitability of the room and the smell of the horses below. When the bed had been made to her satisfaction Beccy explained that she was going to cook Jacques some supper and she would cook enough for the three of them.

'I'll call you when it's ready,' she said, disappearing down the steps. Bruno flopped on the bed and grinned. This was working out even better than he could ever have hoped for. Here he was, only ten minutes walk away from his half brother's home and his sodding, privileged family.

It was almost dark when Beccy came to the foot of the steps and called out to Bruno that supper was ready. She had laid places for the two of them on a small table in the kitchen and while Bruno pulled a cork from a bottle of cheap red wine, Beccy took Jacques' meal upstairs on a tray.

'Poor man,' she said when she returned. 'He's really in pain. Lucky he has an appointment with the doctor tomorrow.' She busied herself serving up the meal for the pair of them, urging Bruno to sit.

'Do you live here?' asked Bruno.

'Good heavens no,' laughed Beccy. 'I'm just helping out, I live a few houses down the street.'

'It's such a steep street,' complained Bruno, pouring the wine.

'I was born here,' replied Beccy. 'I'm used to it.'

'Do you have a husband?' asked Bruno.

'No,' chuckled Beccy. 'Why buy a book when you can join a library.' She laughed uproariously at her own joke. Bruno laughed too, though he didn't know what she meant - or its implication.

At the end of the meal Beccy went upstairs and returned with the tray, complaining that Jacques had hardly eaten anything and was already asleep. The bottle of rough wine was soon empty and they were halfway through a second. Beccy was talkative at the best of times but the wine had certainly loosened her tongue. Bruno was surprised and delighted to learn that Beccy worked for the von Murren's and once again congratulated himself on his good fortune. Beccy might possibly be the connection he needed to infiltrate himself into the family. He asked about Dieter, his wife and each of the children. He particularly liked the sound of the teenage daughter and remembered the attractive girls he had seen in Brandt's photograph. With the second bottle empty, Beccy lurched to her feet and offered a hand to Bruno.

'Come,' she cooed 'We'd better check the horses are all right before I leave.' He grasped her hand and she pulled him to his feet and led him towards the stable; where she chatted to each of the horses and rubbed their noses.

'Okay,' she said at last. 'They'll be fine . . . now lets tuck you up in bed.' Beccy grasped Bruno's hand again and unsteadily pulled him up the stairs; her flimsy morals obliterated by the wine.

Once inside the small, musky smelling room, to Bruno's amazement, she quickly and silently stripped off her clothes and giggling threw herself down on the bed. The dim light of a bedside lamp threw unsettling shadows. Bruno was bewildered; faint memories of the last girl to strip off in front of him, drifted into his consciousness, even though the horrific outcome had long been wiped clean.

'Take your clothes off,' insisted Beccy and when he was naked she reached out a hand and gently pulled him alongside her. He lay unmoving, as Beccy began lathering his face and neck with wet, lingering, alcoholic kisses. She whispered encouragement and soon he responded, each vigorous thrust eliciting a joyful cry from Beccy and an echoing screech from the ancient bed. Before long, the pair of them were drenched in sweat. Beccy's cries and Bruno's groans disturbed the horses below and one of them whinnied loudly, as if complaining. Beccy wrapped her arms around her lover and pulled him even closer. After a moment Bruno struggled free and fell on to his back, gasping for breath. Beccy reached out a hand.

'You made love as if you hated me,' she whispered. She couldn't help but compare Jacques furtive fumbling and this brooding stranger's brutal attack on her thin but hungry body. She was a simple soul and for some reason that she couldn't explain, had found the rough assault unbelievably exciting. Bruno said nothing but his response was to roll the poor woman onto her stomach and start again.

* * *

The following morning when Bruno awoke, he was alone. Sometime during the night Beccy had stolen away. Later, washing his face in the grubby bathroom, he heard her arrive calling out to the horses. Emerging through the door, towel in hand he looked blankly, as Beccy greeted him, wrapped an arm around his waist and rested her face momentarily on his bare chest. She'd made a real effort this morning having washed her hair and added a little lipstick and mascara.

'I'm going to cook you men breakfast,' she said, letting go and strode off towards the house.

Jacques was in the kitchen, when Bruno responded to Beccy's call. He was propped on a chair supping a mug of tea.

'Do you drive" he asked gruffly. Bruno nodded. 'Would you take me to the doctor later? Don't think I can manage it.' Bruno agreed and sat opposite him, the pair tucking into the bread, jam and coffee Beccy had placed before them.

After the simple meal Beccy helped Bruno lead the horses to the field and showed him where to pile up the muck from the stables, after he'd cleaned them out. She then pecked him on the cheek saying that she needed to go, as she was working at the von Murren's all day.

'I'll call in on my way home,' she said, 'to cook you both supper.' With a spring in her step she set off up the hill.

The doctor's surgery was in the nearby village of Metzerlen, Bruno waited in the car while Jacques had his appointment. Later he limped back to the car with a bag full of painkillers, complaining that they were the same as he had bought from the pharmacist, the last time he had a problem.

'At least he's made me an appointment with a specialist,' continued Jacques. 'Think you can drive me there on Tuesday?'

'Of course,' replied Bruno, pleased that he was wriggling his way into Jacques' confidence.

At the von Murren's household, Beccy told Katarzyna about Jacques back problem and how a 'nice young German' was helping out.

'No doubt you will meet him one day,' she babbled, 'if Jacques' arthritis don't get no better.'

Later that evening Beccy, Jacques and Bruno sat around the kitchen table tucking in to the rosti that Beccy had prepared.

'It's not right that Bruno has to sleep above the stable,' she said.

'Why not?' queried Jacques.

'Well for one thing it's damp, there's no heating - and the horses smell.'

'I'm okay,' interrupted Bruno.

It's silly when I've got a spare room,' Beccy went on. 'The nights are getting cooler; no one's used that room above the stable for years. We don't want you getting ill,' she said poking Bruno knowingly in the ribs. Bruno looked at Jacques, who shrugged his shoulders:

'It's up to you … but I still can't pay you.'

'What do you mean?' asked Beccy.

'Well, we had an agreement,' explained Jacques. 'Bruno will help out here, in return for a bed.' Beccy shook Jacques shoulder laughing:

'Good job I'm your friend then. Bruno will work for you and I'll provide the bed.' Once Beccy was satisfied that Jacques was okay to get himself to bed, Bruno collected his holdall and the pair strolled down the hill to the house where Beccy lived. She slid her hand through his arm and murmured:

'This is a much better idea.'

Once inside her cosy apartment, she gave Bruno a towel and pointed him in the direction of the shower. He hadn't had one for several days and it felt good. Afterwards he stood in the tiny hall, a towel wrapped around his waist, wondering where to go. Beccy called his name from her bedroom. Bruno peered around the jamb, she was already in bed.

'You said you had a spare room,' said Bruno.

'Bit silly to dirty another pair of sheets,' said Beccy grinning.

'You can sleep in my bed.'

'I don't have any pyjamas' said Bruno. Beccy laughed:

'Don't be daft,' she said, grabbing the end of the towel and yanking it off. It fell soundlessly to the floor and Bruno climbed into the bed.

* * *

The von Murren's were also in bed, both were reading. Eventually Dieter stuffed the papers he was studying into a folder, dropped it on the floor and turned out his light.

'I'll just get to the bottom of the page,' murmured Katarzyna. A few moments later her light was out and she lay snuggled in Dieter's arms.

'Afraid I'm away on business tomorrow,' he explained. 'I may not be back until Friday.' Katarzyna was used to his regular trips but making conversation, asked where he was going.

'Sweden,' he lied.

'Keep away from those beautiful, blonde Swedish girls,' she murmured. Dieter just grunted.

'Have you been reading the newspaper lately, the Basler Zeitung,' he asked.

'No,' she answered, 'Why do you ask?'.

'So you didn't see the article about me" he questioned.

'They're always writing about you,' she replied. 'But no, nothing lately.'

'Well, this time it's nasty. I've been accused of wrong-doing and the FBI are here making enquiries, as well as people from the European Commission,' Dieter whispered into her hair. Katarzyna stiffened, rolled over and switched on the light. She sat up shocked.

'What do you mean?' she asked anxiously.

'What I said,' replied Dieter. 'I'm going to be charged with price-fixing, manipulating the market, that sort of nonsense.'

'You mean you will be in court?' said Katarzyna horrified.

'Almost certainly,' replied Dieter. 'I have good lawyers but just in case, I want you know that you and the girls will be all right. I've taken care of that.'

'What do you mean, I don't understand,' demanded Katarzyna again, her mind working overtime.

'Please don't worry your pretty head,' he said condescendingly. Katarzyna glared at her husband, her face creased with worry. 'Depending on how things go - I may disappear,' Dieter said dramatically. 'I'm not telling you where, then you can't lie if you're asked.' At this Katarzyna burst out sobbing and Dieter pulled her protesting body into his arms. 'If you have any questions about money or anything, talk to Walter, Walter Klein in Dad's office, he'll help you.' The blunt instructions brought another paroxysm of tears. 'Don't cry,' Dieter whispered. 'Probably nothing will happen . . . but I want you to know that you and the girls will be all right financially . . . and I will be fine, even if we're not together.' His cold matter of fact tone set Katarzyna off sobbing again and a long sleepless night; whereas her husband rolled over and slept like a guiltless child.

The following morning Dieter was on a flight to Madrid, not Stockholm. At the long-windedly named Adolfo Suarez Madrid-Barajas Airport, he caught a connection to the island of Mallorca, where he took a taxi to a modest hotel near the harbour. A couple of hours later he was seated in the comfortable office of one Palma's most prestigious real estate companies. After an hour of studying the details of various properties, Dieter von Murren found what he was looking for: an old farm, desperately needing renovation, adjoining the coast in the north-western part of the island.

The next day Dieter rented a car and left the bustling capital, bound for the town of Pollença, some sixty kilometres away to the north. He hadn't visited Mallorca since he was a child but remembered visiting Cap da Formentor, with its dramatic cliffs and spectacular views. He also had a clear memory of Pollença and racing up all the three-hundred and sixty-five steps that lead from the town-square to the chapel at the top.

It took him less than an hour to reach the attractive town, where he drove through the narrow medieval streets, seeking the office of the local agent, who was to show him the property.

An hour later the pair of them were standing in what was left of a huge barn, there was a hole in the roof and one of the walls was ominously bulging, like a pregnant woman. The actual house was basically sound but the whole place had been unlived in for many years, the agent explained. The elderly man was wearing a formal, though crumpled white suit and a panama hat, which he removed at regular intervals to wipe his sweaty brow with a voluminous handkerchief.

After walking swiftly through the house the pair strolled through a neglected orange orchard, emerging from a tangle of branches to a wonderful white-sanded beach and an azure sea.
'Perfect,' thought Dieter. The perfect place to escape from the idiots who were intent on bringing him down. By the end of the day, Dieter had signed a contract and handed over a cheque, drawn on the account that he held in Madrid, in a false name.

Early the next morning, Dieter was back at the property, together with a cheerful, elderly, bearded architect, that the agent had recommended. They sat at an old picnic table in the shade of an old, gnarled olive tree, where Dieter sketched out what he wanted, and the architect took copious notes.

Back in Pollença, at the architects' office, the man produced an ice-cold bottle of wine and the men toasted the project. The plans would be ready in two weeks time, he had promised. Dieter asked about gaining permission from the local government to extend the property. The architect had assured him that there would not be a problem, he was related to all the influential officials and anyway they would be happy to see the place renovated and used to bring tourists to the area.

'And what about the actual construction, how long will that take?' asked Dieter.

'There's very little work in the area at the moment, so labour isn't a problem,' replied the architect. 'We should have it ready for you in about four months.'

Returning to Basel the following day, Dieter congratulated himself on successfully setting up his bolthole. There had been similar accusations of wrongdoing among Basel's pharmaceutical companies a few years earlier, resulting in mind-blowing fines and key personnel extradited to the USA and later imprisoned. There was no way anyone was going to lock him up. Life was too short. He remembered his father's old adage - there are only two certainties in this life - death and change! At the first sign of prison bars it would be all change. He was going to disappear.

CHAPTER 49

Belloni quietly whooped and smashed his fist into his palm. A young female policewoman had just left his office and fortunately didn't hear the stream of oaths that spewed from his lips. Something else to confront Baumann with, he thought. But he couldn't - it wasn't his case.

The previous day, in the canteen, Belloni had discreetly asked around if anyone knew of any Jews on the force. Someone had mentioned the young woman and Belloni had sought her out and asked if she spoke Hebrew. When she told him that she did, Belloni asked if she could slip into his office before she left work, at the end of the day. She had dutifully turned up and Belloni showed her Raziel Stavi's computer.

'I'm looking for any reference to the Global Vigor Products Company or its CEO, Kurt Baumann,' he explained. 'I believe that the owner of this computer may have done some work for the company, so it may be a letter or possibly an invoice.' The girl nodded and grinned.

'This may take some time,' she said. 'This isn't exactly the latest model.'

However, it wasn't long before she turned to Belloni and told him that there was no reference to either the company or Baumann on the machine. Belloni asked her if she was sure. She confirmed. Baumann had said that Stavi had done some work for the company and that is why he had given him the task of buying a property in the Cayman Islands. So where was the invoice? Later, very reluctantly, Belloni shared this information with Moret.

'Baumann told me that he gave Stavi two-hundred thousand

francs to go and buy a house in the Cayman Islands. And when I questioned him why he had asked Raziel Stavi, Baumann said Stavi had done some work for the company and he trusted him,' explained Belloni. 'There's no reference to Baumann or his company on Stavi's computer - no correspondence, no invoices.' Moret, sitting on the edge of his desk, peered at Belloni, as if to speak. Belloni held up his hand.

'You need to ask Baumann for dates and or proof of payment for Stavi's services,' he said forcibly.

'Baumann's off limits,' replied Moret. 'The Chief made it very clear.' 'Explain to him what I've just said,' replied Belloni, hiding his frustration, 'Tell Steiner, you need to check.' Moret shrugged his shoulders.

'I told you, he explicitly said I was to stay away from Baumann.'

'Okay,' Belloni didn't even bother to hide his frustration. 'Stay away but at least tell the Chief that someone needs to check one of Baumann's claims. It's my belief the man's at least a liar, maybe even worse. We can't just stay away from him because he's pals with the glitterati.'

'The what?' questioned Moret blankly.

'The Haute-monde, the upper-crust . . . you know,' Belloni gushed. And then more slowly, spelling it out: 'The privileged class that pull the strings and make puppets, like you and me, dance to their tune!' Moret looked directly at Belloni and said:

'The Chief made a big issue of you disobeying his instructions and his actual words were that if I bothered Baumann he would have me back in uniform walking the streets.' Belloni swore, spun on his heel and left Moret's office. Walking the corridor towards his own office he admitted to himself that poor Moret's hands were tied. The investigation was stymied.

A couple of days later, Belloni sat slumped in his office chair fingering the business card that the FBI man had left. Jed Hoover, he read. He flipped the card over, saw the Hilton Hotel telephone number and on impulse rang it. Belloni was somewhat surprised when, after the receptionist had connected to the room, Hoover answered.

'I wonder if we could meet?' said Belloni. 'You know . . . compare notes?'

'Sure. Can you come now and we'll have some lunch?'

In a quiet corner of the restaurant, Belloni told Hoover about the need to prove Baumann's claim that Raziel Stavi had done work for his company.

'We've taken a load of files away from Baumann's office,' replied Hoover. 'But I guess if Stavi put in an invoice for his work it would be in the accounts department. I could easily ask.' Belloni expressed his gratitude.

'Any idea of a date?' Hoover enquired. Belloni shook his head:

'Not a clue. In fact,' he continued. 'I don't think Stavi ever did any work for Baumann. I'd just like to prove that he's a liar.'

'He's certainly a complex and unlikable human being,' stated Hoover. 'It helps in this job that I really dislike the man.'

'He certainly has a temper,' said Belloni remembering his last meeting.

'He's actually not around at the moment,' said Hoover, finishing his pasta. Belloni looked puzzled.

'Seems he's taken the company jet to Washington. According to his PA, he's due back on Friday.' Belloni felt a nerve quiver down the whole length of his spine.

'I thought that you might be restricting his movements, taken his passport,' he said apprehensively.

'Well we hadn't really got going,' replied Hoover. 'I needed to ask him a question but when I phoned this morning they told me he left yesterday. Something about appointments at the FDA.' The nerve in Belloni's spine twitched again.

'If I were you, I'd check up that he really has appointments in Washington.'

'You think he's done a runner?' asked Hoover quizzically.

'It seems a bit early in the enquiry but . . . well . . . I wouldn't trust the guy as far as I can throw him,' replied Belloni.

'I'll get my man on to it the moment I get back and let you know,' Hoover added, now feeling worried.

'Please don't leave a message. Speak to me directly. The Chief has banned all contact with Baumann and if he finds out that I'm not looking for stolen cars, he'll have me chucked out of the force.'

'That sounds somewhat bizarre, to say the least,' said Hoover.

'Our friend Baumann moves in very rarefied circles and he's using that influence to keep people off his back.'

'Well that in itself is mega-suspicious,' said Hoover.

'I agree. There's no doubt Steiner is being leaned on from on high.' Hoover looked thoughtful:

'What you said about Baumann's trip. You've got me worried. I think I'll skip coffee, go back to the office and check Baumann really does have appointments in Washington.' Hoover left Belloni to his thoughts and guiltily surveying the desert menu.

Belloni had only been back in his office a couple of hours and was draped over his desk, pouring over the list of stolen cars. The urgent ringing of his phone broke his concentration. It was Hoover.

'I checked up on Baumann,' he began. 'Seems the company jet landed at Washington and Baumann and his crew took a taxi to a central hotel.' Belloni thought Hoover sounded relieved. 'Apparently they have a flight plan to leave Friday morning . . . but I haven't yet been able to discover if Baumann actually has appointments with anyone at the FDA.' Belloni suggested that Hoover contacted Baumann's personal assistant, to ask for his contacts at the FDA offices.

'Good thinking,' Hoover replied. 'I'll get on to it.'

When Belloni arrived at work on the following Monday, the officer at reception told him the Chief wanted to see him. Inwardly he groaned, he'd got nowhere with the stolen cars' problem. He'd no idea what he could say to his boss.

He was surprised to find when he entered the Chief's office that Hoover and Moret were ahead of him. Steiner urged them all to sit but Hoover remained on his feet.

'You all know,' he began, 'that I'm here to investigate Baumann's business affairs. I met him just once, last week, maybe no longer than ten minutes but my men have been to his offices and taken away several boxes of files and a couple of computers.' Steiner started to interrupt. 'Let me continue sir, if I may,' said Hoover authoritatively. 'Baumann went off to Washington in the company jet, telling his staff he had appointments at the Federal Drug Administration's offices in Silver Spring. The company jet arrived back Friday evening but Baumann was not on it.' Hoover paused for dramatic effect. Belloni closed his eyes in frustration. 'It seems he, Baumann, telephoned the pilot and said something had cropped up.

The pilot was ordered to return to Basel . . . and that he himself would return on a regular flight, once he had dealt with the issues that had arisen . . . and he wasn't sure how many days these so called issues would take.'

'I'm sure Doctor Baumann had a good reason to stay. He's not the sort of person to run away from his responsibilities,' said the Chief.

'So you actually know Doctor Baumann, do you sir?' asked Hoover looking Steiner in the eye.

'Well no,' choked Steiner. 'Just met him a couple of times at official functions . . . but he has an excellent reputation . . .' His words hung in the air, as the others stared. Hoover ignored the Chief's outburst of support and continued:

'Baumann told his staff that he had important appointments at the FDA. My enquiries have revealed that he had no such appointments . . . and his own personal assistant can think of nothing urgent that would require this trip to Washington.'

'What are you saying?' asked Steiner.

'I'm suggesting that Baumann, knows that this enquiry I'm conducting, will lead to his downfall,' said Hoover; 'And probably a prison sentence. Your man here,' he nodded at Belloni. 'He thinks there's more. And maybe Baumann is directly linked to the death of the journalist, whose investigation started this whole process.'

'Preposterous!' said the Chief, his face gradually growing pink.

'Sorry sir,' said Belloni. 'But it's not preposterous. I had a whole file of circumstantial evidence that Kurt Baumann failed to adequately explain. And,' he paused: 'almost two-hundred thousand Swiss francs of Baumann's money found in a dead man's flat!' The wind taken completely out of his sails, Steiner sank back in his chair. He looked at Belloni:

Why didn't you tell me this earlier.'

'I tried sir,' replied Belloni. 'But . . . with all due respect, you didn't want to know!' Steiner shot Belloni a sharp look before turning to Hoover.

'Try contacting Baumann's wife and see if he has been in touch and if she knows what has kept him in America and when he is due to return.'

'My German's rusty,' replied Hoover. 'It would make more sense if Belloni here went to see her.' Reluctantly Steiner agreed.

* * *

Early that afternoon Belloni drove out to Gempen and soon found the locked gates at the end of the drive leading to Baumann's house. He parked and rang the bell alongside an intercom attached to the gate pillar. As he waited for a response, he gazed around. The whole area was surrounded by tall trees, casting deep shade. It was dank and dark. He remembered that it was near here, some years earlier, a British plane had crashed. A charter-flight full of mothers from a small, rural English town on a Christmas shopping trip - a trip that left over forty orphan children. It struck him that the whole drab surroundings still seemed to be in mourning. His musings were interrupted by a female voice.

'My name's Belloni. I'm a police inspector. Is that Mrs Baumann?'

'It is,' the woman replied.

'Would it be possible to come in and have a chat' asked Belloni.

'What about?' the woman replied.

'I'll explain when I see you,' Belloni said. The gate swung open. Belloni returned to his car and drove slowly up the rhododendron-lined drive. A blonde haired woman in her early fifties was waiting at the door. Belloni showed Mrs Baumann his identity card and she invited him into a large comfortable lounge, where a log fire burned in the grate. He heard dogs barking in another room, the woman shouted and they stopped.

'I really wanted to speak to your husband,' Belloni began.

'I'm afraid he's not here,' she replied.

'Do you know where he is?' asked Belloni.

'He works in Basel, at GVP, I suppose that's where you'll find him,' she continued.

'When did you last see your husband Mrs Baumann?' asked Belloni. The woman cocked her head on one side and pulled a face.

'Maybe a month ago,' she said.

'You haven't seen you husband for a month?' repeated Belloni, unable to hide his surprise.

'Look Inspector, if you must know. My husband lives here but we rarely communicate.'

'So, you don't actually know if he is in the country or not?'
'No,' the woman replied. 'He could be on the moon for all I know!'

Back in Basel Belloni informed Chief Steiner, Moret and Hoover of his useless visit.

'It was so bizarre,' he complained. 'Living under the same roof but living totally independent lives.'

After listening to Belloni's account, the Chief informed Moret and Belloni that he had telephoned the man Williams, Baumann's personal assistant and insisted that he telephone the moment he heard anything from Baumann; whether that be a telephone call or the fact that he had returned.

Belloni had reluctantly returned to his file on stolen cars, when Moret poked his head around the door.

'I'm at a total loss,' he moaned. 'The trail is totally dead.'
Belloni commiserated.

'It looks like Baumann is our only hope . . . and he's gone AWOL!' The pair talked around the subject for a few minutes before Moret said:

'Listen Silvio. Why don't I ask the Chief to let you take over the case again? You were in right from the beginning.' He struggled to explain his reasoning. 'I've read all the case notes, all the witness statements but you probably have more of a feel for the characters involved. Things that don't show up in the print.'

'I don't mind you asking,' replied Belloni. 'But I doubt he'll change his mind.' An hour later Belloni was summoned to Steiner's office and told to sit.

'I've read all the case notes,' said the Chief. 'Moret seems to be at a dead end.' Belloni shuffled in his chair but said nothing. 'I find it hard to believe that Baumann has anything to do with the journalist's death but the fact that you found the money that he had drawn out of his bank account in Stavi's apartment, does mean he has questions to answer.' Belloni nodded and mumbled agreement.

'His explanation that he gave Stavi the money to buy a house is, well, I suppose, plausible . . . but,' he paused. 'There are questions to answer and facts to be checked.' Steiner looked up.

'I'm sorry that I was harsh on you,' he raised his eyebrows and continued. 'You can guess why. Our friend Baumann, as I'm sure you know, has friends in high places!' The Chief got to his feet and stretched. 'I think it makes sense that you take over the Leman case again. I've talked to Moret, he's in agreement.' Belloni nodded acceptance but in reality, was ambivalent. Part of him was pleased but he knew deep down that he was on to a loser.

CHAPTER 50

Several weeks passed by. For some, particularly Belloni, each day dragged interminably. There was absolutely nothing solid to get his teeth into. But for others the weeks flew by like melting ice in the alpine spring.

Dieter von Murren returned from Spain to discover his assistant, Gloria, in a psychological mess. The sight of three smart-suited, silent officials invading the offices and stuffing boxes with files had filled her with dismay. But when they unplugged the computers in both her office and von Murren's and loaded them into the hired van, the usually, ultra-calm Gloria flipped.

When von Murren arrived at his office, he found Gloria seated at her desk, almost literally counting paperclips. She looked up startled.

'I didn't expect to see you,' she gasped. 'When you didn't show up this week, I thought they'd locked you up.'

'Sorry, I didn't have time to tell you I'd be away,' he said, draping a comforting arm around her shoulder and slipping an elegantly wrapped gift into her hand. She mouthed her thanks, as he kissed her cheek.

'I didn't know what to do,' she said. There were tears in her eyes. 'I cancelled all your appointments for the rest of this week and next,' she looked enquiringly at her boss. 'I hope I did right?' He nodded.

'We have to try and keep going the best we can,' he said. Gloria thought that he looked amazingly calm, considering the circumstances.

'They've taken away our computers,' she repeated, indicating the gaps on their respective desks.

'What about the main office?' he asked.

'No they haven't been in there.'

'Good,' said von Murren. 'At least the business of orders and deliveries can go on as normal.'

For von Murren, he was one for whom the weeks flew by. He held meetings individually with his key staff members. He met twice with Hoover, as well as senior policemen from the special branch in Zurich. He successfully kept his temper, despite the probing questions.

At home, he'd had a greater problem dealing with Katarzyna's questions. She had been like a terrier demanding to know what he meant about disappearing. In the end they had quarrelled, and not for the first time, she slept in another room, only deigning to speak in the presence of the children.

Hoover visited Belloni a couple of times. On his first visit he dropped the bombshell that Baumann had not returned to Basel and that the FBI were busy in Washington trying to trace his movements. It seemed that once he had informed the aircrew that they were to return to Basel without him, he checked out of the hotel and like the will-o'-the-wisp disappeared.

On Hoover's second visit he explained that the team searching for Baumann had drawn a blank. No one of that name had taken a flight from any of the east-coast airports and except for paying his hotel bill; his credit card had not been used. Car rental companies were being checked and some poor soul was trolling through CCTV footage from around the hotel and the airport. To all intents and purposes said Hoover, Baumann had done a Lord Lucan! Hoover also told Belloni that the Swiss police had confiscated von Murren's passport.

'We don't want him skipping the country as well,' he had said.

The loss of his passport really irked von Murren. He cursed himself for not considering this possibility, the lack of a passport would ruin his escape plans. He telephoned his father in Germany and explained that it was imperative that he had a passport to visit clients or his business would suffer. His father's response was one of disgust. He was appalled that his son had broken the law and refused to continue the conversation and put down the phone.

The next day von Murren visited his father's office in Basel and while sitting drinking coffee with Walter Klein, his father's faithful retainer, he explained his dilemma. The old man looked worried but admitted that he did know someone who might know how to go about obtaining an illegal document.

The following Saturday, Katarzyna having taken the girls to town, von Murren decided to go for a hack. He made his way to the stables where a man he did not recognise was helping one of the regular girls to muck out a stable.

'Hello,' he called, 'Who are you?'

'My name's Bruno,' the man replied leaning on his shovel.

'Where's Jacques?'

'He's hurt his back, I'm helping out until he's better.'

'Poor man, sorry to hear that. Give him by best wishes,' replied von Murren. The girl brought the mare from the stable and the pair of them busied themselves fitting the saddle. Bruno returned to his shovelling, at the same time keeping a watchful eye on his step brother; occasionally stopping to watch, seeking similarities. By the time von Murren eventually rode away into the field, he had decided there weren't any. When the girl returned to complete the clean up job, Bruno asked:

'How d'you get on with him?' he nodded his head in the direction of the disappearing rider.

'Hardly ever see him,' replied the girl. 'He's always working.' At that moment Maria Beckett appeared and the stable girl introduced Bruno. She proffered a hand, which Bruno shook.

'So you help out in the house?' he asked.

'Not exactly,' replied Maria. 'I look after the children.'

'How old they?' asked Bruno.

'Stephanie is fourteen and Claudia twelve,' replied Maria. At that moment Beccy Blom appeared and called out a greeting, Bruno nodded. The three women were standing together. Bruno, leaning again on his shovel, ran his eye critically along the line. No matter how good she was in bed, Beccy Blom was a scrawny bitch compared with the others, he concluded. He could do with a change.

Over the next few weeks Bruno found excuses to spend a great deal of time at the von Murren household. Mainly he helped in the stables but he looked for other ways to wriggle his way into favour. The stable girls, Flavia and Simone, were grateful for his help, especially with the heavy jobs. And though they laughed and joked with him, and admired his good looks, they whispered to each other, quietly behind his back, that there was something distinctly odd about the surly, young German.

He'd been introduced to Katarzyna and quite blown away by her fine features and golden hair. She was even more beautiful than she appeared in the family photograph that he had stashed away in his suitcase. He watched like a besotted schoolboy each time she appeared. He was especially moved on the occasions that she came to go riding, wearing her skin-tight jodhpurs. Each time he would stand and stare as she rode off towards the forest. It was like watching a Goddess.

Out in the yard, Bruno took out his frustration by chopping logs and later insisted on carrying the heavy basket into the house. Looking around the luxurious lounge, he could not help but feel anger, when he compared his own lifestyle to that of his brother. It just wasn't fair.

Later, back out in the yard Katarzyna had returned and was bent over scrubbing the mud from her horse's flanks. Bruno ran a lustful eye over the shapely hips contained in the mud-splattered jodhpurs and gulped. He grabbed a brush from Flavia and took over rubbing vigorously on the opposite side of the puffing gelding. At every opportunity he slyly glanced at Katarzyna. The line of perspiration above her lip, the way her clothes clung to her sweating body; he was overwhelmed with desire.

Satisfied that the horse was properly groomed, Katarzyna stood hands on hips and watched, as Flavia led the horse away to the stable. Bruno stood hands clasped behind his head and gazed hypnotised at Katarzyna. Suddenly aware of his intense gaze, Katarzyna smiled, somewhat embarrassed, turned on her heel and headed for the house.

Bruno followed Flavia and the horse into the stable, his head swimming with lust. The stable was one that he had carefully cleaned earlier and the floor was covered in fresh straw. Flavia was continuously talking to the horse, rubbing his nose, as its lengthy tongue flicked out, licking her hand.

'We need to get some hay in the feeder,' she said, pushing past him and into the adjoining loosebox, stacked with bales. Bruno followed, saying that he would carry the hay. He closed the door quietly and the room darkened, lit only by a single shaft of light pouring through a tiny, cobwebbed window. Flavia asked what he was doing and then gasped, as he gathered her into his arms locking his mouth over hers. Nineteen-year-old Flavia was taller than Bruno and athletically built; at first she struggled but gradually succumbed to his darting tongue and roving hands. In an instant she was half naked and sprawled across a hay bale with Bruno deep inside her, pumping like a piston engine; not seeing the plump figure below him but only Katarzyna's smiling face. Flavia, unable to move, flailed about, a hand clapped to her mouth, desperately trying to stifle her ecstatic cries.

Neither was aware when the door opened and Simone stepped into the room carrying a two-pronged pitchfork. When she realised what was happening she held the long-handled fork like a lance and quietly called out:

'Flav … are you okay? Or shall I stick this up his arse?' Crushed under Bruno's flailing body, Simone caught a shake of the head. She closed the door again and stepped nearer, fascinated by the erotic scene played out in the shadows. A spot of brilliant sunlight, reflected by a hanging bridle, played up and down the rippling muscles of Bruno's spine and rhythmic, clenching buttocks. Simone unashamedly watched, totally absorbed. The spell was broken when, with a huge expelling of breath, Bruno climaxed and collapsed onto the near fainting Flavia.

Unwittingly, Simone momentarily laid a hand on Bruno's shoulder. After a few seconds Bruno stood, leaving Flavia exposed and gasping. He turned and leered at Simone. She avoided his eye but bent down and picked up his pants from the floor before she reached out and wrapped an arm around his waist.

'Come,' she murmured and led him into the empty box next door. While Bruno perched on a straw bale, Simone struggled to pull her jeans over her boots. Bruno looked around the stable and noted two rings attached to the wall for tying up the horses. There was a length of rope on the floor. As Simone continued her balancing act, Bruno stood and idly looped the rope through each of the rings, then turned to face the half naked woman.

He stepped towards her and kissed her willing lips, pulling her close. And then, gently, as if leading a temperamental mare, he eased his willing victim towards the rings.

In the adjoining stable Flavia still lay stretched out on the hay bale, her mind a blank but sore and feeling as if she had been run over by a steamroller. Groans and squeals from next door brought her to her senses and zombie-like she slowly began to dress.

Some time later, Flavia staggered out into the yard. Bruno was leaning against a fence sucking on a rolled cigarette. He didn't look at her. She didn't speak. Cigarette finished; he ground the stub under his heel, picked up his jacket and began walking towards the drive leading towards the village.

Just at that moment a gleaming Mercedes pulled up in front of the house and Ferdinand Brandt, Dieter's father, stepped out. Bruno cursed his luck and turned back towards the stables but he had been seen.

'You,' called out his father, his face turning a delicate shade of pink. A woman eased herself out of the passenger door. Bruno presumed his father's wife or latest mistress.

'Come here,' ordered his father. Bruno turned but didn't move. 'What are you doing here?' demanded his father, walking purposefully towards him.

'I work for Doctor von Murren,' replied Bruno flippantly. Brandt suddenly aware that his wife was looking quizzically at him, coughed and urged his wife into the house. Once she was out of sight, Brandt strode right up to Bruno, until they were almost touching.

'What do you mean, you work for my son?' he asked, lowering his voice when he noticed a puzzled Flavia looking at them.

'Haven't you got any work to do?' he bellowed belligerently at Flavia. Embarrassed and annoyed she turned and went into the manége.

'I thought you would like the idea of me getting to know my brother,' grinned Bruno. Brandt snarled angrily, his face now purple, his blood pressure dangerously above normal.

'Wait till my son gets home. I'll make sure he throws you out.'

'I don't think you would really want him to know about poor old me, your other son,' mocked Bruno.

'You're a sick, excuse for a human being. Not fit to be around decent people,' Brandt continued, beside himself. 'I'll tell him you're a criminal. You'll see . . . you'll be out on your neck . . . and good riddance.'

Bruno clenched his fists but before he could think of landing a blow, his father turned and strode angrily towards the house.

Bruno too was fuming, he kicked the shovel across the yard, went inside the first empty loosebox he came to, closed the door and marched up and down, furiously talking quietly to himself. Eventually the anger subsided enough for him to think rationally. If his father did tell his brother he had been in prison, he would be banned from the property and his chances of dragging Katarzyna under his spell would be lost - and after all he had done and all the time he had invested to get near to her.

His eyes alighted on an open toolbox and a cruel, malicious thought rushed into his mind. He almost ran across to the bench, where he rummaged among the tools. Cutters. A large, powerful pair of wire-cutters. He found what he was looking for and tested them, cutting an imaginary cable in the air.

Slipping them into his pocket he wandered nonchalantly outside. All was quiet. The visitors were in the house. His brother was not yet home. He looked around, no sign of the stable girls. In a flash he was on his back and wriggling under the Mercedes. He found the right-hand brake cable and with a struggle cut it clean through. Fluid dripped slowly down his sleeve. He wriggled further under and managed to tear a hole in the other cable but failed to chop it right through. He thought he heard someone shouting and froze. He waited and listened. Satisfied it was quiet again, he rapidly squirmed from under the car, stuffed the cutters into his pocket and sauntered down the drive towards the village. So dear, loving father, let's see what happens, he thought to himself.

Flavia had been really offended by Katarzyna's father-in-law's rebuke. She was not used to being spoken to in such a manner. Inside the confines of the Manége, the indoor riding area, she quietly fumed. Suddenly, she remembered Simone and the fact that she hadn't seen her outside. Flavia made her way towards the looseboxes. Drawing near, she heard sobbing and called out. Fearing the worst, she looked inside a couple of boxes. Nothing.

Throwing open the door on the third box, she stumbled back at the scene that greeted her. Simone was strung up like a side of beef, totally naked, her knickers stuffed in her mouth and uncontrollably sobbing; a pile of clothes at her feet. Flavia untied the rope and Simone fell into her arms.

'The bastard,' she wept. 'The wicked, uncaring bastard. I'll kill him!'

Later that night, Bruno was eating dinner with Jacques and Beccy when it happened. But they were unaware! The solid seventeenth century walls of the old farm so thick, they heard nothing.

Ferdinand Brandt and his wife had kissed their family goodnight and set off down the drive heading for their house in nearby Hofstetten. The car, in low gear, moved slowly down the long, gravelled drive, the headlights casting ominous shadows. Once over the cattle grid, the automatic gearbox moved up a notch and the speed increased. Approaching the ancient water trough, Brandt pushed the brakes and the brake-fluid squirted uselessly on the road. By the time the Mercedes reached Jacques' house it was out of control, with Brandt shouting in fear, as he pumped the brakes to no avail. The incline became steeper. Isobel von Murren was screaming in terror. Houses on either side of the road. Nowhere to go. For a moment Brandt took a hand off the wheel and tried to force the sophisticated gearbox into manual mode. It wouldn't go, he glanced down, just as the front wheel clipped the protruding wall of a house, the vehicle spun wildly round, flipped up onto its roof and summersaulted a dozen times or more to the bottom of the hill, where it crashed through a fence and dropped several feet into a garden, puncturing the petrol-tank in the process. For about ten seconds, after the car came to rest, there was utter and complete silence, such an eerie contrast, after the ear-shattering cacophony - and then the petrol leaked across the hot engine - and the car exploded. Windows were blown out of the nearby house, in what proved to be the loudest explosion and the fiercest fire that the good folk of Burg-im-Leimental had ever experienced.

CHAPTER 51

The following afternoon the charred remnants of the once gleaming Mercedes were taken away for examination. A small crowd gathered to watch, including Beccy Blom.

Gloom had descended on the von Murren household. Katarzyna and the children totally traumatised by the horrifying death of the girls' grandparents. Beccy Blom later explained what she had witnessed at the bottom of the hill. All hoped the tragic couple were dead long before the final explosion and fire.

Dieter von Murren, initially shocked by the death of his parents, overcame any grief that he might have felt, by throwing himself into the business of clearing up the home in Hofstetten and organising his father's business affairs.

A week after the accident, a high ranking policeman visited the von Murren home and explained that the initial examination of the car had proved inconclusive, due to the destruction caused by the flames.

'Mechanical failure the most likely cause,' he had said.

Bruno stayed away from the von Murren's home for a couple of weeks. He wasn't sure whether his father would have said anything to anyone about knowing him. He kept his bag packed, in case he had to make a run for it. He had smiled to himself, as Beccy Blom described the state of the vehicle when the police took the car away. 'Just a shell,' she had said. That, he hoped, meant no evidence of his handiwork.

Bruno's actions had been taken on the spur of the moment, he'd really meant to hurt his father, for the way he had treated his mother, by annihilating those most dear to him - first his wife and then his son. Now with his father and his wife dead, he needed someone else upon which to vent his spleen. The obvious target was

Dieter von Murren, his successful, snotty-nosed-brother.

He lay in Beccy Blom's bed dreaming of hurting his brother through his children and his wife. There would be accidents to his daughters. He planned to get to know them better, to earn their trust. And afterwards, once his brother had suffered the pain of their loss, he too would die. And in her grief, his beautiful wife would look to him, Bruno, for love and comfort. He sighed at the thought, wrapped an arm around Beccy's sleeping body and allowed his imagination to run wild.

Over the following days Bruno busied himself doing odd jobs for Jacques. He had become more confident around the horses and one day Beccy Blom even encouraged him into the saddle of one of the more sedate animals and walked him around the field. He knew that being a competent rider would help him develop relationships with the von Murren girls and their mother and so he strenuously persevered.

* * *

The stable girls Flavia and Simone both lived in Metzerlen, the next village to Burg. Each lived with their parents. One evening they met in the cosy Restaurant Kreuz, found a quiet corner and ordered a beer. They hadn't spoken since the incident with Bruno and were embarrassed. They avoided each other's eyes and talked about everything and anything other than Bruno's assault. They too, were totally shocked about the death of Dieter von Murren's parents and together pored over the story in the restaurant's copy of the local newspaper.

'You know what's funny?' began Flavia.

'What?' asked Simone.

'Well . . . when you weren't there. And the old man and his wife arrived . . . he, the old man, seemed really upset to see Bruno.'

'Why?" asked Simone.

'I dunno but he shouted at him. And then he shouted at me to go away and do something, as if he didn't want me to hear what he was going to say to Bruno.'

'He shouted at you?' queried Simone.

'Yeh, haven't you got any work to do, he said.'

'Cheeky bugger,' said Simone. 'Never did like him.'

'No nor me,' replied Flavia. 'Not that I'd wish him to be fried like he was.'

'Ooh, it don't bear thinking about,' said Simone sipping her beer. 'Talking about that bugger Bruno . . . whatever his name is,' said Flavia, grasping the nettle. 'I mean, are you all right? Stringing you up like so much washing and then buggering off.' Simone stared into her glass.

'Yeh . . . it was my own fault, I suppose. I sort of dragged him off you and into the other loosebox.'

'You don't think we should go to the police then?' asked Flavia, staring at her friend.

'Well I did think about it,' replied Simone. 'I mean his behaviour wasn't natural. He really scared me. He didn't say a word. He was just like some bloody ruttin' animal. If you hadn't come, I reckon he would have left me hanging there to rot,' she swilled the beer around in her glass. 'What about you? He had you too?'

'Makes my boyfriend seem a bit tame,' sighed Flavia, with a giggle. 'Not that I'd let him do it again,' she said firmly.

'Too bloody right,' agreed Simone. She thought for a moment. 'What we should do is tie him up on those rings and leave him there naked for the night.' They both laughed at the thought.

'You know he's staying with Beccy Blom?' said Simone.

'No,' replied the incredulous Flavia.

'Yes, moved out from Jacques' place.'

'Oh well, no doubt that's where he gets his dirty ideas from!' The girls both burst out laughing again, ordered another beer and planned their revenge.

* * *

Police Inspector Silvio Belloni read of the accident in the local newspaper; his interest immediately peeked, when he realized it was von Murren's parents who had died in the shocking accident. For a while he pondered if there could be a connection to the deaths of Joe Leman or Raziel Stavi but in the end decided it made no sense. Nevertheless, he cut out the article from the newspaper and added the cutting to his file.

CHAPTER 52

Following the disappearance of Kurt Baumann, all the weight of the criminal investigation fell on Dieter von Murren. Over the following weeks, after his parents' death, there were either officials sifting through his filing cabinets or his presence was demanded at various hearings. Finally he was issued with a summons and later appeared in court, where he was charged with malpractice, a date for a hearing arranged and granted bail.

Von Murren had gathered a formidable legal team around him but he knew the authorities had their teeth into the case and were unlikely to accept his defence. His lawyers, however were confident and considered that his best chance lay in the fact that the prosecution's case was based on Joe Leman's article, he was dead and all his sources had disappeared. Dieter von Murren was less confident because the FBI had demanded that he be extradited to face trial in the U.S.A. and previous experience had shown that their bullying usually paid off.

* * *

Silvio Belloni was seated alongside the Rhine drinking from a can of coke and scanning the local tabloid newspaper. He was utterly frustrated by the brick wall confronting him, with regards to the deaths of Joe Leman and Raziel Stavi - so he had walked out of his office, seeking fresh air and inspiration.

An article inside the paper detailed the charges against Dieter von Murren; as well as interviews with people who knew him. There were photographs of von Murren leaving his office and entering court, as well as several hazy telephoto pictures taken on his property by a lurking member of the paparazzi. He read a comment from von

Murren's defence lawyer, stating that the evidence was circumstantial; there was no proof of any wrong doing and that he expected the judge to throw out the case before it even got started. From what he'd heard and read of the case, Belloni tended to agree. Even the FBI man, Hoover, had confided that there might not be enough evidence for a conviction.

'So,' thought Belloni, 'If that was the case, why had Kurt Baumann fled?'

Belloni folded the paper and crushed the empty can under his foot and tossed both into a nearby rubbish bin, when a thought struck him. He remembered Maria Beckett saying that she had bugged von Murren's dining room and the resulting tape had caused Joe Leman's Eureka moment. What if Joe Leman had hired bugging equipment from Raziel Stavi? Could he prove it? Might it provide a link to the two deaths? With almost a spring in his step, Belloni headed off back to his office.

* * *

'Okay,' said Belloni, later that day. 'Take me through the process again.' The young policeman, the forces' electronics expert, pointed at several pieces of equipment lying on the large table.

'These sir,' he repeated, 'are sensitive, directional microphones. And this box is the recorder that holds the tape.'

'How many of these recording boxes did we find?' asked Belloni.

'Four,' replied the policeman.

'And they're all empty, no tape in any of them?'

'All empty.'

'What about all this other stuff?'

'These are listening devices you can attach to a telephone,' the policeman responded, pointing. 'This radio is actually a movie camera.' The policeman pointed out all the different devices that formed part of Stavi's spying arsenal.

'And that larger box, what does that do?' asked Belloni.

'It's for playing back the tapes and making copies.

'Making copies?' queried Belloni. The policeman nodded.

'Did you find any tapes?'

'About a dozen, Sir,' replied the policeman. 'Here in this

box.' Belloni opened the lid of the cardboard box. All but one of the tapes was in their original plastic containers and sealed. He picked up the box with the broken seal.

'Can you play this, to check if there's anything on it? The policeman took the tape and spent several minutes fiddling, while Belloni paced impatiently around the room. After what seemed an age, the room was suddenly filled with the sound of a piano. Belloni stopped dead in his tracks. The policeman turned down the volume. Male voices could be heard speaking softly, the murmur of female voices in the background. Belloni's heart skipped a beat when he recognized Dieter von Murren's voice, first singing and humming quietly to the music and then, quite clearly:

'And what about Argentina?'

Later, like Joe Leman, before him, Belloni spent countless hours at his desk, plugged into a pair of headphones, transcribing what was being said on the tape. At the end of the second day, weary from the concentration, he had a typed transcript. Small wonder Joe Leman had been happy with what he heard - Baumann and von Murren were screwed. Belloni reached for the telephone and called Hoover.

* * *

The same evening, von Murren's assistant, Gloria and Maria Beckett were sipping wine in the International Hotel discussing the fact that their boss had now been charged with a long string of offences that, seemed to them, likely to land him in jail. Gloria was concerned for her job, Maria for Katarzyna and the children.

'I overheard Dieter telling his wife that the case would be dropped because there was no proof,' she said. 'He thinks that everything depends on Joe's article and he's not around to explain what he discovered.' Gloria lay a hand over Maria's.

'They've taken so much stuff away from the office,' she said. 'I'm sure they can prove he and Baumann were up to no good.' A short outburst of loud laughter caused Gloria to look up. Two men were standing at the bar, enjoying a joke.

'That's the guy from the FBI,' whispered Gloria, surprised 'He's been in and out of our office, like a fiddler's elbow.' Maria followed her gaze and gasped.

'The other man is the police inspector in charge of Joe's case!' She said. At that moment Belloni half-turned and saw Maria. He took Hoover's elbow and led him towards the two women. He reached out a hand:

'Miss Beckett, Miss Grabic' he said. 'This is a colleague, Jed Hoover. May we join you.' The ladies reluctantly shuffled along the sofa, making room for Hoover, while Belloni dropped into an armchair facing them, across a glass-topped coffee table.

'We've met,' said Hoover to Gloria, oozing charm. 'Sorry, if we've been making your life difficult.' Gloria shrugged.

'And how are you bearing up,' said Belloni sympathetically to Maria. She too shrugged but smiled. The men bought the ladies drinks and ordered more beer. Conversation ebbed and flowed politely between the foursome, until Hoover told a risqué joke, causing Belloni to double up in laughter. The ladies smiled politely, unamused.

'You appear to be celebrating,' said Gloria perceptively.

'Well, our friend Hoover is, that's true,' replied Belloni.

'Afraid, I have no reason to.' He turned to Maria. 'Sorry but there's nothing new.'

'So why are you celebrating, Mr Hoover?' asked Gloria. 'Are you flying home?'

'Naw, not yet,' he laughed. 'Can't get rid of me that easy.'

'Then why,' persisted Gloria. 'Am I going to be out of a job?' Hoover turned to face her.

'I certainly hope not but now we do have the proof that your boss was up to no good.'

'What kind of proof,' asked Gloria. Hoover had drunk too many beers, which had loosened his tongue.

'We have a copy of the tape from the time Maria bugged von Murren's dinner party,' he gloated. He leaned in front of Gloria to look at Maria. Before she could get her thoughts in order, Belloni interrupted.

'I don't think Miss Beckett needs to know this,' he said sharply.

'Oh I think she does,' responded Hoover. 'I want her to say that she is willing to testify in court that she planted the tapes for her boyfriend.' Maria instantly paled and quickly placed her glass on the table before she dropped it. Her head swam. She only half heard

Belloni, as he reached out and held Hoover's arm.

'This is not the time nor the place,' he repeated. Hoover shook off Belloni's hand:

'Can I rely on you Miss Beckett?' Maria, head in hands, was weeping. Belloni climbed to his feet and swept up Maria's coat that was folded over the back of the sofa.

'Come,' he said softly. Took her hand and pulled her to her feet. Like a zombie, she headed for the door, as Belloni wrapped the coat over her shoulders. Gloria watched them go, stood and picked up her own coat.

'It seems sensitivity is not your strongest suit, Mr Hoover,' she said coldly.

'I only asked!' Hoover replied, looking bewildered. 'Please don't go,' he begged, standing and reaching out a hand. 'Let me buy you another glass of wine.' Gloria made excuses; she decided it might be safer not to upset the man, so remained polite but firm.

Outside, the cool air cleared Maria's head. She thanked Belloni for rescuing her.

'He said too much,' he began. 'Let's find a café.'

'No let's just walk,' replied Maria. 'Let's walk towards the Market Square, I can catch a tram there.' For some minutes they strolled in silence until Maria asked:

'Was he serious about me giving evidence . . . about the microphones?' she whispered.

'I'm afraid he was,' replied Belloni.

'What if I refuse?'

'I'm afraid the court would insist,' said Belloni. Maria thought about his reply.

'When would all this happen?' she asked.

'In two or three months, I can't remember the exact date.' A tram rolled noisily by, wheels protesting against the rails, drowning his reply. Belloni repeated what he had said.

'When would Dieter von Murren find out that I was to give evidence?' Would it before then?' Maria's mind was numb.

'Yes, I'm afraid he would. The defence lawyer would know, so he'd advise von Murren what to expect.'

'So I need to resign,' said Maria, tears filling her eyes. Belloni said nothing but reached out and squeezed Maria's hand.

'Where did you find the tape?' she suddenly asked.

'Among Raziel Stavi's stuff,' replied Belloni.

'Oh,' said Maria. 'So it was him that gave Joe the microphones!'

'I guess so,' replied Belloni.

'Why guess? Doesn't Stavi admit it,' questioned Maria. Belloni wrestled with his conscience.

'I haven't seen him yet. He's . . . he's . . . not in the country.' At least that's not a lie, he thought.

They parted at the Market Square tram stop, Belloni promising to be in touch as soon as he knew anything and insisting that if she did leave the von Murren's home, she let him know where he could find her. As the tram pulled away, Belloni watched and waved but Maria's head was down, eyes unseeing, as she pondered the fact that as well as the von Murrens, her life too was about to fall apart.

CHAPTER 53

During the following weeks, life went on as normal in the von Murren household, no one mentioning the shadow of Damocles' sword, hovering threateningly above their heads. Subconsciously, Beccy, Flavia, Simone and Maria were ultra cautious in what they said and in the way they treated each other. Katarzyna put on a brave face such that her joyful, outgoing presence set the tone. The warm, friendly environment only made Maria feel worse. The effort of keeping up with the cheerful atmosphere took its toll and each night she collapsed in tears and cried herself to sleep.

Maria tried hard to plan her next move but couldn't find the mental energy. She knew that she should contact the agency that had placed her in her current job, though she doubted that the von Murren's would provide a reference. Consequently the chance of getting a new job would be slim. It didn't help that she really enjoyed being in Switzerland. She was in love with the scenery, the quality of life and the people; even more so, now that her knowledge of the language was improving. But she knew that she needed to be long gone before the bombshell dropped that she had betrayed them all. Belloni had said it might be several weeks before the legal team informed von Murren that the prosecution had proof. She wished that she could be sure. How much time did she have?

Bruno appeared on the scene again. Beccy had persuaded Katarzyna to set him to work repairing some of the fences around the property and doing other odd jobs. The stable girls kept their distance trying to ignore him. At every opportunity Bruno found excuses to speak to Katarzyna - anything to be near her. It had been his intention to hurt his stepbrother by gradually destroying his family but now he was confused by all the talk of Dieter von Murren being sent to prison. With Dieter out of the way, he would be free to move in on Katarzyna. She would need help and comforting, he smiled maliciously to himself.

It was the middle of a warm, quiet Tuesday afternoon when, without warning, the sky fell in and the day disintegrated into shards of shattered dreams and splintered aspirations. Dieter von Murren arrived in a shower of flying gravel, skidding his 911 to a stop outside the front door. Smart suited, collar undone, tie flapping over his shoulder, he strode into the stable block; his thunderous expression causing Simone to dive into the nearest loosebox, to avoid confrontation. She peered through a crack in the door and watched with trepidation, as her employer grabbed a riding crop and headed into the house, slapping the weapon against his thigh with each stride he took. The moment the front door closed, Simone shouted for Flavia and explained what she had just witnessed, fearing for Katarzyna's wellbeing.

In the hallway von Murren shouted Maria's name at the top of his voice. Eventually Katarzyna appeared from the kitchen, making calming noises and asking what was the matter. Von Murren demanded to know where Maria was.

'Collecting the children from school,' replied Katarzyna. 'Why? Whatever is the matter?' Von Murren began lashing out with the riding crop, beating against the wall, dislodging a picture. Katarzyna clung to her husband, wrapping her arms around him, whispering for him to calm down. She eased him into the lounge, pushed him gently into an armchair, closed the door and eased herself onto his lap. It was quite some time before Dieter calmed sufficiently to tell Katarzyna that he just spent an hour with the lawyer and learned that his house, his home had been bugged and now the prosecution believed they had proof of his wrong doing.

'I'm not a criminal,' he kept repeating. 'Baumann's company was failing in Argentina, he would have pulled out anyway.' Katarzyna didn't know what he meant about Argentina or bugging but ran her hand through his hair and made soothing noises.

'So what's all this got to do with Maria?' asked Katarzyna. At the mention of her name, von Murren pushed his wife from his lap and leapt to his feet, hissing:

'I'll murder the bloody woman when she gets here.' Katarzyna protested. 'Bring her to my study when she gets back - and then,' he said ominously, 'take the girls for a long walk.' He left the lounge, leaving a tearful Katarzyna totally confused.

A few moments later, she glanced at her watch. It was about time for Maria's return. She thought for a moment, made her way to the kitchen where she spoke to Beccy Blom, then slipped on a coat and began walking down the drive.

Maria and the girls were laughing about some incident that had occurred at school, as they approached the end of the drive.

'Look,' shouted Claudia, the younger of the two girls. 'There's mummy!' Katarzyna was perched on the top rail of the fence waiting. Maria drew the Range Rover to a halt and the girls leapt out and hugged their mother. After some minutes Katarzyna said:

'Okay Stephanie, you can drive the Range Rover up the drive but mind Daddy's car. He's home early. Maria and I will walk.' Stephanie was occasionally allowed behind the wheel on their own property and with a joyful cry, she climbed into the vehicle while her younger sister clambered into the passenger seat. As they juddered out of sight, Maria started towards the house.

'Walt a minute,' said Katarzyna, crossing the verge and leaning on the fence. Maria quizzically followed. 'My husband came home about half an hour ago,' she began. 'He was absolutely furious . . . and,' she took a deep breath. 'Threatening to murder you for something that you've done.' Maria's shoulders slumped and tears welled in her eyes. He must know! 'I didn't really understand . . . but he said what you did will send him to prison,' Katarzyna said quietly. Maria sobbed, demanding Katarzyna's forgiveness. 'It's not safe for you to return, with him in this state of mind,' she continued. 'I've spoken to Beccy. She says that that you can stay with her until you decide what to do.' She gave Maria the key to Beccy's apartment. 'I'll pack up your things and Beccy will bring them at the end of the day.' Maria was desolate, standing forlorn, chin on her chest, hands clasped in front of her, visibly collapsing towards the ground, like a melting icicle. 'The girls love you, continued Katarzyna. 'Perhaps when things have settled down, you can return.' She pecked the unmoving Maria on the cheek and wandered slowly up the drive, towards the house and her furious husband.

* * *

Later Maria was cross-examined by the curious Beccy but Maria managed to eventually satisfy her by explaining that Dieter von Murren had taken exception to Maria discussing his private life with a newspaper reporter. Beccy wasn't convinced but realized that Maria was sticking to her story.

'I've left your suitcase at Jacques place,' she said. 'He's got a room over the stable. It'll be more convenient. I cook his meals for him. You'll be all right there.' Beccy was not having the attractive Maria sleeping in her tiny apartment and hearing her nightly ecstatic cries. Besides, she didn't trust Bruno to keep his hands off Maria. She'd noticed the lustful way he looked at other women, she needed to keep temptation as far away as possible.

Just one night in the tiny room, above the stable reeking of horses, was enough for Maria. The next day she telephoned Gloria and explained what had happened. Gloria was sympathetic but said that she and her partner only had one bedroom but she'd speak to her mother, who had a spare room. The following day Gloria took Maria to meet her parents at their apartment in an old building near the city's zoo. Her father was in a wheelchair. The mother, a fussy little woman, showed Maria the room, apologising for its small size. Maria was just grateful to have somewhere to go.

Dieter von Murren had been angry at first when Katarzyna explained that Maria had gone but in the end decided it was just as well, as he would not be responsible for his actions. He soon put her deceit from his mind, as he now had so many other things to think about. In the following days, he spent hours with his production manager, explaining that he wanted him to run the company, as best he could - if the worst came to the worst.

He met with his old school friend, Marco Kaufmann, in their favourite bar, the Fischerstube, in downtown Basel and tried to explain that the case against him was all a mistake. Mistake or not, he continued, the Americans would want him to face charges in their country. There seemed little doubt that he would be locked up. He couldn't bear that, he explained. He would rather die.

'One of these days I'm going to disappear,' said Dieter dramatically, placing his glass on the table. Marco looked startled. 'I'm going to disappear in a way that everyone will think I've drowned.' Marco started to interrupt. 'You'll be the only one that knows that I haven't,' continued Dieter. 'I can't trust Katarzyna, she's too open. She'd spill the beans, even without meaning to.' He smiled and sipped his beer. 'Later, when things have calmed down, I'll contact her.' Marco harangued his friend with the futility of his ideas but Dieter ignored the outburst.

'Can I trust you or not?' he demanded. Reluctantly, Marco nodded: 'Of course you can,' he said.

Thanks,' replied Dieter. 'I knew I could rely on you. I have no idea yet when I'm going but no doubt you'll read about it. When I am settled, I'll telephone you,' said Dieter. 'Walter Klein,' he continued, 'my father's old retainer, will be in charge of everything.'

After a few weeks the head of von Murren's legal team called him to his office in the city.

'Good news and bad,' he began. 'I'm pretty sure the Swiss Prosecutor will decide the taped evidence cannot be used against you.'

That's great news,' beamed von Murren.

'However,' continued the lawyer, 'the Europeans and Americans have decided it can be used.'

'What does that mean?' asked von Murren.

'It means that the Europeans have done a deal with the Americans and they have issued a subpoena for you to face charges in the USA.'

'Already?' protested von Murren. The lawyer nodded.

'And if I don't go?' asked von Murren.

'Diplomatically awkward for the Swiss authorities,' replied the lawyer. 'And if you step outside of Switzerland you'll be arrested.'

'Do you think the Swiss would ship me out, if the Americans issue an extradition order?'

'Reluctantly,' replied the lawyer, 'though they don't like being bullied. But eventually yes, I think they would.'

Driving back to his office, von Murren considered what his lawyer had to say. If he stayed in his home country he would eventually be extradited to the USA - and who knows what the Americans would do to him? If he disappeared perhaps the Swiss authorities would eventually forget all about him? There was nothing for it. The time had come.

Friday morning, after a hasty breakfast, Dieter von Murren kissed his children, wished them a good day at school before placing a soft kiss on Katarzyna's forehead.

'Have a nice day,' he said and left, deliberately not looking back and emptying his mind of anything that might resemble emotion.

In Basel, he parked in a central car park and made his way to Pfauen, a large department store in the main shopping street. In the male department, he bought a change of clothes, as well as a baseball-cap and a pair of sports' shoes. In another section he bought a razor, a pair of scissors, a toothbrush, hair dye and then went looking for a holdall bag. He paid in cash and made his way back to the car. Sitting in the depths of the underground car park, he stared at himself in the mirror for a few moments before winding his way out and towards his office.

Gloria was already busy when he arrived. He greeted her perfunctorily, shut himself in his office and began tying up as many loose ends as possible. Later he walked around the facility, stopping to chat with a number of employees. He issued instructions to Gloria and told her that he would be away for a few days. At the end of the day when everyone had gone, he stood at the window of his office and gazed around. This would be the last time, he thought - and cursed. Leaving the car park, he waved to the security guard and drove his beloved Porsche back towards Basel.

In the city, von Murren parked on the street, switched off the engine and rubbed his hand affectionately over the luxurious leather of the passenger seat.

'Goodbye old friend,' he murmured. 'I'm going to miss you.' He made his way quickly towards the Three Kings Hotel, imperiously perched alongside the Rhine, he was carrying the holdall. He'd visited the luxurious hotel many times and made his way directly to the toilets. It was quite early; he hoped that he would not be interrupted. First of all he set about his beard with the scissors. When he was finished, he gathered up the shavings, dropped them into the toilet and flushed. He then unwrapped the razor, dropping the packaging into the holdall and shaved. Afterwards he sat inside a cubicle and read the instructions on the bottle of hair-dye. This was going to take some time. Nevertheless, he decided he couldn't wait. He removed his suit, and shirt and stuffed them into the holdall and pulled on the new jeans. He opened the door and looked outside, all was quiet. Quickly he filled a basin with warm water and added the dye. Like a submersing diver, he continually dipped his head under water; until he was satisfied his hair was well covered. And then the messy business of drying himself with paper towels and disposing of the evidence down the toilet.

The whole process took in excess of forty-five minutes and before he left, von Murren studied his reflection closely in the mirror. He was satisfied that there had been a transformation, confident there was little chance of being recognised.

Outside of the hotel, von Murren hopped on a tram heading into the depths of Kleinbasel. He had an address written on a piece of paper, reluctantly supplied by Walter Klein, manager of his father's office. It took him half an hour to find the apartment. The dark and gloomy tower blocks matching his mood.

He was expected and soon whisked up to the fifth floor where a seedy, bespectacled man, took his photograph and disappeared into a backroom, leaving von Murren to watch a disinterested, tired-looking woman feed a grumbling baby, wedged in a highchair. The man soon returned with the false Swiss passport, in the name of Axel Ackermann. Dieter hardly recognised the blonde, clean-shaven face peering out from the page. He repeated the name to himself and asked:

'Where did the name come from?'

'He's dead,' came the laconic reply. 'On this paper, there's a bit of history about where he was born and registered.' The man handed over a sheet of paper with a few typed lines. Von Murren handed over the agreed sum of money and left, glad to be away from the smell of babies, stale urine and cigarette smoke. He caught a tram again heading towards the city centre but as it neared the Mittlerebrucke, he got out and strolled alongside the Rhine. After a few moments, in a dimly lit area, he sat on a bench, pulled his suit from the holdall and went through the pockets. Reluctantly, he decided to leave his wallet and car keys in the jacket pocket, hoping that whoever found it was honest enough to leave everything intact and not empty his bank account or steal the car. He left the shirt and shoes neatly folded on top of his suit on the seat, zipped up the holdall containing a few personal possessions, returned to the main street and climbed aboard a tram again. He remained on the tram until it pulled into the square in front of the railway station. He felt conspicuous, as he made his way to the ticket office, not that he needed to; his fellow travellers were only intent on their own destinations and timekeeping. Von Murren bought a ticket to Geneva and made his way slowly towards the platform, he had plenty of time.

On the platform, he found a seat, drew his fleece around him, pulled up the hood and closed his eyes. It was his intention to buy another ticket in Geneva and take a train to Nice. At Nice he would find a train to Barcelona and from there a ferry to Mallorca.

He had never run away from anything or anyone in his life before - and here he was running away from everything that he ever done, all the people he had ever known, a family, a successful business and career - and facing what? He had no idea. Anyone else would, most likely, have wilted at the thought but not Dieter von Murren, his way of dealing with issues, was to empty his mind of all the accumulated detritus and focus on the distant horizon.

CHAPTER 54

Von Murren's disappearance and apparent drowning caused a major stir amongst Basel's business community. There wasn't a single person who thought him capable of taking his own life. The BAZ, the local broadsheet, printed a police statement and a brief history of von Murren's career, together with a single sentence about the accusations being made against him.

The tabloids however had a field day and were full of theories of both murder and suicide. There were long interviews and half page photographs of the young couple who had discovered his shoes and the neatly folded clothes on a bench alongside the River Rhine.

They had been out for an evening stroll; the article quoted, and decided to sit on the bench for a while to watch the lights of the city across the water, when they spotted the shoes and clothes. In the jacket they found a wallet and car keys, so they took everything to the local police station. The article continued that the police telephoned the man's wife and she said he hadn't come home from work. A search of the river had taken place but there had been no sign of a body.

Katarzyna, of course, was distraught. Her husband had gone to work as usual, she told the investigating police officer. There was nothing unusual in his demeanour. The fact that he hadn't come home in time for dinner had not caused her any concern, he worked long hours and had many commitments. Policemen, reporters, photographers seemed to dog her every step; the latter camped out at the end of the drive. The newspapers were full of rubbish, digging under every stone, looking for dirt.

Although all the signs were, that he had jumped in the river and committed suicide, Katarzyna was not convinced. She remembered his dramatic words that night, when he had said that if things got difficult, he might just disappear.

She knew the man; he would fight for his life until there wasn't a breath left in his body. There was no way he would end it all of his own volition. But, she asked herself, had he been murdered, like Maria's reporter friend or gone to join the man Kurt Baumann, wherever he was hiding. Where was Dieter? Why hadn't he told her? Their relationship had been at a low point for some time and although each slept alone, she still loved him and longed for news of his whereabouts.

CHAPTER 55

Two days later, oblivious of the angst and misery he had left behind, von Murren was in Mallorca touring his new domain, together with the architect. It was the first time he had seen the place since the renovations and he was delighted. The elderly architect asked what he planned to do with his new acquisition.

'It will be a guesthouse with a difference,' he had replied and skilfully evaded all the other questions seeking enlightenment. 'I will need some staff,' he said, as they stood in what would become the dining room. 'First a housekeeper and a gardener; do you have any ideas?'

'I have a contact,' replied the greybeard. 'I'll ask him to send you some people to look at.'

The next few weeks were spent furnishing the place. He chose simple, locally built furniture that fitted in well with the rustic surroundings. He'd found a woman to feed him and look after the place and an old man to cut grass and do odd jobs.

In Pollença he'd bought an easel, several large canvases, brushes and paints. Either in the early morning or the late afternoons, when the light was at its best, he set up the easel and painted. Some days he was on the beach, sometimes among the orange trees. He hadn't painted since he was a teenager and he found the process therapeutic and calming. Almost before the paintings were dry he hung them up on the newly renovated walls, confident they would add to the homeliness of the facilities.

He called his friend Marco in Basel from a public telephone and after accepting, without comment, his friend's lengthy haranguing for deserting his family, he urged him to travel to meet him in Barcelona at his earliest convenience. His funds were running low; it was imperative that he started attracting paying guests as soon as possible. He had accounts, located in different countries but he couldn't access them without giving away the fact that he was alive. Later, when the heat eased and if the Swiss decided he had no case to answer, then perhaps he could resurface. But for the moment he had to manage on what he could earn and Marco was the key.

They stayed in the same small hotel, down a quiet side street off the tree-lined street Las Ramblas. Marco was not in the best of moods when he arrived, it had been difficult to convince his wife of the need to fly to Barcelona, when he did so little business travelling. And he hated telling lies.

Later they found an open-air restaurant in in the Port Vell area, sank beers and watched the tenders ferry passengers to and from the moored cruise ships. Marco was still furious with his friend and hammered away at how thoughtless and unkind he was, 'buggering off,' as he put it, and causing his family such distress. Dieter von Murren said nothing; he knew he was in an indefensible position. Eventually the wrath died away and Marco asked how Dieter himself was coping.

'All the things you have said are right, of course,' he said. 'But don't think it's easy for me.' He fingered his chin, as if he still had a beard. 'I told Katarzyna that I might disappear … she'll know I'm not dead.'

'Well she's certainly acting as if you are,' Marco blurted. A waiter arrived with their dinner and meaningful conversation stopped. Later, over coffee, von Murren said:

'Helen, your wife … she's a psychiatrist, right?' Marco nodded.

'She commutes to Zurich, where she has a very successful practice. She has a flat above her consulting rooms, she doesn't always come home'

'Why's that?' asked Dieter.

'Well, she also works in a couple of hospitals and one night a week she has evening clinics,' replied Marco. 'Why the sudden interest?'

'Well,' replied Dieter. 'I've set up this really nice residential place to cater for people with minor psychiatric problems … to escape from the real world for a while,' he explained. 'Not just nutters but folk unable to cope . . . couples with relationship difficulties,' he continued. 'Anyone who needs some rest and relaxation away from it all . . . together with some encouragement and support.'

'What, you have a resident psychotherapist too?' questioned Marco.

'Yes,' lied Dieter. 'A real man of the world.' Meaning himself.

'What an earth gave you the idea?' asked Marco.

'Well, you know how it is,' replied Dieter with a grin. 'I've made a successful career out of manipulating people . . . I'd like to continue.' Marco snorted and finished his beer. 'Let's get back to Helen,' said Dieter. 'Do you think you could persuade her to recommend my place?'

'I could try,' replied Marco.

'Great, I've prepared a few brochures. Perhaps you could ask Helen to give them to her patients and leave a few lying about at the other clinics that she visits.'

The next day Dieter travelled out to the airport with his friend and as they drank coffee, waiting for the flight, the conversation got around to their common passion - Fasnacht, the annual Basel carnival.

'I have every intention of coming next February,' said Dieter. 'I haven't missed one since you twisted my arm to join, all those years ago.'

'You're even more of idiot than I thought,' laughed his friend.

'Not at all. By then the Swiss authorities will have forgotten all about me and if I keep my head down, no one will notice.' They both laughed at his audacity. Shortly afterwards they parted company, Marco to fly back to Basel, Dieter to travel back to the city and his ferry back to Mallorca.

The seven-hour trip to Palma gave von Murren plenty of time to think about his meeting with his friend Marco. He gathered that his company was still trading; the papers were convinced he had drowned and the case against him had been postponed. He also learned that Kurt Baumann was still missing. Where had he gone, he wondered? He pondered whether or not his request for Marco's wife to promote his 'retreat' would bring results. He decided that he had better not rely on this and once he was home began a postal blitz, sending letters and flyers to a long list of Swiss based psychotherapeutic clinics and practitioners.

Gradually his efforts paid off and a slow stream of clients visited his mini paradise set among the orange groves and alongside the azure ocean. There wasn't a single dissatisfied customer, and as each returned to civilisation they spread the word.

CHAPTER 56

When Inspector Belloni discovered that von Murren had disappeared, he inwardly groaned, immediately suspicious. There was no doubt that the lives of Joe Leman, Raziel Stavi, Kurt Baumann and Dieter von Murren were or had been, inextricably linked. There was no question about that. Two were dead, two had disappeared - one an apparent suicide. Well he didn't believe that for one moment. It was an obvious and simplistic ploy.

Belloni grabbed his coat and left the building. On his way out he collected a sheet of paper detailing where von Murren's clothes had been found. It didn't take him long to find the bench alongside the Rhine and with the innate instinct of a born policeman, he began scouring the area, in the full knowledge that probably a dozen or more detectives, on their hands and knees, had probably fingertip combed the whole area days before.

After a while he sank down onto the bench and stared at the river. Muddy-brown water, swirling with mini whirlpools, hiding a multitude of mysteries. One by one he ran through, for the thousandth time, what he knew about the four missing men. Two were accounted for; an Interpol search was on for Baumann - and now von Murren. Wherever Baumann was, he mused, no doubt von Murren had gone to join him.

In fact, Belloni could not have been more wrong. While von Murren was in Mallorca, Baumann was in Argentina, nicely settled in the bustling, leafy city of Mendoza, close to the Andes eastern flank. Baumann had discovered Mendoza many years earlier, when visiting the company's Argentine business interests and had immediately been impressed by the lively city, surrounded with vineyards and olive orchards. It suited his purpose well, with an international airport and links to Buenos Aires and nearby Santiago in Chile. If the authorities did track him down, at least he had escape routes. Using his alter ego, he had long since set up a bank account and had enough cash to keep up a comfortable lifestyle for the rest of his life, like his grandfather before him,

Poor Belloni knew nothing of these facts and as he made his weary way back to the police station, he contemplated asking the Chief if he could return to the car-theft investigation. At least with that, he might get somewhere.

CHAPTER 57

The sweltering summer reluctantly gave way to autumn. Leaves spread joy with eye-catching bursts of colour ranging from vermilion to crimson, before a northerly chill wickedly whipped them from the trees, rolled them into tumbleweed-like balls and shepherded them down the streets and byways. Urban fountains and country troughs were drained. Jacques' horses spent their nights inside. Frost was everywhere, deliciously coating even the hedgerow spiders' webs. The first snow brought smiles to the skiing fraternity, as well as community snowplough drivers, who calculated the overtime that would swell their bank accounts.

The Basel Carnival fanatics began their practices. Cliques clicked. Piccolos were polished. Drums reverently eased from their cases and skins checked for cracks. Poets began writing satire for the mocking, acerbic banners. For many locals, the highlight of the year was approaching fast.

Some inner sense, perhaps like that experienced by the migratory birds, stirred Dieter von Murren's instincts. And when the time came, he flew to Barcelona, rented a car and drove to Basel.

In Basel he rented a room in a cheap hotel and the following evening startled his friend Marco, when at a Clique rehearsal, he settled into the vacant chair next to him and blew a few notes on his piccolo. His presence at rehearsals was not questioned and afterwards each member queued to wring his hand, grateful to have him and his talent back among them.

At 'Moorgestraich', the ridiculous four o'clock start of the carnival, von Murren marched around Basel's narrow back streets with his Clique. They were all dressed as masked harlequins, with long diamond patterned cloaks, each with a thick, black or white ruff. The faces of the long-nosed masks were white, with bright pink cheeks, a sardonic smile painted across the lips. On their heads a

Napoleonic-style hat. Fifers fifed and drummers drummed; the crushed crowd entranced. Three days of music, marching, drinking and camaraderie - von Murren was in his element. And hidden behind his mask, unconcerned that he would be either recognised or apprehended.

On Thursday afternoon, when only men with brooms were on the streets, busy cleaning up, von Murren drove out to his old home in Burg for a tearful reunion with Katarzyna. At first she'd hardly recognised him, without his beard but as he kept a woolly hat on, she didn't know about the blonde hair. He ignored the tears, the pounding of small fists on his chest and the Polish swearwords echoing relentlessly around the kitchen. He was only there, he tried to explain, to check up that she and the children were well and her finances were adequate.

Almost as suddenly as he arrived, he left. Leaving Katarzyna distraught and begging him to stay to see the girls. He made excuses. The authorities were still after him, he needed to keep moving.

'Your telephone number?' she shouted, as he stooped into the car. He shook his head and was gone.

Bruno sheltering from the wind at the stable door watched with amazement and curiosity - and noted the Spanish number-plate. Katarzyna still on the steps, shivering with the cold. Bruno ran across towards her.

'I would have sworn that was Doctor von Murren,' he said. Katarzyna said nothing, overcome with sobbing. Bruno put an arm possessively around her shoulder and gently drew her towards him. 'There now,' he crooned. 'Tears won't help.' For a moment Katarzyna clung to Bruno, afraid her legs would not support her weight. He squeezed tighter. And then it was over. Katarzyna struggled out of Bruno's grasp, ran inside and slammed the door. Bruno stood for several minutes gazing at the solid oak door, with its limp Christmas wreath of holly and ivy still hanging from the knocker. An evil smile spread across his face. 'Well it's a start,' he said aloud and laughed. 'It's a start.'

CHAPTER 58

Later that night, Bruno lay in bed staring into the darkness. Beccy Blom was curled up alongside him in a foetal position, facing away, nursing her wounds from his relentless attack on her willing but aging body.

'So dear brother,' he thought. 'You've run away to Spain.' He pictured Katarzyna's reaction and her pleading for a telephone number, as her husband drove away. 'She obviously doesn't know where he's hiding,' Bruno concluded. He remembered the sensations of holding Katarzyna in his arms and dreamed of more but he reminded himself that he mustn't rush things. He needed to treat her like Beccy had taught him to deal with a shy but skittish pony. Slowly, gently, patiently - until they willingly ate out of your hand.

Katarzyna had been shaking when she picked up her daughters from school. It was apparent that she was distraught; she could hardly see the road for the tears. The girls demanded to know what was troubling their mother. In the end she pulled into a layby and sobbingly told them that their father was not dead and that he had been to see her. It was then their turn to be distraught, angry that he had not waited to see them, angry that he had pretended to die but delirious that he was still alive. Emotion filled the vehicle, the tears and outpourings steaming up the windows.

Both girls admitted to their mother that they had been teased at school about the likelihood of their father being sent to jail. But when the papers had said he was drowned the teasing had stopped and remorse abounded.

Katarzyna was dismayed; she thought her daughters knew nothing of her husband's troubles. Eventually enough calm was restored that windows could be wiped and the journey resumed. But the girls were full of questions, none of which Katarzyna could answer. She didn't know where he was or when he might visit again. Before they left the vehicle, Katarzyna swore them to secrecy. No one else must know that he was alive - otherwise he would end up in prison.

Over the following months Bruno craftily made himself almost indispensible at The Poplars. He was hard working and no job was too much trouble. He had also become a competent rider and occasionally accompanied Katarzyna's daughters on hacks around the area. The stable girls Flavia and Simone kept their distance, his presence made them feel uncomfortable but they watched him like hawks, concerned how lasciviously he eyed sixteen year old Stephanie, Katarzyna's older daughter.

CHAPTER 59

There was more snow than usual that winter. Bruno was kept busy shovelling to clear the paths and also drove a small tractor with a snowplough attached to keep the drive open. More often than not, he was invited into the kitchen afterwards and offered a Kafee Fertig, a strong coffee laced with plum liquor.

Bruno noted that the girl Maria had not been replaced and Katarzyna drove the girls everywhere. He didn't know why Maria had been fired and even Beccy hadn't been able to find out.

When leaning against the Aga in the kitchen, sipping his coffee, Bruno saw that Katarzyna was quieter these days. The lively fun-loving woman seemed to have had some of the stuffing knocked out of her. That made him sad. If only she would love him, she would be happy again.

Some time later, Bruno was very disturbed to see a handsome man visit Katarzyna. When he arrived they had hugged each other longer than was normal, so he thought. And as they walked around the grounds it was clear that she was really pleased to see him. Occasionally holding his hand or he touching her arm. Bruno later found out from Beccy, that his name was Marco Kaufmann, a friend of Dieter von Murren's. After the visit Bruno noted that Katarzyna seemed brighter. He wondered if this Marco man had given her news of her husband? He hoped not, that wouldn't suit his plans. His brother needed to disappear!

Christmas came and went and the good people of Basel's thoughts turned excitedly to the annual carnival - Fasnacht.

Dieter von Murren returned to Basel two days before the celebrations were due to start and joined the rehearsals. On the Sunday evening before carnival started, he drove out to Burg. This time he had telephoned first, Katarzyna and the girls were prepared. Katarzyna had sent Beccy Blom home early; she didn't want her to see her unlikely visitor.

A whole year had elapsed without any contact; Dieter's reception was cool to say the least. The older daughter, Stephanie, was only in the room because her mother had threatened her. She was furious with her father. He had let her down.

Katarzyna was confused, unable to comprehend her flailing emotions. The meeting was polite but Katarzyna and the girls had become accustomed to his absence. They sat slumped in separate chairs around the large room, only speaking when spoken to.

The girls had never seen their father clean-shaven and the fact that he kept a woollen hat on his head, to hide his blonde curls, meant that he seemed like a stranger in their midst.

Each had woodenly hugged him upon arrival and then politely answered his questions about their schooling. After an hour, he made his excuses and, much to everyone's relief, left.

Bruno, lurking around the stable block, had seen the white hire car with Spanish number plates arrive and park in front of the house. The driver was bundled up in bulky coat but he knew who it was.

Earlier, when Beccy told him she had been sent home early, Bruno had become curious to know why and so had made an excuse and walked up to the Poplars and sat in the stable block by a window that looked out towards the front door of the house and waited. Later he crept close to the house and found a window where he could peer in unseen. After several judicious glances he saw his brother sitting in armchair. He laughed.

'So, shaved your whiskers off, have you dear doctor,' he murmured. 'And why are you wearing that silly hat? What have you done to your hair? Shaved that too?'

Bruno returned to the stables and then made his way down the drive, pondering his next move. He stopped at Jacques place, knocked and pushed his way in, calling out. Poor Jacques was still immobile and waiting for an operation to fix a damaged disc in his spine. Bruno was his chauffer these days, driving him to the hospital for examinations as well as to the nearest shops for food, pills and potions. After exchanging greetings Bruno asked:

'Could I borrow your car for a couple of hours?'

'Course you can. Got a date?' chuckled Jacques. Bruno didn't answer but picked up the keys that he knew hung on a nail by the door and left.

He drove to the edge of the village, pulled into a track leading into the forest and waited. There was a huge pile of snow pushed into a heap by a snowplough. It was freezing and the windows soon steamed up. A thought suddenly struck him. Would his brother spend the night in his own home? He hadn't been carrying anything. Not even gifts or flowers. But then it was his own home; he wouldn't need anything. Bruno cursed. He was probably sitting out here in the cold, freezing his balls off for nothing. He looked at the time and decided that he would give him an hour.

Every five minutes Bruno wiped the mist from the windscreen, glanced at his watch and argued with himself. Of course the man would stay. No doubt he was already lying in Katarzyna's arms; he tortured himself. Not a single car had passed in either direction; it was not a night to be out.

Headlamps suddenly caught the glistening trees, casting moving shadows, as if the very trunks were on the move. A quick wipe of the window, as the car drew nearer. A white Audi. Bruno turned the key and cursed when the car didn't start first time. And then breathed a sigh of relief when it did on the second. He pulled out onto the road and began to follow. Being Sunday evening there wasn't much traffic on the main road and Bruno had no trouble keeping his quarry in sight. Eventually, in Basel, Dieter began weaving down narrow side streets towards his hotel. Bruno followed, cautiously. It took several turns around the local side streets before Dieter found a parking spot. Bruno pulled onto the pavement and watched. Dieter climbed out, locked his car and walked to a building across the quiet road. Bruno had not even noticed that the building was a small hotel. Once Dieter had entered the building Bruno left his car and crossed the road. He climbed the steps and pushed open the heavy door. The foyer was small and dark. At the end was a small reception area and a tired-looking woman about to walk into a back office.

'Hello,' called Bruno waving his own car keys. The woman turned, slightly startled. 'The man who just came in - he dropped his car keys.' Before she had time to respond, Bruno continued. 'What's his name and room number? I'll catch him up.'

'No I'll telephone his room,' she stuttered.

'No need to do that. He won't have reached his room yet.' It had been a long day; the woman needed a glass of something strong.

'His name's Ackermann. Two hundred and twenty three.' Bruno took the stairs two at a time until he was out of sight. He waited a few moments and then wandered back down to the foyer. Another customer was collecting his keys. When the man moved away from the counter, Bruno said:

'Mr Ackermann was pretty relieved, I can tell you.' The woman smiled. 'He looked familiar. I was at school with a boy called Ackermann but can't remember his first name.' The woman really did not want to get into a conversation at this hour of night.

'What's this Ackermann called?' She looked at the register.

'Axel,' she said. 'Axel Ackermann.' Anything for a quiet life to get rid of this man.

'Axel,' replied Bruno looking pensive. 'This lad did move to Spain and I see Mr Ackermann is driving a Spanish car.' Would this man never go, thought the woman from behind the forced smile.

'Where in Spain does your Mr Axel Ackermann live?' Bruno demanded. The woman didn't have to look; she'd been on holiday there at least a dozen times in her life.

'Mallorca,' she said. 'Mr Ackermann lives in Mallorca.'

'Really,' replied Bruno. 'You know, I'm sure it's him. You wouldn't give me his address would you? I'd love to drop in one day. Surprise him?'

'His address is on the wall,' replied the woman. Bruno was startled. 'That poster on the noticeboard, he asked if he could put it up.' Bruno walked across to a glass-fronted noticeboard and read.

'Good lord,' he exclaimed aloud. 'Some sort of holiday camp?'

'For those of us who need cheering up and convincing that we are valuable members of the human race,' she said flatly. 'At least, that's what he said to me.'

'Good Lord,' Bruno repeated, baffled. 'Do you have a picce of paper so that I can copy down the address?'

'Better than that,' she replied. 'He left me some brochures.' She reached under the counter and handed Bruno a colourful four-page booklet.

'Well I'll be damned, cunning bastard,' thought Bruno. He

turned to the woman:

'This friend of mine used to play an instrument in a Clique. Do you know if your Mr Ackermann does?' asked Bruno.

'Yes he does,' replied the woman. 'I saw him carrying an instrument case and so I asked.'

'Any idea where his outfit meet?'

'Last house at the end of our street. On the right, in the cellar,' she said.

'Really,' exclaimed Bruno. 'Well, one night I'll drop in and surprise him!' Thanks for this.' He waved the brochure in the air, like trophy, unable to believe his good fortune and strolled back to the car with a jaunty step.

'So Dieter, Axel Ackermann, you live in Mallorca do you?' He sneered. 'And run some kind of holiday camp? Well, that's not exactly keeping a low profile!'

Later, in the solitary security of Beccy Blom's bathroom, he studied the brochure. It really was some kind of holiday camp, he decided; despite a load of crap about catering for those in need of mental sustenance and psychological support, to help deal with today's complex and pressured life. A holiday camp by the sea - no doubt an excuse for the joys of sun, sea and sex for his bastard brother.

Hiding the brochure at the bottom of his battered suitcase, he saw the two brown envelopes containing the money that he had stolen from his father's apartment. He thumbed through the high value notes and decided that he would pay his brother a visit. He could afford it; he'd hardly spent any of the money. That's it, when the weather was warmer he would take a trip, he determined. There might even be an opportunity to dispose of his brother, he thought coldly. Living by the sea could be dangerous, in it or on it even more so. Swimming and boating could be lethal. Accidents happen all the time. Bruno went to sleep dreaming of fatal, maritime mishaps.

CHAPTER 60

It was entirely predictable that the Crossair flight from Basel landed at Son Sant Joan Airport in Palma de Mallorca in a violent, ear-shattering thunderstorm. Bruno was on a dark mission, his aim to annihilate his brother. The weather, clearly in cahoots with his black-hearted intentions.

Bruno had never been on an aeroplane before; his first flight from Basel, on the small, thirty-six seater Saab 340, was uneventful enough, until the plane left the French coast. He was seated by a window and as they descended, he could see nothing but enveloping black cloud, with blinding flashes of lightening reflecting off the raindrops. Water ran horizontally across the glass, thunderclaps could be heard above the sound of the droning engines. Questions were raised in his mind but not apprehension. He didn't understand fear, he'd heard people talk about being afraid; it was not a sensation that he understood or had ever experienced.

Eventually the plane broke through the low cloud ceiling and hydroplaned down the runway in torrential rain, first on one wheel, as a violent gust of wind caught a wing tip. Moments later, accompanied by a relieved communal gasp that ran through the compartment, it dropped safely on to the other. The passengers, almost entirely Swiss, broke into applause, as was their wont on every successful landing, though this time totally justified.

Bruno was only carrying a rucksack and so was quickly through the formalities and into the arrivals area, where he immediately saw a painfully thin woman holding up a board, on which was printed the single word 'Paraíso.' She saw him looking and speaking German asked if he was going to Paraíso? Bruno nodded. She took a clipboard from under her arm and asked his name. He told her and she introduced herself as Martina.

Soon a couple, in their late forties, arrived at which point the woman led them to a nearby restaurant and bought coffee.

'Please wait here,' she said quietly. 'There should be four more people on the next flight and then we can go. With any luck we should be ready to leave in about half an hour.' So saying she headed back to the arrivals' zone.

'My name is Wilfred,' said the man once Martina had left. 'This is my wife Elda.' They shook hands. Elda was a tiny woman with permanent crease marks on her forehead, etched from hours of frowning. Wilfred too was underweight, with a nervous tic.

'You're German,' stated Wilfred. Bruno nodded. 'From Baden-Würtemberg, judging by your accent?' Bruno said nothing but sipped his coffee. 'Is this your first time?' continued Wilfred. 'To, Paraíso, I mean?'

'Yes it's the first time,' replied Bruno.

'It's our third time,' said Wilfred.

'I'm sure you'll find it useful,' said the woman. 'Doctor Ackermann is just,' she struggled to find the right word. 'So inspirational.' She turned to her husband. 'That's right, isn't it Wilfred?'

'Changed our lives, hasn't he dear?' said her husband. The woman reached into her handbag, pulled out a tissue and dabbed her eyes.

'I don't know about changed our lives,' she sniffled. 'He saved our lives.'

'What do you mean?' asked Bruno, not really caring. Wilfred looked at Elda; there was an imperceptible nod. He took a deep breath:

'Our only child . . . our only son, threw himself under a train at Zurich station.' Bruno said nothing. What could he say? 'We don't know why he did it,' whispered the woman. 'But we blamed each other.'

'Our home became a battleground,' said Wilfred quietly.

'That's Doctor Ackermann's phrase,' explained Elda.

'I started drinking,' added Wilfred. 'Our marriage was a disaster.'

'And I was suicidal,' Elda said quietly. 'What was the point of it all?' Wilfred reached out and squeezed his wife's hand.

'We went to a counsellor and after some months she suggested we came to one of Doctor Ackermann's workshops,' continued Wilfred.

'And as we said,' said Elda. 'He saved our lives, our sanity . . . and our marriage.' The pair of them stared at Bruno, looking for a response. He didn't know what to say.

'How old was he, your son?' he eventually said.

'Fourteen,' replied Elda. 'Fourteen years and three months.'

'He'd be twenty five now,' said Wilfred. 'Hard to believe.' Elda drained her coffee and asked:

'And what personal tragedy brings you to Mallorca, Mr Schmidt?' Bruno was spared the problem of inventing a lie, by the appearance of Martina, together with her clipboard and four people, three women and one man, each pulling a suitcase. The two women fell into Elda and Wilfred's outstretched arms.

'We met the last time we were at Paraíso,' explained Elda to anyone who was listening. Each was then introduced to the new couple.

The journey from Palma to Pollença seemed to take forever. The rain had stopped and the road was steaming. Bruno was at the front of the mini-bus, with Martina. The others in the back talked continuously. The two new women asking Elda and Wilfred so many questions about how they were. Doctor Axel Ackermann's ears must have been burning, his name and his good deeds mentioned in every other sentence. The four of them then took turns to quiz the new couple and more whispered tales of personal woe filled Bruno's ears.

'Some bloody holiday camp this,' he thought. He'd have to get the deed over quickly and escape from all these neurotic campers.

* * *

At the opening session, Bruno sat near the back and watched, as the room filled up. His dear brother, wearing a blue singlet and shorts, was standing at the front, encouraging people to sit. Bruno sniggered when he first saw the blonde curly hair and bronzed physique. Was he deliberately trying to look like a Greek God, he wondered? He only needed a laurel wreath on his head and the likeness to Apollo would be complete. Bruno looked around, people were reverently staring at Dieter, as if he were indeed a God, he could sense the veneration.

Bruno's head was so full of questions; he hardly heard what his brother was saying. He was introducing the staff, explaining what each did. Now he was going on about meeting everyone individually to learn about his or her problems. What could he say? He'd have to make something up.

Afterwards, in the orange groves, everyone sat in the shade, some peeling fruit. His brother was speaking. His soothing words easing pain and grief. Bruno was bewildered and immediately reminded of the scriptures that had been forced down his throat at Remand School. Especially the bit where Luke wrote about Jesus healing the sick and then feeding them bread and fish. He looked around him, it was plain to see that these people worshipped his brother; they fed on his every word, never mind the promise of bread and fish in the dining room, later that day.

After he'd been shown his room, Bruno strolled down to the sea. He removed his shoes and sat at the water's edge tossing pebbles into the ocean. Bruno had never actually seen the sea before, only in photographs and in films. Its size and depth made him feel uncomfortable. The sky was spectacular after the storm, but the orange glow, contrasted with the jet-black clouds, went unnoticed.

Getting rid of my brother may not be so easy, he thought. It needed to look like an accident. A knife in the ribs was not what he had in mind. There were too many people about and his brother was always the centre of attention. He walked up onto the headland and looked around. There were no boats anywhere, so no chance of arranging an accident on the water. The sun and the frustration caused a headache to build; he stood for a while in the shade pondering the dilemma before making his way slowly back to the Centre.

Places at dinner had been allocated and Bruno found himself sitting with Wilfred and his wife Elda, as well as the two women who had ridden the bus from the airport. He knew from the conversation on the bus that the two ladies, like Wilfred and his wife, lived in the Zurich area. The two ladies used the same psychiatrist and had become friends after their first visit to Paraiso. They spoke in a local dialect, which Bruno had trouble understanding and so for most of the meal he ate in silence. That suited him; he didn't want to get involved in their petty psychological problems. Throughout his teenage years Bruno had spent hours with psychos, as he called them. He had long since decided that they were a burden on society, serving no useful purpose.

The following afternoon, when Bruno was resting on his bed, there was a knock on the door. He called for whoever it was to come in. Anna the nurse poked her head around the door.

'Mr Schmidt, it's your turn to meet Doctor Ackermann,' she said. 'If you come with me, I'll show you where his office is.' Bruno shuffled to his feet and slid into his sandals. He walked behind Anna, thinking that she was the best looking of a poor lot at the 'camp,' and the only one he would be willing to invite into his bed. Perhaps he would try his luck later.

In Dieter's office, after shaking hands, Bruno slumped uncomfortably in a cane chair.

'So Mr Schmidt,' Dieter began, leafing through the paper-work that Bruno had completed, when he applied to attend the clinic. 'How did you learn about us? You've put here that it was through a friend.'

'Well, not really a friend,' muttered Bruno.

'Can you be more precise?' asked Dieter.

'From a man at work,' lied Bruno.

'Can you give me a name?' persisted Dieter.

'No. He said a relative of his had been here,' Bruno continued.

'But you can't give me a name?' Bruno shook his head. Dieter realised that he wasn't going to get anywhere and changed tack. 'I'm sure that you realise that all the people here, have been through some sort of personal crisis and talking about it helps them come to terms with the problem. Makes them strong. Puts things into perspective, Helps them to face life again.' Bruno was absently nodding. 'Would you like to tell me if anything is worrying you. Or if anything unpleasant has happened?' Bruno didn't like all this interrogation; it reminded him of his teenage years. The questions continued to probe. Dieter launched into generalities of how he understood that some things were difficult or even impossible to voice and that Bruno should take his time. Despite himself, Bruno found Dieter's voice was soporific, his words hypnotic, they elicited confidence. Bruno suddenly didn't trust himself. He stood and without a word walked out. Dieter let him go, it wasn't the first time that a client could not express the trauma he or she was experiencing. But they always came round in the end and opened their hearts.

The next day Bruno was sitting out in the shade of the giant olive tree flicking through a magazine he had picked up in the lounge. It was hot and humid; the print was sticking to his fingers. There were several other people seated around the courtyard when Dieter emerged from inside. He dropped into a chair alongside each of these people and talked for a while before moving on. Bruno watched. It's amazing, he thought. It's as if they are all mesmerised, they're hanging on to his every word, as if they are sugar-coated bonbons. Eventually Dieter dropped into the empty chair next to Bruno.

'So Mr Schmidt . . . Bruno,' he began. 'I hope that you slept well?' Bruno nodded. 'Have you found the sea yet?' Bruno nodded yet again. 'If you decide to swim, remember what I said about the beach shelving quite steeply. There's not much current but you need to take care. Do you swim well?' he asked.

'Yes,' Bruno lied. He'd never been in the sea or a swimming pool in his life and certainly couldn't swim.

'Remember,' continued Dieter. 'When you're ready to tell me how I can help, just come along to my office.'

Bruno muttered his thanks and started to look at the magazine again. Dieter rose and moved on to the next client. Bruno furtively followed his progress, as his brother strode confidently among his flock. His mind was in turmoil. He had come to this god-forsaken place with the express intention of killing his brother. But it had to look like an accident, otherwise he would spend the rest of his life in jail, instead of with his Katarzyna. None of the people at this place would lay a finger on his brother; they adored him. So if anything happened, he would probably be the prime suspect.

The following day, Bruno was in the hall with all the other guests. Dieter was holding forth about the power of meditation.

'It helps you to build resilience,' he said. 'It will provide you with an abiding sense of well-being. It will give you energy and ease the challenges that you face.' You could have heard a pin drop - until Bruno shuffled on his chair. 'The daily yoga sessions help but really you need to find a quiet spot, sit or lie, whichever you find the most comfortable - and focus on an object in your mind.'

At this point Bruno switched off from his brother's voice but focussed his mind on an object. The object was a Technicolour image of a pair of hands around his brother's throat, forcing his head under water. Bubbles spewed soundlessly from the mouth, blue eyes stared wildly into the distance. Yes, thought Bruno, I could meditate on that all day.

The days slipped away and it was already Thursday, the day before Bruno was due to depart. Most of the guests, he discovered, were staying for two weeks. He was overcome with a sense resembling panic. Only twenty-four hours to achieve his goal.

After the morning group session he sat outside in his favourite chair, under the giant olive tree. A robin was chirping somewhere among its branches. Dieter emerged with a group of guests and for a while they stood in the heavy shade, deep in conversation. After a while, Bruno rose and wandered towards them. The group broke up and as Dieter walked away, Bruno called out. Dieter stopped.

'Do you have time?' asked Bruno.

'Of course,' Dieter replied.

'Could we walk down to the sea?'

'Good idea,' replied Dieter. As they walked Dieter never stopped talking. Bruno nodded or grunted but didn't say a word. After a few minutes the pair emerged from under the trees. The wonderful vista of sand and azure sea caused Dieter to say enthusiastically that he never tired of the view.

'Switzerland is such a long way away from the sea,' he sighed. They turned away from the ocean and faced one another. Bruno looked at his step brother. He realised that there was no way he could overpower him in a fight, he was so much bigger and stronger. 'Shall we sit?' said Dieter dropping to the ground, where he shuffled his bare feet in the sand.

Bruno peered around looking for a weapon. A rock? A stone? There was nothing but sand, fine golden sand. He glanced down at his brother's unprotected head. Suddenly Dieter looked up.

'Come, sit down. Tell me what's troubling you because something is,' he patted the ground. 'I'm sure I can help.'

Bruno looked at his hands. With the element of surprise could he strangle his brother? He looked wildly around. It may be his last chance. He tensed his muscles and took a deep breath.

'Hello, you two.' A voice carried on the breeze from the sea.

It was Wilfred. He was waving a snorkel mask at them. Bruno closed his eyes, a silent scream echoed around his head. Wilfred strode awkwardly from the sea in a pair of flippers; successfully imitating a penguin. Bruno turned and headed back into the trees. Dieter called after him but Bruno didn't break stride.

His last night at Paraíso. Bruno lay on his bed fretting. His thoughts turned to his beloved Katarzyna. He would never gain her affection if he didn't remove her husband. It was then he remembered again Beccy Blom's advice about dealing with a wayward pony. The bit about being gentle and patient. The advice he had adopted in his approach to Katarzyna. Now with his brother, he tried to convince himself - he needed to go slowly and be patient in his desire to get rid of him. In the great scheme of things, it didn't really matter if he died tomorrow or in the next few months. The key thing was that he, Bruno, was above suspicion and not caught. He knew that his brother returned to Basel each February for the carnival. That might be the best time to dispose of him. The more he thought about the timing and location, the more he liked it. Big crowds, masks and noise - a knife in the dark. No one would notice - except Dieter, he smiled; and he'd be lying in the gutter bleeding to death.

The following morning, after breakfast, four people and Bruno gathered outside waiting for the minibus that would transport them to Palma. There were tearful farewells and promises to correspond or meet again. Dieter was the centre of attention as usual. This angered Bruno, who stood apart, anxious to leave. The bus arrived with Martina at the wheel. Following more hugs and kisses, the four people piled into the rear. Bruno opened the front door but before he climbed in, he turned towards his brother and stared; his face contorted with hate.

Bruno Schmidt brooded all the way back to Basel. He couldn't get his head around the double life that his brother was leading. He recalled how Beccy Blom had wept when she learned Dieter had committed suicide. The papers had been full of it. Photographs of the riverbank where his clothes had been found. Speculation that he couldn't face up to some crime or other that he was said to have committed. But he'd abandoned Katarzyna - and was living in luxury in the sun. It didn't make sense.

For a while he pondered if it might be simpler to inform the police of his address in Mallorca and let the authorities deal with his brother. Lock him up and throw away the key. However, he mused, because he was a part of the establishment, he would no doubt talk himself out of the charges and walk free.

On the other hand, he suddenly thought, if his brother was supposed to be dead, surely no one would notice if he really did die. He had a new name and he looked different. It would be some dude called Ackermann who died with a knife between his ribs. The more he thought about it, the more he considered he would be able to act with impunity.

* * *

Beccy Blom was really pleased when Bruno suddenly showed up again. She had wondered when he left, saying he had family business to attend to, whether or not she would ever see him again. She knew in her heart that he was a rolling stone. Theirs was an odd relationship. Beccy thrived on having a toy boy in her bed. Bruno content, for the time being, to have a roof over his head and having regular meals cooked for him. Their evenings together and any conversation, almost entirely revolved around what was on the television. Beccy had long since abandoned asking him any questions about his former life. All she knew was that he had been brought up in Germany's Black Forest.

As a young teenager Beccy had once been taken to Titisee, to see all the cuckoo clocks but her main impression of the Black Forest, or as the locals called it, the Schwarzwald, was that the area lived up to its name. A dark, sinister area covered with a canopy of dense evergreen conifers. A place where Grimm's Hansel and Gretel encountered the wicked witch. She didn't even like Black Forest Gâteaux.

Following Bruno's return, life returned to its former ritual of early morning dealings with Jacques' horses, followed by breakfast in his kitchen. Beccy and Bruno would then take the trek up to the Poplars, where Beccy would spend the day in the house and Bruno completing odd jobs around the property.

When the opportunities arose, Bruno followed Katarzyna around the grounds like a lost puppy. If he had completed a particular task he would invite her to come and inspect his handiwork. Katarzyna was grateful to have someone she could rely on to do the heavy work but other than that, she didn't really acknowledge his presence. He was a man of such a few words and when he did speak he always sounded so awkward. Though she did have a slight worry about the way he looked at her, she recognised lust when she saw it.

In Dieter's absence and the need to keep busy, she had bought several thoroughbred mares and a stallion, with the intention of breeding. Jacques had helped her choose the horses. The first foals should be due the following summer. The extra horses meant more work and so Bruno had a solid excuse to fill his days at the Poplars. Katarzyna had been around to the home of the lady who dealt with residents' permits and signed the necessary papers that would allow Bruno a temporary permit to work for her.

Maria Beckett was still living with Gloria's parents but had found a job as a nanny with a Swiss family. The job involved looking after a six-month old girl while her mother was at work. Maria would arrive at the apartment in a fashionable area of Basel at eight o'clock each morning and take care of the child until the mother came home at six each evening. It was not an ideal job but it was giving her time to evaluate where her future might be. She saw Gloria regularly but was rarely invited to the love-nest Gloria shared with the tiny Danish nurse, who worked at a private clinic in the City.

Bruno mentally ticked off the days. In quiet moments he brooded and fretted that time moved so slowly. The end of the year and the Fasnacht carnival still seemed ages away. Keeping busy during the day and roughly using Beccy Blom's body at night, helped the time to pass. But with the dawn of each day he battled to hide the mounting frustration. Beccy was painfully aware things weren't right but was afraid to raise any questions for fear of losing him.

CHAPTER 61

Silvio Belloni was bored. He aimlessly paraded around his tiny office, like a caged tiger. The file he had prepared on car theft had long since been handed over to the French authorities. It seemed a gang based in Lyon were responsible; he hadn't identified a single Swiss citizen being involved. The case against Baumann was in the hands of the FBI but so far, they had failed to locate him. Dieter von Murren's apparent death sent FBI agent Hoover back to the States and if there were to be any charges against von Murren, they were on hold.

For some weeks Belloni had been interviewing possible suspects in a drug smuggling operation. None of the suspects spoke any German or English and using a third party translator made the job unbelievably slow and tiring. It was obvious they were all guilty but they were all mules and he desperately wanted to nail the main man. These guys were plainly scared for their lives; they'd rather stay in custody than talk. He went down to the police garage where the vehicle the four men had been driving was held. He spoke to the man in charge.

'Eric, have forensics finished examining the car?' he asked. The man nodded.

'Show me where the heroin was found.' Eric opened the boot and lifted out the spare tyre.

'Someone had welded a special compartment under here look,' he said. Belloni leaned over the man's shoulder.

'The heroin was in five-hundred gram packages stashed here,' continued the man, pointing. Belloni stretched upright, thanking Eric for his trouble. His eye fell on a large white sheet covering something up against the end wall.

'What have we got under the sheet?' he asked.

'The burnt out remains of a car,' replied Eric. 'It's been there for ages. I keep asking if I can send it to the scrapyard; it's taking up valuable space.'

'Where did it come from?' asked Belloni.

'From an accident, out at Burg,' replied Eric.

'Ah yes,' said Belloni. 'I remember.' He walked across the garage and lifted the sheet. 'Good God,' he exclaimed. 'Not much left.'

'Not much left of the couple inside either; if I remember rightly,' said Eric.

'Do you have a copy of the Forensics' report on this?' asked Belloni.

'Probably,' replied the man. They walked across to his office, where he rummaged in a filing cabinet; eventually pulling out a file stuffed with papers.

'Mind if I borrow it?' asked Belloni. The man produced a slip of paper, which Belloni dutifully signed.

Back in his office, Belloni made himself a coffee, sat in his chair, propped his feet on his desk and settled to work his way through the report. It was very thorough; he looked to see who had written it. The conclusion was that the brakes had failed but due to the intensity of the explosion and subsequent fire, it was impossible to say why. Both cables had been ripped away from the disc brakes and partially melted. One cable, close to the disc, did have a smooth edge that might possibly have been caused by cutters but the surface was so small, as to be inconclusive. The report continued at length to explain that the investigating officer had interviewed all people who might have had access to the car at the property known as *The Poplars*. The immediate family were, at all times, together and indoors. The only other people around at that time were two stable girls and they had not seen anyone interfere with car. No motive had been established that anyone would gain from the death of Ferdinand Brandt and his wife, other than the only son, Dieter von Murren, who would inherit his father's business, as well as his parents' assets.

Belloni drained his cold coffee and pondered. Was this the real reason Dieter von Murren had drowned himself - or fled? He took his feet off the desk, picked up the telephone and dialled a lawyer friend. After exchanging greetings he said:

'Dieter von Murren. Remember him? The FBI were after

him, so he jumped in the river.' His friend recalled the incident.

'Do you remember the charges?'

'Yes, illegal manipulation of the markets. Why?' asked the lawyer.

'If he had been found guilty, how long would he have spent in jail?' asked Belloni.

'Well there is a precedent of a Swiss guy extradited to the USA and jailed for three years - plus a hefty fine.'

'And if he behaved himself, probably let out after two year . . . right?'

'That's about right. Why?'

'Oh nothing' replied Belloni. 'Thanks for that.' He hung up. Would Dieter von Murren really jump in the Rhine for the sake of a couple of years in prison? thought Belloni. 'No way,' he said aloud. But if he had killed his parents, that might have caused him to panic. How could he find out about the relationship between father and son? He thought about Maria Beckett, the young English au pair. Perhaps she might have noticed something.

A couple of weeks evaporated, before Belloni was in a position to hand over a file, concerning the drug runners, to the local prosecutor's office. He was disappointed; he had been unable to find out whom the four men in custody had worked for. Before his Chief could allocate him a new task, he asked if he might have some time to follow up on the apparent accident to Ferdinand Brandt and his wife. Reluctantly he was offered two days. Stupid, thought Belloni but better than nothing. He telephoned the von Murren's home in Burg. Beccy Blom answered. He was surprised to learn that Maria no longer worked for the von Murren's. Beccy advised him to contact Gloria Gabric; she might know where to find her.

Two phone calls later; Belloni had the address where Maria Beckett worked. It wasn't so far away; he decided to walk round to find her. He found the apartment without difficulty and rang the bell. Maria appeared, carrying a baby. She started when she recognised Belloni. Despite his thick policeman's skin, his heart jumped when he saw her. She invited him in and made coffee. The baby was fretful, so she nursed the child while Belloni awkwardly explained that he had only recently learned that she no longer worked for the von Murren's and asked if they could meet up for a drink, or a meal. Maria didn't question his motives and soon a date was fixed and he left. He didn't understand what it was but this woman had the effect of raising his spirits and brightening his day. He looked forward immensely to their date arranged for the following week.

Belloni was halfway through his Tagliatelle pesto, before he asked Maria why she had parted company with the von Murren's. They were seated in a quiet corner of the Mövenpick restaurant on Marktplatz, opposite the crimson coloured Rathause. Maria explained about the hidden microphones and Dieter's fury when he found out. They then discussed his disappearance; neither believed he was capable of committing suicide.

'So you were still there when the terrible accident occurred to his parents?' said Belloni. Maria nodded.

'I was putting the girls to bed when someone from the bottom of the village phoned. Doctor von Murren drove down to see. He was gone for ages but when he did come back he was visibly shocked and distressed,' said Maria.

'You don't mind me asking you these questions?' enquired Belloni.

'Not at all,' replied Maria, sipping her glass of red wine. 'I assumed that's why you invited me out for dinner.' Belloni objected.

'No not at all, I wanted to see you again.'

'It's okay,' replied Maria, unconvinced. 'Fire ahead.'

'Well I did wonder if it wasn't an accident but that someone had deliberately damaged the brakes.' Maria looked up startled, fork halfway to her mouth.

'Surely not,' she said. 'That would be too horrible!'

'Could anyone have interfered with the car while it was parked outside the house?' asked Belloni.

'The family were all inside after Mr Brandt and his wife arrived,' said Maria. 'Flavia and Simone were probably in the stables.'

'Who are they?' asked Belloni.

'The two girls who look after the horses,' replied Maria. Belloni remembered and nodded.

'Not exactly prime suspects then,' he said. A waitress appeared to take away their plates and the subject was dropped.

'Have you ever been to the ballet here?' asked Belloni, as they waited for coffee.

'No,' replied Maria, surprised by the question.

'There's an excellent company here. Very international,'

continued Belloni. 'They're performing Giselle at the moment. If I could get tickets, would you come?'

'Well, yes. I'd love to,' replied Maria. I haven't been to a ballet since I was a teenager.'

'I have a cousin who works in the wardrobe department, she can usually get me tickets.'

'Thank you,' smiled Maria, 'That would be lovely.' She was intrigued that this policeman, whose life seemed to be filled with blood and gore, was interested in something so gentle and delicate, as ballet. Later when Belloni escorted Maria to the tram, he kissed her cheek and promised to telephone, when he had tickets.

The next day Belloni drove out to Burg, it was misty and damp. A typical mid-November day. Katarzyna was out shopping, Beccy Blom told him. He asked where he could find the girls who looked after the horses. Beccy pointed toward the ménage. He thanked her, asked her name and strolled across the gravel drive. Away in the distance he could hear someone with chainsaw.

Inside the ménage Simone was trotting around the perimeter, exercising one of the mares. Flavia was leaning on a shovel watching; when she saw the visitor, she walked towards him. Belloni explained who he was and said that he would like to ask them both a few questions. Flavia waved to Simone who eased her horse to a walk and came towards them.

'This is a policeman,' she said. 'He wants to ask some questions.' Simone slid from the saddle and left the horse to wander.

'How can we help?' she asked and sat on one of several a bales of straw. Flavia settled on another.

'About the day Doctor von Murren's parents were killed,' he began.

'That was terrible,' interrupted Flavia. Belloni agreed.

'Tell me what happened.'

'Well,' began Flavia. 'I saw them arrive and go into the house.'

'Did you see them again?' asked Belloni.

'No, they must have still been in the house when I left. The car was still there,' replied Flavia. Belloni turned to Simone.

'And you Miss, what did you see?'

'I was busy inside the stables,' muttered Simone, reliving her ordeal. 'I didn't see anything.'

'You saw the car?'

'Yes I saw it when me and Flavia went home.'

'What time was that?' queried Belloni.

'About five,' replied Flavia. 'We left together.'

'Was there anyone else around at the time? Did you see anyone near the car?' The girls looked at each other.

'Yes,' said Simone. 'There's a guy who helps with odd jobs and things. He was here . . . but I didn't see him near the car.'

'Ah,' said Belloni. 'And what's his name?'

'His name's Bruno Schmidt,' replied Simone. 'Why are you asking these questions?'

'I wondered if there was a possibility that it wasn't an accident. That someone had interfered with the car . . . perhaps with the brakes,' suggested Belloni. The girls looked first at each other and then Belloni.

'So, what can you tell me about this Bruno Schmidt,' he asked.

'He's a weirdo,' replied Flavia scornfully.

'We really don't know anything about him,' added Simone.

'You should talk to Beccy Blom. He stays with her.'

'What, as a guest?' asked Belloni. The girls sniggered.

'Really couldn't say,' said Simone, with a straight face. 'As I said, you'll have to ask Beccy.'

'That's Beccy Blom, the lady I just spoke to in the house; what's her job?' asked Belloni.

'Housekeeper, cook, head bottle-washer,' replied Flavia.

'And where does she live?'

'In the village. Halfway down the hill,' said Simone. Belloni nodded.

'Can you think of any reason, why anyone would want to kill Doctor von Murren's parents? He asked. The girls shook their head.

'Okay. Thanks ladies,' said Belloni offering his hand. 'Where would I find this man Schmidt?'

'He's up in the forest, cutting wood,' said Flavia. Belloni said goodbye and headed out into the stable yard. The girls followed. The noise of a chainsaw was still echoing through the mist.

'Would that be him?' asked Belloni. The girls agreed. Belloni looked first at his shoes and then the muddy field ahead. After a few moments he said:

'I'll speak to him some other time,' and headed towards the house.'

* * *

'Bruno Schmidt,' said Belloni, 'I believe that he lives with you.' Beccy Blom wasn't the blushing type, which was just as well.

'He's staying with me until he finds somewhere more permanent to live,' she replied.

'What do you know about him?' asked Belloni. They were standing in the hall of Katarzyna's home. Beccy paused and thought of Bruno. He's amazingly good-looking, has the physique of a boxer, is a strong, silent type and totally wears me out each night.

'He's German,' she said.

'What else?' enquired Belloni.

'Nothing really. He's a hard worker. Mrs von Murren seems pleased with him.'

'How did he get on with Doctor von Murren?' asked Belloni.

'They didn't really see each other; Bruno was here when the Doctor was at work,' answered Beccy. Belloni thought for a moment. This wasn't getting anywhere.

'Okay. Thanks very much Miss Blom. I'll be off.' He turned and made for the door, where he stopped and turned. 'By the way. Do you know which part of Germany Mr Schmidt is from?'

'Somewhere near Freiburg, I think,' answered Beccy. 'Not so far away.'

Flavia and Simone watched from the stables as Belloni drove away.

'I wonder if I should have told him about Mr Brandt ticking Bruno off that day?' said Flavia. 'I forgot.'

'Nah, he wouldn't have killed him just for that,' said Simone.

'But he'd only just come,' persisted Flavia. 'He'd only just got here. Nothing had happened that he could have got angry about.'

'You know him. He was always miserable,' replied Simone. 'Don't worry about it.'

CHAPTER 62

Autumn reluctantly gave way to winter. Howling north-easterlies whipped the remaining leaves from the trees. Shoppers huddled inside their padded anoraks, while the skiing fraternity watched the evening news, waiting for forecasts of impending snow. The first of any quantity fell in the Alps in mid December, much to the relief of resort managers. The city of Basel and the surrounding area received a light covering the week before Christmas; pleasing the romantics and exciting the children.

Belloni took Maria Beckett to see Giselle; the romantic tale and enchanting score raising her spirits.

The stable girls Flavia and Simone spent Christmas with their respective families in Metzerlen, where they were reluctantly dragged to church, when they would rather have spent time carousing in the bar at the Kreuz.

Beccy Blom expertly cooked a large salmon and shared her Christmas with Jacques and Bruno. Bruno surprised them both by producing gifts; Kirsch for Jacques and a bottle of Gin for Beccy.

Katarzyna and the children spent a quiet Christmas at home, content with their own company and exercising the horses.

Christmas passed, routines were re-established and immediately supermarkets were full of confetti, streamers, children's masks, and other carnival paraphernalia. Fasnachtsküchlein filled the shelves; large, wafer-like biscuits, which when bitten or broken, shower the gourmand in a fine cloud of mouth-watering icing sugar.

The week before the first day of the carnival, Dieter von Murren bid his staff at Paraiso farewell, flew to Barcelona and hired a car; the prospect of participating in the Basel Fasnacht highly anticipated.

The drive to Basel was a tedious ten hours. He had a reservation at the same hotel, as previous years and on arrival showered and fell into bed, exhausted but pleased to be in his home city.

The following evening he surreptitiously slipped into his cliques' cellar, where Marco hugged him and the others wrung his hand, glad to see him again. Following the music practice he and Marco found a quiet bar and exchanged news and stories. Dieter had made a conscious decision that he would not visit Katarzyna or the children until after the carnival. He would drop in just before he began the long, return drive south.

The music practices went well, ladies arrived and dressed each member with their harlequin costumes, ensuring each was correctly fitted. Masks were checked and any adjustments made. Banners were painted for the traditional lantern, this year poking fun at a prominent, outspoken politician. The clique made an occasional foray around the back streets, practising their pipes, drums and marching. It was in all but name, a military exercise.

On the Saturday before the celebrations, Bruno went to Basel. For days before he had wondered whether or not his brother would be there. As each day passed he had grown tenser, causing a puzzled Beccy Blom to tread very carefully around him.

In Barfüsserplatz he found a public telephone and dialled the number that he had scribbled on a piece of paper. A woman answered.

'Hello,' he said. 'I wondered if you have a guest by the name of Axel Ackermann staying with you?'

'May I ask who's calling?' enquired the woman.

'I'm from the car hire company he's using,' replied Bruno glibly. There was a pause.

'Yes, Mr Ackermann is staying with us but I'm afraid that he's out at the moment.'

'Thanks,' replied Bruno. 'I'll call back later.' Inwardly he cheered and continued on towards the Market Square.

Bruno spent a great deal of time in the kitchen department of the upmarket, Globus department store - choosing a knife. Eventually he settled on a long, broad-bladed, sharp-pointed meat knife that he decided would fit his purpose. Furtively he dropped it into a shopping bag that he was carrying, before merging with the crowd spilling out into the Market Square. Outside Globus the enticing smell of freshly baked bread and warming pies filled the air, while the square itself was filled with stalls selling luscious-looking fruit and vegetables. A couple of buskers, probably music students from the university, were playing Dvorak's Slavonic Dance. One played the flute, the other a violin - accompanied by a full orchestra blasting from a mini boom-box. Bruno bought a sausage-roll from one of the busy market stalls, which he nibbled as he walked towards the area where Dieter's clique met.

He easily found the building the woman at the hotel had described. A solid four-storey house with a small snow-covered garden in front, protected by low, metal railings. An ornate plaque with the number ten was attached to the house, near the door. Bruno stood and stared, how would he be able to recognise his brother in the parade? He knew that all the participants wore costumes and masks. Even now above the distant roar of traffic, Bruno could hear rhythmic drumming coming from inside the building. He opened the gate and walked to the side of the building. He paused at a ground-level window, providing light for the cellar and peered in. He could make out a small group of men drumming, while others sat or stood around. They were all in normal clothes. It was then he spied a rack on which hung black and white harlequin costumes. On a nearby table, neatly arranged, rows of distinctive black hats. He pulled away from the window and leaned against the wall. This wasn't going to be easy.

The evening before Moorgestraich, the early morning start of carnival, many plans were being hatched. Belloni arranged to meet Maria at three-thirty in the morning outside the International Hotel. Gloria was to join them, as her partner would be on duty in the local clinic. Katarzyna packed the girls off to bed early, not that they would sleep. The plan was to take the Range Rover to Flüh and catch the special two-thirty tram into the city. Beccy Blom and Bruno would borrow Jacques' car and catch the same tram.

In the early hours of the morning the good people of the Basel region rose and headed lemming-like towards the city centre, as if drawn by a powerful unseen magnet. The temperature was minus six degrees. The sky was cloudless. There was no moon.

The number ten tram runs from Rodersdorf to Dornach; at almost thirty kilometres, it is reputed to be the longest tram route in Europe. It passes through three Swiss cantons and part of the trip is through France. By the time this early morning tram reached Flüh, there were very few seats. Two stops later it was jam-packed with laughing people, standing cheek by jowl, far too lively for that hour of the day. In the city centre the jolly crowd poured off the yellow and red tram and disappeared into the myriads of side streets; knowledgeable old-timers rushing to find their favourite spots. Beccy led Bruno away from the Market Square.

'If we get separated by the crowd,' she shouted. 'Let's meet up when it's finished at the restaurant Schlüsselzunft in Freie Strasse.' Bruno nodded.

Ten minutes later Beccy was on her own. Bruno was striding out as fast as the crowd would let him towards Number Ten, the building that housed his brother's Clique. The knife that he had recently purchased in Globus, the knife that would end his sick brother's life wrapped in a tea towel, wedged deep in his coat pocket.

Belloni, Maria and Gloria met, as planned, and joined the one-way flow of well-wrapped bodies heading for the old town.

Katarzyna and her daughters found a doorway and stood together. Moorgestraich had always worried her. So many people, so easy to lose each other; Dieter used to laugh at her.

'It's all part of the fun,' he'd said. But today there were strict instructions: 'Stay Close.'

By the time Bruno reached the Clique's headquarters, the shadowy figures of it's members were already lined up in the narrow street. There was very little light. A huge lantern mounted on four poles was carried out of the building and one of the harlequin figures lit the candles to illuminate the dialect script complaining about the pompous politician.

In the distance the clock on the City Hall and three adjacent churches began striking the hour - four o'clock. On the final stroke all the city's lights were extinguished. It was pitch dark. An anticipatory hum from the crowd quickly died and there was total silence; everyone waiting and listening. Bruno heard the drum major quietly issue an order:

'Moorgestraich, forward march.' The drums and pipes burst into action, the lantern was lifted high. Waves of rhythmic music and traditional marches rolled down the alleyways and bounced off walls. The informal, meandering parade had started.

Bruno followed the Clique, fingering the knife in his pocket and wondered which of the pipe players before him was Dieter. The group marched around the narrow streets at a very sedate pace. Occasionally they would meet a group heading the opposite direction and the light from the huge lanterns cast an eerie glow on the masked faces, as well as the crowds pressed against the walls. Later Bruno realised that there was a hideously masked figure following the group, as he was. This was a Waggis. The huge mask was dominated by a vast bulbous red nose, wide lips, glistening teeth and bright green hair. The costume was a smock, hinting that this represented a farmer from the Vosges Mountains of the Alsace. He was carrying a sack of confetti and from time to time would rush into the crowd and stuff a handful down people's necks, particularly those not wearing a plaquette, the simple brooch proving they had donated towards the cause.

Every time there was some light Bruno peered at the piccolo players trying to decide which one was Dieter. Because of Dieter's tall, athletic build, Bruno quite easily narrowed the players down to three. But he needed to get nearer to be sure.

In a particularly dark alley one of the pipe players was suddenly overwhelmed with the need to urinate. Like all his fellow players he had earlier drunk several glasses of white wine to moisten his lips. The man slipped through a narrow gate into a small garden and fumbled with his costume. Bruno quickly followed.
'Good idea,' he said and reached into his pocket. The man was still struggling when Bruno slid the knife into his back and pierced his heart. With barely a cry the harlequinned figure sank to his knees before collapsing prostrate on the ground. Bruno jerked the knife out of the body, rewrapped it quickly in the tea towel and returned it to his pocket. He fumbled in the pitch dark and pulled off the mask and costume. He dragged the pants over his own and struggled into the outfit before feeling around the ground seeking the hat and the pipe that had rolled away.

Back in the lane, he ran through the darkness, eager to catch up with the marching group. It didn't take long and once his eyes adjusted to the light, he pushed his way into the space left by his victim at the rear of the column. At this stage the pipers were resting, just the steady beat of the drums keeping the time.

'Wish you'd gone for me,' grumbled the man next to him. Bruno grunted. This was one of three men he thought might be Dieter. From his voice, he knew it wasn't him. That left two. One to his right, one directly ahead.

For the next thirty minutes or so, the group marched around the streets, Bruno barely pretending to play, hoping his companions would not notice or complain. In a quiet spot where the crowd was thinner, the drum major called a halt.

'Take five minutes,' he said. From somewhere a bottle of wine was produced and some cans of beer. By the light of the lantern, now precariously propped against a wall, Bruno peered at the man next to him. From his build, movement and fleeting comments, he was certain it was Dieter. The man had a can of beer in his hand.

'Marco, do you want a swig?' he suddenly said and handed over the can and walked away. Bruno knew Marco was Dieter's friend. It must be Dieter. He moved behind him.

'Dieter,' hissed Bruno, quietly. The man half-turned. That proves it thought Bruno and instantly plunged the knife up to its hilt into the man's chest. He fell groaning, blood spurting down his black and white costume, his life slowly but surely ebbing away. Someone in the darkness, cried:

'What's happened?' and rushed towards the fallen man. Bruno said nothing but slipped away into the enveloping darkness.

'My God, there's blood,' shouted the costumed harlequin, his voice muffled by the mask. The others crowded round. One of the members knocked on several doors before he found someone at home. He explained what had happened and the victim was gingerly carried indoors.

The city's clocks eventually struck seven doleful times, which marked the end of the early morning celebration. The crowds drifted back into the main square and adjacent streets. Some caught trams heading for home and a chance to return to their beds. Others made for the bustling restaurants, most of which had been open all night. Traditional flour soup was supped, together with cheese and onion tarts. Clique members too gradually filled the bars and restaurants, still in their costumes but with masks removed and piled in the corners, together with instruments and tired looking lanterns. Even at this early hour, beer and white wine swilled down parched throats. Three hours of piccolo playing spawns the most desperate thirst. Laughter, shouting and occasional singing accompanied the drinking - the pattern was set for the next three days.

CHAPTER 63

Bruno found Beccy at their rendezvous, she was cross that they had been separated so early but relieved that he had turned up. She bought coffee and pastries and asked if he had enjoyed himself.

'Oh yes,' he said. 'It was the best day ever.'

En-route to the restaurant he had walked halfway across the Mittlere Brücke, the bridge close to the Market Square, where, under cover of the blackout, he surreptitiously dropped the bloodied knife, towel, costume and hat into the darkness of the swirling Rhine. His body was quivering from his adrenaline-filled veins. He was ecstatic. He'd punished his father for ruining his mother's life and now he had got rid of his brother and could step into his shoes. Oh Katarzyna, he almost sobbed. Oh Katarzyna …'

* * *

Belloni and Maria had long since lost Gloria in the crowds but were enjoying the atmosphere and each other's company despite the hordes. But the enjoyment was wrecked when Belloni received a message that someone had been stabbed. He took Maria's hand and expertly led her through the black back streets until he reached the house where the murdered harlequin had been carried. Members of the clique were standing around, bereft and confused. Telling Maria to wait outside, he pushed his way into the hall, where he met a pathologist just leaving; they recognised each other.

'A blade straight into his heart,' he said. 'The poor man would have died instantly. I've phoned for an ambulance,' he added. Belloni continued into a room where the harlequinned figure was lying on the dining room table, partially covered in a blue-check sheet, that the house owner had supplied. The drum major and two other men were standing alongside the body. Belloni introduced himself.

'Did anyone see what happened,' he asked, looking around. One man spoke up, to say that he was the owner of the house and had been asleep until he had been awoken and asked to help.

'I'm the drum-major,' said an older man. 'We stopped for a break,' his voice wavered, he was clearly distressed. 'I chose the darkest spot, where no one was around . . . I saw nothing.' Belloni turned to another other man. His haggard face was as white a sheet.

'Your name? asked Belloni.

'Kaufmann,' replied the man. 'Marco Kaufman.'

'Did you see what happened?' asked Belloni.

'It was so dark,' began Marco. 'My colleague was drinking a can of beer,' he struggled to construct a picture in his mind of what occurred. 'He then asked if I wanted a drink and held out the can.'

'Did you take it?" asked Belloni.

'Yes, yes I took it,' replied Marco. 'And then he turned away into the blackness, probably to take a pee . . . when he suddenly fell to the floor. It was so dark I couldn't really see. I think one of our colleagues was trying to help him, he sort of had an arm around him.'

'Who was that?' asked Belloni. 'I don't know because as I bent down, he disappeared.

'What do you mean disappeared?'

'Well, just faded into the night.'

'You said one of your colleagues. How do you know that?'

'Well he was dressed like us,' said Marco. 'You know,' he fingered his costume. 'In one of these.'

'And you think he ran away?'

'I was busy trying to find out what was the matter. He may just have moved out of sight. Though in retrospect it's odd that having carefully laid the poor sod down, he didn't shout or help in any way?'

Two paramedics pushed there way into the room wheeling a stretcher.

'I understand that we're too late,' said one.

'Yes,' said Belloni, introducing himself. 'You can take your time.' The men busied themselves loading the victim onto the stretcher and disappeared into the hall. Belloni closed the door and turned to the drum major. 'How many men with you tonight" he asked.

'Thirty-one, counting me,' he answered.

'Are they all still outside?' continued Belloni.

'I expect so,' he replied wearily.

'Can you get them into some sort of order, so you can check,' asked Belloni. The man nodded and together with Marco, went outside. Belloni stood and thought for a moment and then followed.

After the clocks of the city had struck seven o'clock, all the streetlights came on. In the dim light Belloni could see the men lined up in rows of three, the drum-major was working his way down the lines counting. It was then he saw Maria sitting on a low wall. He had forgotten all about her. He rushed towards her:

'I'm really sorry about this,' he said. 'It was supposed to be my night off.'

'The joys of being a policeman,' smiled Maria.

'I promise I won't be long,' he whispered. The drum major came back to where Belloni was standing.

'It seems two men told their friends they were so shocked by what had happened they went home,' he began. 'Two others are unaccounted for.'

'I'll need names and addresses,' said Belloni.

'I have addresses back at headquarters,' replied the old man

'Where's that?' asked Belloni.

'Not far,' was the response. Belloni took Maria's hand and followed, briefly explaining what had happened. The remaining members of the clique followed, subdued and confused.

It was eight-thirty that morning before Belloni took Maria for breakfast. Once again he was apologising for what had happened. Maria dismissing his pleas. He was busy explaining some of the more intricate aspects of Fasnacht when his phone rang. He apologised, took the call and apologised again.

'Sorry,' he said. 'This just isn't fair but . . . but there's another . . . another emergency.' He walked Maria to the nearest tram stop, kissed her hard and promised he would make it up to her.

In the bleak morning daylight, a couple returning home from the celebrations had found a man lying in their garden. At first they thought he was a drunk but upon closer examination discovered his ripped jacket and a large patch of blood stained snow.

When Belloni arrived at the small garden, fenced of with coloured tape and guarded by a uniformed policeman, it was growing light. Steely grey clouds, tinged with pink, were scudding across the sky; the cityscape of towers, steeples, chimneys and roofs in bold silhouette. With a sigh and sense of resignation, he stood and gazed around him. It looked as if there had been a fight, he decided. The snow was scuffed and scraped. The body of a man was lying in a foetal position. He was wearing ski trousers, to keep out the cold; as well as a thick fleece jacket, zipped up to the neck. Belloni flipped open one of the pockets and pulled out a wallet.

'Stephan Graf,' Belloni read the name on the driving licence out aloud. 'Ah, the missing band member,' he said to himself. There were two single one-hundred franc notes in the wallet. 'So robbery wasn't the motive,' he thought. 'And where was the man's black and white diamond patterned costume?'

A team from forensics arrived, unhappy to be called out on what should have been a holiday. While one of the team took photographs, the others searched the immediate area. The same pathologist, whom he had met earlier, appeared. They exchanged greetings and bemoaned the fact that they were both meant to be off duty.

'Well,' said the doctor, after rolling the man over and lifting his clothes. 'He's been stabbed, like the man we saw earlier. This time in the back.' He gently turned the man over again. 'His trousers are undone and wet,' he added, 'he was probably urinating.'

'His name's Graf,' said Belloni. 'One of the two missing band members.'

'Two,' questioned the pathologist, climbing back on to his feet.

'Yes,' replied Belloni. 'After the first killing, two of the band were unaccounted for.'

'You mean there may be another body?' sighed the pathologist.

'Or he's the murderer,' replied Belloni.

'I can't do any more here,' said the pathologist,' removing his rubber gloves. 'We'll get him back to the lab and I'll let you know as soon as I can if it was the same knife that killed the first guy. Though it certainly looks like it.'

Belloni nodded and wandered away, deep in thought. He needed to see the clique's leader again. The man had given him two names but had said he didn't have an address for the second missing man. In retrospect, that didn't make sense. These bands were so well organised. They didn't take just anyone. The old man must have an address, or at least, a telephone number.

Back in his office, Belloni made coffee, slouched in his chair and stuck his feet on the desk. What was happening to his beloved city? he mused. Two murders on, what is usually, one of the happiest days of the year! Two band members dead; one missing - and one of the dead, apparently stripped of his costume? This seemed to indicate an outsider? Belloni was puzzled. Was there a connection between the missing man and the outsider? He fished a business card out of his breast pocket. It was one the old drum major had given him. Cedric Schweinsteiger, Dambuurmaioor, he read. It had an address in the Gellert area of the city and a telephone number. Belloni drained his coffee cup and reached for the telephone. He'd almost given up before the drum major's wife answered.

Belloni explained who he was and said that he needed to speak to her husband. She told him that he was very upset by what had happened and was in bed.

'I really need to speak to him,' demanded Belloni. 'It's very urgent.' The woman grumbled and left Belloni hanging. Several minutes passed before he heard the gruff voice of the drum major.

'Sorry to bother you again Herr Schweinsteiger but I have two murders on my hands. Both members of your band.'

'My God,' the old man gasped. 'You mean poor Willy's dead too?'

'Yes . . . I'm afraid he was stabbed as well,' answered Belloni. There was a muffled sob and the sound of a nose being blown.

'We accounted for the two members who told some of your men they were going home. Which leaves us with this man Ackermann.' Belloni could hear heavy bronchitic breathing the other end of the line. 'You told me that you don't have an address for him.'

'I don't,' said the drum-major,' and before Belloni could say anything he continued, 'Are you suggesting that he murdered the other two?' 'What do you think?' countered Belloni. 'Were you aware of any friction between them?'

'Far from it. They hardly knew each other,' came the instant reply. 'Well it's strange we have two men dead and this man has gone missing. Wouldn't you agree?' said Belloni. Silence.

'Surely you have some contact information for this man

Ackermann?'

'He lives abroad,' Schweinsteiger blurted. 'Which is why I don't have an address.'

'He lives abroad,' echoed Belloni.

'Yes,' the old man said wearily. 'He was a member of the group for years but then he moved away. He usually comes back for the Fasnacht celebrations.'

'Do you know where he stays when he comes back?'

'No. I have no idea.' Poor Schweinsteiger was sweating at the other end of the line. He was an honest upright man. It was not in his nature to be obstructive. Like the rest of the populace of Basel, he had read of Dieter's supposed drowning and had been as shocked as anyone when he suddenly turned up again, with a different name and changed looks.

'Does he have family here?'

'Listen,' continued the drum major, ignoring the question. 'Marco Kaufmann might know more. Why don't you talk to him?'

'Is he one of your Clique?' asked Belloni.

'Yes, he is,' replied Schweinsteiger. 'He and this Ackermann seem to chat quite a bit.'

'Do you have a telephone number for this Kaufmann?'

'Yes but I'll have to find it. I'll call you back.' Putting down the phone, the drum major was feeing relieved that he hadn't given away Dieter's identity. It would now be someone else's problem.

It was early evening before Belloni managed to catch Marco at home. He grew impatient at his vague and evasive answers to his questions and demanded to know where he lived. He then summoned a car and a driver and was soon banging on Marco's front door. Marco's wife answered the door and told Belloni her husband wasn't at home.

'Then I need to speak to you,' said Belloni forcefully and pushed his way inside. He began questioning her about her husband's whereabouts and how well she knew this man Axel Ackermann. She became as evasive as her husband. Belloni snapped and demanded she answer his questions.

'Two men have been murdered and this man Ackermann may well be the killer,' he barked. 'For everyone's sake, I need to find him quickly before he kills anyone else.' At this point Marco appeared sheepishly out of a bedroom, full of apologies; saying that he had been asleep.

Seated in the lounge. Marco told Belloni how Axel Ackermann had suddenly appeared at a band practice. He was someone he had known well for many years until he moved abroad.

'He's not a murderer,' said Marco's wife, interrupting. 'Whatever else he is, this man is not a killer.'

'You may be right,' replied Belloni. 'But I need to speak to him. He may have vital information. Do you know where he's staying?'

'He's at a small hotel behind the Market Square,' said Marco, 'The White Hart.' Belloni could picture the place and nodded.

'Does he have family here,' persisted Belloni. Neither answered. Belloni repeated the question. The pair looked at each other.

'Tell him,' said the wife. Marco gazed at the floor.

'Mr Kaufmann,' demanded Belloni.

'Actually,' whispered Marco, 'Axel Ackermann is a pseudonym for Dieter von Murren.' Belloni started, dropping the pencil that he was holding.

'Von Murren?' he questioned, disbelief written all over his face.

'When he came to the band practice, I tried to persuade him to hand himself in,' said Marco. 'But he wouldn't listen. 'His family live out at Burg,' continued Marco.

'I know all about his family,' said Belloni. 'So . . . Axel Ackermann is really Dieter von Murren.' Marco nodded, ashamed to have given his friend away. 'Well I'll be damned,' Belloni said aloud, quite blown away by this revelation. After some moments Belloni asked: 'These two men who were stabbed, can you think of any reason why anyone would want them dead?'

'Not at all,' replied Marco. 'They were a couple of quiet family guys. Not the sort to upset anyone.' Belloni rose to his feet and made for the door.

'There will be further questions to answer later. You may well face criminal charges. You know that don't you?' Marco and his wife paled but said nothing. At the hotel Belloni drew a blank. Ackermann was not in his room. Back outside, he instructed his driver to take him to Burg. En-route he telephoned and requested back up; another car and two uniformed policemen.

CHAPTER 64

Shortly after seven o'clock, when Moorgestraich had finished, Katarzyna and the children took the tram straight back to Flüh, where Katarzyna had left her car. Later, at home, they sat around the kitchen table, drinking hot-chocolate and laughing about their early morning experiences. Afterwards they sat in the lounge, read and watched videos. It wasn't long before all three of them had dropped off to sleep. After lunch, feeling refreshed, Claudia, the younger daughter suggested a ride and it wasn't long before the three of them had saddled their horses and rode off through the light covering of snow towards the surrounding forest.

Bruno Schmidt and Beccy Blom arrived back in Burg soon after midday. Beccy made tea and then announced that she was going to bed for a couple of hours. The early morning start had worn her out. She tried to persuade Bruno to join her but he declined. Destructive adrenaline juices were still flowing. He made the excuse of returning Jacques' car. Instead he continued past Jacques' home and up the long drive leading to his prize - Katarzyna.

The Poplars was quiet when he arrived. The Range Rover was parked outside the house but the front door was locked. He checked the stables and quickly saw that three of the horses and their tack were missing. He walked back towards the house; it was growing dusk, they wouldn't be long. At the rear of the fine old building, he found the backdoor unlocked and let himself in.

Like the master of the house that he now purported to be, Bruno strolled leisurely from room to room. In the lounge, he sat in a large armchair in front of the television, running his hands over the fat, comfortable arms. He found the remote and switched on the television. Not stopping to watch, he moved into the kitchen, running his fingers possessively along the edge of the central, island worktop. He noted a wooden block filled with knives of every size and for every purpose. He wandered into the dining room, tried the chair at the head of the table. It felt just right.

Bruno wandered out into the hall and deliberately made his way upstairs. The first bedroom he walked into must be the youngest child's, he decided. It was filled with teddy bears and soft toys. The next room was more interesting; it had posters of rock and film stars on the walls - obviously Stephanie's room. He opened a wardrobe and ran his hands over the hanging dresses. After a few moments, he carefully closed the door and made his way out onto the landing again. One of the guest bedrooms was obviously little used and had a rowing machine taking up space at the foot of the bed.

Inside the master bedroom, Bruno stopped and gazed around. He had never seen such a tasteful, sumptuous looking room in all his life. The drapes, the bedcover, the pillows, the cushions, and the thick-pile carpet - all spelled out luxury. He walked past the bed and into the large, gleaming bathroom. Oh how I will enjoy soaking in the shower, he thought, intrigued by all the jets designed to spill water at every level of one's body. There was another room off the bedroom, Katarzyna's dressing room. Bruno slowly pulled open drawers; one was filled with lingerie. Here he lingered, fingering, smirking, sniffing, imagining.

Gently he closed the drawer, returned to the bedroom where he stretched out on the bed, hands behind his head and gazed at the ornate light fitting, allowing his mind to run riot. He turned onto his side and in his imagination pulled Katarzyna close, wrapping his arms around her breasts: 'I love you,' he whispered aloud - and fell asleep.

CHAPTER 65

Earlier, while with his Clique, Dieter von Murren had heard the muffled cry and reached out in the darkness, as the man near to him stumbled backwards into his arms. It was pitch black, he had no idea what was happening. He tried to hold the man upright but he was a dead weight. He gently lowered the man to the ground when he heard Marco call out. Dieter had something sticky all over his hands - blood. He moved away and peered into the gloom. Someone shouted:

'He's dead . . . my God . . . he's dead.'

'Who is it?'

'I can't see . . . a light - someone . . . a light.' A cigarette lighter was produced and by it's feeble flame, the man identified.

'He's soaked in blood,' came the distraught cry.

'Lift his clothes,' came an authoritative shout. 'Try to stem the blood.' A few moments later a quieter, unbelieving voice:

'Poor Rudi. He's been stabbed in the chest . . . he's not breathing.' A slight pause and then - 'He's dead, Rudi's dead!'

Listening in the dark, Dieter was bewildered. Whatever it was that happened, the law would be summoned. Soon the whole area would be filled with police. He had to get away. He ripped off his mask and hat and fought to get the smock-like costume over his head. He rolled them into a bundle; tucked them under his arm and thief-like crept away.

In the light of the reception area of the hotel, he saw the blood covering his hands. He hid them and ran upstairs to his room where he dived into the bathroom and peered in the mirror. There were smudges of blood on his face. Quickly he washed his hands and face, piled his few belongings into a case and went downstairs. A woman appeared sleepily from the room at the rear of the reception desk. Apologising that there was an emergency and that he had to leave, he thrust a bundle of notes into the unwilling woman's palms and ran, leaving her shouting and bemused. Dieter rushed down the dimly lit street until he reached his car. He threw his case on the backseat and gingerly made his way out of the city deciding that he must get out of Switzerland, as soon as possible and into France. He needed to cross the border where there was no control. They might be looking for him. There was an unmanned crossing near his old home at Burg, he remembered. That's where he'd go.

* * *

Katarzyna and the girls returned from their ride and spent half an hour brushing down their horses before they cheerily made their way indoors. Katarzyna instructed them to go and shower, while she started supper.

The sound of laughter woke Bruno with a start and wondering where he was. A quick glance around the room quickly reminded him and the memories came flooding back. He lay tense, listening. He could hear the girls were in the bathroom.

He rose and peered around the door before walking quickly towards the girls' bedrooms, where he opened the doors and removed the keys. He quickly returned to Katarzyna's bedroom and waited. After a few moments the bathroom door opened. He peeped through a crack in time to see a figure wrapped from head to toe in a huge towel disappear into a bedroom. The shower was still running. Bruno nipped out, quietly slipped the key into Stephanie's door and turned the lock. A few moments later when the younger child returned to her room, he locked her in too.

At this point Bruno slowly sauntered down the stairs, silently whistling to himself. In the hallway he stopped and listened. He could hear Katarzyna was in the kitchen. He walked to the door and looked in. The woman of his dreams was unromantically washing lettuce at the sink. She was still wearing mud-spattered jodhpurs. He loved the way they emphasised her hips. He crept up behind her and threw his arms around her, enfolding her to his chest. She screamed out in surprise. Bruno nuzzled his face in her golden hair murmuring in her ear. All the time Katarzyna was struggling to see who her attacker was and demanding to be let go. After several minutes, realising that she had no chance of escaping, she went limp. Bruno took this for acquiescence.

'That's right, don't fight me,' he murmured. One of his hands slipped from her waist and cupped a breast. 'You're mine now . . . your husband's gone out of your life . . . forever.'

Katarzyna suddenly recognised the voice. It was the man who helped in the garden. What did he mean about Dieter? She took a deep breath and shuddered, remembering the way he always looked at her. She thought of the girls.

'Bruno,' she said in the steadiest voice she could muster. 'Bruno, please let me go . . . I'm trying to get supper.' Bruno laughed and eased his grip. Katarzyna wriggled round to face him but before she could speak he kissed her so hard, her lips hurt. One hand was behind her head, he crushed her against the worktop struggling with his free hand to undo her belt. She had never felt so helpless. Soon the treasonable belt was undone, his rough hand cupping her buttocks. He was bruising and biting her lips - the animal was out of control.

CHAPTER 66

Dieter arrived in the village of Metzerlen, close to his home and turned right towards Burg. He was breathing hard, concentrating on the black ribbon of road that wound through snow covered fields, interspersed with dark conifer woods and cherry orchards. It was pitch black but the bright starlight threw everything into silhouette.

The border between the two countries was on the back road leading from Burg to the small French village of Biederthal. There was nothing to mark the border, except a couple of small signs. There was no actual border post. He remembered once discovering that occasionally the customs sent out a battered Volkswagen van with a couple of men to do nothing more than check peoples' shopping baskets.

Once down at Biederthal, he would make his way to Ferrette and pick up the motorway heading south, near Belfort. He remembered with a sigh that the road was slow and twisty and it was many years since he had been that way. He really needed a map.

For the first time he thought about Katarzyna and his daughters. He had promised himself that he would call and see them. He had totally forgotten the previous year's cold reception.

He could kill two birds with one stone, so to speak. Say hello to Katarzyna and pick up a map, which he knew should be in his study. Why do hire cars never have maps he rued? By the end of his musings he was already in Burg, at the bottom of the hill leading up through the village to his home, The Poplars. For a second he stopped and gazed at the spot where his parents had met their horrendous demise. Should he risk getting a map or not? He made up his mind, slipped the car into first gear and started up the steep hill. Oh for his old Porsche, instead of this silly little Toyota!

In the courtyard in front of the house, he turned his car around, in case he needed to make a quick getaway, stepped out and pulled his coat tight around him. He recognised Jacque's old pickup parked next to the Range Rover. It was trying to snow. He stopped at the front door wondering for a moment whether or not he should knock. He decided against it and went inside, closing the door quietly behind him. He was just about to call out when he heard continuous banging and shouting coming from upstairs. It was the girls and they sounded hysterical. Some inner sense filled him with apprehension. He peeped round the door of the lounge. Empty. He made his way to the kitchen.

The sight that greeted his eyes filled him with rage. Katarzyna was wedged against a worktop while some man with his trousers flapping around his knees was urging her to cooperate. In an instant he could see this was no love tryst and charged towards the couple bellowing at the top of his voice. He wrapped a massive bicep around the man's neck and dragged him off, as if he was some wild beast. Katarzyna collapsed in a heap to the floor, sobbing. Bruno struggled, continually jabbing at Dieter with his elbows.

Suddenly Bruno lashed out backwards with his foot and caught Dieter with a painful blow on the knee. He wriggled free and as Dieter hobbled on one leg Bruno lashed out at the other, bringing Dieter crashing heavily to the floor. By now Katarzyna was on her feet and as she lunged towards the ornately carved wooden block full of knives, Bruno got there first. He shoved Katarzyna away and selected the most lethal weapon he could see. Dieter was seated, propped against a kitchen cabinet, his forehead bloodied. For a moment there was silence.

'Why aren't you dead?' hissed Bruno incredulously. 'You should be dead!?

'You!' gasped Dieter ignoring the question and struggling to his feet. Suddenly he recognised Bruno from his visit to Paraiso.

'He works here,' said Katarzyna, still winded from her fall.

'You should have died this morning,' screamed Bruno kicking out at Dieters good leg, causing him to fall again. 'Why aren't you dead?' His wild eyes glinted with anger and frustration; the involuntary tic in overdrive.

'The men that died in Basel - that was you?' shouted Dieter, struggling to balance and sit up. 'You were really trying to kill me? Why?'

'Why?' hissed Bruno. 'You ask why.' He stood threateningly

above Dieter, waving the knife. 'Because . . . because dear brother. You've had everything handed to you on a gilded plate. My poor mother died in poverty thanks to our father.' Dieter interrupted Bruno's outpourings.

'What do you mean . . . brother?' he shouted.

'I mean dear Doctor von Murren that you and I were both fathered by that sick old fart who went up in smoke.'

'I don't understand,' stuttered Dieter.

'Of course you do. It's simple and not exactly original. Our dear father - one family here; another there. Only one gets treated like royalty. The other like dirt.' He lashed out at Dieter's head with a foot, almost knocking him out. Katarzyna stifled a scream, still thinking of the girls and relieved they weren't witness to this.

'I need some string,' shouted Bruno, at Katarzyna. She didn't stir. Bruno made a threating move towards her.

'String . . . or your fancy girls will suffer,' he hissed. Katarzyna fumbled in the drawers until she found a ball of string. As Bruno reached out to take it from her, he attempted a smile, as he caught her wrist and pulled her towards him.

'It'll be all right,' he said calmly. 'I'll take care of you.' He bent to kiss her bloodied lips but she turned her head away. 'Get used to the idea,' he said gruffly. 'There's no getting away from me.' His laugh sent chills down her spine.

Dieter came round to find his wrists tied together behind his back. He tried to sit but the pain in his leg prevented it. He could just see that Katarzyna was also on the floor, trussed up like a chicken, her wrists tied to her ankles, so that she couldn't move, a tea-towel stuffed into her mouth.

'Wake up you,' said Bruno, kicking Dieter's ribs. 'We're going for a short walk.' He was still holding the large kitchen knife. He helped Dieter to his feet and pushed him towards the door.

'Wait. Where are we going?' mumbled the bloodied Dieter.

'Well, dear doctor. You're meant to be dead; first drowned and then with a knife between your ribs - third time lucky, as they say.' He laughed, a hollow, sinister sound. 'There's that old slurry pit at the top of the field,' he chuckled. 'Exactly the right place for a shitty arsehole, like you.'

'But I don't understand why,' blurted Dieter. 'I didn't even know you existed.'

'You didn't know I existed.' mocked Bruno. 'You didn't even know I existed.' He shoved Dieter and leaned his face closer, until their noses were almost touching.

'Well it was our father I was really after,' snarled Bruno. 'He was meant to make amends for ruining my mother's life. But he upset me and I got angry . . . so he died,' Bruno voice was as cold as the icicles hanging from the outside gutters.

'I still don't understand,' cried Dieter. 'What's that got to do with me?'

'You've had everything you ever wanted. You've thrown it away and so . . . and so I'm taking over your life. Your home, your wife your children I'm going to live the life I've never had.'

'If it's money?' implored Dieter.

'Get out,' said Bruno, pushing Dieter towards the door. 'It's not just money - its everything that you and your family stand for.'

There was a sudden movement at the kitchen door, both Dieter and Bruno turned. Inspector Silvio Belloni stood framed in the doorway. Bruno screamed in anger.

'Get out of the way, if you know what's good for you.' He wrapped his arm around Dieter's neck, so that the lethal looking knife hovered close to his jugular.

'I presume that you must be Bruno Schmidt,' Belloni said quietly.

'May I suggest that you put down the knife before anyone gets hurt.'

'Who the hell are you,' asked Bruno.

'I'm Police Inspector Belloni . . . and I'd like a chat.' Bruno cursed, his plans were all awry. He could kill the man in his grasp and make a run for it . . . but that would be the end of his dreams of life with Katarzyna. A stream of frustrated oaths filled the air. Perhaps, he thought, he could take Katarzyna as a hostage - and then somewhere, far away from all this, they could set up home together.

'What did you want to talk to me about?' he asked, playing for time.

'Well actually, I wanted a chat about Doctor von Murren's parents - and the unfortunate accident,' Belloni said. Bruno grunted, he'd spotted a uniformed policeman behind Belloni waving a gun. His head was in a whirl. The back door that he had used to enter the house was behind him. There was nothing for it, he'd have to make a run for it. Giving the unsteady Dieter a violent push into Belloni's arms he dived through the door and out into the icy air. In the dim light thrown by an outdoor lamp he could see two armed policemen making their way towards him. He cursed and eased his way through the bushes towards the courtyard.

Behind him Bruno left a room full of confusion. The policeman could not get a clear shot but strode awkwardly over Katarzyna and chased out through the rear door. He soon began bellowing to his colleagues and they met on the rear patio before heading off towards the stables. In the kitchen, Belloni found a knife and cut through the string binding Dieter's wrists before bending to cut Katarzyna free.

Dieter scrambled painfully to his feet. He was in a dilemma. He needed to get away. There was nothing he could do here; the madman would soon be caught. Katarzyna would be fine. The children were unharmed, though occasional exhausted knocking could still be heard. Perhaps he could just slip away. He watched carefully, as the crouching Belloni sliced through the string around Katarzyna's wrists and backed away, an inch at a time towards the door leading to the hall.

A breathless cry from Katarzyna indicated that Belloni had removed the towel from her mouth. He was gently reassuring her, as Dieter tiptoed down the hall, through the front door and outside. He waited. The beam of a torch reflected through a distant window; the policemen were searching the stables. Still on tiptoes, he moved towards his hire car; pausing for a moment before slipping into the driving seat and releasing the handbrake.

The courtyard was on a gentle slope leading to the drive. He slowly silently coasted away from the mayhem. Once he was well clear of the house, he started the engine and drove carefully down the steep narrow street. Five minutes later he was across the border, into France and with a sense of relief, making his way towards the sleepy little town of Ferrette.

Questions filled his head. Would Belloni ask the French authorities to look out for his car? Did they even have details of his number plate? He hadn't had a chance to find a map but should he keep clear of the motorways? In the end he thought that it would take too long to reach Barcelona if he didn't use the motorways and so decided to take the risk, stick to his original plan, head for Belfort and the route south.

The road was slow and winding but with very little traffic. His thoughts turned to the episode at the Poplars. So his father had produced another child. That in itself was not so surprising, seeing that the old man spent so much time apart from his wife. But why was this man Bruno so angry? Angry enough to want to kill him. The pain in his knee reminded him of how near to death he had been. And the man had admitted that he had murdered his parents in cold blood? He was obviously mad. He needed to be locked up. He hoped that by now the police had found him. It was incredulous that the man had visited his centre in Mallorca - why? What an earth did he do that for?

His thoughts turned momentarily to his new home in Mallorca. There would be a new intake of patients next week, a warm glow spread through his veins at the thought. For a second he thought of Katarzyna. He felt no guilt at leaving her. She would be fine. She had a nice home, her children and her horses. She didn't need him.

He had just negotiated his way through the small town of Altkirch and following the signs to Belfort and the motorway, when he heard a slight rustling sound coming from the rear. He peered in the mirror - nothing. Nevertheless, the hair on the back of his neck sprang involuntarily to attention. And then . . . and then . . . the touch of icy-cold steel rubbing against the skin beneath his ear.

Dieter jumped like a scalded cat, momentarily losing control, causing the car to swing wildly across the road. He braked hard, fighting with the steering wheel and all the time a continuous, loud, chilling laugh painfully filled his eardrums.

'So dear brother,' laughed Bruno. 'Somewhat ironic, don't you think? Here we are running away from the law together.'

Dieter, now with the car back on the correct side of the road, breathless, his heart pounding so fast, he feared for his life.

'I'm really looking forward to living with you at your nice little set up in the sun,' whispered the voice in his ear. 'What do you call it - Paraiso - paradise? Oh brother dear . . .! The voice was almost whining. 'We'll have a great time together. Just you and me. We have such a lot of catching up to do.' And as Dieter drove down the pitch-black country roads, the sound of Bruno's hysterical laughter rang incessantly in his ears.

CHAPTER 67

They were fast approaching the motorway La Comptoise. A sign said five kilometres. Dieter's mind was working overtime. He determined that this madman was not going to have the chance to ruin his life. He was not going to destroy everything he had so carefully set up. But what could he do?

Bruno was leaning over the passenger seat, using the knife like a brush, as he painted the life that he and Dieter would lead together. His incoherent rambling convinced Dieter the man was not just unhinged but totally mad. He thought about his parents and their horrific end; together with the two random, heinous deaths that morning. He made a decision and slipping one hand down the side of his seat, surreptitiously tightened his seatbelt. The road was quiet. They hadn't seen another vehicle in the last half an hour. Dieter peered ahead seeking the right spot.

Bruno was blathering about his time in jail. Dieter not listening; only concentrating on the road ahead. In the headlights, another sign . . . it read motorway five-hundred metres . . . and then he spied a solitary tree. Dieter slowed and checked the speedometer fifty, it read fifty kilometres an hour. That should do it.

He said a silent prayer, yanked the wheel and aimed the car directly at the tree. The car bounced wildly over the grass-verge, brambles lashed and screeched protestingly against the sides of the vehicle. Bruno yelled and swore. Dieter grabbed a deep breath, gritted his teeth, drew his feet under the seat, desperately threw his arms around his head and clamped his eyes shut.

CHAPTER 68

Probably no more than five minutes elapsed before Dieter came round. His head was filled with the mind-numbing screeching noise of crumbling metal, smashing glass, an exploding airbag - and a brief, very high-pitched human scream.

His chest hurt from where the safety belt and airbag had done their job. Gently he shook away the shards of glass, which covered him from head to toe. He blew away the bits that covered his face before gingerly testing each arm, each leg and slowly rotating his head. Thank God, miraculously nothing was broken. He tried to open the door. It was stuck.

Eventually using his shoulder, he managed to force it open and clambered drunkenly out into the bitterly cold air. He stretched and breathed deeply, the memory of why he had risked life and limb rushing like the oncoming tide into his brain. He staggered slowly and carefully around the steaming pile of metal that had once been his escape route. Oddly, despite the damage, one headlight was still drunkenly beaming out into the darkness. In the stage-like spotlight he could clearly see Bruno splattered across the trunk of the tree, his head twisted at an unnatural angle. He'd obviously flown straight through the windscreen and was probably dead before he hit the tree.

Dieter gulped, tore his eyes away from the macabre scene before him and rescued his case from the rear of the car. Following one last look he hobbled down the road towards the ethereal glow, illuminating the unmanned toll barriers of the motorway.

Drawing nearer he could see a couple of trucks on the car park. The driver of the one with a Spanish name on the tilt was just strolling back from the toilets towards his cab. Dieter called out in perfect Spanish.

'Hi. How far are you going? Any chance of a ride?' The man turned:

'Madrid. Si. Hop en!' came the cheerful answer. Dieter smiled, limped up to the driver and shook his hand.

'Un milliom de gracias,' Dieter said. And he truly meant it - a million times.

Postscript

Inspector Silvio Belloni was also in the bath, when he had his Eureka moment; only unlike Archimedes, as far as we know, he was sharing it with an attractive lady: Maria Beckett. They were facing each other having been there some time and the water was cooling.

'You look tired,' said Maria caressing Belloni's foot. 'You should be in bed. I'm going to lead the way.' Nimbly she climbed to her feet, stepped out and into a voluminous towel.

'Be with you in a moment,' called Belloni to the retreating, swathed figure. He was still sore and bruised. His superior officers had hauled him over the coals and reprimanded him for losing both von Murren and Bruno Schmidt. He wasn't so worried about von Murren, his crimes were technical and someone else's problem. But Schmidt?

Katarzyna von Murren had told him how Schmidt had burst in and tried to assault her until her husband appeared. About how the men had fought and how he claimed to be her husband's brother and then proudly announced that he had killed their parents and was responsible for the deaths at the carnival. What did all this have to do with anything?

For the millionth time Belloni's mind scrolled through all the facts he had accumulated regarding the deaths of Joe Leman and Raziel Stavi. He was still missing something and in his own mind hadn't proved a truly positive link between Baumann and Stavi.

With a shiver, he climbed to his feet, pulled the plug, wrapped a towel around his shoulders and stared at the water between his toes spiralling clockwise into the vortex. Perhaps it was the spinning foam that triggered the thought of a camera reel, for suddenly, with a jolt, he remembered the video camera set up over the gates at Baumann's home.

'Yes!' he exclaimed aloud. 'Perhaps this might reveal the clue he was seeking!'

The next day Belloni, accompanied by a young policeman, drove out to Baumann's home near Gempen. At the fancy gates he gazed at the camera and rang the bell. Once inside he persuaded

Baumann's wife to show him the security equipment and was relieved to see a modern high tech recorder. He explained that he was taking the cassette for examination and fitted a spare. Later he asked for permission to examine her husband's study.

Belloni closed the door, once the woman had left, sat in an uncomfortable armchair and methodically gazed around the room. Standard fare, he thought. Bookcases full of unread books, a glass-fronted cupboard full of neatly-ordered files and a wonderfully ornate writing desk sporting a crystal decanter of whiskey and a tumbler.

What are we looking for, sir?' asked the policeman.

'Good question,' replied Belloni, his eyes drawn again to the desk. He rose to his feet.

'Take a careful look at the desk constable,' he ordered. 'A really careful look. I'm going to check some of those files.'

The stuff in the files was boring. Pages of ideas about company strategy; as far as Belloni was concerned, meaningless gobbledygook! His attention had turned towards examining the bookshelves when his companion let out a low whistle.

'Look sir,' he whispered excitedly. 'A secret compartment!'

The ingeniously hidden drawer contained a solitary envelope addressed to Baumann, a business return address across the top and a gaudy stamp that Belloni didn't recognise. Inside was a single sheet of paper, which Belloni read. Moments later the young policeman leapt in shock, as Belloni punched the air and yelled with delight.

Later back at Headquarters, Belloni set the hapless, junior policeman the task of ploughing through the video recording, checking who had been visiting the Baumann's in the last few months.

Feet propped on his desk, coffee in hand, Belloni read and reread the letter he had found in Baumann's desk. It was from an Argentinian lawyer in somewhere called Mendoza and dated some twenty years earlier. It was brief and to the point: Kurt Baumann was named the beneficiary, in his grandfather's will, of a valuable property with an address in Mendoza.

Belloni's gleeful musings were interrupted by the young policeman bustling in waving a photograph.

'It's him sir,' he almost shouted. 'It's Stavi standing by the gate!'

Belloni leapt to his feet, ignoring the half-empty coffee cup rolling its contents across his desk. He peered at the grainy photograph and cheered.

'By God, you're right. Good man,' he cried, punching his colleague's shoulder.

Later, calm restored, Belloni pulled out Jed Hoover's business card from his desk drawer and dialled the telephone number.

'This is a job for the FBI,' he said aloud. 'I'm sure our friend Hoover will enjoy a trip to foreign parts!'

A further two months elapsed before Belloni learned of Bruno Schmidt's death. The report from the French authorities said that the stolen car he was driving left the road, crashed into a tree and Schmidt was killed immediately. There were no witnesses and no reason to suspect foul play. Belloni decided justice had been served, placed the report in Schmidt's file and dropped it into the back of a filing cabinet - case closed.

ABOUT THE AUTHOR

The author was born in Much Wenlock and spent his formative years in Bridgnorth, Shropshire. Following National Service in the Royal Air Force, he attended Saint Pauls' College in Cheltenham and later Bristol University. He worked as an educator in the U.K., Bermuda, Indonesia, France and Switzerland. His other books include:
Java Jaunt, published in 2012;
Pink Sand and Parasites, published in 2013
Belgian Blues published 2018
All available from Amazon and other on-line retailers, as well as major bookshops.
Follow Java Jaunt, Pink Sand and Parasites, Missing Genes and Belgian Blues on Facebook.

If you enjoyed this book, you may enjoy the author's other books. All available from Amazon and other on-line retailers, as well as many bookshops – and on Kindle.

PINK SAND AND PARASITES

A powerful tale of love, intrigue and heart-stopping drama, set on the exquisite island of Bermuda.

Jack Cross, a recently widowed teacher, arrives in Bermuda in the early Seventies to teach in one of the Islands' schools. After the trauma of losing his wife, it's not long before he believes his luck has changed and he has arrived in paradise - the sun, the sea and the people beguile him and soon he is captivated by the Islands' enveloping charm.

He meets a variety of colourful characters including the mysterious Eloise; Marsha a bigoted young lawyer and Dilly a charismatic neighbour.

Jack discovers Bermuda has a dark underbelly and before long he is caught up in a web of deceit that threatens his life

Racial tension, threats, abductions, violence, murder and finally the assassination of the Islands' Governor leave Jack and his friends wondering what the future might hold.

JAVA JAUNT

The book describes life in the mega city of Jakarta, West Java and Bali in the 1980's when the author was Director of the British International School. As well as painting a picture of everyday life through amusing anecdotes, the book has chapters charting the development of the international school and travel through this fascinating country.

BELGIAN BLUES

Belgian Blues are an important breed of cattle, they are also what you suffer when your carefully planned holiday through the Belgian countryside goes awry - and the vacation of Silvio Belloni and his girlfriend totally falls apart when he discovers a corpse in an otherwise idyllic village. A village that he soon discovers hides many dark secrets.

Chief Inspector Silvio Belloni of the Swiss police, (you may remember him from the novel Missing Genes), finds himself pressganged into helping the local authorities and is quickly drawn into a web of sophisticated crime, art theft and espionage, as the case twists, turns and progresses - so does the body count!

37446929R00174

Made in the USA
Columbia, SC
05 December 2018